BOOK TWELVE IN THE RAIDING FORCES SERIES

STRATEGIC SERVICES

PHIL WARD

A RAIDING FORCES SERIES NOVEL

This book is a work of fiction. Names, characters, businesses, organizations, places, events and incidents are either a product of the author's imagination or are used fictitiously. Any resemblance to actual persons, living or dead, events or locales is entirely coincidental.

Published by Military Publishers LLC
Austin, Texas
www.philwardauthor.com

Distributed by Military Publishers LLC
For ordering information or special discounts for bulk purchases, please contact Military Publishers LLC at 8871 Tallwood, Austin, TX 78759, 512.346.2132.

DEDICATION

This book is dedicated to Janis Helm Cartwright, my friend and business partner for over thirty-five years. Janis and I met while I was teaching land development at the Academy of Real Estate in Austin, Texas and she was manager. We soon formed a partnership, purchased the school and renamed it USA Training when we ventured into other projects in other states. Our relationship is built on trust as well as respect.

From the beginning, we have had distinct roles. Janis runs the day-to-day operations. And I'm glad she does.

Over the years we have enjoyed more success than we ever expected, and I am thankful for having met Janis. She is family, and that says it all.

RANDAL'S RULES FOR RAIDING

RULE 1: The first rule is there ain't no rules.

RULE 2: Keep it short and simple.

RULE 3: It never hurts to cheat.

RULE 4: Right man, right job.

RULE 5: Plan missions backward (know how to get home).

RULE 6: It's good to have a Plan B.

RULE 7: Expect the unexpected.

RAIDING FORCES ONGOING OPERATIONS

OPERATION BOMBSHELL. Named after pilot Pamala Plum-Martin. Resulted in more than one hundred Luftwaffe and Regia Aeronautica pilots being killed.

OPERATION GOLDEN FLEECE. "Pinch" operations to capture Nazi encoding/decoding equipment. Lt. Cdr. Fleming's project, aka OPERATION RED INDIAN.

OPERATION JUBILEE — OPERATION RUTTER RENAMED JUBILEE. A large raid originally planned by General Bernard Montgomery and the largest combined operation of the war to date. Planned as a frontal assault on an enemy port in order to discover difficulty of landing ashore and capturing a port city. Rutter was intended to be a live-fire training exercise, a raid with a planned withdrawal and no intention to stay. RUTTER was canceled and then revived as OPERATION JUBILEE.

OPERATION LEAF EATER. Illegal diamond buying (IDB) interdiction program.

OPERATION LIGHTFOOT. The second battle of El Alamein.

OPERATION LONG LEGS. Anti-diamond-smuggling mission assigned to Raiding Forces by the Office of Strategic Services. Mr. Treywick is the point man in Cairo and Alexandria and responsible for going after smuggling caravans into Turkey.

OPERATION OVERTHROW. A series of meaningless landings on meaningless beaches that appear to be reconnaissance in advance of a major invasion.

OPERATION PURPLE. Mission to obtain serial numbers from German tanks in an attempt to determine how many are being manufactured each month.

OPERATION RAYON. An A-Force deception.

OPERATION RED INDIAN. Cover name for OPERATION GOLDEN FLEECE.

OPERATION RODEO. Anti-illegal-diamond-buying mission assigned to Raiding Forces by the Office of Strategic Services in West Africa. Captain McKoy heads up the effort.

OPERATION TORCH. Largest armada in U.S. history to set sail with intention of invading a foreign power. The most ambitious, complex, high-risk amphibious operation ever attempted by U.S. military up to that point in time.

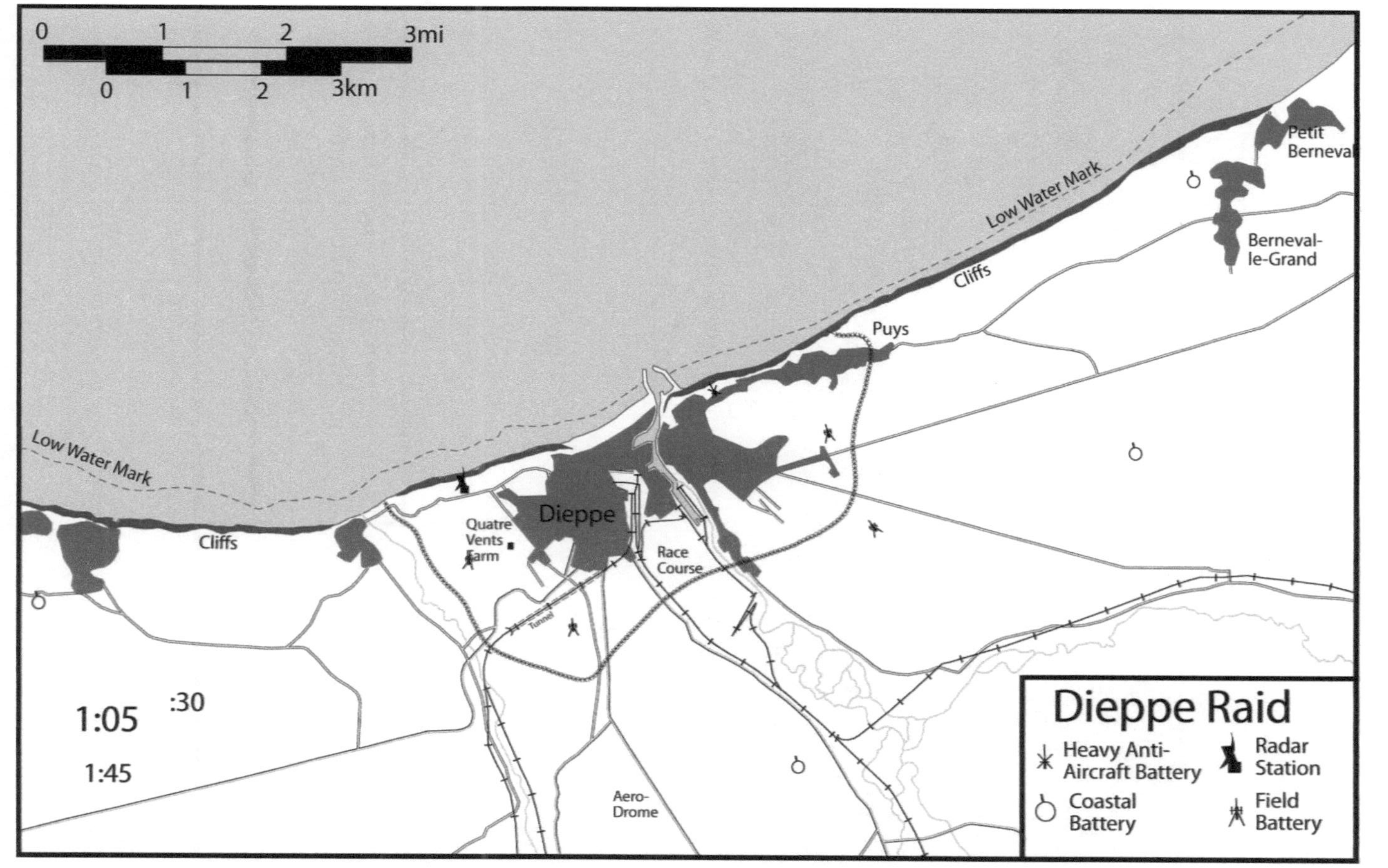

Dieppe Raid
Heavy Anti-Aircraft Battery
Radar Station
Coastal Battery
Field Battery
0 1 2 3mi
0 1 2 3km
Petit Berneval
Berneval-le-Grand
Low Water Mark
Cliffs
Puys
Dieppe
Quatre Vents Farm
Race Course
Tunnel
Aero-Drome
Low Water Mark
Cliffs
1:05
:30
1:45

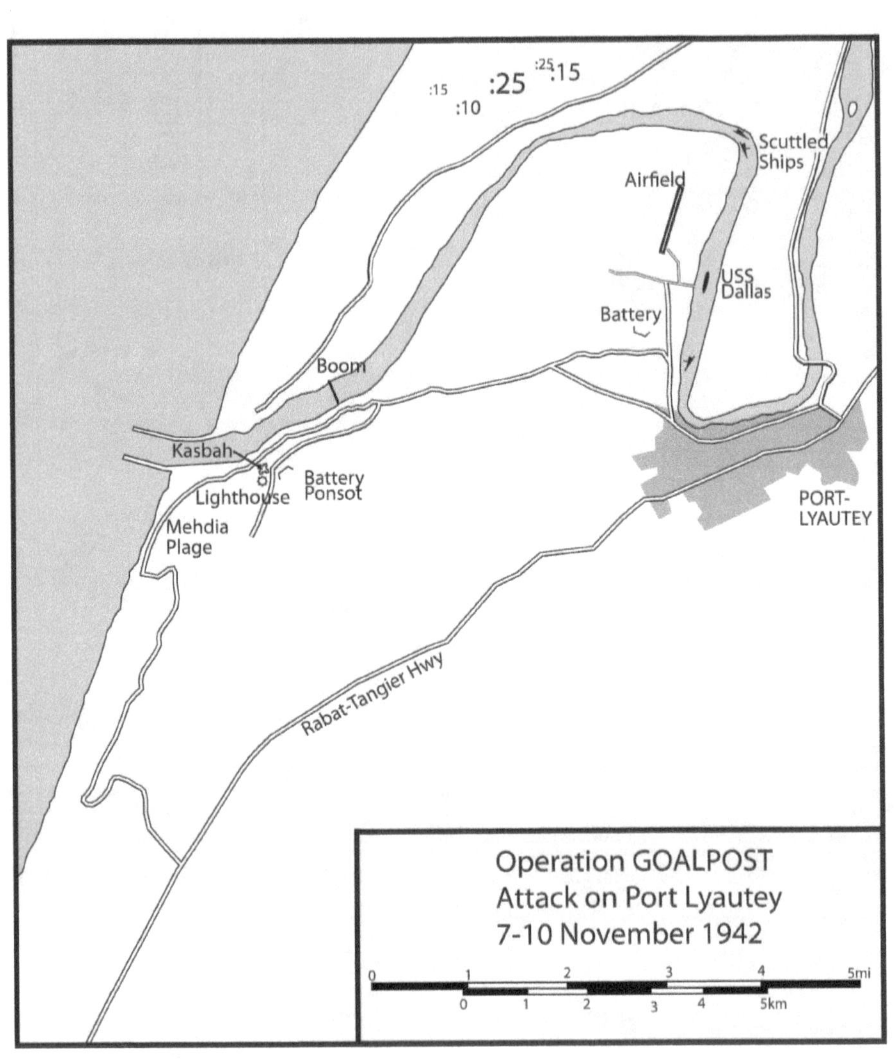
:15
:10
:25
:25
:15
Scuttled
Ships
Airfield
USS
Dallas
Battery
Boom
Kasbah
Lighthouse
Battery
Ponsot
Mehdia
Plage
PORT-
LYAUTEY
Rabat-Tangier Hwy
Operation GOALPOST
Attack on Port Lyautey
7-10 November 1942
0
1
2
3
4
5mi
0
1
2
3
4
5km

1
DEATH FROM ABOVE

VICE ADMIRAL LOUIS "DICKIE" MOUNTBATTEN, DSO, RN, ARRIVED UNANNOUNCED AT Raiding Forces' departure airfield in the RESTRICTED ZONE that encompassed all the county surrounding Seaborn House—Raiding Forces Headquarters (Europe). The timing could have hardly been worse. OPERATION JUBILEE, the division-plus-sized raid on the French port of Dieppe, was scheduled for dawn. The last thing Colonel John Randal needed was a visiting "fireman." However, senior officers are wont to show up to motivate men they are sending off on a hazardous mission, even though the troops are seldom impressed with fake hearty pep talks from someone who is not going to share the risks with them.

U.S. Army personnel take an especially dim view of such military theatrics.

VAdm. Mountbatten assembled C/1/575 around his automobile while he stood on the running board. "When my destroyer was sunk by Stukas, while possibly not the last man off, I did abandon ship by jumping over the side. My chief petty officer bobbed up next to me and said, 'Ain't it amazing, sir, how the scum always rises to the top'."

This drew a laugh from the paratroopers.

"The Stukas then proceeded to machine gun my sailors in the water. When you American Rangers go in shortly, there is no reason to treat the Nazis gently on my account."

The Admiral then climbed back in his staff car and was driven away. The speech was an unparalleled command performance. Fortress Europe still seemed impenetrable in the summer of 1942, but there were Nazis who would soon regret that VAdm. Mountbatten had stopped by to have this little chat with Raiding Forces.

0245 HOURS. "WAY TOO EARLY THIRTY, SIR," CAPTAIN BILLY JACK JAXX SAID. HE struggled to his feet when Colonel John Randal and Major the Lady Jane Seaborn, LG, OBE, RM, walked up to the Pathfinders' C-47 that would be transporting them to a drop zone "somewhere in France." The team had been catching a few last minute ZZZZ's. The Rangers did not seem the least bit discomfited about not having any idea where they would be jumping.

Col. Randal knew the name of the target only because Lady Jane and Lieutenant Mandy Paige, OBE, RM, recognized the location from prewar gambling trips to the casino in the port city. Everyone else would find out once their aircraft was airborne. Shortly after takeoff, the senior officer on board each plane would open a sealed set of orders that would identify the OPERATION JUBILEE objective. Not that it mattered. C Company, 575th Parachute Infantry Regiment, "Rangers" would be dropping six miles west of the main objective.

Lt. Mandy and Beverly Blackwell walked up, carrying red-filtered flashlights as the Pathfinder Team prepared to board their aircraft. There was a loud pop, followed by the wheezing sound as a prop turned over. Then the port engine thundered into a full-blooded roar, soon followed by the starboard engine. Capt. Jaxx and four of his Small Operations Group (SOG) operators were flying out thirty minutes before the main body in order to jump in and mark the DZ.

Col. Randal was about as worried as he had ever been prior to a mission. The intelligence provided by Combined Operations Headquarters (COHQ) had not been impressive, noting only that the enemy defending Raiding

Forces' objective possessed a masked battery of three 240mm guns.

The Rangers had virtually no time to rehearse the actions on the objective of the raid. In accordance with Raiding Forces Rules for Raiding, tactics were kept "short and simple" by necessity. However—and this was significant—Col. Randal was violating his long-standing policy of not attacking hard targets.

Every spare minute had been spent in transitioning C/1/575 from a class of commando students back into a three-platoon airborne rifle infantry company under Captain Earl Longstreet, Lieutenant Tom Green and Lieutenant David Granbury.

Most senior commanders of paratroops would have said staging a complex mission against a hard target on such short notice was impossible. It did not help that the Rangers were exhausted from the arduous training they had completed at the Special Warfare Training Center only two days previously. Sleep and food deprivation being a key element of the program, the Rangers had spent as much time as possible since graduation eating and catching up on sleep—which was not very much considering all the tasks they had to accomplish prior to the jump.

"Drop in," Col. Randal said, "mark the DZ with flares in the shape of an L with the short leg indicating wind direction."

Col. Randal's instructions were redundant. Capt. Jaxx knew his assignment. He also knew that the Pathfinder job was as close to a suicide mission as Raiding Forces had ever taken on. Five men parachute into enemy-occupied France in the immediate proximity of a German fortified port under cover of darkness and then light glowing red railroad flares to mark a drop zone for the follow-on company of paratroopers arriving a half hour later.

"SOG will be on board the lead aircraft with me," Col. Randal said. "You pick up your people on the DZ when we land. Then head out immediately to effect our link-up with Lord Lovat and Butch Hoolihan, dropping off guides to lead us in along the way. Questions?"

"Negative, sir."

"See you on the drop zone."

Lt. Mandy's red-filtered torch illuminated the pistol in Capt. Jaxx's shoulder holster, "Is that a *nude* photo of Rocky?"

Lady Jane said, "It's very tastefully done."

Beverly Blackwell studied the photograph in the pistol grip. "You're a wild one, Billy Jack."

The Pathfinders laughed.

Jack Cool.

Lady Jane did something completely out of character—she hugged Capt. Jaxx.

Women of Lady Jane's class are groomed from birth to never show any emotion in public except joy. When she turned away, Col. Randal saw a single silver tear running down his fiancée's cheek, reflecting the moonlight. He was more shaken by the sight than he would have cared for anyone to know.

Lady Jane was having a hard war—not something he had considered before. Her husband, Mallory, had been listed as KIA. When that turned out not to be the case, MI-9 had arranged to rescue Mallory from enemy-occupied France—Col. Randal brought him out. When Lady Jane filed for divorce, her husband had accused her of being a Fascist spy—Rommel's "Good Source."

Despite all the marital drama, Lady Jane had been working nonstop on the war effort, Raiding Forces being her pet project. Col. Randal realized at that moment that having a relationship with him could not be easy. He spent most of his time away on operations. He had once been in Abyssinia for over six months, listed for part of that time as MIA—presumed dead. Two recent trips that should have been vacations had been cut short by Raiding Forces missions that came up unexpectedly.

As the Pathfinders loaded up, Col. Randal, Lady Jane, Lt. Mandy and Beverly proceeded to the Dakota aircraft SOG would be jumping. It was the lead plane in the serial, and Col. Randal would jumpmaster the stick. Behind them, the Pathfinders' C-47 rolled down the runway and took off into the night. Capt. Jaxx and four Rangers flying off to invade the continent of Europe all by themselves.

Col. Randal put his arm around Lady Jane's shoulders.

"We'll be back in time for a late breakfast, Jane. As soon as I arrive, the two of us are headed to the Bradford Hotel. Not doing a thing for one whole week. Unless, of course, you decide to go shopping—deal?"

"Agreed," Lady Jane said. "I shall hold you to your promise, John Randal."

"Word of honor."

COLONEL JOHN RANDAL CONDUCTED A JUMPMASTER INSPECTION OF THE RANGERS WHO would be on Chalk 1, the lead aircraft in the serial. There were fourteen SOG operators broken down into two teams, led by Lieutenant Eddy Ryder and Lieutenant Clint Hays. The SOG, all carefully selected men, had seen a lot of action since being assigned to Raiding Forces. They called themselves "Jack Cool's Boys."

SOG was remarkably calm.

Col. Randal took his time with the inspection. This was a chance to spend a few minutes with each of the Rangers. He never wasted an opportunity to talk one-on-one with his men. The jumpmaster inspection gave him the chance to do that *and* evaluate the morale of his troops without appearing to do so.

SOG was good to go.

When the inspection was completed, Col. Randal and his entourage—which now included James "Baldie" Taylor in addition to Major the Lady Jane Seaborn, Lieutenant Mandy Paige and Beverly Blackwell—went around and visited the troops waiting to board each of the other five C-47s. This was not going to be a typical jump.

There were not enough officers to jumpmaster each plane and have them combat loaded in the configuration called for by the mission. King had originally been slated to drop in with the Pathfinders. That plan had been scrapped. Now he was the jumpmaster on Chalk 2—the second aircraft in the serial.

The Merc's jumpmaster inspection was not as touchy-feely as Col. Randal's.

Although the tension in the air was thick enough to cut with a knife, Captain Earl Longstreet's reconstituted C/1/575 was ready. The men were veterans of one previous combat jump and four two-week gun jeep patrols. At this point, they were as highly trained as any paratroopers in the world, having worked in jungle, desert and mountainous terrain. And they were graduates of the British Special Warfare Training Center—which meant, among other things, they were extremely well-versed in amphibious operations.

C/1/575 consisted of three small, understrength airborne rifle platoons but only had two platoon leaders. So tonight, Capt. Longstreet would be leading one of them. Col. Randal would be in overall command. The company was tasked with taking out three 240mm gun emplacements.

All three platoons had satchel charges prepared by Captain "Pyro" Percy Stirling, DSO, MC. The charges were to be placed on the breech of each cannon once the battery was overrun. Capt. Stirling would supervise the demolitions. For once, no one cared how big a bang might result from his efforts.

In fact, the bigger the better.

CAPTAIN "GERONIMO" JOE MCKOY WAS AT SEA ON THE HIS MAJESTY'S YACHT *ARROW* with two motor launches—ML 978 and ML 783—in concert. He had with him Lieutenant Marvin Johnson and four men from the U.S. Army's 1st Ranger Battalion. His mission was to land ashore, secure the beach, and bring out Raiding Forces when they arrived on Orange Beach 2.

The *Arrow* and the two MLs were in a convoy with 4 Commando under command of Lieutenant Colonel the Lord Simon "Shimi" Lovat, DSO—arguably the best unit commander in the 1st Special Service Brigade. The Commando command party was on board HMS *Prins Albert,* an infantry landing ship originally built for the Belgian government and converted for special service in 1941. It had a capacity of 350 military personnel (all ranks) and carried eight Landing Craft Assaults (LCA). Each LCA was forty-one feet long with a ten-foot beam, powered by two Ford V-8 engines and capable of carrying thirty-five fully armed men.

Touchdown on Orange Beaches 1 & 2 for the Commandos was 0450 hours, ten minutes before beginning morning nautical twilight (BMNT). Priceless moments of darkness Lt. Col. the Lord Lovat considered vital to the success of the operation. Precise, pinpoint navigation was an absolute necessity. He was a military perfectionist. Having refused the initial operations plan for 4 Commando put forward by Combined Operations staff, Lord Lovat drew up his own—and rejected the first navigator proposed by the Royal Navy.

The *Prins Albert* and 4 Commando enjoyed the luxury of having been able to conduct intensive rehearsals together. The Royal Navy sailors and the Commandos worked together with the precision of a finely tuned Swiss watch. Captain Butch "Headhunter" Hoolihan, DSO, MC, MM, RM, was on board as liaison from Raiding Forces.

For the raid, Lt. Col. the Lord Lovat was armed with his favorite red stag 7x57 Mannlicher-Schönauer carbine and a Colt 1911 Model .45 pistol. The handgun was a gift from Major William O. Darby, commander of the 1st U.S. Ranger Battalion (Provisional), delivered to him by the Rangers attached to 4 Commando for the raid.

"When intelligence is available, only fools fail to take advantage of such information," Lt. Col. the Lord Lovat said to Capt. Hoolihan. "Since this is the second go around for OPERATION JUBILEE—at least our part of it—we know the range and the distance to be covered and have learned every fold and terrain feature on the ground from exhaustive map study. We are going in wearing gym shoes and leggings for speed and stealth.

"Our demolition squad is trained to the point of being able to set the charges to blow up the gun breeches of the cannon on the objective in their sleep. Wireless communications have been tested and countertested. Every weapon has been fired over measured marks.

"Snipers have zeroed telescopic sights, Boys Anti-Tank riflemen, Bren gunners, riflemen and Tommy gunners all burned up mountains of ammunition practicing their marksmanship. Rifle grenadiers fired No. 68 grenades from cups on reinforced rifles until they wore out their original weapons and had to be issued replacements. The two-inch mortarmen can drop eighteen out of twenty rounds in a twenty-five foot square at 200 yards. Our heavy mortars are capable of the same accuracy out to 600 yards using field phones to adjust their fire.

"We have practiced crossing concertina obstacles by throwing rolled rabbit wire over the defensive aprons. We trained with Bangalore torpedoes to blast our way through wire entanglement obstructions in the two defiles we intend to use as exits leading off the beach.

"Junior officers changed places with supposedly wounded or killed superiors. Landing craft were sunk—in theory—to test improvisation carried out on the fly with no delay."

Capt. Hoolihan said, "Raiding Forces is basically winging it."

"Unfortunate," Lt. Col. the Lord Lovat said. "The devil is always in the details—contingency planning is paramount for raiding. Like the fact your Rules for Raiding, of which I have a copy, stipulate, "It's good to have a Plan B." Well, we have plans C, D, E, and F.

"Whoever sprang this mission on your colonel needs to be imprisoned in the Tower of London—or at least be ordered to accompany Raiding Forces on its drop."

3 COMMANDO, THE MOST BATTLE-EXPERIENCED BATTALION IN 1st SPECIAL SERVICE Brigade, meaning in the British Army, would have taken umbrage with the notion that Lieutenant Colonel the Lord Simon "Shimi" Lovat was a better commander than their own. No. 3 was also at sea, traveling to its objective in small motor launches called Eurekas. The assignment was

to land on the opposite side of the port, scale a cliff and take out a gun battery—a twin mission to that of 4 Commando.

Unknown to Colonel John Randal at the departure airfield, Lt. Col. the Lord Lovat at sea, or anyone else not on board the small boats transporting 3 Commando, it had bumped headlong into a convoy of Nazi trawlers sailing out of Dieppe. In the resulting engagement, the Eurekas scattered. There were a number of casualties, several boats were damaged, and only a handful of men of 3 Commando, including two G.I.s from the 1st Ranger Battalion, were able to continue the mission.

This was the first indication that the raid was not going to go like clockwork—the element of surprise had been compromised before it started.

C/1/575 PARACHUTE INFANTRY REGIMENT, "RANGERS," TOOK OFF RIGHT ON TIME—TO the minute. Colonel John Randal was on board the lead C-47 being piloted by Lieutenant Colonel Ralph Livesay. The plan called for the serial of six planes to fly a circuitous route, the idea being to circle around deep into France in order to approach the DZ at low level heading back toward the English Channel and the U.K.—mimicking RAF bombers returning from their night bombing missions, not intruders carrying paratroops.

This was not the first time the seaside resort Dieppe had been invaded. Vikings, the Spanish Navy, freelance marauders, buccaneers, privateers, and more recently the German Army had attacked the port. Now Raiding Forces was going to come calling.

The SOG Rangers on board were silent—lost in their own thoughts. They were heavily armed. Every third man was carrying either a .30 cal. Johnson M1941 LMG or one of the cut-down R80 .30 cal. BAR "Monitors" Captain "Geronimo" Joe McKoy arranged to have modified for Raiding Forces by the U.S. 27th Ordnance Company in Egypt. Virtually everyone else was armed with a .45 Thompson or a 9mm MAB-38A submachine gun. There were a handful of .30 M1 Garands carried by men who preferred rifles. However, for fast close work in the dark, high-capacity automatic weapons were much in vogue.

Tonight, or more accurately this morning, they were jumping X-type parachutes with no reserve, weapons exposed. The 575th Rangers had come to prefer the British chute because it had no opening shock but did have a quick release system. The gentle deployment of the canopy prevented weapons and other equipment from being ripped off and lost in mid-air as often happened when the U.S. T-4 chute violently cracked open. And the quick release let the jumper drop his harness to his feet upon landing by popping the safety clip and giving the device on his chest one hard blow with the palm of his hand.

There was no need for a reserve chute. SOG would be jumping at 350 feet. While it might be possible to deploy a reserve at that altitude, it would be too late for it to do much for the paratrooper.

Jumping from an aircraft in flight in the dark of night behind enemy lines at low level is not without peril nor for the faint of heart.

AFTER WATCHING THE AIRCRAFT DEPART, MAJOR THE LADY JANE SEABORN, LIEUTENANT Mandy Paige, Beverly Blackwell and James "Baldie" Taylor boarded Lady Jane's white Rolls Royce for the trip to the port of Portsmouth where Raiding Forces would return following the raid. Lady Jane drove.

Anxiety was running high. Time, which had been flying by for the last forty-eight hours, seemed to stand still.

Jim was particularly silent. He had met with "C," Colonel Stewart Menzies, DSO, of MI-6, the British Secret Intelligence Service, earlier at his club, White's. In past meetings, Col. Menzies had been protective of Colonel

John Randal and Raiding Forces, having earmarked them for Top Secret strategic missions of national importance with intelligence implications.

Jim was surprised when Col. Menzies showed no unease when briefed on Col. Randal's involvement in OPERATION JUBILEE. Baldie would have expected Col. Menzies to be concerned that Raiding Forces was being misused on a mission impossible-type operation—something the chief of MI-6 had issued him strict orders to ensure never, ever happened.

The lack of a reaction from "C" set off immediate alarm bells—something else was going on here and Jim did not know what it was.

And he did not like it.

THERE WAS GOOD NEWS AND BAD NEWS ABOUT THE PLAN TO FLY A CIRCUITOUS ROUTE TO the drop zone masquerading as Wellington bombers returning from a mission. Everyone, meaning the occupying German Army and most French citizens, hated the Allied bombers. The U.S. bombed by day and the British bombed by night. Enemy-occupied France was being pounded around the clock.

As Captain "Geronimo" Joe McKoy famously had noted, "Friendly fire ain't real friendly." No one likes getting bombed. Every German and some angry Frenchmen who had illegal access to firearms blazed away at any bomber on the return trip, when they were flying low to avoid night fighters. The Dakotas started taking fire almost as soon as the flight looped around, dropped down to 350 feet and started back in the direction of the DZ.

Tracers crisscrossed the sky. An occasional flak gun opened from time to time. The lead C-47 was buffeted by the antiaircraft artillery fire. The explosions lit up the interior of the cabin. Fortunately, it is hard to hit an airplane sailing past at night, but the experience did nothing for the morale of the SOG Rangers on board Colonel John Randal's aircraft.

As usual, at this point in the mission Col. Randal was running through the sequence of events in his mind—meaning the actions on the objective and withdrawal phase once Raiding Forces jumped. The plan was simple.

C/1/575 would exit the aircraft and assemble on the drop zone. SOG would be taken under command of Captain Billy Jack Jaxx and make a beeline to make contact with 4 Commando. The linkup was crucial. It was imperative there be no blue-on-blue between the Commandos and the Rangers in the dark and confusion—both units being known to have a tendency to shoot first and ask questions later.

That was very important.

While SOG was making the linkup, the three C Company platoons would assemble on the DZ and proceed independently to attack the German 240mm gun battery, which was Raiding Forces' main objective. If the guns were not neutralized, OPERATION JUBILEE did not stand a chance of succeeding and a lot of good men would die. The problem was, time had been short. Col. Randal only had aerial photos to work from, no intelligence of any real value, and rehearsals had been simplistic in the extreme—meaning virtually nil.

Each platoon was expected to locate the specific gun emplacement it was assigned to attack. In the dark and confusion it was going to be difficult. Especially if the Rangers were getting shot at.

Once the guns were destroyed, Raiding Forces would assemble on the objective, move out to link up with SOG and 4 Commando, exfiltrate to Orange Beach 2, rendezvous with Capt. McKoy, board the *Arrow* and the two motor launches, then sail away home to Portsmouth.

Raiding Forces would be gone by the time the Canadians' main attack commenced.

Sometimes plans work out the way they are supposed to—they had in the past. Col. Randal knew only a fool expected that result going in. Most plans do not survive the first shot fired in anger. There were a lot of things that could go wrong.

The red light came on.

Col. Randal stood up, "TEN MINUTES!"

The troops sat up straight. They began running their hands over their equipment for at least the one hundredth time since the airplane had taken off. There is no such thing as being too sure—not that they could do anything about it at this point. No matter how many times you checked, there was always the sudden stab of panic you had forgotten to bring something vital—like your primary weapon.

Col. Randal did not have to worry if he had brought his. On this jump he was carrying one of the R80 .30 cal. Colt Monitors. It weighed sixteen pounds, which was eight pounds lighter than a standard issue BAR. However, the weapon was more than twice the weight of his favorite 9mm MAB-38A left back at Raiding Forces Headquarters (RFHQ) Egypt—he was supposed to be on a working leave.

Col. Randal had the big automatic rifle slung across his chest right to left, barrel down under the canvas straps of his parachute harness. Since the barrel was only eighteen inches long with an additional four inches of custom Cutts compensator, the weapon was fairly manageable in the confines of the aircraft. Paratroopers in their chutes with all their gear are always packed in like sardines, so the R80 Colt Monitor's maneuverability was an important aspect that he noted. So far, except for the weapon's weight, he was impressed with it.

It was a little early in the process, but Col. Randal decided to begin his jumpmaster check. He moved to the door, which the USAAF loadmaster had opened. The wind was howling. He could see tracers streaking through the sky from what looked like miles out. Sporadic fire coming from armed angry individuals, not organized antiaircraft batteries.

The adrenaline rush kicked in early.

Lacing his fingers in the rims of the door and wedging his canvas-topped raiding boots on each side of the door frame, Col. Randal arched his body outside the aircraft. Clearly, Colonel Ralph Livesay had the plane down below the 350-foot jump altitude to make it a smaller target. The C-47 was almost brushing the treetops and was going like a bat out of hell.

He looked ahead, although it was too soon to see the drop zone at this low altitude. On the other hand, Col. Randal did not see any signs of a firefight taking place in the distance where the DZ should be. He took that as a good sign—unless the Pathfinders had already all been killed or put out of action.

While no one wants to land on a hot drop zone, the theory is "big sky, little bullet"—a concept most likely dreamed up by some armchair commando who had never jumped out of an airplane while being shot at.

Tracers were coming up from time to time, but they always curled off. The occasional bursts of antiaircraft artillery intensified as the Dakota neared the coast. Col. Randal could see the Channel glimmering in the moonlight off in the distance.

He thought about the single tear running down Lady Jane's drop-dead gorgeous cheek. Then way ahead he saw the burning "L."

Jack Cool—stud.

Col. Randal swung back inside the aircraft. "SIX MINUTES!"

There was the sound of a metallic rattle like someone was tossing a handful of pebbles against the skin of the C-47—machine-gun fire. One engine was hit. It started flaming.

Col. Livesay pulled the stick back, feathering the prop at the same time and the C-47 swooped up to 350 feet with the engine still burning. The maneuver was a cool move to get the plane to jump altitude while it still had power or before the wing fell off. However, it tossed the jumpers around like rag dolls.

"STAND UP, HOOK UP AND CLOSE ON THE DOOR!" Col. Randal ordered, modifying the jump commands. There was a good chance he was going to need to get the troops out before they reached the drop zone.

The jumpers struggled to their feet. The aircraft was yawing and skidding, buffeted by flak—there being more Germans with heavy firepower the closer they came to the coastline. The Rangers clamped their snap link on the steel cable running the length of the fuselage open side *away* from the skin of the fuselage. Some instructor long ago and far away had explained that was important, but Col. Randal could not remember why exactly.

There was no need to "check their equipment" or "sound off for equipment check"—everyone was going to jump.

"CHECK STATIC LINES!"

Machine-gun fire tore through the floor of the aircraft and stitched holes in the roof of the C-47. If anyone was hit, they did not sound off about it. The Rangers began rattling their static lines back and forth, making a terrible racket—the signal they were eager to jump. Everyone wanted out of the airplane.

Col. Randal braced his arm across the door in front of Lieutenant Eddy Ryder. He did not want him to go early. Then one quick glance out to the front and the DZ was right there, a half mile ahead. To the rear he could see the other planes had closed up and were flying straight and true even though they were taking heavy fire.

Col. Randal swung back inside, "ONE MINUTE!"

The loadmaster grabbed Col. Randal's arm and pointed out the open door. The flames from the engine had flared up white hot, eating into the wing. Not waiting for the green light or bothering with the rest of the sequence of jump commands, Col. Randal turned his head and shouted, "LET'S GO!"

Then he was out the door with the Rangers thundering after him, some leaping over the man in front of him in their eagerness to get out of the burning Dakota. Without any warning, the C-47 did a wing over, crashed into the ground and exploded in a massive fireball, killing the USAAF crew and Raiding Forces Special Operations pilot acting as navigator.

Col. Randal's parachute cracked open. He took one swing and slammed into the ground. He went in head first, which is not how you are supposed to make a front parachute landing fall (PLF). Somehow, he managed to twist in the air and hit all the approved points of contact—in reverse order starting with the small of his back. You are not supposed to do a PLF like that.

It really hurt.

Around him the Rangers were slamming down. Capt. Jaxx ran up going full speed, SOG having landed far short of the DZ. He arrived as Col. Randal had recovered enough to hit his quick release and disengage himself from his parachute harness.

"I got a good count on the jumpers, sir," Capt. Jaxx said. "All my boys made it clear. No one else on the plane got out."

Meaning the aircrew and Raiding Forces Special Operations pilot who was acting as an additional navigator. Five men dead, and the mission had not started yet.

"Grab your people and take off, Jack," Col. Randal ordered. "Get going."

King came trotting up looking for Col. Randal. The follow-on planes in the serial were roaring overhead, discharging their jumpers on the DZ. The three C/1/575 platoons began assembling as fast as they landed.

Captain "Pyro" Percy Stirling arrived. He would be traveling with Col. Randal's command party. Once the battery was taken, Raiding Forces legendary demolitions officer had been instructed to make sure it was thoroughly out of commission.

An order that gave brave men pause.

Lieutenant David Granbury was away first, followed by Captain Earl Longstreet, then Lieutenant Tom Green. Col. Randal, King and Capt. Stirling came right behind them.

Raiding Forces had never assembled and cleared a DZ any faster—tonight might have been a record.

2
QUAKER GUNS

COLONEL JOHN RANDAL COULD NOT HEAR ANY FIRING. THE THREE C/1/575 "RANGER" platoons should have reached the objective by now. He would have expected to hear the crackle of small arms and grenades going off.

Could all three platoons have become disoriented?

"Something is not copacetic, Chief," King said. "We have already traveled the correct distance. I have the pace count."

Col. Randal glanced at the Panerai wrist compass Brandy Seaborn's late husband, "Dickey the Pirate," had captured from a team of Italian underwater saboteurs and given to him. It was a precision instrument made for the Regia Marina on contract by Rolex. "Right on azimuth—all three platoons can't be lost."

Captain Earl Longstreet appeared out of the dark. "You're not going to believe this, Colonel. You know why those cannon barrels looked as big as telephone poles— they *are* telephone poles."

"You're kidding."

"Negative, sir," Capt. Longstreet said. "Quaker guns—decoys. Raiding Forces jumped on enemy-occupied France to attack a dummy position."

"Let's take a look," Col. Randal said.

When he arrived on the objective, it was clear the 240mm guns were a deception. Logs and sandbags. No wonder the battery had only recently turned up in aerial photos. Probably had not taken the Nazis more than a few hours to set up the decoy gun emplacement.

It was not even well-constructed.

Quaker guns are the oldest trick in the book—back to the days of the invention of gunpowder. COHQ fell for it. So did he.

"Assemble your troops," Col. Randal commanded. "Move out, link up with Captain Jaxx's guides. Order of march as briefed." Which meant Capt. Longstreet's platoon, Col. Randal's HQ element, followed by Lieutenant Tom Green's platoon, with Lieutenant David Granbury's platoon bringing up the rear.

C/1/575 Rangers had not patrolled far before they heard a brief burst of automatic weapons firing to their front. To the discerning ear, it was easy to distinguish the U.S. .30 caliber BARs, .30 caliber Johnson M1941 LMGs and .45 caliber Thompson submachine guns engaging with no return fire. It sounded not unlike a brief rain squall—angry, violent and over.

Captain Billy Jack Jaxx had made contact.

A runner from Capt. Longstreet came back down the column looking for Col. Randal. "The Captain reports he has linked up with Jack Cool . . . I mean Captain Jaxx's guides, sir."

Col. Randal asked, "Any idea about the firing?"

"Negative, sir—up ahead somewhere."

"Tell Captain Longstreet to continue to march."

The column had hardly resumed travel before an SOG messenger arrived at the HQ element. "Captain Jaxx sends his compliments, sir. He requests you order Captain Stirling and all explosives forward ASAP, sir."

"He say why?"

"Negative, sir—the Captain only said, 'on the double'."

"Do it, Percy," Col. Randal commanded. "No telling what Jack's run into."

"SIR!"

The 17th/21st "Death or Glory Boys" officer started jogging back toward the tail of the column. When he reached Lt. Granbury, he ordered, "Send forward your demo team. Have them collect all the spare explosives in your platoon on the way and bring it along. I shall be with Lieutenant Green.

"Make it snappy, Lieutenant."

"Yes, sir!"

No one had any idea what was happening. The gun battery turning out to be a decoy had been a letdown. The prospect of imminent action had everyone keyed up again.

As soon as the two demo teams reported, Capt. Stirling said, "Follow me."

When he came past the command element, Col. Randal said, "King is up ahead rounding up the demolitions team from Captain Longstreet's platoon. We're coming with you, Percy."

In the far distance, heavy firing broke out. And this time it was not all in one direction. 4 Commando was fighting its way ashore against opposition.

By the time Col. Randal, Captain "Pyro" Percy Stirling and the three demolitions teams reached Capt. Longstreet's point element, another SOG runner had arrived. "Captain Jaxx wants me to lead the company around the German position up ahead, sir. We're in contact with one of "Headhunter" Hoolihan's guides on the far side who will take over from there."

This was valuable information. It meant 4 Commando had landed, were fighting through to their objective, and Captain Butch "Headhunter" Hoolihan had been able to infiltrate a guide for C/1/575 and SOG past the gun battery. From the sound of the firing, it was clear the Commandos had not assaulted their objective yet. They were still fighting their way forward.

Col. Randal thought, not for the first time, *you can always count on the Headhunter.*

"Take charge of the company, Captain Longstreet. Link up with Captain Hoolihan's guide and stand by. Inform him I'll be there with SOG and the demo teams as soon as possible."

"Yes, sir."

At that instant, the six 150mm guns of Battery *Hess*—4 Commando's objective—opened fire. No one knew what it meant, however, when almost simultaneously there was a tremendous secondary explosion. C/1/575 Rangers could see the blast. The guns went silent.

The demolitions teams, with Col. Randal and King walking point behind the SOG guide, broke off from the main column. The moon was still up, but the sky was starting to lighten—BMNT. They made their way across country, moving at the double.

"Halt," Lieutenant Eddy Ryder commanded out of the haze. "Who goes there—HI—HO?"

"SILVER," the SOG guide responded, giving the countersign to the challenge.

"Advance and be recognized."

"Stand easy, Lieutenant Ryder," Col. Randal ordered. He knew the young officer had his finger on the trigger of the .30 caliber Johnson M1941 LMG he was carrying on the raid.

"Roger that—glad you made it, sir."

Capt. Jaxx appeared, "Demo teams stand fast—Colonel, if you'll come with me, sir.

"We stumbled across a bunker, sir. Only it's not a fighting position. We shot everyone inside as they tried to flee—caught 'em completely by surprise."

"What is this place, Jack?"

"Some sort of signals installation, sir," Capt. Jaxx said. "Kriegsmarine—heavily camouflaged—there's grass planted on the roof.

"When I got inside, some idiot in blue silk pajamas with little yellow butterflies on them tried to shoot me with a 9mm Artillery Luger—eight-inch barrel looked about a mile long, sir. I think he was the commanding officer.

"Happened so fast," Capt. Jaxx said, "I didn't have time to take him prisoner, Colonel."

"So why do you want all the explosives, Jack?" Col. Randal asked.

"RED INDIAN, sir," Capt. Jaxx said. "When I got inside, I saw one of those typewriter devices Commander Fleming's always trying to get his hands on. So, I shooed everyone out and searched the place.

"There's a private bedroom suite occupied by the dead guy in the silk pajamas. Under the socks in one of the drawers, I found code books encased in celluloid containers, sir. Jimmied the lock on his desk and found what looks like some kind of code sheets."

Col. Randal said, "Whatever they're paying you, Jack, it ain't enough."

"Pure accident we stumbled across this place in the dark, sir."

Col. Randal and King followed Capt. Jaxx inside the bunker. It was hard to say what the installation was. It could have been a secret signals post or possibly a Kriegsmarine listening station monitoring Royal Navy traffic in the channel. There was a lot of radio equipment.

As advertised, a dead man in blue silk pajamas sporting little yellow butterflies was laying sprawled on the floor in the door to the bedroom. Col. Randal noted the man was wearing a hair net. It was not the first time he had seen dead enemy personnel or even live prisoners, taken by surprise when they were in bed, wearing silk PJs or hair nets.

Capt. Jaxx said, "Nazis take their sleeping attire seriously."

"King," Col. Randal ordered, "bring up the demo teams on the double. Keep everyone outside except Captain Stirling until we call for 'em."

"On the way, Chief."

Col. Randal and Capt. Jaxx looked around while they waited. They did not find anything else of intelligence value. The 9mm P08 "Artillery" Model Luger with its eight-inch barrel lying next to the dead Nazi was the only thing unusual in the room besides the ridiculous little yellow butterflies on the pajamas.

"I'll keep this handgun for Roy Kidd," Capt. Jaxx said. "He likes exotic weapons."

Capt. Stirling and King came inside with packs containing explosives. The Merc emptied one on the floor. Capt. Jaxx put the wooden box containing the RED INDIAN device inside one of the packs along with the ancillary signals books and closed it up. Raiding Forces had been given strict orders for the handling and transport of "pinched" enemy signals equipment: "carefully packed and forwarded to the Director of Naval Intelligence Vice Admiral John Godfrey, London, by the quickest possible route under officer guard and are not to be touched or disturbed in any way except for removal and packing."

RED INDIAN pinches fell into three categories according to Commander Ian Fleming: 1. Design: An extensively planned, sophisticated special operation. 2. Opportunity: An attractive target of opportunity comes into reach on land or sea, which requires hasty planning followed by rapid execution. 3. Chance: Incidental capture during the course of an unrelated action.

Capt. Jaxx's pinch fell into Cat 3.

"Make this bunker disappear," Col. Randal ordered Capt. Stirling. "I want what's inside to vanish."

"We have enough explosives to blast everything in the interior into a fine mist, sir," Capt. Stirling said. "Not enough to destroy the structure. This is reinforced concrete. We may be able to bring part of the roof down but that is about all to hope for with the limited amount of demolitions I have available."

Col. Randal said, "Make it happen."

While the demolitions charges were being set, Capt. Jaxx said, "Never heard firing or explosions from your objective, sir."

"The battery consisted of three telephone poles and a pile of sandbags," Col. Randal said. "Teddy's going to get a big laugh out of this story."

"We made a low-level night combat jump behind the lines to take out some telephone poles, sir? Crazy," Capt. Jaxx said. "How could COHQ get something so wrong?"

Col. Randal said, "I have no idea."

"The Nazi in the silk PJs," Capt. Jaxx said, "You should have seen him waving that hand cannon. Looked like Wyatt Earp's Buntline Special.

"Boom!"

Jack Cool.

WHEN SOG REJOINED C/1/575 "RANGERS," CAPTAIN BUTCH "HEADHUNTER" Hoolihan's "guide" turned out to be the Headhunter himself. After coming ashore, he had fought his way up one of the exits that 4 Commando had cleared by blasting the wire obstructions with Bangalore torpedoes. The beach had been defended. However, the Germans were caught by surprise.

The Commandos struck so swiftly that they were on the Nazis before they were able to deploy from their quarters and reach their prepared fighting positions. A vicious close-range firefight ensued. All of Lieutenant Colonel the Lord Simon "Shimi" Lovat's meticulous planning and intensive training paid off. Every man knew his job and the job of everyone else. When one officer was shot down, another stepped in, took his place, and continued the attack with no loss in momentum.

Unfortunately, so many Commando troop leaders were killed or incapacitated by wounds that one of the liaison officers, Captain Pat Porteous—already wounded twice himself—led the final charge on the battery. He was shot a third time but kept going forward until he passed out. At the end, the fighting was hand to hand.

While that was taking place, Capt. Hoolihan shot his way past the objective with his cherished .45 Caliber Thompson submachine guns. When 4 Commando went in for the final assault, the Headhunter skirted the main objective, moving inland to attempt to locate C/1/575 Rangers. It was beginning to get light, which helped. Still, making the linkup between two armed groups with a tendency to shoot first and ask questions later was a dangerous task.

As soon as Captain "Pyro" Percy Stirling shouted, "Fire in the hole," SOG, with the demolitions team in trail, moved out at a trot to rejoin Captain Earl Longstreet and C/1/575.

"I wasn't expecting you, Butch. You were supposed to *send* a guide," Colonel John Randal said when he arrived. "How'd it go with 4 Commando?"

"Pretty stiff fight initially, sir," Capt. Hoolihan said. "The Commandos went straight in. Nothing was going to stop Lord Lovat from taking Battery *Hess.*"

WHUUUUUMPH!

"That's "Pyro" Percy taking out a bunker Billy Jack found," Col. Randal said. "We're ready to move out as soon as you are, Captain."

"No time like the present, sir," Capt. Hoolihan said. "Colonel Lovat is not going to want to spend any more time in France today than absolutely necessary. Number 4 has taken quite a few casualties. He will want to evacuate them as soon as possible."

Col. Randal ordered, "Captain Longstreet, send out a point element/security party for Captain Hoolihan. Let's roll."

"Yes, sir."

C/1/575 moved out in a platoon column formation, with SOG bringing up the rear. Col. Randal's HQ element traveled at the front with Capt. Longstreet. The sun was coming up. Everywhere the Rangers looked, they saw devastation from the naval bombardment.

The column had not moved far when the point spotted a large formation of German soldiers, presumably from the 302nd Infantry Division known to be in the area, assembling ahead. The Nazis gave the appearance of forming up to launch a counterattack on 4 Commando. Preoccupied, they never noticed the arrival of C/1/575. The lead Rangers immediately stopped, went to ground, and sent word back.

The German Army was known for its blitzkrieg tactics, but in fact, counterattack was its true forte. According to Wehrmacht doctrine, whenever a position was lost, an immediate counterattack was required—under penalty of death by firing squad should the senior German officer present fail to do so—which is a powerful incentive. No military organization in the world was more competent at conducting hasty counterattacks.

The assembling 302nd ID troops was a dangerous development. 4 Commando was in a vulnerable position as it prepared to withdraw with its dead and wounded. The Germans were between Raiding Forces and Captain "Geronimo" Joe McKoy's Motor Launches and the *Arrow* waiting on Orange Beach 2 to take them home.

When the "enemy to our front" message arrived, Col. Randal ordered, "Captain Longstreet, set up a base of fire—stand by for my command to commence. King, inform the platoon leaders to bring up our follow-on platoons."

After that, things happened fast.

The Rangers double-timed forward, Lieutenant Tom Green's platoon tying in on the right flank of Capt. Longstreet and Lieutenant David Granbury's on the left.

C/1/575 engaged the instant Col. Randal gave the order, "Light 'em up!"

A massive volume of fire at virtual point-blank range was directed at the surprised Germans, who had no idea there was an enemy force to their rear. Every Ranger was in action. Col. Randal had the Colt Monitor to his shoulder with the selector switch on semi-automatic, firing as fast as he could work the trigger. Nazis were being knocked over like pop-up targets.

When he heard the roar of firing break out, Captain Billy Jack Jaxx brought up his SOG personnel at a dead run, looping wide to the left. Not a prerehearsed movement to contact—Jack Cool was improvising his tactics on the move.

The Small Operations Group came in and hit the Nazis on their flank, catching the would-be counterattackers in enfilade. Then Capt. Jaxx put in an assault.

When he saw what was taking place, Col. Randal ordered C/1/575, "SHIFT YOUR FIRES—RIGHT!"

The hasty attack by SOG—driven home with speed, superior firepower, and the element of surprise—rolled up the German line. The enemy was thrown into panic. In less than thirty seconds the entire action was over. The German artillerymen from the 302nd ID preparing to retake Battery *Hess* had been caught in the open. They never stood a chance.

Dead or dying Nazis littered the ground—over a hundred of them.

There was no time to get an accurate count. However, typically the Rangers liberated all the Nazi pistols, knives, and wristwatches they could find as they passed by. Col. Randal surveyed the carnage. It was one of the most perfectly executed small unit actions he had ever participated in.

The 575th Parachute Infantry Regiment Rangers had become a highly adaptable organization. One minute a para/glider infantry battalion, the next transformed into eighteen-man jeep patrols, then broken down into individual students at the Special Warfare Training Center, and finally reorganized as a company of paratroopers for a night combat drop. And so far, the only casualties the Rangers had sustained on the raid were jump-related due to the low-level exit—there were a lot of those but most were relatively minor.

Col. Randal was well pleased.

4 COMMANDO HAD CONSOLIDATED ON THE OBJECTIVE BY THE TIME C/1/575 RANGERS arrived. Lieutenant Colonel the Lord Simon "Shimi" Lovat had already begun evacuating his dead and wounded to Orange Beach 2. *Hess* Battery had clearly been the scene of a desperate battle. One of the first mortar rounds fired by the Commando Support Group, engaging from Orange Beach 1, had scored a lucky hit on the Nazis munitions locker, causing a tremendous secondary explosion that knocked the battery out of action.

Lt. Col. the Lord Lovat was preparing to pull out. He was as cool as ice.

"Move when ready," Colonel John Randal said. "We'll cover your withdrawal."

"Any problems on your objective, Colonel?"

"Telephone poles," Col. Randal said. "Didn't put up much of a fight."

"Bloody COHQ," Lt. Col. the Lord Lovat said. "What was that firing a moment ago?"

"A company of Germans forming up didn't see us coming," Col. Randal said. "They won't be interfering with our withdrawal."

"Outstanding, old boy," Lt. Col. the Lord Lovat said. "I owe you a debt of gratitude."

In the distance, from the direction of Dieppe six miles away, the faint sound of a battle could be heard when the wind blew right.

Col. Randal said, "Let's get the hell out of Dodge."

"Well said," Lt. Col. the Lord Lovat said. "We played our part to perfection. Time to exit stage right. Are you aware General "Ham" Roberts informed his officers when the 2nd Canadian Division goes in 'it will be a piece of cake'?"

"I heard that," Col. Randal said.

"I lost twenty-three of my lads KIA," Lt. Col. the Lord Lovat said. "Still no complete report on the wounded. A handful of people are missing. 'Piece of cake'. My guess is the general shall rue the day he uttered those words."

4 Commando began pulling back to Orange Beach 2, a thousand yards distant. C/1/575 Rangers set up a defensive position to cover them during this extremely vulnerable phase. Battery *Hess* was in shambles. The lucky hit on the Germans' munitions locker had been devastating.

Two green Very flares went up from the vicinity of Orange Beach 2, signaling that 4 Commando had completed embarking. C/1/575 Rangers were cleared to withdraw.

Col. Randal ordered, "Lead out, Captain Jaxx."

SOG took off for the beach on the double. The plan was for Raiding Forces to leapfrog to the beach by platoons. At this stage in every raid—mission accomplished—all everyone wanted was to go home. Lieutenant David Granbury's platoon went next, followed closely by Lieutenant Tom Green's. Col. Randal, Captain Butch "Headhunter" Hoolihan and King waited with Captain Earl Longstreet's platoon to give them time to board the two motor launches.

It felt lonely being last.

Col. Randal ordered, "Move out, Earl."

Capt. Longstreet's squads started moving by bounds down to Orange Beach 2. Once at the water's edge, they found Captain "Geronimo" Joe McKoy pacing back and forth. Lieutenant Marvin Johnson of the 1st Ranger Battalion, with four of his men, were on one knee providing security. Captain Billy Jack Jaxx was already on board the *Arrow* with his RED INDIAN device concealed in the demolitions pack.

Not even the Rangers were cleared to know he had captured it.

The other two platoons and SOG were already loaded on the MLs. The 1st Battalion Rangers boarded the *Arrow.* Col. Randal and Capt. McKoy were the last two men to depart Orange Beach 2.

Capt. McKoy said, "By the way, John, we think the electricians installed the degaussing gear on the *Arrow* backwards."

"Does that mean we're attracting mines instead of diverting 'em?"

"Yep," Capt. McKoy said. "Adios, France."

THE LITTLE CONVOY CONSISTING OF MOTOR LAUNCH 978, MOTOR LAUNCH 783 AND THE *Arrow* arrived at the dock in Portsmouth a long six hours later. Normally the trip would have taken a little over three. They had been diverted to act as Air/Sea Rescue for the massive air battle taking place. The delay did not comply with Naval Intelligence Division's (NID) standing orders relating to RED INDIAN pinches to "carry by hand of officer by the quickest route." However, the exigency of the situation dictated that the *Arrow* maintain radio silence so there was no way to alert the NID and there were a lot of Royal Air Force (RAF) pilots being shot down who needed to be fished out of the Channel.

All the airmen they rescued were British—not a single German.

"I thought the Royal Air Force wanted to draw the Luftwaffe into a major air battle as part of this-here raid," Captain "Geronimo" Joe McKoy said. "Looks to me like the RAF's gettin' its ass kicked."

The dock was an ugly scene of pandemonium. Landing Craft Assaults that had gone over carrying the 2nd Canadian Division were coming back filled with dead, wounded, and dying men. The sight of the Dieppe survivors was worse than Colonel John Randal's return from Calais when the Dunkirk evacuees were being disembarked.

Ambulances were everywhere. Doctors and nurses were everywhere. Bloody, wounded soldiers were everywhere. Bodies were everywhere. People were shouting. Men were in shock, staring through glazed eyes. Some were crying. Others were sprawled on the pier, too exhausted to walk.

OPERATION JUBILEE was a disaster.

Officers were angry. NCOs were angry. Men were angry. The press allowed to accompany the raid to report on it were angry.

The blame game was already in progress. Fingers being pointed. Whose idea was this? "Piece of cake"? The 2nd Canadian Division was shattered. Had the division been sacrificed? Did the Germans know they were coming? Was it a command failure? An intelligence failure?

Heads were going to roll.

As Colonel John Randal was walking up the pier, holding his .30 caliber Colt Monitor over his shoulder by the barrel, he spotted Commander Ian Fleming, RNVR, disembarking from the destroyer HMS *Fernie.* The normally suave naval intelligence officer was disheveled, walking like he was physically ill—pale as a sheet.

"Rough day at the office, Fleming?" Col. Randal said.

"Everyone is dead," Cdr. Fleming said, wild-eyed in shock. "Abandoned on the beach to be captured."

Col. Randal clicked on. Why was the commander here?

"JUBILEE was a cover to capture one of your RED INDIAN devices," Col. Randal said. "You had a GOLDEN FLEECE target in Dieppe—sacrificed a division to try to get it."

"Colonel . . ."

Col. Randal said, "Captain Jaxx, give the Commander his present and let's get the hell out of here."

Captain Billy Jack Jaxx swung the pack he was carrying over one shoulder to the ground. "Brought you a toy, sir."

"That what I think it is?" Cdr. Fleming asked in disbelief.

"Roger that," Col. Randal said. "You owe Jack—make sure you square it, Fleming. How's it feel sending men on a suicide mission you observe from a long way off?"

"I can explain . . ."

"Not to me," Col. Randal said. "I'm on vacation."

Major the Lady Jane Seaborn came running down the pier, pushing her way through the crowd. She threw herself on Col. Randal, kissing him with tears streaming down her drop-dead gorgeous face. Lieutenant Mandy Paige and Beverly Blackwell were right behind her, crying as well. No stiff upper lips today. "Keep Calm and Carry On" being a bit much to ask for, all things considered.

The women had been firsthand witnesses to the homefront side of a national disgrace.

Col. Randal said, "We lost Colonel Livesay and his crew. Our plane was shot down. My stick jumped at low level so some of us are dinged up a little—maybe all of us. Other than that, Raiding Forces made it home with no casualties."

Lt. Mandy said, "Lower than the insane three hundred fifty feet you planned on?"

"Yeah."

Lady Jane asked, "Was it bad, John?"

"Not a shot fired on our objective," Col. Randal said. "Lord Lovat had a stiff fight. 4 Commando lost over twenty men."

"The idea," Lt. Mandy said, "was to spirit you out of Egypt for a quiet rest cure, John. Not have you parachuting out of crashing airplanes at treetop level while invading France."

"Some planners we are, huh," Beverly said.

Col. Randal said, "Well, I'm rested."

COLONEL JOHN RANDAL WAS STRETCHED OUT ON THE COUCH IN MAJOR THE LADY JANE Seaborn's suite on the private floor of London's exclusive Bradford Hotel, which she owned. He was dressed in a white T-shirt, faded blue jeans and the cowboy boots he had owned since high school—the ones that were so soft they could be rolled up in a ball. Col. Randal was semi-napping, beginning to feel the stiffness and pain kick in from that morning's low-level jump—he had smoked in hard.

There was a style show in progress. Lady Jane, Lieutenant Mandy Paige and Beverly Blackwell were trying on formal gowns for a reception the prime minister's office had prevailed upon Lady Jane to host at the hotel. The event was for visiting U.S. Army Major General George S. Patton Jr. He was in London to confer with Lieutenant General Dwight D. Eisenhower, the recently appointed commander of the United States Armed Forces European Theatre of Operations (ETO), about the first American invasion of WWII by the United States Army.

No one had any idea who Maj. Gen. Patton was, though Col. Randal vaguely recalled having heard the name.

And no one had a very good idea about how a man who had been General Douglas MacArthur's clerk a little over two years ago had managed to go from the "bowels of the War Department," as the general told Col. Randal on

Corregidor, to become the commander of the ETO. That was some jump in rank.

Col. Randal intended to stay as far away from ETO headquarters as possible because he knew it had caused a bit of a stir when the gold-tooth-filled head of "Smiling Jack" had ended up on then-*Major* Eisenhower's desk in Manila after Col. Randal had shot the Huk bandit. Fortunately, Lt. Gen. Eisenhower was not able to attend tonight's event.

The only other member of the U.S. Army invited was Colonel Lucian Truscott, a cavalry officer currently attached to COHQ as an observer.

Clothiers and their assistants were delivering gowns to the suite from boutiques all over London. The three girls were playing, having fun. They would try on a dress in Lady Jane's bedroom, then come out to model it for him—wanting his approval—not necessarily his opinion. Col. Randal was enjoying the show, though how three women as beautiful as they were could be so concerned about how they looked was a mystery.

He could feel the stress of the last twenty-four hours—or maybe it was the last twenty-four months—evaporating. The fact was, Col. Randal was exhausted. Everyone knew it but him.

The task of hosting the party had fallen to Lady Jane because the Prime Minister was currently in Cairo on an inspection tour. In fact, Churchill was staying in her rooms at the Mena House Hotel. The PM was less than pleased with the progress of the war in the desert. The loss of Tobruk had been a blow—he claimed his low point—in a war that so far had seen defeats at Narvik, Dunkirk, Dakar, Greece, Crete, Singapore, Hong Kong, Rangoon, Gazala, and as of today, Dieppe.

Prime Minister Churchill had learned of Tobruk's surrender while standing in the Oval Office of the President of the United States. It was, he told President Franklin D. Roosevelt, one of his blackest moments. British Forces had been defeated by a numerically inferior Afrika Korps.

The PM immediately departed the U.S. for Cairo. He intended to shake things up. Time for new generals.

Tonight, Lady Jane had invited families of her Royal Marines, the Wrens, and junior officers serving in Raiding Forces to attend the reception. Then she filled out the rest of the guest list with an open invitation to the Beaufort Hunt—the most influential political cabal in all of England. The event would be a glittering assemblage of Great Britain's titled, landed gentry and power elite. Maj. Gen. Patton, whoever he was, should be suitably impressed.

Brandy Seaborn arrived. She had flown in to brief the MI-5 Security Executive Council on the hunt for—and elimination of—Rommel's signals intercept genius Captain Alfred Seebohm. Tonight, she had been dragooned to be Maj. Gen. Patton's dinner companion.

Scooting onto the couch and putting her arm around Col. Randal's shoulders, she said, "Enjoying the show, handsome?"

"Well, yeah."

"You wait," Brandy laughed. "Jane will try on every single dress, then wear a simple black—or possibly a white—sheath she already has in her closet. I wager it will be black—Jane's new favorite color because it makes the twenty-five-carat Sheba diamond you gave her flare when she crosses her arms.

"Jane loves her ring."

Beverly Blackwell came out in a dark green strapless evening gown that fit like a snakeskin with a heart-shaped top and a long slit revealing most of one golden leg. The blond Texas beauty queen was tanned and fit.

Col. Randal said, "I think we have a winner."

"Thanks, John—you have exquisite taste."

"Are you bringing Jack tonight?"

"I've never actually dated Billy Jack. He's two years younger," Beverly laughed. "Love him as a friend. Mandy and I are planning to keep you company while Lady Jane's busy hosting the reception."

"Commander Fleming is downstairs in the side bar introducing our hero to a chorus girl with the IQ of a peanut," Lt. Mandy said, modeling a yellow sheath that looked like it might be hard to breathe in. "Jack Cool will not be attending tonight's festivities."

Col. Randal said, "Good for him."

MAJOR GENERAL GEORGE S. PATTON JR. WAS STANDING IN THE LOBBY OF THE BRADFORD Hotel when the private elevator doors opened. He was magnificent. Beautifully tailored U.S. Army greens, jodhpurs in a color the army called "pinks," highly polished riding boots, pistol belt made by Sam Myres of El Paso, Texas, encasing a Colt Single Action Army .45 sporting ivory grips with "GSP" carved on the handle on one hip and a Smith & Wesson "Registered Magnum" *aka* .357 Magnum with matching ivory grips on the other.

The Colt .45 had two notches carved on the handle indicating the demise of a pair of bandits shot during a gunfight at a rancho in Mexico during the Punitive Expedition.

Major the Lady Jane Seaborn introduced herself, Colonel John Randal, Brandy Seaborn, Lieutenant Mandy Paige and Beverly Blackwell.

Maj. Gen. Patton studied Col. Randal's superbly cut Pembroke Military Tailors uniform sporting a pair of Lady Jane-designed Raiding Forces parachute wings sewn above the left breast pocket with a pair of silver U.S. Parachute Wings pinned above it.

"You are out of uniform, Colonel."

"Sir?"

"I understand you have been decorated," Maj. Gen. Patton said in his squeaky high-pitched voice, which he hated. "It's un-American for a soldier not to wear his medals. What the hell's the matter with you, Colonel?"

Lady Jane walked over to a phone in the lobby.

"Sir," Col. Randal said, "any awards I have were earned by the troops under my command . . ."

Ignoring him, Maj. Gen. Patton said, "Now that I take a look at it, that's the best damn cut uniform I ever saw. I want you to introduce me to your tailor."

The private elevator doors opened. Sergeant Major Maurice Chauncy stepped off, carrying a U.S. Army uniform jacket over one arm. Col. Randal removed the blouse he was wearing and was helped into the replacement. All his brass, awards, and decorations were in the proper place—highly polished, gleaming.

Maj. Gen. Patton's eyes bugged out.

"Thank you, General," Lady Jane said. "I can never convince John to wear his medals."

"If I had that many," Maj. Gen. Patton said, "I'd sleep in mine."

Captain "Geronimo" Joe McKoy arrived, resplendent in a white buckskin jacket and yellow alligator cowboy boots with an ivory-handled .45 Colt Peacemaker stuck in his belt in front. Maj. Gen. Patton looked like he had seen a ghost. "I heard you got killed in Nicaragua."

"Georgie Patton," Capt. McKoy said. "The army must be scrapin' the bottom of the barrel to make you a major general. Saw your picture on the cover a' *Life* magazine standin' in a tank wearin' a gold football helmet—looked like the Green Hornet."

Col. Randal did not say anything, but now that Captain McKoy mentioned it, he had seen the same copy of *Life* at RFHQ. And, he also remembered where he had heard of the general before. "Geronimo" Joe had named the mule he rode in Abyssinia after him.

"I can't believe it's you, Joe," Maj. Gen. Patton said. "Let's go have a drink to settle my nerves. I'm used to making speeches to troops where you give it to 'em dirty—not the aristocracy. Wouldn't do to create an international incident on my first trip to London.

"You kick me in the pants, Lady Seaborn, if I get off track tonight."

"Never fear," Lady Jane laughed. "You shall not offend anyone in this crowd. Be yourself, General."

Maj. Gen. Patton said, "That might be a mistake."

There was a long receiving line. Brandy did the honors, introducing each of the guests to Maj. Gen. Patton, Lady Jane, Col. John Randal and Capt. McKoy. The line moved slowly because so many of the couples in attendance had sons or daughters serving in Raiding Forces. The parents all wanted to have a word with Col. Randal, whom they had read about in letters home from Egypt but had never met. One glamorous blond in a slinky silver evening gown introduced herself as Raquel St. Ledger, "Bentley's mother—she tells me parachuting is better than sex."

"Bentley told you that?"

"Says you assigned her to beat your two female slaves, Colonel."

"I don't actually have any female slaves, Mrs. St. Ledger."

"That is *not* what Bentley claims."

Lady Jane came to his rescue. "John was simply teasing, Raquel. He *really* likes Bentley—we all do."

As the line moved on, Col. Randal said under his breath to Lady Jane, "You don't think Bentley's actually beating Rita and Lana, do you?"

"You gave her the order."

Raquel shook hands with Capt. McKoy, taking note of the ivory-handled Colt Single Action Army .45 revolver he had tucked beside the sterling silver belt buckle on the supple horsehair belt made by prisoners in the Wyoming State Correctional Institute.

"Are you expecting trouble tonight, Captain?"

"No ma'am," Capt. McKoy said. "If I was expectin' trouble, I'd a' brought my shotgun."

Maj. Gen. Patton turned out to be a charming, entertaining raconteur. His talk was all fire and fury about "killing Nazis," a policy everyone in the room heartily endorsed. The guests were being bombed, blacked out, and rationed. Most of them were on Hitler's death list in the event that England was invaded, which was still a possibility.

There were quite a few uniforms in the audience. Many of those not on active duty, men and women, were involved with war work. Everyone had at least one family member in the service, many several.

Some had lost loved ones.

"Killing Nazis" sounded like a jolly good idea. The quicker the better. Maj. Gen. Patton was everything an American general should be. Big, tough, brash, bloodthirsty and armed to the teeth.

Lady Jane's reception was a huge success.

After it was over, Col. Randal found Maj. Gen. Patton and Capt. McKoy in the smoking salon. The room was a dark teak-paneled, Indian rug-covered enclave dedicated to male conversation, ancient brandy and the enjoyment of fine cigars. Women were rarely allowed in—and then by invitation only, a practice frowned upon by the management.

The two old soldiers were refighting the shootout at San Manuelito during the Punitive Expedition, which was where the two notches on Maj. Gen. Patton's ivory-handled Colt had been earned—or maybe not. When the General was not looking, Capt. McKoy gave Col. Randal a wink. They had both been shooting at the Mexican bandits.

It was clear to Col. Randal that Maj. Gen. Patton still wanted Capt. McKoy's approval, even after all those years.

There were several versions of the gunfight story. What was consistent was that six soldiers from the 6th Infantry Regiment, under the command of then-Lieutenant George S. Patton Jr.—Major General John J. "Black Jack" Pershing's aide-de-camp—attacked a hacienda at a rancho known to be frequented by a famous bandit, General Julio Cardenas—commander of Pancho Villa's personal bodyguards, the Dorados. The U.S. Army troops, guided by Joe McKoy, chief of scouts, arrived unannounced and unexpected at a high rate of speed in three Model A Fords.

And that was when Lieutenant George S. Patton Jr. shot Cardenas' horse.

Three bandits, including the general, were killed. Who shot who and when was a matter of debate. Not in question was that Lt. Patton had carefully planned the raid in advance, thoroughly briefed the three carloads of soldiers on the exact scheme of maneuver they were to carry out upon arrival at the rancho, and then, leading the charge, executed the operation to perfection.

The gunfight made Lt. Patton a national hero—called the "Bandit Killer" in the press. It earned him the distinction of commanding the first mechanized infantry attack in history. The photo of the three Model As with the dead bandits strapped to the fenders like trophy deer was on display at the Cavalry School at Fort Riley Kansas. Col. Randal had seen it when he was an officer student at the school after graduating from ROTC.

The manager appeared at their table.

"Colonel Randal," he said, "two young ladies in the lobby request your permission to join you, sir."

He seemed genuinely pained by the prospect.

Col. Randal leaned around him to see who was at the door—Lt. Mandy and Beverly were peeking in.

"They're with me."

Which meant Lady Jane, and she owned the hotel.

The two girls walked in, ignoring the frowns from the other smokers in the room. "Thanks, John. We didn't think it was fair for you boys to be having all the fun," Beverly said.

Maj. Gen. Patton and Capt. McKoy grinned at being called "boys."

Lt. Mandy opened her small bag and took out two of Waldo Treywick's custom-rolled cigars. Capt. McKoy held out his brandy snifter. The girls dipped the ends of their cigars in the brandy, and Col. Randal offered a light from his battered U.S. 26th Cavalry Regiment Zippo.

Maj. Gen. Patton said, "You ladies carry cigars in your purses?"

"We saw the three of you in here, General," Beverly laughed. "Mandy and I snuck up to John's room and raided his stash."

"Pack pistolas in them little handbags," Capt. McKoy said. "Couple-a' regular gun molls—girls can shoot."

"Mandy's MI-5 and Beverly's OSS," Col. Randal said. "That's classified, sir."

"In that case, I can relax," Maj. Gen. Patton said. "If the Germans invade while we're in here smoking cigars, you two secret agents can provide my security."

Mandy and Beverly rewarded him with magnificent smiles, clearly enjoying themselves. They liked the general. Even if he did have a squeaky voice.

Maj. Gen. Patton turned to Col. Randal. "I've been studying everything I can lay my hands on about the Eighth Army's operations. I'm a student of maneuver warfare—made it a point to read everything ever written about mobile combat going back to antiquity. You tell me, Colonel, how the hell does Rommel manage to win all those battles against the numerically super British with the 1,500-mile-long supply line he has to contend with?"

"I don't know much about strategy, sir," Col. Randal said. "Afrika Korps *tactics* are easy to understand. Rommel deploys his infantry, antitank guns and armor in a combined arms team," he said.

"The Desert Fox sets up defensive positions with his antitank artillery, primarily German 88s, stationed in the rear, heavily camouflaged. The infantry, which is mechanized, is positioned in front of the antitank artillery, with the panzers advanced some distance forward, seemingly all alone by themselves.

"What happens is this, sir," Col. Randal said, "the British cruise around the desert in armored formations looking for someone to fight. They spot Rommel's tanks and charge. The panzers retreat, picking up the infantry as they go, appearing to run away. The British tanks give chase, only to be drawn onto the antitank screen where they are shot to pieces by the 88s.

"Then the panzers counterattack. The infantry mops up. Works every time, sir."

Maj. Gen. Patton said, "That's it?"

"Rommel can count on the Luftwaffe having Stuka JU-87s stationed close to the front on call as flying artillery, sir," Col. Randal said.

"Don't chase the tanks without having scouts out. Everything you need to know 'bout fightin' Afrika Korps, Georgie," Capt. McKoy said, "in a nutshell."

Maj. Gen. Patton said, "I would like to discuss this with you in more detail at a later date, Colonel."

"My pleasure, sir."

Lady Jane walked into the smoking room, not waiting for an invitation. The three men at the table stood up. "General, I would like to invite you to be my guest to ride with the Beaufort Hunt tomorrow at 1100 hours. You shall be able to renew your acquaintance with more than a few of tonight's guests. Mandy and Beverly are riding as well."

"I would be delighted," Maj. Gen. Patton said. "Promptly at eleven. Very gracious of you, Lady Seaborn."

"Time to wrap it up, gentlemen," Lady Jane said, "John's been going for over twenty-four hours—as have you, Captain McKoy. Bed time."

And that was that.

Maj. Gen. Patton pulled Col. Randal aside as the group walked out into the lobby. "Colonel, it's no secret I'm to command one of the Task Forces that attacks the Axis somewhere, sometime in the future. I could use a good commando type unit when we do.

"You interested?"

"Sir," Col. Randal said. "Raiding Forces is a small, highly specialized outfit spread out from England to Egypt. I doubt we're what you have in mind."

Maj. Gen. Patton asked, "Are you aware of any U.S. Army unit with amphibious special operations capabilities I might be able to get my hands on?"

"There's one, sir," Col. Randal said. "The 10th Ranger Battalion. Captain Dance, their commander, currently has them at a place called Little Creek, Virginia, attending the navy's Scout and Raider School. No one seems to have a mission for the battalion."

Maj. Gen. Patton said, "They do now."

"Two things I'd like to mention, sir, based on our conversation," Col. Randal said. "If you're serious about studying operations in Middle East Command, try to get your hands on Colonel Bonner Feller's daily messages to the War Department. He was the U.S. Military Attaché stationed in Cairo until recently.

"Probably classified material, sir—you did not hear it from me."

Maj. Gen. Patton said, "What's the second thing?"

"Your signals officer may be your most valuable asset," Col. Randal said. "If you'd like to send someone out to take a look at Raiding Forces' commo setup, we'll show him how it works. We have excellent communications all over the desert, as well as to Washington and London.

"The rest of Eighth Army can't even talk to itself."

"I'll be taking you up on both those suggestions," Maj. Gen. Patton said. "When I get my command organized, would you be available to fly to the States to talk to my people? I'd like my officers to hear firsthand what they're going up against, the way you explained it to me—short and simple. Like it says in your Rules."

"Sir," Col. Randal said. "I was asked to brief the Airborne Training Center at Fort Benning about British parachute developments. The staff didn't care to hear one thing I had to say."

"My men will listen," Maj. Gen. Patton said, "or I'll kick 'em in the ass."

"In that case," Col. Randal said, "love to, General."

The next morning a huge bouquet of flowers was delivered to Lady Jane's room from Maj. Gen. Patton, as a token of thanks for hosting the reception. There was a book for Col. Randal, *On War* by Carl von Clausewitz, with a note.

"Time to start learning strategy."

THE ENIGMA DEVICE CAPTAIN BILLY JACK JAXX CAPTURED DID NOT CONTAIN THE HIGHLY sought-after fourth rotor wheel.

3

STRAFER GOT STRAFED

COLONEL JOHN RANDAL WAS IN THE SUITE HE SHARED WITH MAJOR THE LADY JANE SEABORN AT RFHQ. She was away in Cairo, about a ninety-minute drive, but they were to meet later for lunch. Rita Hayworth and Lana Turner were sunbathing nude out by the private pool, with Happy, the German shepherd, keeping them company. Lady Jane had explained that the girls did not want tan lines because they were resuming their undercover work for MI-5, dancing at the Kit-Kat Club. The two were minor celebrities among the fast set.

Col. Randal was not able to see any bruises, which was a good thing. Apparently Sub-Lieutenant Bentley St. Ledger had *not* been beating them—or at least not hard enough to leave marks—he was afraid to ask.

He was reading a brief synopsis of the military situation worldwide and a stack of reports prepared for him by Lieutenant Stephanie Fawcett-Tatum, RM, about events that had taken place while he was in England. In the China–Burma–India Theatre of Operations, the Japanese were threatening India. The Germans appeared to be on the verge of defeating the Russians and then being able to cut through Persia to get at the Iraqi oil fields.

Rommel was digging in at El Alamein.

A lot had happened in the time he was away. Afrika Korps had been rushing supplies to Panzerarmee Afrika around the clock by any means possible, using the secondary tracks as well as the Via Balbia, when Col.

Randal departed for England. Now, Rommel was stalled out at El Alamein, and the RAF Desert Air Force was joining in conjunction with the U.S. Desert Air Task Force to focus on flying air/ground attack missions around the clock. The patrol reports indicated the bulk of enemy convoys had shifted back to the coastal hard-topped highway.

The Axis trucks were running almost exclusively at night. Raiding Regiment patrols, who were night stalkers by choice, would notify Wing Commander Ronald Gordon, *aka* "Flash Bang", at Oasis X when they had a target. He would dispatch the pair of captured Regia Aeronautica Ro.63s followed by a pair of A-20 Havocs configured as night fighters. These gunships had their four Hispano 20mm cannons replaced with a package of six Browning .50 caliber machine guns, giving the aircraft a total of eight forward-firing guns firing rounds the size of cigars. The patrol on the ground would put out flares marking the direction to the target, the Ro.63s would drop parachute flares illuminating the enemy convoy, then the A-20s would roll in with all guns blazing.

It was clear from the patrol reports that Lieutenant Colonel Sir Terry "Zorro" Stone, KBE, DSO, MC, and W/Cdr Gordon had been hard at work refining air ground cooperation. An attached note said they were experimenting with adding an additional four forward-firing .50 caliber machine guns to the A-20s in "blisters" of two guns each on both sides of the cockpit to increase firepower. The RAF, after a long history of refusing air cooperation to attack ground targets, was being remarkably supportive for a change and willing to experiment.

Before departing for England, Col. Randal had issued orders for the Raiding Regiment's patrols to concentrate on truck busting. Those instructions had been followed to the letter—and to good results—brought about by a handful of Raiding Forces personnel.

Desert Patrol, Lancelot Lancer Yeomanry Regiment, 2 RAF Company, the 575th Ranger Regiment and the Raiding Regiment all sounded like large formations. However, the names were intentionally misleading—designed to confuse. All up, Lt. Col. Stone had fewer than 250 men. Those troops, mounted on gun jeeps, had been hammering away at Panzerarmee Afrika convoys. In addition, Captain Roy Kidd's Scout Patrol I and Captain Dan Morgan's Scout Patrol II specialized in long-range truck plinking with scoped Boys .55 Anti-Tank rifles.

The patrols had been shooting up a lot of trucks—more than Raiding Regiment's actual troop strength would have led anyone to believe possible. They were going to have to. An intel report marked SECRET noted Panzerarmee Afrika had captured over 6,000 trucks from the British Army. The United States of America was supplying the Allies *and* the Axis. An addendum noted Y-Service intercepts indicated Rommel preferred the British and U.S. Lend Lease trucks to his German models which had dual axel rear wheels because they experienced fewer problems with stones becoming stuck in the back tires.

Col. Randal was pleased to read that Raiding Regiment was not taking casualties at the same rate it had during the disastrous CRUSADER period.

Captain "Geronimo" Joe McKoy walked in.

"That was a dang good R&R, John. I'm feelin' fresh as a daisy."

Which was a strange remark to be coming from a man who, while on leave, had participated in one of the most disastrous military operations in modern history. Slightly fewer than 5,000 Canadians had gone on the raid to Dieppe; just a little over 2,000 had made it home. The exact numbers had not yet been established but were in the 60 percent casualty range. The RAF reported 106 planes lost, seventy-one pilots and ten aircrew killed or missing in action. The Royal Navy lost one destroyer, thirty-three landing craft and 550 sailors.

4 Commando was the only unit in OPERATION JUBILEE to accomplish its mission—unless you counted Raiding Forces taking out a dummy battery of telephone poles. The Dieppe raid was a national military disaster and an embarrassment of arms. Repercussions were reverberating throughout Allied Armed Forces.

The official line was that the raid on Dieppe was a test designed to determine how difficult it was for an amphibious force to capture a Nazi-defended port on the coast of France. That story was a lie. What was amazing was that anyone actually believed it.

In fact, Col. Randal knew, the raid on Dieppe was a large-scale cover operation designed by Combined Operations at the request of the Naval Intelligence Division (NID). The sole purpose of OPERATION JUBILEE was to conceal the true purpose of the raid, which was to capture one of the latest model Enigma encoding/decoding machines with the new four-rotor wheel installed—the fourth rotor now being used by some units of the Kriegsmarine made cracking it statistically impossible. Who would ever guess an entire reinforced infantry division would be deployed to hide the fact that a small party of NID Commandos was carrying out a clandestine mission? Certainly not the officers and men of the 2nd Canadian Division assaulting the beach or Numbers 2 and 3 Commando supporting it.

Commander Ian Fleming's new RED INDIAN Commandos failed to capture the Enigma machine. Most of them did not even make it ashore. And the sacrifice of the 2nd Canadian Division on the beaches at Dieppe proved it was suicide to attempt to invade a defended port city by head-on amphibious assault.

OPERATION RUTTER also demonstrated beyond any reasonable doubt that playing at Special Operations was a guaranteed formula for failure. Experienced leaders and highly trained men were required.

Col. Randall's angry reflections about the Dieppe raid were interrupted by the sound of cheering from outside. He had been hearing it from time to time all morning. "What's going on out there, Captain?"

"Beverly Blackwell was teachin' Lady Jane and some a' her Marines how to barrel race," Capt. McKoy said. "Them little Arab ponies turned out to be real good at runnin' the barrels. The girls are lovin' it—Lady Jane's about ready to go on the rodeo circuit. Mandy ain't half bad.

"Pretty soon they had 'em an audience, and as you know we got us quite a few cavalry boys in Raiding Forces, since you recruited the polo teams of the Life and Horse Guards for your first bunch a' men. Some of 'em wanted to give barrel racin' a try. But they couldn't keep up with Beverly timewise.

"Words was exchanged, one thing led to another, then Beverly accepted a challenge from one of the ex-polo team players to try his game—a one-on-one polo match."

Col. Randal said, "Beverly knows how to play polo?"

"Her daddy has hisself a team," Capt. McKoy said. "Rich south Texas ranchers play some, likin' any sport has to do with livestock. Beverly says he takes his southwest Texas squad up the East Coast and competes in tournaments against them New England blue bloods."

"Really?"

"Her daddy's big rich."

"One-on-one polo against an Olympic-class player," Col. Randal said. "How's she doing?"

"Beverly failed to mention her father owned a polo team—beat the daylight outta that poor trooper—believe he was a Blue," Capt. McKoy said. "She was polishing off her third victim when I was comin' up here.

"Got a story for you, John."

"Let's hear it," Col. Randal said, sticking one of Waldo's long, thin cigars between his teeth.

"You know we, meanin' the U.S. of A., supplied the Eighth Army with a bunch a' Grant tanks."

"I do."

"Well, there's lotsa problems with 'em. Maintenance record's pretty spotty. The tanks is too tall to take up much of a hull-down position, which ain't good when the opposition's a- shootin' at you. That said, Eighth Army loves the Grant. It has a 37mm gun *and* a 75mm main gun, which allows 'em to outmatch the Nazi tanks distance-wise for the first time ever. They're callin' the Grant the 'ELH' tank for 'Egypt's Last Hope'.

"The thing is, the U.S. M-72 armor-piercing ammo fired by the Grant's 75mm main gun ain't much good against the German Mark III tank's frontal armor. The solid steel shot shatters on the panzer's face-hardened plate."

Col. Randal said, "That's a problem."

"Yeah," Capt. McKoy said. "But the British ordnance boys hit on a plan. Eighth Army had captured a monster stockpile of Nazi 75mm armor piercing rounds no one knew what to do with. So they used the 75mm armored tip to cap the U.S. M-72 rounds. The reloaded AP shell fit the Grant's breech like a glove—shot through those Mark III's frontal armor like a knife cuttin' hot butter. Problem solved.

"Modified a ton of U.S. M-72s."

"That's good," Col. Randal said.

"Well, not really," Capt. McKoy said. "Rommel recaptured all of 'em."

COLONEL JOHN RANDAL AND MAJOR THE LADY JANE SEABORN WERE SITTING AT A TABLE IN THE back of the Gezira Club's restaurant, partially hidden by a palm. The place was packed. A substantial number of officers from the United States Army Air Force Desert Task Force were at the bar, crowding out some of the bearded pretenders from General Headquarters (GHQ) staff. More Americans were arriving in Cairo every day.

The atmosphere had changed in the few weeks since they had last visited. Resolve had replaced the despair that had hung in the air after Panzerarmee Afrika's last offensive. Eighth Army had Rommel stopped on the El Alamein line, a place in the middle of nowhere—named by the Bedouins for the two red flags the railroad surveyors had placed in the sand to mark the end of the tracks.

Which, up to now, was probably the most interesting thing to ever take place there.

Eighth Army and Panzerarmee Afrika had fought to a draw. The opposing forces were lying up, eyeing each other while licking their wounds and doing their best to regroup, resupply and reconstitute. The next phase of the battle was going to be decisive.

Do or die.

As usual, Lady Jane was entertaining Col. Randal with a story.

"Prime Minister Churchill stayed in our suite at Mena House. We shall never get all the cigar smoke out. Hotel staff tells me he left behind a pile of empty brandy bottles to rival the Great Pyramid.

"He fired Auchinleck," Lady Jane said. "Replaced him with General Sir Harold Alexander."

Col. Randal said, "The Auk would have made a brilliant Eighth Army commander, but he never had any business being commander-in-chief."

"Agreed," Lady Jane said. "After conducting interviews with a number of corps and division commanders, the PM came to the conclusion that the senior Eighth Army officers had lost confidence in the Field Marshal.

"Not that our troops showed much enthusiasm for Winnie either."

"Really?"

Lady Jane's green eyes started sparkling, "When the Prime Minister inspected the 9th Australian Division, one of the soldiers—possibly from your friend Colonel 'Hard-as-Nails' Hammer's 48 Battalion—shouted, 'When are you going to send us home, you fat old bastard?'"

Col. Randal said, "Those are tough troops."

Lady Jane said, "'Strafer' Gott was elevated to take over Eighth Army. On the way to Cairo to assume his post, the general's plane was shot down. He was killed when the Germans machine gunned it on the ground. Now someone named Bernard Montgomery will command the army."

"The Strafer got strafed," Col. Randal said.

"Exactly."

"What's all this mean for you personally, Jane?"

"Sir Harold asked me to stay on as his social secretary," Lady Jane said. "I agreed on a limited basis. One of my Marines, possibly Stephanie, can fill in during my absence.

"My desire is to focus on developing Raiding Forces' relationship with OSS."

"I see," Col. Randal said. Which meant he did not have a clue where this was heading. Lady Jane had a plan.

Brigadier Raymond J. Maunsell—who liked to be called "R. J."—and James "Baldie" Taylor arrived at the table.

R. J. said, "Colonel, I am here to solicit your assistance on a matter of some importance."

Col. Randal clicked on, so much for a quiet lunch with his drop-dead gorgeous fiancée.

R. J. said, "With Colonel Fellers out of the picture, Captain Seebohm dead, and Eighth Army holding at El Alamein, Rommel is floundering. The Field Marshal seems to have lost his legendary, highly exaggerated 'finger touch' for the battlefield."

"Gee," Col. Randal said, "that's too bad."

"Not for the home team," R. J. said. "The Desert Fox is finding it to be rather more difficult to be a military genius when we are not telling him all our plans in advance. Now, with Panzerarmee Afrika stalled, the time has come to turn our attention to other matters."

Col. Randal said, "Like what?"

"We have three problems," R. J. said. "Each one has national strategic implications and all three pose a threat to the Allies' and/or the Axis' ability to conduct the war. Your mission is to resolve all three in our favor. For reasons I will not go into, this needs to be an OSS operation. MI-6, MI-5, SOE, SIME and all branches of the British military will support you to their fullest ability.

"Needless to say, we are not having this conversation."

It was the last thing Col. Randal wanted to hear. Raiding Regiment was running patrols around the clock. Sea Squadron had units out nightly and had been forced to relocate from its base in Alexandria because of Rommel's last big push east. The Royal Navy had panicked, raised anchor and sailed for safer harbor, taking the squadron with it. And Raiding Forces was in the process of settling in after a period of extensive reorganization. Now was not the time to be distracted by a new mission—or was it three new missions?

Col. Randal said, "Lovely."

R. J. said, "There is a thriving black market in illicit diamonds centered here in Cairo. The stones are purchased in the bazaars by the criminal element and hidden on merchant ships to be transported up the West African coastline: French Guinea to Sierra Leone, Liberia, Ivory Coast and the Gold Coast. We turned a blind eye to the trade up until now because it was relatively harmless. Small businessmen, West Africans, Syrians, Jews, Vichy French, Irishmen, the odd American and a fair share of expatriate Englishmen all trying to eke out a living in the decrepit port towns along the coast see nothing untoward about the time-honored business of smuggling, even if the end user is the enemy.

"The black market traffic in diamonds was petty enough in the beginning. As always happens when the money is good, the trade becomes more and more organized. Major crime organizations became involved.

"Diamonds fall into two categories: gemstones and industrial diamonds. We have little interest in the gems as they have no strategic value unless they are ground up, which is cost prohibitive. Our concern is industrial diamonds. We, as well as the Nazis, need them to harden the tips of tools and to manufacture precision instruments.

"The diamonds are purchased in Cairo and then secreted aboard merchant ships that ply the West African Coast. When the steamers reach a neutral port, the stones are spirited ashore and sold to German agents.

"More than a few of our RAF pilots have become ensnared by the smugglers—paid extravagant bribes to carry diamonds on board their aircraft when they have a flight to Gibraltar. Once there, the stones are clandestinely deplaned, whisked across the border to Spain and straight to Germany."

"The Third Reich has no diamond mines of its own. The Nazis are wholly dependent on the illegal traffic to supply their industrial diamonds. However, Hitler can—and does—rely on private purchases from DeBeers, *aka* The Diamond Company, through their offices in Switzerland."

Lady Jane gasped, "Surely that cannot be true!"

R. J. said, "Sadly, it is. The British-managed South African conglomerate has a worldwide monopoly on the diamond industry—over ninety percent of the market. Our intelligence indicates DeBeers is supplying industrial diamonds to both sides, though the company vehemently denies trafficking with the enemy.

"The United States is infuriated with DeBeers. The Diamond Company's board of directors recently declined a request to increase the allocation of industrial diamonds the firm sells to America. President Roosevelt, concerned England might still be invaded, has quite reasonably asked DeBeers to transfer its commercial stockpile, which is being stored in a vault in London, to the U.S. or Canada for safekeeping.

"DeBeers claims the vault in London was damaged in an air raid. The Diamond Company says it is not possible for the doors to be opened.

Apparently, money, greed and maintaining their iron-fisted control of the market have blinded the directors to reality. What they believe will happen if Hitler wins the war is a complete mystery.

"While the sordid DeBeers saga is played out at the highest levels of government on three continents," R. J. said, "it is of little interest to us except for background information.

"At this stage, things have become so heated between The Diamond Company and the United States government the President has threatened to cut off shipment of military airplanes to Great Britain if the Prime Minister does not force DeBeers into line."

Col. Randal said, "That's some story."

"Next—gold," R. J. said. "The Nazis need gold to purchase the industrial diamonds.

"Gold from all over Africa is being smuggled to Cairo primarily by ship but by other means as well. The gold is sold in the bazaars here in the city, where it sells for up to thirty times the going rate. Then it is spirited overland to Turkey by camel caravan and on across the Aegean to Greece by ship, then moved to Germany. Once the Nazis obtain the gold, it is transported by rail to Switzerland where the diamond buy takes place."

R. J. said, "Polish Air Force pilots in Middle East Command were the first to be involved in smuggling early on. They are making a bloody fortune off the Nazis who invaded their country, murdered tens of thousands of their fellow officers, confiscated their properties, etc.

"Some of our RAF pilots have since fallen in with the traffickers, victim to the enormous bribes being paid. They smuggle gold to buy the diamonds the Nazis then use to make bomb sights to bomb their homes in England."

"Pretty cold," Col. Randal said. "Sounds crazy."

"Stand by," R. J. said. "The tale I am going to tell you next is so bizarre you will have trouble believing it."

Lady Jane said, "I am having trouble accepting that DeBeers sells to both sides and our lads in the RAF are trafficking with the enemy."

"I feel the same way," R. J. said. "As I mentioned, industrial diamonds are used to manufacture precision instruments. For example, premium grade watches such as that Rolex you are wearing, Colonel. In Great Britain, we do not possess the manufacturing capability to make timepieces of equal quality. Our high-end luxury watches originate in Switzerland, Germany or Italy and are imported. The war put a stop to that.

"The RAF in Middle East Command is desperate for precision timepieces. Navigators require them. According to Air Chief Marshal Tedder, more planes are lost due to navigational errors than enemy action. With the war on, we can only obtain premium watches from the Swiss. Unfortunately, Switzerland is completely surrounded by the Nazis and we have no commercial flights into or out of the country."

R. J. said, "The Germans want gold and diamonds. We have—or can lay our hands on—gold and diamonds. The Nazis have access to German, Italian and Swiss watches. What to do?

"About a year ago, some enterprising RAF lads loaded up a Lend Lease Liberator with gold and diamonds while some equally enterprising Luftwaffe lads loaded up a JU-52 with watches. Both planes landed in Lisbon. An exchange of cargo was made. Everyone was satisfied and there were no international repercussions, Portugal being a neutral country. Both aircraft flew back to their respective bases—mission accomplished.

"That practice has continued to this day."

"You're right," Col. Randal said. "That one's hard to believe."

"Your mission, Colonel," R. J. said, "is to put a stop to the illicit trade in gold, diamonds and timepieces."

Jim said, "The RAF still needs the watches."

Lady Jane said, "The Royal Air Force is engaging in trade with the enemy?"

"With the tacit approval of Air Chief Marshal Tedder and SOE, who coordinates the arrangements with the Nazis," R. J. said, "Tedder is angst-ridden by the incongruity. He has requested a private audience with you, Colonel, to explain in person the desperate plight his air crews find themselves in."

"The RAF is trading gold to the Nazis for watches to buy the diamonds to make the bombsights the Luftwaffe uses to bomb RAF airbases," Lady Jane said. "Seriously, is everyone a traitor or are they all simply insane?"

R. J. said, "I can only speak for myself—mark me down as totally insane."

"Why me?" Col. Randal asked.

"Because the United States, and you specifically, in your capacity as the senior OSS officer in Middle East Command, are the only person to have clean hands at this point," R. J. said. "However, count on USAAF pilots getting caught up in the black market trade in diamonds and gold sooner rather than later. The profits are enormous and the bribes irresistible."

Jim said, "I am flying to Washington this afternoon to brief 'Wild Bill' Donovan on the situation. I am one hundred percent confident he will greenlight Raiding Forces' involvement."

"Let me get this straight," Col. Randal said. "You want all three smuggling operations closed down by OSS?"

R. J. said, "I do not care how you go about it, what it costs, or who you have to kill."

A RED-TABBED STAFF OFFICER WEARING THE BADGES OF THE 1st ROYAL TANK REGIMENT (KINGS) was waiting to see Colonel John Randal when he and Major the Lady Jane Seaborn returned to Raiding Forces Headquarters from Cairo. Lady Jane introduced him as "Major Desmond Barrymore, General Alexander's senior aide."

Maj. Barrymore said, "General Alexander asked me to brief you on certain pressing concerns GHQ has, sir. Is there some place we can have a private conversation?"

Col. Randal said, "Sure, come up to our suite."

When they arrived on the third floor, Flanigan was on duty at the desk. Col. Randal said, "No visitors."

"Sir!"

Once inside, Col. Randal said, "If you'll give me a minute, Major."

"Yes, sir."

He went into the master bedroom with Lady Jane.

Col. Randal said, "Ring the Operations Room, have Stephanie or whoever has the duty contact Admiral Ransom, Mr. Zargo, Major Sansom, Captain McKoy, Waldo and King. Set up a meeting here as soon as possible."

"I would very much like to sit in," Lady Jane said. "At last, Raiding Forces has a project I can be involved with from the start."

"Fine," Col. Randal said. "Might as well add Mandy to the list too. There won't be any keeping her out of this."

"Why not include Beverly . . . she *is* OSS," Lady Jane said. "If nothing else, as my assistant. We shall want Brandy and Parker involved as soon as they return from London."

"Your call," Col. Randal said.

"I shall contact R. J. and ask him to attend as well," Lady Jane said. "Bound to be questions we do not have the answers to."

"Good idea."

When Col. Randal returned to the living area, Maj. Barrymore did not waste time. He immediately began a rundown of the current military situation in Middle East Command.

"Some day in the distant future, sir," Maj. Barrymore said, "historians will make sense out of everything that has taken place in the last few weeks. Put it all into perspective nice and neat with names, dates and times for every action.

"In truth, sir, there has been a series of confused seesaw battles between Eighth Army and Afrika Korps. No one, at least on our side, really understands everything that has occurred. The last month has been characterized by chaos, confusion and the fog of war wrapped in a kasmin.

"A lot of mistakes have been made, sir. Communications have been horrific, causing blunders resulting in unintended battles occurring in places of no strategic or tactical value. Vital positions paid for in blood intended to be held at all costs were withdrawn from—given up without a fight.

"Our commanders have been at each other's throats. The Australians refused some orders, only to carry them out later on their own authority exactly as originally issued. The New Zealanders threatened to refer assignments they do not agree with to their government, as is their right. The South Africans have either fought hopelessly or brilliantly—the 1st South African Division CO, Dan Pienaar, does not get along with anyone, but he is a good battle commander. Our infantry hates our armor for swanning off and abandoning them. The list goes on.

"Eighth Army is a Commonwealth coalition; the army squabbles among itself almost as ferociously as it fights the enemy. However, it stopped the Desert Fox in his tracks and with a little luck—just a little—could have completely destroyed Panzerarmee Afrika. Rommel's offensive has run out of steam. His troops are exhausted. His excessively long supply lines are under constant attack.

"And he is out of fuel, sir.

"The Desert Fox does not have enough to advance and he does not have enough to retreat. The Axis army is digging in because they have no other option.

"General Alexander ordered me to come here today to provide you these details, sir, knowing you have been away, and to request that Raiding Forces concentrate its efforts on knocking out Rommel's capacity to deliver fuel to the front.

"It is understood at GHQ your patrols have been concentrating on attacking wheeled transport to good effect, sir. The General has no wish for you to stop going after enemy trucking. Only, while you are at it, he would like you to do everything you possibly can to attack fuel storage depots and fuel carriers."

"We can do that," Col. Randal said. "Tank farms are soft targets. We know where a lot of them are located. Tanker trucks . . . that's another story. Unless we have specific intelligence, it's hit or miss on ambushing convoys transporting fuel."

"Understood, sir," Maj. Barrymore said. "I shall pass that information along to General Alexander.

"On another subject, Colonel, a situation is brewing among the private armies, causing unnecessary friction that needs to be resolved. The Long Range Desert Group and the Special Air Service are feuding. Once the SAS obtained its own vehicles and gained enough experience to navigate their way in the desert, they became a law unto themselves. They do not play well with others.

"As you probably know, sir, the LRDG is carrying out a sensitive mission called 'Road Watch', which is pure reconnaissance, requiring stealth, patience and a high degree of skill.

"SAS has been provided the coordinates where LRDG will be conducting operations at a given time and place to avoid a clash between the two units. David Stirling simply ignores the information, sir. If a target is 'juicy', as the Major puts it, he attacks—regardless of the problems it creates for the Road Watch.

"General Alexander would like your assistance brokering a peace treaty between SAS and LRDG, sir. He wants everyone working off the same page. The word is you are the man to make that happen."

"Colonel Dudley Clarke would be who you need for the job," Col. Randal said. "Dudley works with both the LRDG and the SAS."

The last thing Col. Randal wanted was to get involved in a turf war.

"Actually, sir," Maj. Barrymore said, "Colonel Clarke suggested you."

"The General have any advice," Col. Randal said, "on how to go about it?"

"Not exactly, sir," Maj. Barrymore said. "General Alexander instructed me to say, 'Tell Randal he has my full backing to do whatever he feels is necessary to bring peace to the LRDG and SAS. The only thing off limits is shooting either Stirling or Pendergast'.

"Your reputation has preceded you, Colonel."

"Consider it done," Col. Randal said. "Now, if there's nothing else, Major, I'm extremely pressed for time."

"There is one other issue, sir," Maj. Barrymore said, as he was standing up to leave.

"Rommel never attended the German General Staff course. Apparently he failed to read Clausewitz either. If he had, the Desert Fox would have never handled Afrika Korps and later Panzerarmee Afrika in the manner he has chosen, knowing full well the farther he extended his operations from his logistical base the weaker and more vulnerable his army would become. Not only has the Field Marshal outrun his ability to deliver fuel to his attacking force, but he also pushed Panzerarmee Afrika past the range of the Luftwaffe to provide close air support, sir.

"The Luftwaffe is in a frenzy attempting to leapfrog improvised desert landing grounds east in order to keep their JU-87 Stuka dive bombers within range. General Alexander wants to put as much pressure on these new airstrips as possible. My, or his, question to you, sir, is: can he depend on the SAS to be able to handle the assignment since they claim to specialize in raiding airfields?"

"No."

"Why not, sir?"

"They're cowboys," Col. Randal said. "One of my NCOs went on the SAS raid to Benghazi as an observer. He reported that instead of conducting a deliberate approach march, Stirling made a mad dash across the desert at full speed in the middle of the night, like he was on a joy ride. The jeeps were virtual wrecks by the time the SAS reached the objective—lucky to make it back.

"Not only were the jeeps rendered combat ineffective, the inflatable boat they were carrying to attack shipping in the harbor was so damaged it couldn't be inflated. That part of the mission had to be scrubbed. SAS blew up a couple of warehouses, three or four fuel storage tanks and limped home."

"Not the way the newspapers described it, sir," Maj. Barrymore said. "They claim the Benghazi raid was a great victory."

"You believe what you read in the papers?"

"Negative, sir."

Col. Randal said, "Tell General Alexander I'll put advanced Luftwaffe landing grounds back on Raiding Forces' priority target list."

Maj. Barrymore said, "A pleasure doing business with you, Colonel."

LIEUTENANT MANDY PAIGE AND BEVERLY BLACKWELL CAME THUNDERING UP THE STAIRS. THE two girls were wearing cut-off blue jean shorts and peewee cowboy boots. Colonel John Randal clicked on the instant they charged into the room.

Lt. Mandy said, "Stephanie asked us to hand-carry this to you, John. The message is so hush-hush, she put it in an envelope and sealed the flap to keep us from reading it."

Beverly said, "Maybe it's a secret mission."

Col. Randal said, "All our missions are secret, Beverly."

He produced a switchblade jump knife, slit open the envelope and took out the flimsy inside. It was marked, "GOLDEN FLEECE"—the most highly classified code word identifier to which Raiding Forces was authorized access. It meant drop everything and execute immediately.

> STAND-BY TO CONDUCT RED INDIAN RAIDS ON SHIPS IN HARBOR AND GERMAN SIGNAL INSTALLATIONS ASHORE LOCATED VICINITY OF MARSA MARUTH, EGYPT/DERNA, LIBYA AND/OR ISLAND OF CRETE STOP DETAILS TO FOLLOW BY HAND OF OFFICER STOP SIGNED FLEMING STOP

4
CLAUSEWITZ

COLONEL JOHN RANDAL WAS IN THE SMALL BRIEFING SECTION OF HIS THIRD-FLOOR SUITE. Lieutenant Stephanie Fawcett-Tatum, RM, was helping him put up a map of the continent of Africa. It took up nearly one whole section of a wall. He sat in a chair with one of Waldo's long, thin cigars in his teeth and stared at the map, more or less in shock.

"How far is it from here to the west coast?"

"Three thousand miles, John," Lt. Fawcett-Tatum said.

"Well," Col. Randal said, "we're going to have to conduct operations in West Africa, Stephanie."

"The distance I gave you is as the crow flies," Lt. Fawcett-Tatum said. "There is a lot of German, Italian and Vichy French territory in between. Have to fly or sail around it."

"Yeah," Col. Randal said, "going to take some planning."

Lt. Fawcett-Tatum said, "Who is our best logistician?"

"Jack Merritt," Col. Randal said. "But he's a ground transportation man. This is going to require RAF and naval experience."

"I'm sure you shall find someone, John. You always do."

"Lady Jane mentioned," Col. Randal said, "you might be headed to General Alexander's staff."

"We have discussed the possibility," Lt. Fawcett-Tatum said.

"I hate to see you go, Stephanie," Col. Randal said.

Lt. Fawcett-Tatum had been the third Royal Marine to join Lady Jane's detachment. She and Lady Jane had nursed him back to health after he had been wounded in the "Gunfight at the Blue Duck." Col. Randal liked having the tall, good-looking brunette around.

"Oh?"

"I realize your social pedigree is impeccable," Col. Randal said, "which would be a good thing for the General. However, unless you tell me not to, I'm going to request you to be allowed to stay here—maybe I can talk Lady Jane into a promotion."

"She has promoted me, John," Lt. Fawcett-Tatum said. "We have not announced it yet."

"Really?"

"I shall tell Lady Jane my preference is to remain in the job I have."

"You're sure?"

"Absolutely."

"Congratulations, Captain," Col. Randal said. "Have a cigar."

"I do not believe it's standard procedure to give female marines a cigar when they are promoted," Capt. Fawcett-Tatum laughed. "But I shall keep this one and treasure it forever."

Major the Lady Jane Seaborn, Veronica Paige and Beverly Blackwell walked in.

"I've just talked your new captain into staying here at RFHQ," Col. Randal said. "If you look at the map, Jane, you'll see we're going to need to keep all the talent we can get around here to handle our operations in West Africa."

Capt. Fawcett-Taylor said, "I would very much like to remain at RFHQ full-time to see how John manages to pull this one off."

"You are welcome to serve anywhere you wish, Stephanie. As for you, John, the promotion was supposed to be a secret," Lady Jane said. "I wanted to surprise the Marines."

Col. Randal said, "Uh-oh."

Beverly laughed, "Now that you've told us, does that mean you have to kill us?"

Col. Randal said, "I'm going to get King to do it."

"Colonel Donovan sent me a confidential message," Lady Jane said, ignoring him. "The U.S. Army has assigned OSS responsibility for Escape. General Hap Arnold, Chief of Staff, USAAF, is making inquiries about the status of the program now that American pilots are beginning to be shot down and going into captivity.

"Wild Bill wants to know what your reaction to being asked to assume the added responsibility might be—under the mantle of 'special projects'.

"You're kidding," Col. Randal said.

Lady Jane said, "Donovan would like to inform the U.S. Army Air Force he already has a senior officer in Middle East Command organizing Escape and Evasion. He believes General Arnold is trying to embarrass OSS—inter-service rivalry."

"In that case, message Wild Bill," Col. Randal said, "Can do.'

"Why not create a joint US/UK Escape organization?" Lady Jane said. "Veronica can head it up. Beverly will be her American counterpart—on paper. I'm not giving her up."

"I like it," Col. Randal said. "Assign 'The Great Teddy' to the project. He makes things appear and disappear—we'll see what Ensign Hamilton can do with POWs.

"While you're at it, bring in Hawthorne Merryweather too. The captain's a political warfare mastermind. Maybe he'll have some ideas on how to use our POWs to disseminate misinformation or plant fear and despondency in the hearts and minds of the bad guys from their prison camps."

"You *have* been giving thought to MI-9," Veronica said. "I believed you were simply being polite, John, when you said you were going to help me get organized—no one else seems interested."

"The idea," Col. Randal said, "is to turn a lemon into lemonade. You'll get all the support Raiding Forces can give, which isn't going to be much."

"Very good, John," Lady Jane rewarded him with one of her heart attack smiles. "Any other suggestions?"

"Negative," Col. Randal said. "I'm mentally bankrupt."

COLONEL JOHN RANDAL WAS SITTING IN COLONEL DUDLEY CLARKE'S OFFICE AT A-FORCE HQ. Major David Stirling, the commanding officer of the Special Air Service, was in the lobby cooling his heels, waiting to be summoned. He was going to have to stand by a while longer. It had been a while since Col. Randal and Col. Clarke had had an opportunity to talk and they had a lot of catching up to do.

The two men had known each other from the early days of the war when Col. Clarke was heading up MO-9, tasked with organizing small raids on the French coast. Col. Randal, then a lieutenant just back from Calais following the evacuation of Dunkirk, had applied first aid to Col. Clarke when he earned the distinction of having created, named, planned, taken part in *and* been wounded during the first British Commando raid.

Following the mission, which was a total fiasco, Col. Clarke authorized the raising of the unit that would become Raiding Forces. The two were old friends, though it was said Col. Clarke still harbored ill feelings about Major the Lady Jane Seaborn, who he had been pursuing until she met Col. Randal in the Blind Eye pub near Seaborn House.

And there was some truth to the belief the A-Force commander did not really care much for Americans—unless they were famous.

The one subject not open for discussion was Col. Clarke's fairly recent adventure in Spain, where he had been arrested in drag. No satisfactory explanation for what he was doing dressed as a woman in a neutral country had ever been given, though officially he had been playing at being a secret agent. Still undisclosed was the identity of the person he claimed to have gone there to meet. There was not even the whisper of a rumor about who it might have been, which did nothing to quash speculation.

Col. Clarke was not telling. It was a mystery.

Col. Randal asked Col. Clarke to arrange the meeting with Maj. Stirling because the A-Force commander had not only sponsored, but also named, the Special Air Service—in effect the SAS worked for him. However, first things first. The two officers had a lot to talk about.

Eventually the subject got around to Rikke Runborg, *aka* Rocky.

Col. Clarke said, "Now that you eliminated Seebohm and Bonner Fellers has been recalled to the States, Rommel has lost his eyes and ears in our camp. Once again, Rocky is in position to be our most valuable misinformation intelligence asset if we play our cards right. R. J. and I have been working to rehabilitate her in the Desert Fox's eyes ever since she tricked him into being out of the country when CRUSADER kicked off.

"Rocky is all Rommel has left in the way of a highly placed agent in Cairo. He *wants* to believe she is reliable. Wanting to believe anything is a fatal flaw in a commander—gives the opposition something to work with."

Col. Randal said, "Well, you would know."

"We have big, big plans for Miss Runborg," Col. Clarke said. "Ensure her safety at all costs, Colonel. Even more so than ever before."

Col. Randal said, "Rocky has been living at Oasis X under tight security lately. However, she's flying back to RFHQ this afternoon. I'll have rotating protection on her twenty-four hours a day."

"Perfect," Col. Clarke said. "On another note, I understand you reorganized your gun jeep patrols into the Lancelot Lancer Raiding Regiment."

"We did," Col. Randal said. "Called the Raiding Regiment for short."

"I also heard you named the U.S. Army Paratroopers the 575th Ranger Patrol?"

"Roger," Col. Randal said. "That's deceptive. There are actually six patrols in its TO&E."

"I would rather you modify the name to 575th Ranger *Regiment* Patrol," Col. Clarke said. "Or better yet, simply the 575th Ranger Regiment. It suits A-Force purposes to keep up the illusion that we have a full U.S. Army Parachute Infantry Regiment in Egypt."

"We can do that," Col. Randal said.

"That is settled, then," Col. Clarke said. "Time to have Stirling in and get the unpleasantries over with."

Maj. Stirling was a tall, rawboned officer. It was said that he had gone into his cabin on the troopship out from England and slept the entire voyage to Egypt. His nickname was the "Big Sloth."

He may have been lazy, but no one had ever accused Maj. Stirling of being a coward. The commanding officer of SAS was badly injured attempting to teach himself how to parachute. Two of his men were killed before calmer heads had prevailed and called in Captain Roy "Mad Dog" Reupart, an experienced parachute instructor, to teach the SAS how it was done.

Maj. Stirling's command had been practically wiped out on two previous operations he had led—both of which were basically suicidal from the inception. Still, the Special Air Service never gave up, never quit. The SAS's main problem was missions planned by Middle East Command's Joint Planning Staff, who had no idea of the limitations of special operations troops.

Some claimed Maj. Stirling was overly ambitious. Officers who did not go along with GHQ staff's proposals were rumored to damage their prospects for promotion. He never refused a mission.

The Special Air Service was wholly owned by Col. Clarke; however, he typically left it to its own devices until he had a specific task for Maj. Stirling to perform. Maj. Stirling proposed to raise a unit to raid enemy airfields, and the A-Force commander had agreed to sponsor it when no one else was interested in the idea. In exchange, Maj. Stirling had to agree to name the unit the "Special Air Service Regiment" to foster the impression there was a substantial British airborne capability in Middle East Command. And SAS had to drop whatever it was doing to carry out missions for A-Force from time to time.

Now with SAS up and running, Maj. Stirling had come to resent the fact that he had to answer to Col. Clarke, considering it a pact made with the devil.

When Maj. Stirling walked in the office, it was clear he did not appreciate having been kept waiting. Col. Clarke made the introductions. While Col. Randal had seen the SAS officer at the bar at the Gezira Club on numerous occasions, the two had never formally met.

Col. Randal said, "General Alexander asked me to resolve a conflict between the SAS and the LRDG."

"What bloody conflict?" Maj. Stirling snarled.

"It's a big desert," Col. Randal said. "Apparently not big enough. The LRDG has complained that SAS is interfering with its Road Watch reconnaissance operations."

"Who bloody cares what the bloody LRDG complains about?" Maj. Stirling said.

"I do," Col. Randal said.

Maj. Stirling could not think of anything to say to that.

"Here's what's going to happen," Col. Randal said. "We'll draw a line across the middle of the desert north to south to the west of Benghazi. SAS can raid any target west of that line from Alexandria to Benghazi, provided it does not conflict with any operation Raiding Forces has going. I'll station a liaison officer or NCO at your headquarters to make sure nothing you plan interferes with our patrols."

"Bloody hell you will!"

"LRDG," Col. Randal said, "will shift its Road Watch west of Benghazi. There will not be any more problems. Is that clear?"

"What happens if I choose not to bloody agree?" Maj. Stirling said. "This is bloody highway robbery."

"I'll relieve you of command," Col. Randal said. "The SAS will be amalgamated into Raiding Forces. You'll be shipped home by non-priority, space-available, surface transport—which could take several months."

Maj. Stirling looked at Col. Clarke, desperate for some sign of help.

There was none to be had.

Col. Randal said, "I'm going to replace the jeeps you totaled on your Benghazi raid—wreck those and you won't get any more.

"A motion picture news crew will be arriving at SAS HQ in Kabrit sometime in the next few days. You're going to be famous—the 'Phantom Major'. Tell 'em how you wiped out all those Nazis on your Benghazi raid.

"Now, if there are no more questions," Col. Randal said, "I'm pressed for time."

After Col. Randal departed, Maj. Stirling said, "Not such a bad bloke actually, for a Yank."

"I have the impression the Colonel believes you are the man to turn the SAS into a valuable raiding organization once you get your legs under you," lied Col. Clarke, the world's master of deception. He was perfectly aware Col. Randal knew "Phantom Major" was a derisive nickname the SAS troops had bestowed on their commanding officer.

The name had been born while the troops trained in the burning hot desert and their boss was partying in Cairo.

COLONEL JOHN RANDAL WAS IN CONFERENCE WITH CAPTAIN "GERONIMO" JOE MCKOY, WALDO Treywick and King in the third-floor suite at Raiding Forces Headquarters. This was a meeting before the meeting. He was briefing three of his closest confidants on the various elements of the smuggling operation Raiding Forces, or in this case OSS, had been tasked to attack.

The three were ideal for the assignment: A law enforcement officer, a semi-reformed ivory smuggler and a mercenary with shadowy connections to Switzerland.

"How do you want to handle this deal, John?" Capt. McKoy said. "Prioritize or all at once?"

"I've been giving it thought," Col. Randal said. "You men are my key players. We'll set up what we'll unofficially call 'TASK FORCE', consisting of three sections. Each of you will head up a section—operate independently. We'll work together as necessary.

"Lady Jane has informed me she wants in. Jane can make sure we all stay on the same page. She's good at that.

"I want TASK FORCE to have a strictly limited 'Need to Know' list—operate outside normal Raiding Forces channels. We're not going to pay attention to constraints like the Geneva Convention."

Capt. McKoy said, "Good way to set it up—clandestine."

Col. Randal said, "King, you're on the Swiss watch problem. The RAF needs the shortage resolved. I'm hoping you can come up with a plan. I don't have a single suggestion.

"Waldo, link up with Major Sansom at SIME. He'll be working with you—at least in an advisory capacity. First tackle the illicit gold and diamond trade operating out of the bazaars here in Cairo. Then follow wherever the trail might lead.

"Captain, you've dealt with smuggling rings, bootleggers and gun runners along the Mexican border. I'm giving you the toughest assignment—responsibility for interdicting the industrial diamond and gold smuggling on the West African Coast.

"Questions?"

"Well, hell yes, John. We all ought to have a whole bunch," Capt. McKoy said. "Only you didn't give us enough information to come up with any."

"There's one other thing," Col. Randal said. "TASK FORCE is an Office of Strategic Services mission. British Intelligence doesn't want any part of it, officially.

"My guess is, sooner or later it's going to become crystal clear why that might be. As soon as one of you suspects you know the answer, tell me. Something's not right with this picture."

Capt. McKoy said, "You ain't wrong about that, John."

Waldo said, "Might be a profit to be made, Colonel."

"Go ahead," Col. Randal said, "No one's going to care as long as we accomplish the mission. You men have a completely free hand—do what you have to do. Keep Lady Jane informed."

"You're giving us a lotta rope," Capt. McKoy said.

"Take all you want," Col. Randal said. "Just get it done."

The phone rang. "Brigadier Maunsell and Major Barrymore to see you, sir."

This was not expected. Col. Randal had already met with both officers separately. The two walked in as Capt. McKoy, Waldo and King were leaving. They were clearly not making a social call.

Col. Randal clicked on.

"Y-Service intercepts," Brigadier Raymond J. "R. J." Maunsell said as soon as they were alone, "have alerted GHQ that Rommel is preparing to counterattack during the next full moon period."

This was not exactly true. The intelligence came from an Ultra decryption.

Neither Col. Randal nor Major Desmond Barrymore were cleared to know that information.

R. J. said, "Most likely Rommel wants to test General Montgomery before he has time to settle into his job as Eighth Army commander. But the Desert Fox has a problem.

"Panzerarmee Afrika does not have sufficient petroleum, oil and lubrication to make the attack. Herculean efforts are being made to ship POL from ports in Italy to North Africa. However, the Royal Navy, assisted by elements of the U.S. Navy and the combined air forces of both countries, are making a maximum around-the-clock effort to prevent the fuel from arriving. The problem is some ships always manage to slip through and it only takes one or two tankers reaching Panzerarmee Afrika to keep the panzers rolling."

R. J. said, "'Smiling Al' Kesselring, Rommel's boss, attempted to alleviate the crisis by flying in a massive fuel allotment aboard JU-52 transports. The planes landed in the Tripoli area. The fuel was pumped into 10-ton tanker trucks and convoyed east down the Via Balbia to El Alamein. Our Y-Service reports seventy-five percent of Field Marshal Kesselring's *entire* resupply ration was used up to fuel the lorries simply hauling the gas the fifteen hundred miles to the front.

"After that painful lesson, Panzerarmee Afrika is now attempting to utilize small Italian merchant marine steamers to ship POL down the coast to ports where it can be unloaded closer to the front. Unfortunately for Rommel, the Italian merchant ships are extremely vulnerable to attack.

"The bad news for our side is the small steamers are extremely difficult to locate sailing singly at night, unescorted, hugging the coastline like blockade runners. What General Alexander ordered me here to inquire is if your Sea Squadron would be able to aid in interdicting the Italian tankers . . ."

Col. Randal said, "Hold up right there, R. J."

He reached for the phone and dialed the Operations Room, "Stephanie, is the Admiral in his office? Good. Would you patch me through?"

"Lieutenant St. Ledger, sir,"

"Bentley, put the Admiral on the horn."

"Admiral Ransom."

"Sir," Col. Randal said, "could you come up to my suite?"

"Is this urgent, Colonel?"

"You might consider it a *Frogspawn,* sir."

"Shoving off now."

While they waited, Maj. Barrymore said, "The German 164th Division, the Italian Folgore Parachute Division, and the German Ramcke Parachute Brigade were flown from Italy to Africa during July. The paratroopers arrived without any motor transport. Now Rommel has more troops to haul, more mouths to feed, more ammunition to be delivered and no additional vehicles.

"You may remember, sir, I brought up Clausewitz in our last conversation."

"I do," Col. Randal said, not bothering to mention he had been reading the copy of *On War* given him by Major General George S. Patton. "The farther an attacking force advances from its supply base, the weaker it becomes. Something like that . . ."

"Outstanding, sir," Maj. Barrymore said. "General Alexander sent me back here with the Brigadier to make absolutely certain nothing we discussed in our previous meeting about Raiding Forces attacking fuel storage depots and Luftwaffe landing grounds gave you the impression you were to cease going after Rommel's overland convoys. Trucks are strategic targets. Panzerarmee Afrika's thin-skinned transport is in *critical* short supply."

R. J. said, "Some of the radio messages Y-Service intercepts are most entertaining. The airborne units flown in for the offensive Rommel personally promised Hitler would carry Cairo, which failed. They are elite shock troops; however, the men had no previous desert experience. Some of their equipment proved to be quite unsuitable.

"For example, they brought wood-burning stoves to cook on. There is no wood in the desert."

Col. Randal said, "Hate it when that happens."

Vice Admiral Sir Randolph "Razor" Ransom, VC, KCB, DSO, OBE, DSC, arrived, moving fast.

R. J. made the introductions. "Admiral, this is Major Barrymore—General Alexander's senior aide. The Major has been coordinating with

Colonel Randal on select targets for Raiding Forces to concentrate on when Eighth Army launches its next offensive—LIGHTFOOT.

"Panzerarmee Afrika is starving for fuel. As I am quite sure you are aware, the Kriegsmarine is attempting to ship POL from the tip of Italy to North Africa. The Nazis have decided to switch to having the Italian merchant fleet slip the POL down the coast at night to ports closer to El Alamein rather than truck it down the Via Balbia.

"General Alexander asked me to inquire if Sea Squadron would be able to assist in trying to interdict the tankers skirting the coastline."

VAdm. Ransom was the Royal Navy Director of Operations (Irregular). Not only had he sailed these waters in days past, his post put him in a position to know everything there was to know about the North African coast from Tripoli to Tobruk. He was also cognizant of the fact that the Royal Navy—even with the added support of the U.S. Navy—was stretched far too thin to adequately cover the long coastline in any meaningful way.

"Sea Squadron," VAdm. Ransom said, "consists of one Motor Gunboat, two captured Italian MAS boats and a Landing Craft Tank. They can contribute to the effort; however, none of them are armed with torpedoes. Afraid we will not be of much help, Major."

R. J. said, "I was hoping you would offer up Hornblower's squadron. GHQ is frantic to prevent the Nazi fuel resupply from reaching Rommel. The fate of the upcoming campaign very well could hang in the balance."

"Actually, I did. A normal torpedo boat or gunboat squadron consists of a dozen boats," VAdm. Ransom said. "Randy's three stationed along the length of that stretch of Mediterranean coastline are going to be like fleas in the Great Sand Sea."

R. J. said, "Admiral, can we step over into the living room for a moment? I require a word with you in private."

VAdm. Ransom glanced at Col. Randal to check his reaction to being left out. Getting no visible response, he said, "As you wish."

When the two were out of earshot, R. J. said in a tone barely above a whisper, "Admiral, we are able to supply Special Intelligence that gives you the location of the Italian merchantmen. However, we have an ironclad requirement that no surface attack can be made on any enemy ship until it has first been sighted by an aircraft."

VAdm. Ransom knew "Special Intelligence" was a term meaning material gleamed from an Ultra decrypt. Having the information was a game changer but no guarantee of success. The merchantmen still had to be sunk.

VAdm. Ransom said, "Advise General Alexander, subject to Colonel Randal's approval, Sea Squadron will cooperate in any way possible. However, be aware that even with Special Intelligence, the chances of our locating and sinking those Italian tankers is still a long shot."

MAJOR TAYLOR CORRIGAN, DSO, MC, THE COMMANDER OF SEA SQUADRON, AND CAPTAIN Billy Jack Jaxx arrived. They were waiting on the landing outside with Flanigan until the meeting in Colonel John Randal's suite broke up.

Vice Admiral Sir Randolph "Razor" Ransom said, "Drop by my office, Major, as soon as you conclude your business with the Colonel. We have another Sea Squadron mission in the offing that is going to require heavy lifting."

"Yes, sir!"

"Come on in," Col. Randal said. "Shut the door. Flanigan—no interruptions. I need a word with the Admiral, then I'll be right in."

Admiral Ransom waited on the landing until they were alone.

Col. Randal asked, "Not having torpedoes—is that going to be a problem, sir?"

"Negative, torpedoes are not necessary to sink trawlers," VAdm. Ransom said. "We shall pack so many guns on board Randy's boats, each one shall have a broadside the equal of a destroyer. If Hornblower manages to intercept one of the fuel tankers, Colonel, you can feel sorry for the unfortunate Italian sailors manning it."

Col. Randal said, "I'd like to go along some night."

VAdm. Ransom said, "Let me know when. I shall sail with you."

Col. Randal returned to the suite. The three men moved into the briefing area/map room.

"A nonspecific RED INDIAN alert has arrived. As you are both aware, any mission prefixed by that particular code word takes priority over everything else," Col. Randal said. "Raiding Forces has been ordered to be prepared to conduct raids on targets, aboard ships or shore installations located at Marsa Maruth, Egypt; Derna, Libya; and on the island of Crete—a Sea Squadron assignment.

"Major Corrigan, you will be in overall command."

"Yes, sir."

"Captain Jaxx, your Small Operations Group, with Duck Patrol attached as needed, will form the raiding element. You will be responsible for evaluating the targets and planning the concept of the operation phase of the missions—keep me in the loop. Major Corrigan will provide you all the assistance in his power to deliver."

"Yes, sir!"

"RED INDIANS are challenging under the best of circumstances," Col. Randal said. "These are not the best of circumstances. Intelligence indicates Rommel is planning to attack. I've been drawing up a target list at the request of General Alexander—we're going after Luftwaffe and Regia Aeronautica airfields and fuel storage facilities, and we have a requirement to keep up pressure on the Via Balbia.

"Your Sea Squadron, Major, is about to be tasked with an additional high-priority mission. Admiral Ransom will explain to you in greater detail when you go downstairs."

"Colonel, you must have been really bored to dream up all this," Capt. Jaxx said. "We're going to need a scorecard to keep up. Maybe I should have flown straight home and taken you on a gun jeep patrol to keep you entertained instead of hanging out in London for an extra week to party with Commander Fleming, sir."

Col. Randal said, "I was sitting right here in this room minding my own business . . ."

He had not even mentioned diamonds, gold or Swiss watches.

5
SNAKES

A CLASSIFIED BRIEFING WAS TAKING PLACE IN THE SUITE COLONEL JOHN RANDAL SHARED WITH Major the Lady Jane Seaborn on the third floor of Raiding Forces Headquarters. Present were: Col. Randal, Lady Jane, Vice Admiral Sir Randolph "Razor" Ransom, Major A. W. "Sammy" Sansom, Captain "Geronimo" Joe McKoy, Captain Pamala Plum-Martin, DSO, OBE, DFC, RM, Captain Penelope "Legs" Honeycutt-Parker, OBE, GM, RM, Lieutenant Mandy Paige, Mr. Zargo, Brandy Seaborn, Red, Waldo Treywick, King, Rita, Lana and Beverly Blackwell.

Brigadier Raymond J. "R. J." Maunsell briefed. You could have heard a pin drop in the room. The audience was mesmerized, stunned to learn about the existence of a thriving Cairo-based black market trade in industrial diamonds with the Nazis. Everyone present was fighting the war with every fiber in their body. It defied belief to discover that British, Polish, American, French and who knew who else war profiteers were selling strategic materials to the enemy that would be used as weapons back against them, their families and their country.

Hearing that the illustrious DeBeers Diamond Company was price-fixing and might be facilitating—or at least turning a blind eye to—the sale of industrial diamonds to the Third Reich was a shock. When R. J. reached the part about the RAF and Luftwaffe exchanging gold and diamonds for watches, a sound came from the group that was like a gigantic gasp.

Col. Randal stood up at the end of R. J.'s presentation. "We're forming a group we'll call TASK FORCE. I'll be in command, with Lady Jane and Beverly acting as my deputies. Information will flow through them. Since operations will be simultaneously taking place all over Africa, parts of the Mediterranean and in Europe, it's vital for each of you to keep in touch with Lady Jane and/or Beverly at all times.

"For the record, this is a United States Office of Strategic Services operation. British Intelligence will be acting in an advisory capacity, supplying access to sources, local contacts and working alongside us. Everything we do is restricted to 'Need to Know'. No one not physically present in this room has the need to know, with the single exception of Jim Taylor, who is currently away in the U.S.

"Do not discuss our intentions, plans or ongoing operations with anyone.

"Initially, TASK FORCE will be broken down into a HQ and three field sections. Mr. Treywick will head up the team that deals with the gold and diamond market in Cairo. Captain McKoy will be in charge of the group interdicting gold and diamond smuggling along the West African Coast. And King will tackle the watch problem for the RAF.

"As the operation develops, each of you will have a role. Exactly what that may be is not clear at this stage. If any of you have any suggestions, my door is always open.

"The implications of our own people trading gold and industrial diamonds to the Nazis are staggering. Consider anyone involved a traitor. The Geneva Convention is not applicable. Wire taps, opening the mail, harsh interrogations—standard operating procedure. We will not be arresting anyone.

"Is that clear?"

"CLEAR!"

BEVERLY SAID, "WHAT DID YOU MEAN YOU WON'T BE ARRESTING PEOPLE, JOHN?"

She and Lieutenant Mandy Paige had remained behind after the briefing broke up.

Colonel John Randal said, "Exactly that."

"Snakes," Beverly laughed. "Daddy always says, 'A dead snake is a good snake'."

Col. Randal said, "That's what I mean."

"What do you have in mind for me, John?" Lt. Mandy asked.

"I'm planning to use you and Beverly as female assassins," Col. Randal said. "Put Jane on the kill team when and as needed."

Major the Lady Jane Seaborn rolled her eyes.

"You'll be working with Waldo and Major Sansom in Cairo," Col. Randal said. "Rita and Lana are going to be assigned directly to you, Mandy. They're excellent undercover operatives."

"'Right *Girl,* Right Job'," Lt. Mandy said, paraphrasing Raiding Forces Rules for Raiding. "Love you, John."

Beverly said, "Does this mean I don't get to be a hit woman?"

"Not right now," Col. Randal said.

Lady Jane said, "I want you to be careful, Mandy."

"Roger that," Col. Randal said. "Most dangerous assignment you've ever had—money and greed. Lethal combination."

"Worse than being surrounded by ten thousand bloodthirsty Iraqis," Lt. Mandy said, "who wanted to gang rape me and then sell me into a life of slavery?"

"Well, maybe not that bad."

"Wow!" Beverly said. "Were you totally terrified, Mandy?"

"I was until John showed up," Lt. Mandy said.

Red walked in. She had recently returned from the U.S. where she had been advising the Office of Strategic Services on how to best employ airline stewardesses as Secret Intelligence (SI) agents. The stunning Clipper Girl took a seat on the couch.

"The girls flying BOAC have all been approached about smuggling diamonds, John. Until now airline management has turned a blind eye, considering the trade harmless. The numbers of stones and amounts paid have been trivial."

"No kidding," Col. Randal said, sticking one of Waldo's cigars between his front teeth. "So, you've known this trade was going on?"

"It's not really a secret," Red said. "We all thought the diamonds were worthless. They look like gravel. The girls were warned not to buy any because the stones were not gem quality or could even be outright fakes. No one dreamed the Nazis would end up with them or that they had any strategic value."

"Starting now you're in charge of putting a stop to diamond smuggling on commercial flights, Red," Col. Randal said. "Tell me what you need to make it happen. Report directly to Lady Jane."

"Yes, sir!"

Col. Randal said, "My guess is, sooner or later you're going to trace the supply of diamonds back to a sophisticated smuggling ring. When you do, we'll make a plan."

Red said, "I was horrified when R. J. explained what the diamonds were being used for. The stones seemed so harmless."

"Beverly, ask Red if she was scared at Habbaniya," Lt. Mandy said. "The Iraqis were holding her hostage."

"Terrified," Red said. "Even after John shot the Security Service thugs. Once he rescued me, the RAF base was still surrounded by the Iraqi Army. The soldiers of the Golden Square had bad intentions for the women."

"How about you, John," Beverly asked, "were you afraid?"

"I was on vacation."

COLONEL JOHN RANDAL AND VICE ADMIRAL SIR RANDOLPH "RAZOR" RANSOM FLEW TO Alexandria on board a Walrus piloted by the Vargas Girl look-alike Royal Marine, Captain Pamala Plum-Martin, with Beverly Blackwell as co-pilot. The place was a comparative ghost town. The port city had been stripped of combat troops, who had all been shipped east to the Eighth Army. All nonessential military personnel and as many civilians as could afford train tickets or find other transportation had evacuated. The Royal Navy had weighed anchor and sailed for safer harbor.

Panzerarmee Afrika was a little over an hour's drive due west up the Via Balbia. Fortunately, Rommel halted at El Alamein. The panic among the Egyptian civilian population had abated somewhat. However, it was claimed some of them had painted large white swastikas on the tile roofs of their houses to signal the Luftwaffe not to bomb them. Just the word *Rommel* was enough to send shivers down people's spines.

The Walrus splashed down in the harbor and taxied to the semi-abandoned naval maintenance dock. There were two U.S. Navy Lend Lease 77-foot Elco Patrol Torpedo (PT) boats undergoing frenzied modifications. Dockworkers were swarming all over them like ants. VAdm. Ransom had threatened the dock foreman that the PT boats would sail with the workers still on board if the work was not completed by sundown. The civilian workmen were highly motivated not to let that happen.

Sparks were flying from the welder's torches.

VAdm. Ransom had located the two PT boats and requisitioned them for Sea Squadron. One had been a pleasure craft used by Field Marshal Auchinleck. The other had seen service as an RAF Air/Sea Rescue craft.

Neither boat was armed.

Major Taylor Corrigan, DSO, MC, met them on the dock. He gave the group a tour of the work that was transforming torpedo boats into miniature battleships.

"Originally," Maj. Corrigan said, "the PT boats came armed with 4 Mk-XIV torpedoes and a pair of .50 caliber Browning M-2 machine guns. The weapons were removed because the boats were not employed in the patrol torpedo role.

"Admiral Ransom shanghaied the boats under his authority as Deputy Royal Navy Director of Operations—Irregular. He ordered each of them to be equipped with a pair of 20mm Oerlikon automatic cannon, another pair of 20mms staggered back flanking it, two pair of .50 cal. M-2 Brownings port and starboard amidships and a twin 40mm Bofors aft. We have extra air-cooled Browning .30 caliber machine guns we can add to the mix if there is any way to sandwich them in."

"Impressive firepower," Col. Randal said.

VAdm. Ransom walked up. He was supervising the dock work, "Checked with the U.S. Navy. There is no standard TO&E gun package for PT boats. It is amazing how many guns you can pack on one of these boats. You taught me the 'P-for-Plenty' formula, Colonel."

"That was 'Pyro' Percy Stirling, sir," Col. Randal said. "If one of these PTs do locate an Italian fuel tanker, Admiral, they can definitely light it up."

"That is the plan," VAdm. Ransom said. "Randy enhanced the armament on his three boats some time back. He likes to cruise along the shore and shoot up truck convoys far west up in Libya as they travel down the Via Balbia."

"Where are you going to find crews, sir?"

"Royal Navy Volunteer Patrol Service," VAdm. Ransom said. "A lieutenant commander I know, Adrian Seligman, lost his destroyer escort, sunk by Stukas. Drafted him to recruit two crews. The Commander will command one PT boat. I will take the other."

Col. Randal said, "Should have seen that coming, Admiral."

"Desperate times," VAdm. Ransom said, "require drastic measures. Sea Squadron *must* stop fuel from reaching Afrika Korps. I intend to make sure we do."

Col. Randal said, "You believe Rommel's hurting that bad, sir?"

"Checked on the POL story, Colonel," VAdm. Ransom said. "R. J. did not exaggerate—never does. Panzerarmee Afrika is experiencing a catastrophic fuel crisis of epic proportions. Our side can win this thing right here and now if we do our duty."

"Should any Italian tankers make it down the coastline," Maj. Corrigan said, "Sea Squadron will be the absolute last hope of preventing those ships from getting through. We are planning to make a maximum effort. Even the

King Duck has orders to patrol."

VAdm. Ransom said, "The entire fleet of Raiding Forces aircraft will be airborne tonight searching for a target. With a little luck, the RAF may be able to scrape up a few more planes to assist."

Col. Randal said, "I'll pull 'Guns' off gun jeep patrol duty, Admiral. Put him on your boat. He's the best fast-firing cannon man in the Royal Navy."

"Thank you, Colonel," VAdm. Ransom said.

"Try not to get him sunk again, sir," Col. Randal said. "'Guns' doesn't like to swim."

COLONEL JOHN RANDAL, MAJOR THE LADY JANE SEABORN AND BEVERLY BLACKWELL WERE sitting in the Gezira Club in the back behind a palm leaf. The restaurant was crowded. Officers in from the desert were taking a short break before returning to rebuild units shattered in the heavy fighting around El Alamein. Pilots who had flown missions that morning were at the bar having a drink to aid their descent from coming down off the adrenalin rush. The Desert Air Force, working in conjunction with the newly activated, renamed United States Army Air Force in the Middle East, had gained air superiority over the battlefield for the first time in the war. The combined air forces were flying around the clock.

Most of the men at the bar would be carrying out a second mission later in the afternoon. Some of the fighter pilots would even squeeze in a third before nightfall.

Officers in the uniform of at least five different countries were all hoping to strike up a conversation with one of the BOAC stewardesses at the bar on layover. Or possibly a WREN, or maybe—if they were really lucky—one of Lady Jane's Royal Marines. The odds were not good.

Captain Pamala Plum-Martin was at a table having lunch with a much-bemedaled Royal Air Force Group Captain sporting an impressive mustache.

Since the snow-blond Vargas Girl look-alike Royal Marine did not wear any decorations except her Air Transport Auxiliary (ATA) flight wings and Parachute Wings, her dinner companion had no idea she had more valor decorations than he did. She made eye contact with Col. Randal across the room and waved, wiggling her fingers.

Beverly said, "Admiral Ransom—he's Randy's grandfather, his mother Brandy's father?"

Lady Jane said, "Correct."

"Daddy would *love* to meet Brandy," Beverly laughed. "We better make sure that never happens. He has a roving eye."

"What's your father doing," Col. Randal asked, "now there's a war on?"

"He's a colonel in the Air Force Reserve," Beverly said. "Commands a training base at Big Springs—calls it 'flying a mahogany bomber'. Daddy's not a happy camper. They won't let him in fighters any more—too old."

Col. Randal said, "What's too old?"

"Forty-one," Beverly said. "USAAF policy says you can't fly fighters past the age of twenty-six."

"Really?"

"He shot down over a dozen Germans in WWI," Beverly said. "Daddy always calls it 'the Great War'. I think it was because of all those French girls he met at the *Folies Bergère* in Paris."

There was a stir in the room as King escorted Air Chief Marshal Sir Arthur Tedder, Commander-in-Chief of the Royal Air Force, Middle East, back to the table behind the palm tree.

Lady Jane made the introductions.

"Sir Arthur, this is Colonel Randal and Beverly Blackwell. I believe you know the Colonel, at least by reputation—Beverly is with the U.S. Office of Strategic Services assigned to Raiding Forces."

ACM Tedder looked mildly surprised when King took a seat at the table.

Col. Randal said, "Mr. King is a freelance soldier with connections to Switzerland. He is my Number Two on operations and handles certain sensitive assignments for Raiding Forces from time to time—he also has an ancillary contract with Lady Jane to be my bodyguard, sir."

Lady Jane said, "You are not supposed to be aware of that contract, John."

"An impressive resumé," ACM Tedder said.

Col. Randal said, "King will be working on the RAF watch problem, sir."

ACM Tedder said, "There is no RAF watch problem. There has never been an RAF watch problem. If anyone claims there is or was an RAF watch problem at some later date, I shall deny it."

"I see," Col. Randal said. Which meant he did not have a clue what had just taken place. The Air Chief Marshal had requested the meeting to discuss a shortage of precision wristwatches for his navigators. And, it was thought, to explain why the RAF was flying planeloads of industrial diamonds and gold to neutral Portugal and trading them for Swiss, German and Italian watches flown in by Luftwaffe pilots.

ACM Tedder was said to be happier sitting on a desert airstrip smoking his pipe and talking to his pilots than sitting behind his desk. It was also said that he knew every squadron leader by name. And that any squadron leader in his command could call him on the phone and he would take the call.

ACM Tedder said, "This conversation is not taking place."

Col. Randal said, "What conversation?"

"That's the spirit," ACM Tedder said, taking out his unlit pipe and sticking it in his teeth. "We British have lost the art of manufacturing precision timepieces. All of ours are imported. With the war on, naturally we cannot buy them directly from Italy or Germany since they are the enemy and one would *never* traffic with the other side no matter how desperate the situation.

"In order to do their calculations, my RAF navigators require chronometers which do not lose more than four seconds within a twenty-four hour time period. As you have probably already heard, I have more men killed in plane crashes resulting from poor navigation than due to enemy action."

"For a problem that doesn't exist, sir," Col. Randal said, "sounds to me like a big problem."

"Quite," ACM Tedder said, producing a typed page of paper. "This is a list of the Swiss companies who produce watches meeting our minimum standards."

He handed the paper to Col. Randal, who glanced at it and then passed it to King. The list read:

Buren
Lemania
Jager-LeCoultre
Longines
Record
Timor
Vertex
Enicar
Eterna
IWC
Grana
Omega
Cyma

"You will note there are some famous watchmakers not on the list, such as Rolex for example, for the simple reason the firms do not manufacture enough timepieces to be able to obtain them in bulk—but if you can obtain some, we shall be delighted to have them."

Col. Randal said, "Anything else we need to know, sir?"

"Two things," ACM Tedder said. "First off, the RAF will pay any price for wristwatches that meet our standards. We do not care how you acquire them. We do not have any objection to you using middlemen, nor will we make inquiries into the identities of any agents who help expedite the transaction.

"Can you fund the initial purchase or will you require RAF to supply the buy money?"

Col. Randal said, "We have resources."

ACM Tedder said, "Splendid—reimbursement to you will be made in gemstone diamonds or gold, Colonel, which is untraceable. The transactions will have never happened.

"No one will ever be reading about RAF timepieces, the lack thereof, or any illicit trade between my pilots and the Luftwaffe during WWII in any history book—ever."

Col. Randal said, "What's the second thing, sir?"

"I am aware of the gypsy fleet of mostly obsolete or captured airplanes Raiding Forces has assembled," ACM Tedder said. "The exception being two Hudsons that seemed to have disappeared from RAF books and the A-20s you have on loan. I must say, very creative employment of aircraft no one else has much use for. However, for this operation you require extreme long-range aircraft and experienced crew capable of flying anywhere in the world.

"Do you remember Tony Dudgeon from your days during the siege of RAF Habbaniya?"

"Yes, sir. He won that battle almost single-handedly. Whatever medal the RAF gave him, it's not enough."

"Afraid he was not decorated," ACM Tedder said. "By the time the battle was over, Tony managed to alienate virtually everyone on Habbaniya over the grade of flying officer. Had the quaint idea senior RAF officers should actually have taken part in the base's defense by flying operationally, there being such an extreme shortage of pilots."

Col. Randal said, "Some senior officers were not flying, sir."

"Instead of a gong, I promoted him," ACM Tedder said.

"Tony is a burn-out case—too many combat missions. In fact, he was at Habbaniya for a rest cure when the Iraqis attacked. We found the perfect assignment for him. Now Wing Commander Dudgeon commands a way station airfield in the middle of nowhere, ferrying planes to all points on the compass.

"Not much paperwork, very little responsibility, and he can requisition any plane he takes a fancy to passing through, fly it anytime, be away for as long as he wants with no questions asked."

"Sounds like you took care of Tony, sir," Col. Randal said.

ACM Tedder said, "Wing Commander Dudgeon finds himself faced with a dilemma. He desires to be married. Unfortunately, his bride-to-be is in India. Regulations prohibit travel to Middle East Command for unmarried women unless there is a job with the military waiting here upon arrival.

"If you can arrange for Tony's fiancée to find suitable employment qualifying her to come to Cairo, then I shall authorize him to transport

Raiding Forces personnel anywhere they need to fly, anytime, no strings attached.

"It is my understanding your command has other commitments in West Africa that require air transportation. This would resolve air travel for you, forever."

Lady Jane said, "General Alexander requires an assistant social secretary. I shall put her name forward today. No one will question a member of the GOC's personal staff traveling to Egypt."

ACM Tedder said, "An elegant solution, Lady Jane."

"Next time you see Wing Commander Dudgeon, sir," Col. Randal said, "ask him to tell you the story about how he and I cut the Iraqi telephone lines to Baghdad by intentionally flying through the wires. Chopped 'em up with his propeller."

"Tony did that?"

"Oh yeah," Col. Randal said.

COLONEL JOHN RANDAL WAS TALKING TO CAPTAIN "GERONIMO" JOE MCKOY, WALDO Treywick and King in the third-floor suite he shared with Major the Lady Jane Seaborn at Raiding Forces Headquarters. Beverly Blackwell was being allowed to sit in on the conversation, which was, in fact, a high-level TASK FORCE strategy session.

Everyone except Beverly had one of Waldo's custom-rolled unlit cigars in their teeth. She might have wanted a cigar but did not ask.

Col. Randal said, "OK, give me a report."

Capt. McKoy said, "I've been studyin' on this assignment, John. Need to get out to the Gold Coast, put boots on the ground and see what's goin' on. Got a couple a' ideas. This ain't my first rodeo when it comes to busting smugglers, but I want to scope it out first."

Col. Randal said, "What are you thinking?"

"What I'm probably going to do is get some retired U.S. Marshals and stick 'em in the U.S. Counsel's office in all the colonies along the coast. They'll be my point element—good law enforcement men. Figure out the trafficking angle, identify the players and be on hand to assist when we make our move."

Col. Randal said, "Sounds like a plan."

"This could be an ongoing, long-term proposition," Capt. McKoy said. "Ain't gonna be real easy. Lotta ways to hide diamonds on a ship. I may need to bring in some boys from the Port Authority used to lookin' for hidden contraband to show us the tricks."

Col. Randal said, "Where do you intend to start, Captain?"

"Accra," Capt. McKoy said. "They already know me there as the Secretary Treasurer of the Southwest Cattleman's Association's Chapter of the American Philatelic Society from our OPERATION LOUNGE LIZARD days."

Waldo said, "What . . . ?"

"Stamp collector," Capt. McKoy said. "It's a dang good cover."

"I woulda taken you for a butterfly man," Waldo said. "Bein' an outdoorsman."

"OSS Headquarters in Washington runs three field bases out of Africa," Beverly said, to everyone's surprise. "Accra covers the Gold Coast, Cape Town is responsible for South Africa, and Addis Ababa has Abyssinia.

"Africa Project #7, Secret Intelligence's office in Accra, not only has the Gold Coast but it also keeps an eye on Liberia and the Belgian Congo. AP#7 is headed up by Major Doug Bonner—he's not a real army officer. Colonel Donovan gave him the title."

"A lotta minin' goes on in the Belgian Congo," Capt. McKoy said. "Could be where some of the diamonds gettin' smuggled come from.

"Real good information, Miss Texas Ten Most. I'll be addin' Leopoldville to my itinerary."

Col. Randal said, "How do you know all that, Beverly?"

"I told you, John, when those Ivy League snobs at OSS heard my Texas accent they deducted ten points from my IQ," Beverly said. "Everyone thought I was a dizzy blonde, so they assigned me to the Africa Section. There is no functioning Africa Section. The intelligence file on West Africa is nothing but old yellow newspaper clippings from the *New York Times.*

"I pointed out to David Bruce, OSS Chief of Secret Intelligence, that I didn't know one thing about Africa except Daddy liked to go there on safari, and he said, 'Who does?'"

Col. Randal said, "You said there was no Africa Section but you just laid one out in detail."

"I said *functioning,*" Beverly laughed. "Originally OSS recruited a PhD in ornithology from the American Museum of Natural History in New York—he wrote the book *The Birds of the Belgian Congo*—to head up AP#7. The 'Outfit' likes to hire bird watchers and anthropologists for some reason. However, before the doctor could go out to Africa, Colonel Donovan had to divert him to Ascension Island in the South Atlantic to solve a bird problem for the USAAF.

"Birds called sooty terns nest on the island. They pose a menace to air operations. The birds lay their eggs in nests on the ground. Every time a plane at our base on Ascension would take off or land, the birds would rise up in a giant cloud, which is not good for airplanes.

"First the OSS bird person tried smoke candles. Failed. Dynamite blasts. Failed. Then he got creative and flew in a planeload of house cats to eat the birds. Failed—something ate the cats. Finally, our man on Ascension decided the only option left was to break all the sooty tern's eggs in hopes they would leave the island—forty thousand of 'em. He formed up the troops from the base on line and they marched out, stepping on the bird's eggs."

Waldo said, "How'd that work out?"

"Like a charm."

Capt. McKoy said, "That's a lotta eggs to stomp."

"Too many for the sensitivities of the author of an exotic bird book," Beverly said. "Upon arriving at his post in Accra, the doctor started organizing a network of undercover operatives and was making good progress when he suddenly had a nervous breakdown. Guilt-ridden over the sooty tern egg massacre.

"Being Secret Intelligence," Beverly laughed, "the doctor did not keep written notes or records. He kept everything in his head. OSS had no way to know who his contacts were after he was evacuated home."

Waldo said, "Uh-oh!"

Capt. McKoy said, "Dang good story. Too bad we can't tell it, bein' classified and all."

Col. Randal said, "What do you have to report, Mr. Treywick?"

"Been talkin' to Major Sansom, Mr. Zargo and Joe," Waldo said. "We all agree the way to go about takin' down the diamond- and gold-buying in the bazaars here in Cairo is don't take it down, take it over. What we do is step in and buy up all the gold and diamonds in Cairo—cut out the middlemen. We become the end buyer.

"Then once we capture the market, we sell our product at thirty times the cost to Nazi straw men who plan to smuggle the contraband from here across the desert to Turkey, then on into Nazi-occupied Greece.

"Once it's sold," Waldo said, "We double-cross our buyers by havin' Raiding Forces patrols intercept the caravans carryin' the loot to Turkey. Or alert the Turkish Security Services and they can pick up any that gets past us for a cut a' the take. Mr. Zargo says he can set that deal up with the Turks.

"Now, here's the part I like best," Waldo said. "Once we get a load a' diamonds and gold back, we resell it to the same Nazi money men. They ain't gonna know the difference—a diamond's a diamond, especially industrial grade, and gold, well, it's gold.

"Ain't no way to tell any of it apart."

Col. Randal said, "You think the underworld cartel buying and selling gold and diamonds in Cairo is just going to step aside and let you take over?"

Waldo said, "Could be the point in the deal where we need you to come in, Colonel."

"King?"

"I have to travel to Switzerland."

"You have a plan to get there?"

"I do, Chief."

"Sounds like we've got the beginnings of a plan," Col. Randal said. "I like it."

Capt. McKoy said, "Everybody bear in mind—we have to be real clandestine. It's a lot easier to let the cat outta the bag than to stuff the cat back in the bag. This here ain't your normal sneak and peek."

Waldo said, "You got that right, Joe."

King said, "We do not know—and may never know—who we can trust."

"Affirmative," Col. Randal said. "You men are going to need the weight of the United States government behind you.

"Stand up, assume the position of attention and raise your right hand."

Capt. McKoy, King and Waldo stood up and raised their hands.

"Repeat after me," Col. Randal said. "I do solemnly swear to faithfully uphold all the rules, statutes and bylaws of the Office of Strategic Services—so help me God."

The three droned, "I do solemnly swear to faithfully uphold all the rules, statutes and bylaws of the Office of Strategic Services—so help me God."

Col. Randal said, "Consider yourself all duly sworn agents of the OSS."

"What are the rules, statutes and bylaws we have to uphold?" Waldo asked.

Col. Randal said, "How would I know?"

Capt. McKoy said, "I recommend we consider Rule #1, Raidin' Forces Rules for Raidin' to be in full force and effect for Task Forces purposes—'the first rule is there ain't no rules'."

"Agreed," Col. Randal said.

"Since we got sworn," Waldo asked, "does that mean we're on the government payroll?"

"Affirmative," Col. Randal said. "Dollar-a-year men—thank you for your service."

Beverly stayed behind after the three brand-new OSS agents left the room.

"That ceremony didn't sound very official, John."

"Best I could do on short notice," Col. Randal said. "Where did your father like to do his big-game hunting?"

"All over Africa," Beverly said. "Stays on safari for three weeks at a time, then always wraps up with a week in Nairobi."

"Really?"

"He had a good friend there, some expatriate earl who always took him partying at the Muthaiga Club—Daddy called it a 'den of iniquity'," Beverly laughed. "Daddy has always had a weakness for places like that. He told me they have a saying, 'Are you married, or do you live in Kenya?'"

"I've heard that."

"Daddy won't be going back, the earl got shot by his fiancée's husband," Beverly said. "Things like that can happen when you get engaged to a married woman. You ever worry, John?"

Wanting to change the subject, Col. Randal said. "Excellent briefing on the OSS African Project #7, Beverly. Clearly more to you than just a pretty face."

"When I got the job offer from Colonel Donovan," Beverly said, "Daddy told me to keep my eyes and ears open . . . and my mouth shut."

"Sound advice," Col. Randal said. "Only I don't want you to be reluctant to tell me your thoughts. Don't hold back because you might think I'll laugh at you."

"In that case," Beverly said, "I think something's going on in the Belgian Congo."

"Yeah, like what?"

Beverly said, "The office there is an independent operation within the Theatre Command of Project #7. The Chief of Station reports directly to OSS HQ in Washington DC, bypassing the Accra office. The incoming messages have a classification above Top Secret."

Col. Randal said, "So, what do you *think* is going on?"

Beverly said, "The war on gold smugglers and illicit diamond buying could be a cover to distract attention away from some other more important project we don't know about."

"Let's keep that thought between us," Col. Randal said. "You can tell Jane."

"Might be difficult working in the Congo," Beverly said.

"Why might that be?'

"The country has 242 languages."

Col. Randal said, "Could be a problem."

"One more thing you should know," Beverly said. "The State Department hates the Office of Strategic Services. I don't think they're going give Capt. McKoy's men diplomatic cover. Swearing everyone into the OSS might not have been such a great idea."

Col. Randal said, "I can always un-swear 'em."

THE HEADLINE READ, "MARINE RAIDERS HIT JAPS ON MAKIN ISLAND."

Major the Lady Jane Seaborn, dressed in one of her trademark simple black sheaths, was fixing one of her diamond ear studs. She glanced over at what Colonel John Randal was reading: "Jimmy Roosevelt's men—2nd Raider Battalion."

Col. Randal, already dressed in his Class A uniform the U.S. Army called "Pinks and Greens," looked up from the newspaper. "Good for him."

Lady Jane said, "Wing Commander Dudgeon's fiancée is set to be General Alexander's social secretary. I intend to let her run the show and merely check in from time to time."

"Hope you're not mad at me about Stephanie," Col. Randal said.

"Once you informed Captain Fawcett-Tatum you wanted her here," Lady Jane laughed, "there was no way she was ever leaving to work for the general. You were nice to one of my Marines . . . how could I be mad at you."

Brandy Seaborn, Captain Penelope "Legs" Honeycutt-Parker, Veronica Paige and Rikke Runborg (her friends called her "Rocky"), had been in and out of the suite for the past hour, getting ready for the mother of all private cocktail parties in Middle East Command. Lieutenant Mandy Paige and Beverly Blackwell had been camped out in the bedroom trying on Lady Jane's jewelry.

Tonight's guest list was short but impressive. Lieutenant General Sir Harold Alexander, accompanied by his wife, Lieutenant General Bernard Montgomery, Air Chief Marshal Sir Arthur Tedder, newly arrived in country, United States Army Air Force Major General Lewis H. Brereton, Brigadier

Robert J. Mansell, who liked to be called "R. J.," and Colonel Dudley Clarke. The party was not intended to last overly long.

It was a photo op.

Rocky was to be Lt. Gen. Montgomery's dinner companion tonight, though there was not actually going to be any dinner—drinks only, photo shoot and over. The idea being that, in all likelihood, Rommel would be extraordinarily interested in any and all news related to his brand-new opposite number at Eighth Army. So he would undoubtedly pay close attention to the photo spread of the party that would appear in the social section of the *Egyptian Gazette* newspaper tomorrow morning and land on his desk within two days—Col. Clarke had the ability to make that happen.

The purpose of the exercise was to have Rocky at Lt. Gen. Montgomery's side in the pictures. The Desert Fox would have that in mind when he received a clandestine radio transmission from her sometime in the next few days stating that the Eighth Army commander had confided he would not be ready to attack before the fourth week of October. That piece of information was the answer to the question Rommel had asked his most highly placed agent in Cairo to discover.

FM Rommel was not well and wanted to fly home to Germany for medical treatment. He needed to know when the attack was coming so he knew when to time his trip back to Germany. Rocky had already tricked him into being out of the country for the beginning of CRUSADER. Could she do it again?

Possibly.

Rocky was not going to be telling the truth. OPERATION LIGHTFOOT, the second battle of El Alamein, was actually laid on for early September.

No one in Raiding Forces was aware of any of these machinations. The "Need to Know" rule was in full force and effect. Tonight they were merely bit players in one of Col. Clarke's elaborate deceptions.

6
THE SEXY PART

COLONEL JOHN RANDAL AND CAPTAIN BILLY JACK JAXX WERE ON THE BEACH OUTSIDE RAIDING Forces Headquarters, firing their pistols. Their target was one that Captain "Geronimo" Joe McKoy had made for them—something he called the Texas Star. There were five arms, like a star, mounted on a rotating wheel with steel plates welded on each one.

There were two ways to attack the Texas Star. You could shoot a plate, which caused the wheel to rotate, providing moving targets. Or, you could spin the wheel by hand, step off your distance and fire at really fast-moving plates.

Col. Randal saw no point in trying to print small groups with a handgun even though he had been on the U.S. 26th Cavalry Regiment's Pistol Team, which shot bull's-eye targets for score in competition. In his line of work, pistols were serious weapons used primarily for shooting people who were generally not holding still for him to put a bullet in them. Often they were shooting back, seldom at a known distance but generally at close range with everything happening fast.

The only exception to moving targets Col. Randal ever indulged in was to shoot at tiny targets at long range, which is hard. A shooter who is able to hit a quarter at fifty feet with a pistol is deadly against a man-sized target at half that distance. He knew if you could hit small targets at long range, the ability to shoot large targets up close would never be in question.

The only trick being to remain calm, focus on the front sight while working the trigger and achieve *several* hits fast. Col. Randal also knew from experience in gunfights, even though he used the sights he seldom, if ever, actually saw them. The most important aspect of pistol shooting is confidence. And that comes from practice.

Col. Randal worked with his handguns every day. In his opinion, pistol drill needed to be done in private. Except when he could find another shooter who could match his skills. Then the two could push each other . . . and that was the best practice of all.

Jack Cool was a crack shot.

To wrap up the session, Col. Randal and Capt. Jaxx took turns operating a small, portable clay pigeon thrower. The targets were thrown, flying straight away. The clay pigeons were traveling fast and were almost impossible to hit with the Colt 1911 Model .38 Super both officers preferred, a .22 High Standard Military Model D or Col. Randal's 9mm Browning High Power *aka* P-35.

The operative word being *almost.* Knowing you *could* hit one was a true confidence builder.

After they wrapped up, as they walked back to RFHQ, Col. Randal asked, "How's it coming on the RED INDIAN missions, Jack?"

"R. J. has requested an intelligence dossier from SOE," Capt. Jaxx said. "They're not being cooperative, or they don't have what we need. I think we're dead in the water until Jim gets back from the States to deal with them, sir."

"I'll message Commander Fleming," Col Randal said. "If he wants us to take down RED INDIAN targets, he needs to come out to Egypt and head up the intelligence mission."

"I don't think you'll have any trouble getting him to comply, sir," Capt. Jaxx said. "The Commander confided to me he wants to know Beverly better."

Col. Randal said, "Who's to blame him?"

"I'm pretty sure Commander Fleming's wasting his time, sir," Capt. Jaxx said. "She likes men twice her age and I don't think playboys like the

Commander stand much of a chance. Beverly had a relationship with the head of the UT Art Department, who was in his late fifties. And, there was a Hollywood movie producer who used to fly in to Austin to see her."

Col. Randal said, "You might be right about that, Jack."

"The art professor did a bust of Beverly. It's on permanent display in a glass case in Old Main," Capt. Jaxx said. "Want to hear the sexy part, sir?"

"You know I do."

"Beverly made a sculpture as an art project—her nude torso," Capt. Jaxx said. "Donated it to the UT Art Department, to be displayed only in the event of her death. Good too—kept under lock and key, sir."

"How would you know?"

"I went out with her art professor's student aide," Capt. Jaxx said. "We snuck into his office late one night and she showed it to me. Don't let Beverly know I told you, sir. She'd murder me."

"You're supposed to swear me to secrecy," Col. Randal said, "*before* you reveal the secret, Jack."

"You're not going to say anything to Beverly, sir?"

Col. Randal said, "I have to tell Jane. She's going to love this story."

"As long as you advise her it's classified, Colonel."

"I can do that."

"No problem then, sir," Capt. Jaxx said. "Lady Jane can keep a secret."

Now what did that mean?

THE SUN WAS GOING DOWN IN BRILLIANT COLORS. THE DESERT WAS COOLING OFF FAST. COLONEL John Randal, Major the Lady Jane Seaborn, Lieutenant Mandy Paige, Beverly Blackwell, Veronica Paige and Happy, the dog, were sipping iced tea as they sat under a blue striped pavilion outside Raiding Forces Headquarters next to the improvised polo pitch. The women were dressed in jodhpurs, riding boots and matching pink T-shirts. All four were equestrians, played polo and had been taking on all comers. The girl's squad acquitted themselves well against the Life Guard and Horse Guards brigade polo team members.

Now, the 575th Parachute Infantry Regiment Rangers of Captain Billy Jack Jaxx's Small Operations Group had taken the field and were engaged in a fierce scrimmage. Since the men came from states all across the nation, most of them could not ride horses. SOG was playing their match on bicycles.

The Rangers were hilarious.

There was a lot of action, but the match was a low-scoring game. Steering, pedaling and swinging a polo mallet on a bicycle with any degree of accuracy was proving difficult. It had not taken long for the Rangers to figure out it is impossible for your opponent to score if he is crashed, laying on the ground, which gave a whole new perspective to playing defense.

Everyone at RFHQ not on duty was on hand cheering on the bicycle polo players.

Sub-Lieutenant Bentley St. Ledger, WRNS, arrived and whispered in Col. Randal's ear, "Sir, Pamala . . . I mean Captain Plum-Martin would like to see you and Beverly right away."

Col. Randal made eye contact with Beverly. The three made their way to the Operations Room where they found Captain Pamala Plum-Martin standing in front of the giant wall map of Egypt, Libya and the tip of Italy. The Vargas Girl look-alike Royal Marine was studying the Mediterranean coastline.

Captain Stephanie Fawcett-Tatum saw them come in and walked over to be of assistance if needed.

"Last night a pair of Fairy Albacores located an Italian fuel tanker approximately one hundred miles west of Tobruk," Capt. Plum-Martin said. "One of them managed to damage her with an aerial torpedo. The ship beached in this isolated region here."

She tapped the map with a scarlet nail.

"Sea Squadron has been alerted to dispatch MGBs and PT boats to blow up the tanker before Afrika Korps can salvage the fuel on board. However, they are unable to sail until nightfall. Randy's boats are listed as being capable of forty knots, but my guess is they are not able to maintain that speed for any length of time.

"The RAF advised GHQ it might be faster to insert a demolitions party by float plane. Grey Pillars has inquired if Raiding Forces is capable of sending a team."

Col. Randal asked, "Why not bomb the ship?"

Capt. Plum-Martin said, "RAF is not confident nighttime aerial bombing can be relied on to guarantee total destruction of the freighter. This mission has to be one hundred percent. We need boots on the ground to ensure it is."

Col. Randal asked, "What's your plan, Pam?"

"Every single pilot Raiding Forces has plus the ones the RAF loaned us are scheduled for night patrol on a grid search in the Mediterranean, hunting for blockade runners. Beverly and I are the only two not flying. A pair of Navy Walruses are the only amphibious aircraft available. Unfortunately, both planes had been mothballed because they were declared surplus/obsolete.

"They are being serviced as we speak."

"Is searching for other Italian fuel tankers more important than going after the one that's beached?" Col. Randal asked.

"It is," Capt. Plum-Martin said. "GHQ is frantic not to let a single drop of fuel slip through."

Col. Randal said, "Any idea of where the *King Duck* is steaming?"

"A long way from there, John."

"What's the nearest Raiding Regiment patrol, Stephanie?"

"Major Beauchamp's A-Patrol," Capt. Fawcett-Tatum said. "Approximately thirty miles from where the ship is beached."

"They can't travel until last light either," Col. Randal said, knowing thirty miles was a long way to travel cross-country at night in close proximity to the Via Balbia. There were secondary roads that would have to be crossed en route to the target, and that took time.

"Alert Major Beauchamp to start that way as soon as his patrol is under cover of darkness. In the event A-Patrol sees the tanker blazing from a distance of five miles, they are to stop and commence firing a single parachute flare every fifteen minutes for ninety minutes. In the event the landing party is unable to return on the Walruses for any reason, they can march inland and link up with A-Patrol.

"Inform the Major that if a pair of A-20s or the two Ro.63s overfly his patrol at low level," Col. Randal said, "he can cease firing the flares and continue his original mission."

"What are your instructions," Capt. Fawcett-Tatum asked, "in the event Major Beauchamp does not see the tanker on fire?"

"In that case," Col. Randal said, "A-Patrol is cleared to attack."

"Roger."

"Beverly," Col. Randal said, "are you willing to fly a mission tonight for OSS?"

Beverly flashed her best beauty queen smile. "Love to, John."

"Stephanie," Col. Randal said, "Captain Stirling is on leave in Cairo. Find him and get him back here ASAP if not sooner."

"Yes, sir."

"I'll order Billy Jack to put together a SOG team," Col. Randal said. "Stephanie, make sure Sea Squadron is placed on notice that we'll be conducting a raid on the beached tanker. This operation is going to require coordination. I don't want the cavalry to arrive with all guns blazing while we're standing next to the ship placing our charges."

"Understood, John."

"You said 'we'," Capt. Plum-Martin said. "Will you be along tonight?"

"Someone has to keep Beverly company," Col. Randal said. "You'll be flying lead and have your navigator with you. We wouldn't want one of Texas' Ten Most bobbing around all alone in an empty Walrus behind enemy lines after SOG shoves off."

"You are not going ashore?"

Col. Randal said. "I will not be landing, Pam."

"We are all concerned about you, John," Capt. Plum-Martin said. "Your vacation did not work out so well."

Beverly said, "That's an understatement."

Col. Randal said, "Lighten up, ladies."

Line-of-Departure Time was scheduled for 1930 hours. The planes would take off precisely to the minute. Straphangers started showing up long before the appointed hour. Col. Randal had his work cut out dealing with everyone who wanted in on the raid.

Lt. Mandy requested permission to go.

"No."

Lady Jane asked if she could because Beverly was flying.

"No."

Captain "Geronimo" Joe McKoy, Waldo and King arrived.

"Can do."

Major Desmond Barrymore, General Alexander's aide, drove in from Grey Pillars to accompany the mission.

"No."

Brigadier Raymond J. "R. J." Maunsell appeared and made a rare request to observe.

"Negative—sir."

Capt. Jaxx, the mission commander tonight, gave his Raid Order at 1800 hours.

"Situation: Rommel is short on fuel for his tanks. The Italian Merchant Marine is trying to run fuel tanker ships down the Mediterranean coast at night to resupply. The Italian tanker *Abruzzi* was torpedoed last night and managed to beach herself approximately one hundred miles west of Tobruk.

"Mission: A ten-man team of SOG operators transported in two Walrus amphibious aircraft will land, paddle ashore and place demolitions on the *Abruzzi* . . ."

Brig. Maunsell, Maj. Barrymore and Capt. McKoy were standing at the back of the audience of Raiding Forces Raiders who would be going on tonight's mission.

R. J. said quietly, "The Desert Fox gambled his logistics would improve and lost. Rommel has never understood that when a ship is sunk, it is more than simply fuel and crew that goes down. The Axis have a finite number of merchant ships. They are irreplaceable, as are the sailors. Rommel has never grasped the complexities of *why* he has a fuel shortage—blames the Italian Navy for lack of organization and efficiency when, in fact, it is making a valiant effort."

Capt. McKoy said, "Man believes his own press. Thinks he's a military star. Win on guts, determination, and his magic 'finger touch for the battle' alone."

"I concur," R. J. said. "The Field Marshal does not seem to comprehend the reality of the situation now that the U.S. has entered the war. The RAF and the Royal Navy, ably assisted by highly aggressive units of the USAAF and the U.S. Navy, are strangling the sea lanes between Italy and Africa."

Capt. McKoy said, "He'll figure it out sooner or later but there ain't much the man can do when he does."

R. J. said, "Hope you are right, Captain. That stipulated, we have to intercept every tanker. Even a solitary ship can carry enough fuel to provide Rommel what he needs to make one more desperate counterattack. With a brand-new Eighth Army commander who has never fought in the desert, we would rather not have that occur."

"Cuttin' off Rommel's fuel supply should do the trick," Capt. McKoy said. "A tank division bone dry ain't nothin' more than a junkyard."

Maj. Barrymore said, "As a former member of the 3rd Royal Tank Regiment who spent nearly two years fighting Rommel, I could not agree more."

"A most colorful description, Captain," R. J. said. "I shall plagiarize it at the first opportunity when I bring General Alexander up to speed on Raiding Forces plans later this evening."

Capt. McKoy said. "Make yourself happy, R. J."

In the front of the room Capt. Jaxx said, "This concludes my briefing. What are your questions?"

TEN RAIDERS WERE GOING ON THE MISSION TO DESTROY THE *ABRUZZI*. CAPTAIN BILLY JACK JAXX, with Captain "Pyro" Percy Stirling and three of his SOG operators, would travel in the lead aircraft flown by Captain Pamala

Plum-Martin. Colonel John Randal, Captain "Geronimo" Joe McKoy, King, Waldo and Lovat Scouts Lionel Fenwick and Munro Ferguson would be in the second, flown by Beverly Blackwell.

Locating the ship should not be difficult.

Raiding Forces' pair of captured Italian Ro.63s were on scene keeping an eye on the *Abruzzi* and had been orbiting overhead ever since it was discovered. They would mark the target with flares for the two Walrus amphibians when the raiding party approached the beached tanker.

Capt. Plum-Martin said, "In the event our ground party fails to completely destroy the ship with demolitions, Wing Commander Gordon will attempt to finish the job with the A-20s. Concurrently, Admiral Ransom and Randy will be at sea, en route, to provide support as needed."

Major Desmond Barrymore said, "Appears you plan to go for layered overkill—exactly the enthusiastic response General Alexander was hoping to hear from Raiding Forces."

"Redundancy is good, Major," Col. Randal said. "There's no such thing as overkill on a Commando raid."

"Major, you tell your general," Captain "Geronimo" Joe McKoy said, "When our outfit gets involved, too much ain't enough. Especially with Captain Stirling in charge a' demolitions. When 'Pyro' Percy blows somethin' up, it stays blown up."

Maj. Barrymore said, "I shall pass along your assessment of the situation to General Alexander."

Major the Lady Jane Seaborn, with Happy riding in the back of the jeep, drove Col. Randal to the dock where the two former Air/Sea Rescue Walruses were tied off. The seats in the back had been removed, so everyone would be sitting on the floor of the aircraft. Capt. Plum-Martin and Beverly were already on board, going through their pre-flight checklists.

Lady Jane said, "I understand this is a vital mission, John, but you stay on the plane like you promised."

Col. Randal said. "I'm just along to keep Beverly out of trouble."

Lady Jane said, "Who is to keep *you* out of trouble?"

The troops loaded onto the aircraft. Every man was an experienced

Commando or Ranger. There was little talking.

Demolitions were carried on both Walruses, though Capt. Stirling was the only person qualified to set the charges. In the event both aircraft did not reach the target, the one that did would have enough explosives to destroy the Italian tanker. At least that was the plan.

The Raiders were armed to the teeth.

On Beverly's plane, Col. Randal was carrying his favorite 9mm MAB-38A submachine gun, as was Capt. Jaxx. Waldo had his cut-down 12-gauge Browning A-5. Capt. McKoy brought his .30 caliber Colt Monitor BAR. King was armed with a .30 caliber Johnson M1941 LMG. And Lovat Scouts Fenwick and Ferguson both were armed with .30 caliber U.S. M1 Garand semi-automatic rifles they had come to prize for close- to medium-range work.

Col. Randal held his 9mm Browning High Power slung over his shoulder on a canvas pistol belt.

Lady Jane kissed him on the cheek, "Be safe."

The two museum-piece amphibians cranked up their engines.

Time to go.

Col. Randal made his way to the cockpit and slipped into the copilot's chair. "What weapon did you bring tonight, Beverly?"

"My .32 Remington Model 51."

"Buckle this on," Col. Randal said, handing her his 9mm Browning P-35. "We're going to have to get you outfitted with a serious handgun when we get back."

Following the lead Walrus's phosphorescence wake, Beverly began to make her take-off run. The little amphibian was capable of lifting off in a remarkably short distance. The Texas cowgirl seemed very comfortable at the stick of the plane.

Col. Randal said, "Where did you learn to fly amphibians?"

"Daddy liked to go hunting and fishing in Alaska," Beverly said. "While he was in the woods, I hung out with the bush pilots. They let me fly. Really fun landing on those smooth-as-glass, high mountain lakes."

The night was dark. Only a sliver of moon. The two Walrus airplanes stayed slightly out to sea but in sight of the coastline. They were skimming along, barely above the waves.

It was a beautiful night.

Thirty minutes out from the *Abruzzi*, Beverly said, "Pam has broken radio silence to report she has to abort the mission, John."

Col. Randal, who was not wearing a headset and could not hear the transmission, said, "What's the problem?"

"Her engine redlined," Beverly said. "She's not sure she can make it all the way back home."

"Tell her I said good luck," Col. Randal said, running through a mental checklist of options. Capt. Stirling was now out of the picture. Col. Randal was pretty sure no one on board this airplane had ever trained to place explosive charges on a ship.

"What do you want me to do?" Beverly asked.

"You up to continuing the mission?"

Beverly said, "Come on, John."

"OK," Col. Randal said, "let's do this."

Beverly said, "Do you know how to blow up something as big as a fuel tanker?"

"I have no idea," Col. Randal said. "We'll fall back on the P-for-Plenty formula."

"You mean the 1/2 P-for-Plenty formula," Beverly laughed. "Pam's carrying half the explosives."

"Yeah—Roger that."

Col. Randal climbed in the back of the plane to explain the situation to the team. No one seemed concerned. The men were used to things not going as advertised. They would have been more surprised if everything worked out according to plan.

Col. Randal handed Waldo his 9mm MAB-38A submachine gun and his ammo pouches, "Give me the 12-gauge. I'll let Beverly have it."

Handing over the sawed-off semi-auto A-5, Waldo said, "What are you goin' to be carryin'?"

"My Colts," Col. Randal said. "There shouldn't be any shooting."

"John . . ." Beverly called from the cockpit.

Col. Randal slid back into his seat, "Here's a Browning 12-gauge. It used to be mine but Waldo appropriated it when we were in Abyssinia. Change two, I want you to taxi up on the beach. Keep it with you while we . . ."

"We have a situation," Beverly said, interrupting him.

"What kind of situation?"

"Oil pressure," Beverly said. "We won't be flying home in this airplane, John."

"Why the mechanical problems all of a sudden?" Col. Randal asked. "Our Walruses have always been reliable."

"These two planes had not been flown for over a year," Beverly said. "The RAF tried to get 'em airworthy. Didn't happen."

"Can you get us to the target?"

"I'll try."

"Since we've already broken radio silence," Col. Randal said, "are you able to raise Wing Commander Gordon?"

"I think so."

"Tell him to break off his grid search and strafe the *Abruzzi* as we come in," Col. Randal said. "Make one gun run, then buzz the ship until we can get on board and deal with any Italian guards."

"Roger."

Col. Randal went back to explain developments to the team. The men remained unfazed. Professionals.

When he returned to the cockpit, Beverly said, "Ronnie says, 'Can do'—there's a campfire about a mile from the ship the Ro.63s have been keeping an eye on. He's going to attack it after hitting the *Abruzzi.*"

"Probably the crew," Col. Randal said. "No Italian in his right mind is going to stay on a beached tanker full of fuel and wait for the RAF or the USAAF to show up and bomb it."

"Beverly said, "Who's to blame 'em? I wouldn't sit on the *Abruzzi* and wait to be bombed either. Would you?"

"No."

"Ten minutes, John."

"Can you contact the Phantom team with A-Patrol?"

In a moment Beverly said, "I'm in touch with Phantom. What's your message?"

"Order Major Beauchamp to head straight for the *Abruzzi.* Tell him he's our ride home."

"It's good to have a Plan B," Beverly quoted from Raiding Forces Rules for Raiding.

"That's a fact."

"John, the engine's ready to cut out any minute now," Beverly said. "It's running really rough."

"Can you make a dead stick landing?"

"We're about to find out," Beverly said, way cool.

Up ahead the black shadow of the Italian freighter swam into sight. The two A-20s were blasting it with everything they had, which was a lot. The twelve .50 caliber Browning machine guns per plane were putting out an awesome amount of firepower.

"Get us as close as you can," Col. Randal ordered.

"Yes, sir."

"Prepare to land," Col. Randal shouted over his shoulder. "We're coming in hard."

Beverly attempted to gain as much altitude as possible. The Walrus swooped up. The engine cut out.

The Walrus was going down. The tanker was dead ahead. Beverly attempted to put the airplane on a gradual glide path, but it was sinking fast. While the little amphibian was one of the ugliest airplanes ever built and looked about as aerodynamic as a rock, it flew well. She had the plane under control, but they were going to crash.

Beverly laughed, "Are we having fun yet, John?"

"I can't speak for anyone else on board," Col. Randal said. "I know I sure am."

Beverly stretched the glide path as far as possible. The beach was coming up fast. Then she intentionally slammed the plane down hard at the edge of the breakers. When the floats touched, they caught the sand and the supports crumbled. The forward momentum carried the Walrus up the beach, skidding on its belly—the pusher-type engine with the propeller mounted high on the roof was a nonissue even though the prop was auto-rotating.

Except for the initial hard bump and the *idea* they were crashing, the landing was about as smooth as a lot of others Col. Randal had made. When it skidded to a stop, the Italian tanker was so close it was almost possible to reach out and touch her. He could see the *Abruzzi's* bow was on the beach and her stern was in the water.

"Nice job," Col. Randal said. "Guess you know how to make a dead stick landing."

"Beginner's luck, John."

Col. Randal noted there were tiny beads of sweat on her upper lip. Apparently the crash landing had not been as easy as Beverly made it look. The Walrus could have nose-dived into the Mediterranean. It could have plowed into the sand or flipped over on its back.

In the distance, the pair of A-20s were in the process of strafing the camp where the fire could be seen burning. Then, the Havocs returned to the *Abruzzi* and began buzzing it at low level to keep anyone who might happen to be on board's head down. The roar of the powerful airplane engines screaming overhead at low level was deafening.

"Stick with me, Beverly," Col. Randal ordered as he kicked the door of the Walrus open.

The five men in the back, completely unruffled by the crash landing, were already standing on the beach, going about the business of unloading the demolitions from the cabin. When Beverly stepped out of the plane, they all stopped what they were doing and clapped. No one could say this team of SOG hard cases did not have a sense of humor.

King had inventoried the explosives once he received word the Walrus carrying Capt. Stirling had aborted. He had them divided up. There were twelve prepared charges and enough det cord to go around the *Abruzzi* twice.

Capt. Stirling took redundancy seriously.

"Col. Randal said, "I'll take Beverly, go on board the *Abruzzi* and clear the deck. Captain McKoy, you supervise placing charges down the length of the ship—port and starboard. I have no idea if that's going to work but it's the only thing I can think of."

"Sounds like a plan," Capt. McKoy said. "We need to blow this Walrus at the same time."

"Make it happen."

Everyone moved out on their appointed mission.

As Col. Randal and Beverly were climbing the boarding ladder, he asked, "You can shoot a shotgun?"

Beverly laughed, "I was the state champion .410 class skeet shot when I was thirteen."

"We won't be shooting skeet," Col. Randal said. "You stay behind me. Close up so tight you're pressing against my back. Anything so much as wiggles if I haven't shot first, let 'em have it, no questions asked."

"Yes, sir."

Col. Randal was taking Beverly with him because it was the safest place he could think of to put her while the charges were being set. He was not expecting to find anyone on the tanker. The sailors knew it was only a matter of time before the *Abruzzi* was bombed or taken under fire by a war ship. While the Italians were not the cowards some liked to portray them as, anyone staying on board for long was a dead man and they were not known for suicide missions.

The bridge was abandoned. What Col. Randal was looking for was the radio shack. There was a slim possibility signals intelligence might be found there.

Three Italian sailors appeared out of nowhere, firing .32 caliber Beretta M-34 side arms—the little pistols barking furiously.

Col. Randal chopped down two of them with his 1911 Colt .38 Super. Then Beverly fired over his shoulder twice, *BOOOOOM! BOOOOOM!* The 12-gauge buckshot rounds at virtual contact range knocked the third sailor off his feet. He fell over the railing, down to the steel deck of the ship below.

Col. Randal said, "Top off your weapon."

He could hear the *click, click* as Beverly inserted shells into the A-5's magazine.

There were no more enemy personnel on the *Abruzzi.* Why had the three sailors been on board? Col. Randal considered the idea that maybe they had been sent back to recover something left behind.

A quick search of the ship's radio room turned up a wooden box that held one of the RED INDIAN typewriter devices. There were several signals books and some loose sheets of paper they scooped into a canvas sack. Then it was time to get off the *Abruzzi.*

It was not a great feeling to be standing on top of what amounted to a giant incendiary bomb, with people down below attaching explosives to the sides. As Col. Randal and Beverly were making their way down the ladder, Major Everard Beauchamp rolled up with A-Patrol, 575th Ranger Regiment. One of his corporals had been a combat engineer before transferring to airborne infantry.

He knew about demolitions.

Unfortunately, the corporal had never been trained to blow up a ship either. After the former engineer inspected the work and signed off on it, meaning the explosives and detonation cord had been placed so they would ignite, it was time to light off the fuse. No one knew what was going to happen.

Capt. McKoy pulled the ring on the fuse lighter, "Fire in the hole!"

There was a sharp, but not particularly loud, *CRAAACK.* Then the smell of burning cordite.

"We got us fifteen minutes, boys," Capt. McKoy said. "Let's make the best of it. We can carry on the rest a' this here conversation someplace else."

There were six jeeps in A-Patrol. Col. Randal and Beverly climbed in Maj. Beauchamp's, with Col. Randal at the wheel. The Major climbed in the back and let Beverly ride in the front passenger seat. The rest of the team dispersed across the patrol, which proved not to be a problem. It was understrength.

"Where to, Major?" Col. Randal asked, sticking one of Waldo Treywick's long, thin cigars between his teeth.

"Mr. Diamond had a target for us before the message to rendezvous with you arrived, suh," Maj. Beauchamp said. "However, my orders are to take you straight back to Oasis X, Colonel."

"What kind of target?"

"A fuel storage tank farm, suh."

"Really," Col. Randal said. "How far away?"

"About an hour's drive, suh."

In the distance behind A-Patrol, the charges on the *Abruzzi* cooked off like a string of dominoes, making loud ringing explosions against the steel hull. That series of detonations was followed by a secondary explosion. Everyone in the jeeps turned to observe.

What they saw was the ship completely encased in a thick, white fog that looked exactly like a giant upside-down onion. Then without any advance warning, a sudden brilliant flash, a tremendous eruption and a giant, golden-orange mushroom cloud appeared as if by magic. It seemed to be a mile high. The explosion lit up the night. The fuel on the Italian ship detonated all at once. The tanker, hidden by the white fog, completely disintegrated in a massive fireball.

The sight was as magnificent as it was terrifying. No one present had ever been witness to anything as fantastic. It was hard to believe they had been the cause—but then most of them had felt that way before when blowing things up that had a bigger result than anticipated.

In a few minutes A-Patrol felt the heat from the blast. Everyone was still shaken by the suddenness and violence of the explosion. They were all night-blind from the flash.

Unlike the time when Col. Randal's patrol had blown up the underground landmine storage cave, resulting in a monstrous black cloud rising miles high that kept growing for the entire day, this event was over in an instant.

Patches of fuel oil rained down and were burning on the beach.

"Epic," Beverly said, in a little girl's voice.

Rommel was not going to be recovering any fuel from the *Abruzzi.*

Pointing to the wooden box with the typewriter device inside, Capt. McKoy said, "Captured enemy intelligence is worthless if the opposition knows you've got it."

Col. Randal said, "Not much chance of that."

Coming down low overhead, the two A-20 Havocs roared past the patrol, rocking their wings. They disappeared into the night. W/Cdr. Gordon and his wingman were heading out to sea to resume the search for more Nazi blockade runners.

"Beverly," Col. Randal said, "how would you feel about taking a side trip to shoot up an enemy fuel depot before we go home?"

"Can I drive?"

"I'll drive," Col. Randal said. "You operate the pair of .303 Vickers K machine guns mounted on the hood in front of your passenger's seat."

Beverly laughed, "What are we waiting for?"

COLONEL JOHN RANDAL ORDERED, "MAJOR, HAVE YOUR PHANTOM OPERATORS CONTACT RFHQ and see if Pam has made it back yet."

A-Patrol was halted approximately one mile south of the Via Balbia. The tank farm was less than a quarter mile ahead. The massive fuel storage tanks could be seen as shadows in the distance, dotted across the desert. While he waited for a response to his query, Col. Randal sat with one of Waldo's unlit cigars clenched in his teeth, making an estimate of the situation.

Fuel was precious to Panzerarmee Afrika—its lifeblood. For that reason the fuel tanks *should* be heavily guarded. However, it was impossible to completely secure something as big as a tank farm without deploying hundreds of troops. Rommel did not have hundreds of troops to spare for securing each of the fuel storage facilities scattered down the 1,500-mile length of the Via Balbia.

Therefore, this target was vulnerable.

Major Everard Beauchamp walked up. "Captain Plum-Martin has ditched at sea. Air/Sea rescue is searching for her plane at this time, suh."

Col. Randal went to the Phantom jeep to do something he should have done before. "Send the following message: "RED INDIAN."

"Yes, sir!" The Phantom team had no idea what a RED INDIAN was. They just knew it was important.

"You men let me know the minute you hear Captain Plum-Martin has been picked up."

"Wilco, sir."

Captain "Geronimo" Joe McKoy, King and Mr. Diamond were waiting at the command jeep when Col. Randal returned, "Major, how do you want to make this happen?"

"I'd say, suh," Maj. Beauchamp said, "we ought to drive in from the south as far away from the Via Balbia as we can. Then come on line, get the machine guns working and drive through the farm shooting up fuel tanks as we go."

"Sounds like a plan," Col. Randal said. "A single pass and head for the barn."

"That was my thought, suh."

Col. Randal, Capt. McKoy, King and Beverly boarded the second jeep in a quick patrol reorganization. Maj. Beauchamp, his driver, Mr. Diamond and Lovat Scout Lionel Ferguson were in the lead command jeep. A-Patrol moved out, looping south.

While there was only a sliver of moon, visibility was reasonably good for night work. Tank farms, especially when they were over a hundred miles behind enemy lines, are virtually never secured in strength. The sentry's posts had to be a long way apart. Fixed installation security was the responsibility of the Italians, who did not like to be out and about at night. So, while guard posts or roving patrols might be planned, the troops did not actually carry them out. The men would find a nice, safe place to hide from any inspecting officers—who would not be coming around checking at night, there being the off-chance of running into an Arab scavenger with a big knife. Everyone would go to sleep until it was time to be relieved by another patrol, which was not actually going to do any patrolling either.

Italian guards had the art of night security duty down to a science.

That did not mean that A-Patrol could take things for granted tonight. If patrols were out, sleeping or not, once it opened on the fuel tanks there was always the possibility the Italians might return fire and get lucky. The Raiders knew from experience it is never smart to hold your enemy in contempt.

Col. Randal drove, following Maj. Beauchamp in the lead jeep. Beverly was on the twin Vickers K .303 machine guns on the hood in front of the right front seat. King was on the pair on the pedestal mount in back, and Capt. McKoy had his Colt Monitor BAR and a canvas satchel full of spare magazines.

Maj. Beauchamp's driver pumped his brake lights three times. The signal to come on line. Col. Randal pulled up to the left of the command jeep with about ten yards spacing between them. The rest of the patrol moved into position.

Several of the fuel tanks were now only fifty yards away. Maj. Beauchamp's pedestal gunner opened fire, which was the signal for the patrol to move forward on line and engage targets as they came to bear. One of the fuel tanks immediately caught fire, lighting up the night.

Col. Randal said, "Now would be the time, Beverly."

She commenced firing, touching off short, crisp bursts as instructed. However, the Vickers Ks were such fast-firing weapons it was difficult to get really short bursts. Col. Randal watched as Beverly vectored in on a giant storage tank as they rolled slowly forward. First, tracers laced into the container and then armor-piercing rounds mixed with incendiary rounds.

The fuel tank disintegrated into a massive fireball. *KAAAAABOOOOM!*

King was firing on another one that exploded.

Capt. McKoy was shooting over Col. Randal's head and the hot brass from his .30 caliber Colt Monitor was dancing all over the front two seats of the jeep. One shell casing fell down the collar on Col. Randal's neck and for a second he thought he had been wounded.

Realizing what had happened and ignoring the pain, Col. Randal began firing on a fuel tank. He was being careful with his driving. It would not pay to have strayed too close to one of the two-story petroleum containers when it exploded. A lot was going on, but the action seemed to be taking place in slow motion.

The tank farm was a massive complex. Unlike some that Raiding Forces had attacked, these fuel tanks were well spread out. Six jeeps spaced on the SOP ten-yard intervals was sixty yards of concentrated firepower. However, there was no way A-Patrol could possibly engage all of the targets.

The night had turned snow white. Tracers were crisscrossing. Storage tanks were burning. Vickers K machine guns were screaming, making their distinctive, high-pitched whine.

A-Patrol was performing like the veteran desert raiders the 575th PIR had become.

Col. Randal was impressed with the Ranger's fire control discipline.

He glanced over to see how Beverly was doing. She was shifting from target to target. The Tri-Delta sorority girl was as laid back as if she were in a shooting gallery at the Texas State Fair trying to win a kewpie doll. Beverly had her left arm held vertically across her body, grasping her right wrist and stabilizing her gun hand wrapped around the pistol grip of her twin Vickers K's, exactly the way Col. Randal had shown her in the few minutes before A-Patrol launched its attack.

He was impressed with Beverly's performance too.

The only problem was, she did not know how to reload the drum magazines. Beverly finally expended all her rounds. Col. Randal saw her pull out the 9mm Browning P-35 and keep firing.

When Capt. McKoy realized what had happened, he climbed over the seat, being careful to stay well out of King's line of fire, and balancing himself, changed the Vickers K's magazines. Without a word, Beverly holstered the pistol. The 9mm rounds had not been doing any damage but demonstrated warlike intent.

She went back to firing her machine guns.

Col. Randal kept driving and firing. After what seemed like a long time but was only a few minutes, they were through the tank farm and headed out into the desert. The ironclad rule was one pass and gone.

"Let's go back," Beverly said, "I want to do that again."

Col. Randal said, "Not a chance."

Maj. Beauchamp led A-Patrol out into the desert for a mile, then stopped to get a check on his troops. Other than minor scrapes, abrasions and the usual burns from brushing against hot gun barrels, there were no casualties. The Rangers were dazed by the immense volume of firing and the enormity of all the enormous flash explosions.

Everyone's night vision was destroyed.

A lot of damage had been inflicted in a short amount of time. No one reported taking any return fire. As A-Patrol looked back, the desert seemed to be burning.

Rommel did not know it yet, but he was not having a good night.

Col. Randal was well pleased with the performance of A-Patrol. No one could have done it any better. He instructed Maj. Beauchamp to inform the men of his thoughts at the first opportunity.

As Col. Randal was talking to Maj. Beauchamp, one of the Phantom operators ran up, "Sir, we received a message with a God-high priority, ordering you to move to a location to be extracted by air—may have originated from the Chief of the Imperial General Staff or maybe the King."

Col. Randal said, "Mr. Diamond, do you know of a location where a plane can land?"

"There's one of the old abandoned Regia Aeronautica emergency landing strips about ten miles from here, Colonel."

"Get with Phantom," Col. Randal said. "Give them the coordinates. Maj. Beauchamp, it looks like it's time for us to get the hell out of Dodge."

Maj. Beauchamp said, "The men are going to miss Beverly, suh."

"I bet they will."

7
CANNIBALIZED

CAPTAIN PAMALA PLUM-MARTIN WAS PILOTING THE HUDSON COMING TO EXTRACT COLONEL John Randal, Captain "Geronimo" Joe McKoy, Waldo Treywick, King, Beverly and the two Lovat Scouts. Just as the sun was coming up, she landed the Hudson on the Regia Aeronautica auxiliary airfield on the edge of the Great Sand Sea. Major the Lady Jane Seaborn was on board with Happy, the German shepherd. Capt. Plum-Martin had demanded to fly the mission after the Walrus she had been piloting went down with engine failure and was towed in by a passing U.S. Navy destroyer escort.

There was also a man in a dark suit on board. He did not bother to introduce himself. The stranger took immediate possession of the wooden box containing the RED INDIAN typewriter device and the canvas bag of material Col. Randal and Beverly had recovered from the *Abruzzi's* radio room before it was vaporized. He went to the rear of the plane and sat all alone.

As the Hudson was taking off, the man in the suit opened the wooden box and inspected the Enigma encoding machine inside. He was not pleased. The device did not have the highly-sought-after fourth rotor wheel—a fact he did not share with anyone.

"Cuthbert Bowlby, chief of station, Cairo office, MI-6," Lady Jane whispered in Col. Randal's ear.

Col. Randal gave an almost imperceptible nod, the only sign he had heard

Lady Jane. He walked up to the cockpit, "You OK, Pam?"

"Fine, John. We almost made it all the way back to RFHQ before the engine conked out." The Vargas Girl look-alike Royal Marine flashed a smile over her shoulder. "Sorry I was unable to continue on to the *Abruzzi.*"

Col. Randal said, "Well played, Captain Plum-Martin. You brought everyone home."

"Thanks, I felt I let you down."

"Negative—not your fault."

Col. Randal shoved Happy out of the seat next to Lady Jane that the animal had claimed the instant he had left it to walk to the cockpit. The German shepherd curled up on the floor, put his chin on one of Col. Randal's canvas-topped raiding boots and looked up innocently with big brown eyes. "Don't think you can soft-soap me. You're not a very loyal dog."

"Yes, he is," Lady Jane laughed. "Happy simply likes me better."

Col. Randal said, "Nice airplane . . . leather seats, art deco interior. How did we rate this?"

"Belongs to General Alexander," Lady Jane said. "Chief Air Marshal Tedder loaned it to us for this one trip only since both of our Hudsons were out on patrol. He wants it back."

"I can see why he would."

"We were worried about you, John," Lady Jane said, wrapping her arm around his shoulder, "Wing Commander Gordon reported Beverly's Walrus to be a total write-off."

"True," Beverly laughed. "It *was* after Captain McKoy blew it up."

"Waste a' explosives," Waldo said. "Beverly crash-landed right next to the Italian ship. When the tanker lit off, it flat toasted our airplane. Thought I was witnessin' the 'end a' times' them fire and brimstone Baptist preachers used to rant and rave about back in Mississippi before I run away to see the world."

Capt. McKoy said, "Bein' around 'Pyro' Percy as long as I have, you'd think I'd be immunized to big bang excitement by now. But, well, that ain't the case. Too bad ole 'Pyro' couldn't a' been there hisself to see the show."

Beverly said, "Took my breath away."

Lady Jane said, "Admiral Ransom reported it was a massive blast. He and

Randy arrived off the beach about the time the *Abruzzi* went up. They landed a shore party to check on you, but A-Patrol had already departed the area."

Lovat Scouts Lionel Fenwick and Munro Ferguson were the only people present besides Col. Randal who had been on the mission the night Captain 'Pyro' Percy Stirling blew up the lighthouse at the conclusion of the raid on TOMCAT—unaware of its fully topped-off two-story acetylene fuel tank. The Scouts had been debating which explosion was more impressive.

"What say you, sir," Scout Fenwick asked, "*Abruzzi* or lighthouse?"

Col. Randal said, "I know which one scared me the most."

"Accolades have been pouring in," Lady Jane said.

"Why?" Col. Randal said. "My guess is the Desert Fox wrote off the *Abruzzi's* cargo the minute he heard the ship beached."

Capt. Plum-Martin called over her shoulder from the pilot's compartment, "Check out the window, John. A couple of little friends would like to say thanks."

Col. Randal craned his neck in time to see a pair of Hurricane fighters screaming past doing Victory rolls.

"What the . . ."

Raiding Forces had not had a fighter escort since the raid on TOMCAT two years earlier.

"Tedder sent the Hurricanes, too," Lady Jane said in her cut-glass accent. "Not everyone agrees that crash landing a hundred miles behind enemy lines in the dead of night to blow up a ship full of POL bound for Panzerarmee Afrika is much ado about nothing—as you seem to, John."

Lady Jane had clearly had enough of heroics.

Col. Randal wondered how she was going to take the news that A-Patrol had made a detour to raid a fuel depot after picking his team up instead of heading straight back to Oasis X as ordered. And there was the little matter of his and Beverly's encounter with the Italian sailors on board the *Abruzzi.*

Oh well.

COLONEL JOHN RANDAL WAS IN HIS THIRD FLOOR SUITE TALKING TO CAPTAIN "GERONIMO" JOE McKOY. The topic under discussion was "illicit diamond buying (IDB)." IDB was the term DeBeers used to describe diamond smuggling on the West African Coast—or diamonds being sold anywhere else on the planet when The Diamond Company did not get paid a commission on every sale.

From its headquarters in South Africa, DeBeers made its best effort to enforce an iron-fisted monopoly on diamond sales worldwide. However, somehow industrial grade diamonds were still making their way to the Third Reich in adequate amounts to meet its annual needs. Which begged the question—was it through smuggling or was DeBeers selling them to the Nazis?

Flanigan stuck his head in the door, "Sergeant Beckwith to see you as requested, sir."

Master Sergeant Mack Beckwith marched into the room ramrod straight. Most sergeants did not look like they had stepped off of a recruiting poster. MSgt. Beckwith did.

He snapped to attention and saluted, "Master Sergeant Beckwith reports, sir."

Col. Randal returned the salute, "Have Raider Patrol ready to take the field, Sergeant Major. I want to fly out to Oasis X tomorrow morning at 0530 hours. We'll pull out same evening."

"No can do, sir."

"What?"

"Colonel Stone cannibalized Raider Patrol to use as replacements. Promoted everybody except the Lovat Scouts, the Phantom Team and GG because they're SOG. Guns is serving on the Admiral's PT boat, sir."

"You're kidding?"

"Negative, sir," MSgt. Beckwith said. "Been hating to tell you, Colonel."

Col. Randal did not say anything, but he suspected Lady Jane had a hand in this development.

"Sounds to me," Capt. McKoy said, "like you done been benched, John."

"Flanigan," Col. Randal called, "go find Captain Jaxx and have him report to me on the double."

"Yes, sir."

Suffering fewer losses than CRUSADER did not mean *no* losses. Col. Randal should not have been surprised. Ordering light jeep patrols to attack hard targets or ambush heavily armed convoys with virtually no break in operations was a misuse of their skill set. The strategy would inevitably lead to Raiding Regiment being ground down through attrition.

He had warned it would.

Raiding Regiment personnel were highly trained, experienced desert warriors. There was no pool of replacements to draw from to make up losses. That was one of the reasons Col. Randal was always careful not to take unnecessary risks with his troops.

The key word being *unnecessary.*

He realized the situation in Middle East Command was at the tipping point. Victory hung in the balance. Everyone had to do their part. Every man, every unit, every piece of equipment was expendable. Raiding Regiments patrols had to keep going out and keep going out.

Sea Squadron sailed nightly. Duck Patrol was taking losses as well.

Col. Randal could see Raiding Forces was in a death spiral. To make the situation worse, he had a long list of diverse missions to accomplish. All of which were Top Secret, high priority, high risk, execute immediately.

"Zorro disbanded Raider Patrol without you knowin'," Capt. McKoy said. "He shouldn't a' done that, John."

"Well," Col. Randal said, "he broke up your White Patrol too."

"When did that happen?"

"I authorized it before we shipped out to England," Col. Randal said. "You're out of the patrolling business, Captain. We have other plans for you."

"Yeah, I know," Capt. McKoy said. "Kinda hard to give it up, though. Livin' wild and free out in the blue like kings—strikin' outta nowhere, doin' bad things to bad people, then disappearin' into the dark and long gone. Showin' up someplace else the next night and doin' it all over again."

"The one constant in war," Col. Randal said, "nothing ever stays the same."

Capt. McKoy said, "Don't mean you have to like it."

Col. Randal said, "Roger—that's a fact."

Captain Billy Jack Jaxx arrived.

"You wanted to see me, sir?"

Col. Randal said, "How would you like to go on a patrol with Capt. McKoy and me tomorrow, Jack?"

"Yes, sir!"

"Raider Patrol and White Patrol have been broken up to make up for Raiding Regiment's combat losses," Col. Randal said. "What say you and the Sergeant Major survey what's left, combine the two, then fill in the empty slots with your SOG operators?"

"Broke up Raider and White, sir," Capt. Jaxx said. "That's crazy. Why would Raiding Regiment do that?"

"Pretty sure Lady Jane wants me to be more of a commander than a patrol leader. And, Captain McKoy will be departing for duties in West Africa in the near future," Col. Randal said. "But that doesn't mean we can't pull one last patrol together."

Capt. Jaxx said, "What's the plan, sir?"

Col. Randal said, "Raiding Regiment has been assigned the primary responsibility of going after Axis landing grounds. SAS has been raiding airfields for the last six months, and the bad guys may have improved their defenses. We may need to rethink our tactics."

"Best idea I've heard in a long time," Capt. Jaxx said. "I'm all for it, sir."

"Captain?"

"Nothin' I'd rather do, John."

"Maybe we'd better avoid mentioning our plans to Lady Jane," Col. Randal said.

"No problem, sir," Capt. Jaxx said. "As far as anyone will know . . . I'll be taking out one of the patrols."

After Capt. Jaxx and MSgt. Beckwith left the suite, Capt. McKoy said, "You need me to do anything in particular?"

"Get with Mr. Zargo," Col. Randal said. "Work up a target list."

"I'll get on it," Capt. McKoy said. "This is goin' to be good, John. One last ride."

Waldo Treywick showed up about ten minutes later, Capt. McKoy having informed him about the patrol after swearing him to secrecy as to who would be on it.

"You're not going, Mr. Treywick."

"Why not, Colonel?"

"I need you to stay here. Link up with Major Sansom," Col. Randal said. "You two start working on your plan to infiltrate the gold and diamond bazaars in Cairo. I'm putting Mandy on your team. Major Sansom has been her counterintelligence mentor, and they have an excellent relationship. Rita and Lana are assigned to her—they're good undercover operatives, but primarily I want the girls to be her bodyguards."

"Good idea havin' Rita and Lana watchin' Mandy."

"Don't tell her they're doing that," Col. Randal said. "Mandy thinks she can take care of herself."

"When do you want me to get the ball rollin', Colonel?"

"It's your operation, Mr. Treywick," Col. Randal said. "You're in charge. Go when ready."

"How long are you and Joe plannin' to be out?"

"A week to ten days," Col. Randal said.

"Me and Sansom will make us up a plan. Have it ready for you to review when you get back," Waldo said. "I'll do a deep dive into the seedy underbelly of the city while you're gone, reconnaissance bein' my forte. Give you my personal report on Cairo's criminal underworld. Could be real interestin'."

"Could be," Col. Randal said.

"I may be in charge a' the Cairo end like you say," Waldo said, "but you can count on me checkin' with you for advice on a regular basis, and I do mean regular, Colonel. I ain't never done nothin' like this before."

"Well, neither have I," Col. Randal said. "Imagine you and P. J. Pretorius had discovered an organized ring of competitors poaching Portuguese ivory in the territory where you were poaching back in the day. Just do what you two studs would have done, Mr. Treywick."

"Yeah," Waldo said, "If nothin' else, we can always fall back on 'the problem is the solution' like Joe's correspondence course says. Glad we had us this little talk, Colonel."

"There you go," Col. Randal said. Sometimes command responsibility is more than giving orders or leading the way—it's about instilling confidence.

King arrived. He had heard about the patrol.

"Chief, I'm not going to be able to accompany you."

"Oh?"

"Flying out tomorrow morning," King said. "Back to Seaborn House first. From there, one of the Special Operations pilots will fly me to a clandestine airstrip in enemy-occupied France. Then I catch a train to Switzerland."

"You can do that?"

"My Swiss passport makes it possible."

"There's train service between France and Switzerland?"

"Never interrupted—war or no war," King said. "Commerce between the two countries has continued nonstop."

"I didn't realize that."

"Everyone wants to make money off WWII, including certain members of the British royal family, Mussolini, and Hitler," King said. "Chief, I am not sure you fully comprehend the witches' brew we are about to stir up going after the illegal diamond trade."

Col. Randal said, "I'll keep that in mind."

The Merc said, "From this point forward, never count on anyone that's not a badged member of Raiding Forces when it comes to DeBeers. It may not even be possible to rely on everyone in the unit—to include people you would normally trust your life to."

"I see," Col. Randal said. Which meant he did not have any idea what King was talking about, but he did not like the sound of it.

King said, "With a little luck, I can pick up information on diamonds being smuggled into Switzerland while I'm there, in addition to setting up a line of supply of precision watches. I seriously doubt my mission will be as complicated as the RAF has made it out to be."

"What makes you think that?"

"Everybody wants to make money."

"Have a good trip," Col. Randal said, "Get back as quick as you can. I've got a feeling I'm going to need your services in a big way, King."

Thirty minutes later, Col. Randal had his 9mm Browning High-Power disassembled on a piece of newspaper on the coffee table, dusting it with a shaving brush lightly dipped in oil. The pistol components were spread across the front page of a newspaper featuring a photograph of the stage-managed cocktail party at RFHQ. Lieutenant General Bernard Montgomery and Rikke Runborg were sitting side by side.

It was the perfect shot. Rocky was wearing a low-cut black evening gown with spaghetti straps. In the photo, Lt. Gen. Montgomery appeared to be attempting to sneak a peek down her dress.

Col. Randal laughed out loud when he noticed the picture. Rommel would definitely see this newspaper. Colonel Friedrich von Mellenthin, Panzerarmee Afrika's Intelligence officer, would make sure of that.

Lieutenant Mandy Paige rolled in, wearing a super short pair of blue jean cutoffs and little heeled sandals, "We need to talk, John. Do you like Beverly better than you do me?"

Col. Randal immediately clicked on. Though it was clear no one was going to die or even be injured in this situation, a wrong answer could still be dangerous. It paid to be careful when dealing with Lt. Mandy.

"Why do you ask?"

"You have been spending a lot more time with her lately than you have me," Lt. Mandy said, plopping down in one of the sofa chairs and dangling a shapely tanned leg over the overstuffed arm. She worked out with Rocky's crew of Raiding Forces women every morning and was extraordinarily fit.

"Well," Col. Randal said carefully, "you've been busy catching spies."

"Is it true," Lt. Mandy asked, "the two of you got into a gunfight on the *Abruzzi?*"

"I'm not sure you would describe it as a gunfight, exactly," Col. Randal said.

"When you come face to face with three hostile combatants blazing away at you with pistols at five-feet range," Lt. Mandy said, "what would you call that, John?"

"Ahhh . . ."

"Beverly shot one of them?"

"She did," Col. Randal said. "Beverly is reliable in a tight spot. As are you."

"I spoke to Waldo. We plan to meet with Sammy this afternoon and start crafting a strategy to infiltrate the illicit gold and diamond market. A great assignment."

"Mandy," Col. Randal said. "I know you think you're bulletproof, but you're not. The criminal element in Cairo is as vicious and brutal as any city in the world. Be alert at all times."

"John . . ."

"Never go anywhere without either Rita or Lana, preferably both. That's an order."

Mandy said, "Lady Jane is going to let Security train Happy to be an attack dog."

"Good," Col. Randal said. "Take him with you too."

"I am not sure Happy has the temperament."

"Might be surprised."

"John, you worry too much."

Col. Randal said. "You'll be dealing with cold-blooded killers and assassins . . ."

"So?" Lt. Mandy said. "I hang out with you and King all the time."

COLONEL JOHN RANDAL WAS READING AN INTELLIGENCE SUMMARY. ITALIAN ROYAL NAVY, *Decima Flottiglia Mezzi d'Assalto* (10th Assault Vehicle Flotilla), operating out of a clandestine house in supposedly neutral Spain had made a failed attack on Allied shipping at Gibraltar, using three-man "human torpedoes." The phone rang. It was Captain Stephanie Fawcett-Tatum.

"Air Marshal Tedder's office called," Capt. Fawcett-Tatum said. "The Air Marshal inquired if it would be convenient for you to see him this afternoon."

"Roger that," Col. Randal said. "It'll take me about two hours to get there because of all the military traffic on the roads."

"I shall so inform the Air Marshal, John."

Beverly Blackwell came into the suite in her off-duty uniform of cut-off jeans and pee wee cowgirl boots—some combination of which most of the Royal Marines and Wrens had adopted after seeing the photos of the Tri-Delta sorority girls at the University of Texas. She looked none the worse for the long night.

Col. Randal said, "I have to go to Cairo. Would you like to have lunch with me?"

"Fun," Beverly said. "Give me a minute to go change."

The phone rang again.

Capt. Fawcett-Tatum said, "Colonel Clarke called. He wants to know if you can drop by his office this afternoon, John."

"Tell him," Col. Randal said, "I have a meeting with Air Marshal Tedder, then Beverly and I are going to lunch at the Gezira. He can meet us there or I can come by his place later."

"Stand-by one, John," Capt. Fawcett-Tatum said.

The Royal Marine officer came back on the line, "Colonel Clarke said he will see you at the restaurant."

Col. Randal said, "Try to find Lady Jane and ask if she would like to meet us as well."

Beverly returned in jodhpurs, boots and a khaki blouse—her Raiding Forces walking-out dress. She was wearing U.S. officer's insignia on the points of her collar, which did not signify a thing. That was the idea.

"Ready, John?"

"Not quite, Beverly," Col. Randal said. "OK, Miss Texas Ten Most, now's the time—tell me at what point last night you realized our Walrus was not going to make it to the objective and back."

"Almost from the time we lifted off," Beverly said. "Those two airplanes were not airworthy. Pam's plane was in worse shape than the one I was flying."

"Let me get this straight," Col. Randal said. "You knew we had a one-way ticket?"

"Roger," Beverly said. "But I understood how important it was to reach the *Abruzzi* to make sure the fuel on board never reached Rommel's panzers.

"Besides, you had a Plan B to get us home."

Col. Randal said, "Don't you think you should have informed me as soon as you had your doubts? We could have made a joint decision to continue the mission or abort."

"John," Beverly asked, "are you chewing me out?"

"Yes, I am."

"You're being very nice about it."

Col. Randal said, "I'm also recommending you for an award for valor."

"Wow!"

AIR CHIEF MARSHAL SIR ARTHUR TEDDER'S JUNIOR AIDE ESCORTED COLONEL JOHN RANDAL TO the Air Marshal's office. The young officer could not race back to the lobby fast enough to keep Beverly Blackwell entertained while she waited. The Texas beauty queen never mentioned she had been flying since she was twelve years old while he was dazzling her with hair-raising tales of combat missions in Bristol Beaufighters.

ACM Tedder was chewing on his pipe when Col. Randal reported. He returned his salute with a casual wave.

"Have a seat, Colonel," ACM Tedder said. "Thank you for coming on such short notice. Before we get started on the reason I asked you here today, I would like to take the opportunity to tell you that in my opinion, there is no way to truly estimate how many of our lad's lives were saved by you destroying the *Abruzzi.* Quite a lot would be my conjecture.

"Quite impressive to continue on to the target after Captain Plum-Martin was forced to turn back."

"You met Beverly Blackwell, sir," Col. Randal said. "She piloted the aircraft. Even though Beverly knew from takeoff our Walrus was not airworthy enough to fly to the target and return to base, she flew the mission."

ACM Tedder said, "Are you jesting?"

"Negative," Col. Randal said. "She's an accomplished pilot. A full report will be on your desk in the next few days, sir."

"I shall look forward to reading it," ACM Tedder said. "Now, Colonel, the reason I asked you here today is because Wing Commander Gordon has briefed me on your OPERATION BOMBSHELL—the targeting of enemy pilots at places where they congregate. I understand the mission has been temporarily stood down."

"Out of necessity, sir," Col. Randal said.

"I would like you to ramp BOMBSHELL back up again. The idea is to go after enemy air at every level—pilots, aircraft, and fuel, nonstop. Air Intelligence will assist with as much intel as we can gather," ACM Tedder said. "Pilots are the Luftwaffe's weakest link—not enough of them in the pipeline being trained.

"As you are already aware, I put in a request for Raiding Forces to return to attacking enemy airfields. When the balloon goes up, top priority is to the landing grounds hosting Stuka dive bombers. The idea is to significantly reduce Rommel's flying artillery. Two additional A-20s modified as gunships will be assigned to Wing Commander Gordon to assist in the effort.

"Strange fellows, the U.S. Army Air Force," ACM Tedder said. "Their doctrine calls for close ground support utilizing fighter bombers, and their pilots are enthusiastic about providing it. The Yanks have gone all in on the concept of heavy bombers pounding strategic targets. However, they do not have much use for medium bombers like the A-20 Havoc which, for some reason, our side insists on calling the Boston. The USAAF will provide the RAF with as many as we can find pilots to fly.

"Wing Commander Gordon will, in all likelihood, be knighted for his influence in convincing the RAF Desert Air Force to provide close air support to Eighth Army, which we are now calling our 'total air doctrine'. I am confident Ronnie and Raiding Forces, working closely together as you have, will put the A-20s to good use."

Col. Randal said, "I'm heading out on patrol in the morning to evaluate enemy landing grounds. The SAS has been responsible for attacking airfields for the past six months. I want to check if we need to modify our tactics due to any defensive adjustments that may have been implemented during that time period."

"Jolly good idea," ACM Tedder said. "Forward thinking of you, Colonel."

"That may be a matter of opinion, sir," Col. Randal said. "In the event you should happen to run into Lady Jane between now and 0530 hours in the morning, don't mention we had this conversation."

"Wilco," ACM Tedder said. "Read you loud and clear."

Col. Randal and Beverly walked into the Gezira. Heads turned as the two made their way to the back of the restaurant. She did not seem to notice.

In that respect, Beverly and Lady Jane were alike.

They stopped by the table where Brandy Seaborn, Captain Penelope "Legs" Honeycutt-Parker and Veronica Paige were having lunch.

Col. Randal said, "Ladies."

Brandy said, "Jane heard you were sneaking out on a date with Beverly. You shall find her hiding in ambush behind the usual palm, John."

Beverly laughed, "You don't think Lady Jane would shoot me in front of all these witnesses?"

"One never knows with Jane," Brandy said. "Normally not the jealous type. However, John is the exception and she is armed. We are all quite proud of you, Beverly. Parker and I want you to come and spend more time with us."

Beverly said, "I'd like that."

Capt. Honeycutt-Parker said, "Lady Jane has her old flame, Dudley Clarke, with her, John. Any cause for alarm?"

"Don't know," Col. Randal said. "After she guns down Beverly, I'll have to ask."

When they arrived at the table in the back, Lady Jane said, "I have been telling Dudley about your exploits, Beverly. He filled me in on certain details of last night's events that you and John left out of the story."

Col. Randal said, "I was . . ."

Coming to his rescue, Colonel Dudley Clarke said, "The reason I wanted to visit with you is to discuss a new A-Force commitment that requires us to coordinate certain upcoming operations both in the Middle East Command area and out of England. Need to conduct them more or less concurrently."

"What kind of targets?" Col. Randal asked.

"For reasons of operational security," Col. Clarke said, "I am not at liberty to provide you specifics at this time. However, the missions will be similar to things Raiding Forces has done in the past. For example, raiding enemy airfields—say, on Crete—conducting reconnaissance on certain coastal beaches in enemy-occupied France or possibly Sardinia.

"More details will be revealed at the appropriate time."

Col. Randal said, "Raiding Regiment is being misused again in a role that armored cars could just as easily perform. Sea Squadron is out every night. We have a backlog of other high-priority tasks and are on standby for even more.

"My people are stretched to the breaking point. The last thing I need is another assignment."

"Understood," Col. Clarke said. "When I am able to reveal to you why the missions need to be conducted, I am confident you shall be eager to take part."

Col. Randal said. "I want to make one thing perfectly clear. Raiding Forces won't be parachuting into the interior of any island the size of Crete where it will take several days' march following the raid to reach the coast for extraction."

"Nor will you be asked to," Col. Clarke said. "Not to worry. We can always get Stirling's lads for those type missions."

"You do that."

"On another subject," Col. Clarke said, "I understand you ordered Ensign Hamilton to work with MI-9."

"I did."

"The Great Teddy," Col. Clarke said, "is currently involved with Douglas Fairbanks Jr. and the best-selling author John Steinbeck on a Top Secret sonic deception project. I would like to temporarily propose an alternate officer in his place for the MI-9 program."

Col. Randal made eye contact with one of the waiters. The man was at the table in an instant.

"Would you invite Mrs. Paige to join us?"

"Right away, Colonel Randal, sah."

"I've been promising Veronica help on her MI-9 Escape program for months and haven't been able to follow through," Col. Randal said. "She knows Ted from RAF Habbaniya and wants to work with him. Not about to let her down this time."

Col. Clarke said, "I have a suitable temporary substitute."

"If the man you propose is acceptable to Veronica, fine. If not, The Great Teddy will have to quit hobnobbing with the rich and famous and start helping her figure out how to break our POWs out of prison," Col. Randal said.

Col. Clarke said, "I need the Ensign to finish up his project."

Col. Randal said, "It's not like the old days, Dudley. I work for more than one boss now. Escape has become a priority with one of 'em."

"Understood," Col. Clarke said. "Fair enough."

Veronica arrived at the table, "You wished to see me, John?"

"Col. Clarke has plans for Teddy," Col. Randal said. "He'd like to propose another officer to help you with MI-9 on a temporary basis."

Col. Clarke said, "Ensign Hamilton is working on an extremely high-priority project with a couple of U.S. Navy types—Lieutenants Douglas Fairbanks Jr. and a friend of his, an author named John Steinbeck who is a war correspondent turned unofficial civilian volunteer Commando. Possibly you have heard of them."

Veronica said, "Who has not?"

"Do you know of Jasper Maskelyne?"

Veronica said, "The world-famous illusionist?"

"Maskelyne works for me," Col. Clarke said. "As incredible as it sounds, he is hopeless at military deception. You can never believe a word the bounder says, the absolute biggest liar in the world. But he is a wonderful showman."

Col. Randal thought the liar part might be over the top. Col. Clarke commanded A-Force, which was the cover name for "Deception." His military occupational specialty was misleading people. *He* was the "biggest liar in the world."

Col. Clarke said, "Maskelyne is just the chap to help you design ways to slip things like compasses, hacksaw blades, etcetera, into POW camps. You might want to use him to travel around to air bases, put on shows. Teach pilots and air crew the secret techniques MI-9 will be using to conceal parts to build radios, maps and other escape items in Red Cross packages sent to prisoner of war camps in order for the lads to know what to look for if they become captured."

"Your call, Veronica," Col. Randal said.

"If 'Maskelyne the Magician' does not work out, I can still have Teddy?"

Col. Randal said, "That's the deal."

"I accept," Veronica said. "Getting MI-9 running has been a long, frustrating process. I shall take what help is offered. Escape has been three steps forward, two steps back."

"I promise your work shall be well worth the effort, Mrs. Paige," Col. Clarke said. "Do not become discouraged. This is going to be a long war. Your services shall be in high demand before it is over."

Veronica said, "We shall see."

Beverly said, "Is there is anything I can do to help?"

Veronica said, "I am confident we can find something for you, Beverly. When we start putting on demonstrations for the RAF and the USAAF, you would be perfect."

At that moment, Captain Pamala Plum-Martin walked into the restaurant with a U.S. Army Air Force lieutenant colonel. They were escorted to a table. The Vargas Girl look-alike Royal Marine spotted them and waved.

Col. Randal glanced at the waiter.

"Sah?"

"Ask Captain Plum-Martin if she would mind stepping back here to speak to me for a moment."

"Yes, sah."

The snow-blond pilot offered excuses, then made her way to the table. Col. Randal stood up and the two walked to a corner in the far back where they could have a private conversation.

Col. Randal said, "Air Marshal Tedder asked if we could crank up OPERATION BOMBSHELL. He offered to have Air Intelligence locate suitable targets. Are you interested in heading up the project again, Pam?

"Absolutely," Capt. Plum-Martin said. "I shall meet with Air Intelligence straightaway to see what they have—gin up my other intel sources."

"Keep me in the loop," Col. Randal said. "Have a nice lunch."

"John, you have been going without a break for ages and now another high-priority assignment," Capt. Plum-Martin said. "Concerned about you, love, as you already know."

Col. Randal said, "Captain McKoy, Billy Jack and I are going on safari. Get away for a few days."

It was sort of the truth.

8
THE BIG FIVE

AT 0530 HOURS COLONEL JOHN RANDAL WALKED OUT OF RFHQ AFTER AN EARLY BREAKFAST. HE had his gear slung over his shoulder. Captain the Lady Jane Seaborn had been asleep when he slipped out of their suite. So, he was more than a little surprised to find her curled up in the passenger seat of the jeep he was driving to the airstrip for the flight to Oasis X.

"You forgot to say good-bye."

"Not true," Col. Randal said. "I kissed you on the forehead while you were sleeping before I left."

"I was not asleep," Lady Jane said. "Besides, that does not count."

Col. Randal said, "I can see how it wouldn't."

Lady Jane said, "No matter how I have tried to arrange time when you can take off and relax, it always goes terribly wrong."

"We're going on a reconnaissance patrol," Col. Randal said. "Sneak and peek—a camping trip. I'll be back in a week to ten days . . . tanned, fit and rested."

"You are such a bad liar," Lady Jane said. "I still love you, though."

"Well, I love you, too," Col. Randal said. "But don't tell anybody I said that."

"Your secret is safe with me."

As soon as the melodrama was concluded, Lovat Scouts Lionel Fenwick and Munro Ferguson appeared out of the dark into which they had retreated when Lady Jane showed up. At the last minute, Waldo showed up with his gear.

Col. Randal said, "What do you think you're doing?"

"You said I was in charge a' Cairo," Waldo said. "Bein' a big-picture man, I delegated Mandy to take my place at the meetin' with Major Sansom. Them two can work out the details."

"Throw your stuff in the back," Col. Randal said. "I should have known better than to try to leave you behind, Mr. Treywick, you being such a fire-eater."

"I ain't no fire-eater," Waldo said. "Ain't real big on sittin' around in meetin's neither. I'll do that dive into the underbelly a' Cairo's criminal element when we get back."

Col. Randal drove.

Even though it was pitch-black, the road was clogged with military traffic. Eighth Army was gearing up to go on the offensive. It was only a matter of time—momentum was building for a battle. However, its new commander, Lieutenant General Bernard Montgomery, would not be rushed.

Captain Penelope "Legs" Honeycutt-Parker had briefed Col. Randal that her friend, Colonel Francis "Freddie" de Guingand, formerly the Chief of Military Intelligence and now recently promoted to be Eighth Army Chief of Staff, had described his new boss, Lt. Gen. Montgomery, as a peerless planner who was doing a masterful job of traveling around to all the units, outlining what he expected of them in the upcoming battle.

None of the senior officers were particularly drawn to the man—Lt. Gen. Montgomery seemed a bit odd. However, the commanders of the major maneuver elements appreciated his taking the trouble to visit with each of them personally to explain the battle plan and to answer questions. No previous army commander had done so before.

According to Capt. Honeycutt-Parker, there should be no misunderstanding about what was expected of the Eighth Army officers and men when the balloon went up. There always had been confusion in the past. Confidence appeared to be growing that after two years of setbacks, the war in the desert was getting ready to turn around. The British Army was maturing from an army of military amateurs composed of independent regiments—almost a confederation of tribes—into a hard-hitting, unified fighting force to be reckoned with.

The patrol with no name departed Oasis X within an hour of landing. Lieutenant Colonel Sir Terry "Zorro" Stone saw them off. Just before driving out, Col. Randal broke the news about Raiding Regiment retaking the responsibility to attack enemy airfields.

"What am I to do, old stick? You know how stretched Raiding Regiment happens to be at present."

"I have no idea, Terry. You'll think of something."

The patrol drove all day. Instead of using the Great Sand Sea as a safety buffer, Col. Randal decided to cross it now, then skirt along the northern edge fifty miles, more or less, from the Mediterranean coastline. He did not want to waste time crossing, then recrossing, the vast obstacle. Besides, if the patrol ran into trouble, the jeeps could always make a dash into it for safety. Neither the Germans nor the Italians would likely follow them.

No matter how long Panzerarmee Afrika had been in Libya and Egypt, neither the Nazis nor the Fascists were ever comfortable outside the narrow fifty-mile-wide strip of mostly hard "good going" running along the coast. The Italians, who had been in the region for decades, had only a handful of small units capable of penetrating the immensity of the Great Sand Sea.

Both the Germans and Italians disliked operating at night.

Knowing these things gave Col. Randal and the troops of Raiding Regiment a slight edge. Jeep patrols could negotiate the Great Sand Sea with relative ease. And Raiding Forces fought at night almost exclusively.

As the sun was going down, the patrol linked up with the intelligence operative known as Club. The mercenaries who worked for Mr. Zargo had a habit of appearing out of nowhere with detailed information about enemy forts, fuel installations, military stores, dumps, airfields and the like located in their area of operations. The intelligence operatives were perfectly at home in the vastness of the desert.

Club climbed into the passenger seat vacated by Scout Fenwick, so he could brief Col. Randal.

"What kind of targets are you interested in this trip, Colonel?"

"Airfields," Col. Randal said. "We need to know if there have been any significant changes in Axis landing ground defenses since Raiding Regiment quit attacking them."

"Not much," Club said. "The SAS only work against the ones found along the Via Balbia and they keep going back to the same targets because they know where to find them. As a result, one would think those airfields in the vicinity of the hardball would have beefed up their ground security. Not the case . . . an extra strand of barbed wire is about the extent of it, Colonel.

"The Regia Aeronautica and Luftwaffe air strips farther inland have not even upgraded with the strand of wire."

"Hard to believe," Col. Randal said.

"What has always worked best for SAS is to infiltrate a landing ground by stealth late at night and plant explosives on individual aircraft. Slip in and slip out unnoticed," Club said.

"Lately the SAS has abandoned that tactic in favor of a large party of jeeps traveling in formation like a convoy of warships—they call it a 'gangster style' attack. The jeeps slowly cruise up and down the runway with all guns blazing. It works, but the SAS take casualties every time. Even Italian defenders can manage to find the courage to fire the odd machine gun burst or drop a mortar round or two down a tube in the dark."

"We've done the same thing on a smaller scale," Col. Randal said. "I ordered Raiding Regiment to cease the practice for exactly that reason."

"You may recall I went on a couple of those beatups with you," Club said. "In answer to your first question, Colonel, there are five active enemy landing grounds currently operational in my AO."

"That's what I needed to know," Col. Randal said. "We'll take a look at all five.

"When we complete this patrol, I need you to keep the air strips under observation, Club. What I'm looking for is up-to-date intelligence on where Stukas are based. In future, we're going to be specifically targeting dive-bombers."

"Consider it done," Club said. "This trip is strictly reconnaissance, then.

We will not be attacking the landing grounds?"

"Negative," Col. Randal said. "We're going to hit 'em all."

THE PATROL WITH NO NAME PULLED INTO A REMAIN OVERNIGHT POSITION (RON) AFTER DARK. Patrol members went about their appointed tasks. Before long, Colonel John Randal, Captain Billy Jack Jaxx, Waldo Treywick, Club and Wing Commander Ronald Gordon *aka* "Flash Bang" —who had come along to experience how a gun jeep patrol operated and to see an enemy airfield up close and personal—were sitting in folding canvas chairs smoking cigars, with Captain "Geronimo" Joe McKoy holding court.

A million stars sparkled overhead. It was a nice night, if a trifle cool.

"Good judgment is the single most important quality a patrol leader or combat commander can have," Capt. McKoy said. "I'll give you boys an example a' what I'm talkin' about.

"Back in the day, Luke Short really was short, which may have gotten him into altercations and dangerous encounters from time to time with people thinkin' they could take advantage of his diminutive size. He was best known for being a gunfighter, but what Luke really was, was a sportin' man—a gambler. Horses, cards, boxin' matches, you name it. At games a' chance, he was a genuine Western success story and a highly respected individual. Though, he did get run outta Dodge City one time, when he was part owner of the Long Branch Saloon, for bein' an 'undesirable' after shootin' at a local policeman.

"Never one to let anyone get the bulge on him, Luke contacted some a' his pals, to include Bat Masterson, Wyatt Earp and a few other *pistoleros* a' note and callin' themselves 'the peace commission." They took the train to Dodge, where the local city administration unanimously decided, pretty much on the spot, to let bygones be bygones. After all, Luke *had* missed the policeman.

"However, the place just didn't hold much allure for Luke anymore. So, he sold out his interest in the Long Branch and relocated to Fort Worth, where he opened a bar and gambling emporium called the White Elephant.

"Life was good . . . almost.

"Trouble showed up in the form of this ex-cavalry scout, ex-mining guard, former lawman named Jim 'Longhair' Courtright. Jim was sole proprietor of the T. I. C. Detective Agency. Now, Detective Courtright didn't do much detectin'. What he mostly specialized in was extortion. Longhair proposed to provide protection to the White Elephant, for a price. He was makin' the same offer to the sportin' houses all over town, and since Jim had killed four men in New Mexico and four more in Texas, people were inclined to hire him, being intimidated considering Wild Bill Hickock had only killed eight men hisself.

"Not Luke. He figured having a mankiller like Longhair hanging out in the White Elephant might have a chillin' effect on his gamin' crowd, which would be bad for business. So, he telegraphed Bat Masterson to come to Fort Worth to consult, which Bat did.

"Luke and Bat was upstairs in the White Elephant discussin' the situation when Jim paid a unexpected call. Demanded to see the proprietor—that bein' Luke Short.

"A reasonable man woulda declined to have his meetin' interrupted, Jim a certified shootist and all. Word was he could hit coins tossed in the air with his Colt .45 Peacemaker. And it was widely known Longhair had performed with his pistols in Buffalo Bill's Wild West Show for a tour or two.

"Not Luke—like I said—he wasn't afraid a' nobody.

"Luke and Bat walked downstairs to see what the detective wanted. Jim suggested they step outside for a chat. The three men strolled down the sidewalk to the alley stopping out in front of the Ella Blackwell shootin' gallery—no relation to Beverly, I don't think.

"At that point, Jim repeats his demand that Luke hire his detective agency, meaning him, to provide security for the White Elephant. Luke demurred, claimin', with some justification, he could protect his own establishment. All the while he had been standin', talkin' with his thumbs in the loops of his suspenders, innocent and nonthreatenin' like.

"Suddenly Luke drops his arms straight down by his side.

"Longhair says, 'You needn't be gettin' out your gun'."

"Luke said, 'I ain't got a gun, Jim'—but a'-course, he did.

"Courtright immediately reaches for his pistol but the hammer spur gets tangled up on the fancy gold watch chain dangling from his vest pocket. Luke draws his gat and 'bang', shoots Jim's thumb off.

"It bein' impossible to cock a single action revolver without a thumb, Longhair tries to do the border shift, which is tossing your gun from one hand to the other, and in the process Luke plugs him through the gizzard—five times.

"So, what it boils down to, boys—good judgment comes from experience," Capt. McKoy said, rolling his cigar between his fingers. "Most experience comes from bad judgment."

Capt. Jaxx said, "I've been to the White Elephant. It's still in business."

"So, Joe," Waldo said. "How's 'the problem is the solution' rule you learned in your correspondence course play out on that Fort Worth gunfight?"

"Well, let's give 'er a try," Capt. McKoy said. "The problem was Longhair Courtright. The solution . . ."

Waldo said, "Works every time."

W/Cdr. Gordon looked confused.

Col. Randal drew on his cigar, looking at the stars and not saying a word.

One of the Phantom operators brought Colonel John Randal a flimsy. It read, "Move to the emergency Regia Aeronautica landing ground located ten miles north of your present position. Aircraft to arrive at 0230 hours."

This was not part of the plan. Col. Randal had no idea what it was about. He handed the message to Captain Billy Jack Jaxx. "Give everyone a chance to finish their meal, then let's move out."

"Do you know what's going on, sir?"

"Negative."

The patrol motored to the landing ground. The gun jeeps set up a perimeter and most of the troops went to sleep. The patrol was on twenty-five percent security, which meant one in four of the men had to be on watch. This was Raiding Forces' lowest state of alert.

The patrol was only about fifty miles straight line distance from Oasis X. No one was expecting any trouble, unless a band of marauding desert nomads wandered by. It was always a good idea to remain on guard to that possibility. Nomads had a well-deserved reputation for attacking those who were weak, unsuspecting, or not able to defend themselves.

Shortly before 0230 hours, Capt. Jaxx and Master Sergeant Mack Beckwith set out red railroad flares marking the landing ground. Soon the sound of a low-flying aircraft could be heard in the distance. A single Ro.63 aircraft approached, lined up on the flares and came in for a landing.

Raiding Forces SOP called for its planes to fly in pairs in case one went down. However, tonight this flight inbound from Oasis X was so short that the precaution was not deemed necessary. If the Ro.63 piloted by Captain Pamala Plum-Martin and Beverly Blackwell did not return within a certain amount of time after it radioed it had taken off from its rendezvous with Col. Randal, then search parties could immediately be sent out from both the Oasis and the patrol along its line of flight.

Col. Randal walked up to the captured Italian aircraft. The door opened, and he climbed inside. Brigadier Raymond J. Maunsell, who liked to be called "R. J.," Major A. W. "Sammy" Sansom and Lt. Mandy Paige were the passengers. Beverly joined them in the cabin.

R. J. said, "A plan to effect the takedown of the illicit diamond trade has been decided on. Simple, easy to implement, and one hundred percent guaranteed to work. We came to pick up Mr. Treywick."

Col. Randal said, "That was quick."

Maj. Sansom said, "There are five major crime lords in Cairo's extensive underworld, which covers all of Egypt and most of Libya. Two Egyptians, a

Syrian, a Palestinian and a Jew. Their crime families control the city, with tentacles reaching from Turkey to Tripoli to West Africa and beyond. Prior to the war, all illegal activity was controlled by what is called the 'Big Five'.

"Once the war started, the illicit trade in diamonds—both gemstone and industrial grade—exploded. As has the brokering of gold, but to a lesser extent. The crime bosses never saw it coming. The Big Five were not prepared for the tidal wave of small operators who arrived in Cairo, eager to barter gold and diamonds in the bazaars. As a result, from their criminal overlord perspective, the small dealer trade has spiraled out of control."

R. J. said, "The crime bosses are seething. The competition from the influx of small dealers is eating into their earnings. However, the Big Five are apprehensive about crossing Major Sansom and doing anything about it. As chief of field security, Sammy has clamped down on criminal activity in Cairo with an iron fist never experienced before."

"Most of my efforts," Maj. Sansom said, "have been centered on identifying and eliminating enemy agents. To be frank, by necessity I have come to an unspoken understanding with the Big Five. I leave the crime bosses to their dirty business as long as the mobsters stay out of the newspapers and continue to provide me with counterintelligence on German and Italian spies.

"There are certain provisos—like not harming Allied troops on leave who frequent their night clubs, gambling casinos, red-light houses, etcetera."

"That is background," R. J. said. "Now the plan.

"Major Sansom is going to call a sit down of the Big Five. At the meeting, the Major will introduce them to a new player from the United States, "Mr. Big." At that time, Mr. Big will inform those present he has negotiated an accommodation with Major Sansom's Field Security Police, the chief of Security Intelligence Middle East—meaning me—and the Office of Strategic Services.

"In short, the deal is, Sammy and I shall look the other way while the crime bosses eliminate their diamond and gold competition. We believe the Big Five's response shall be . . . enthusiastic."

Maj. Sansom said, "After a suitable period of time has passed, a follow-up meeting is to be called. At that time Mr. Big will inform the Big Five starting from that point forward, they have to conduct all of their diamond and gold transactions through him. He is the new kingpin under the protection of His Majesty's Secret Services and the U.S. Office of Strategic Services.

"The crime bosses are not going to be able to make as much profit per transaction on diamonds. However, they are astute businessmen. They will realize it will be possible to make up for the per-transaction loss by the increase in their volume of sales when competition from all the small operators is eliminated."

"That is cold," Col. Randal said. "You dream this up, Major?"

Maj. Sansom said, "Mandy's idea, actually."

Col. Randal said, "What do you need Waldo for?"

"'Mr. Big'," Maj. Sansom said.

"Oh," Col. Randal said. "That's good."

R. J. said, "All of the crime lords have attempted to bribe Maj. Sansom and been roundly rejected. In their eyes, Mr. Big must be someone special—possibly aligned with DeBeers—to have made it happen. The Big Five will respect that.

"I intend to make a guest appearance at the second summit. Reasonably certain we shall want you to attend as well, Colonel."

Col. Randal said, "I like it."

R. J. said, "We came to take Mr. Treywick back to Cairo with us."

"No problem," Col. Randal said. He leaned out the door. "Captain Jaxx, have Waldo saddle up and report to the Ro.63 on the double. Duty calls."

"Yes, sir."

Col. Randal said, "What part in this operation are you two ladies playing?"

"Not quite sure yet, John, maybe we can pretend to be gun molls," Lt. Mandy said. "Sounds fun."

"Not if you're a small-scale diamond or gold broker," Col. Randal said. "Beverly, you are to stay away from Mandy. She's turning into a bad influence."

Beverly laughed, "Daddy would love this story."

THE PATROL WAS LAAGERED IN A WADI THREE MILES FROM A LUFTWAFFE AIRFIELD. IT WAS located right up on the edge of the Via Balbia. While not a large base, the landing strip had recently been extended to accommodate heavily loaded bombers. A squadron of Regia Aeronautica Savoia-Marchetti SM.79 medium bombers—tasked with operating against Malta—were stationed on the field. Club and Master Sergeant Mack Beckwith had managed to work their way to within a mile of the landing ground before sunset to perform a last-minute reconnaissance. The sun was to their back. There was no way anyone on the airfield could see them.

The two reported back to Colonel John Randal there were no signs of alarm at the field, no heightened state of alert, no indication the enemy forces had any idea a Raiding Forces patrol was in the area.

The report did not seem credible to Col. Randal since he knew the Special Air Service had raided this particular landing ground on two previous occasions. The bad guys had to know Eighth Army was getting ready to attack in the near future. They should have beefed up security. However, counting Abyssinia, he had been operating against Italian airfields for two years and by now nothing the Italians did or did not do really surprised him.

A dozen prepared explosive devices were made ready with thirty-minute fuses. A simple tactical plan was crafted. The SM.79s were parked along one side of the air strip with fifty-yard spacing. There was a large fuel dump situated away from the aircraft on the far east side, almost next to the perimeter wire. And there were underground bomb dumps on the north end of the runway about 200 yards from five round-topped hangars.

The operations center, barracks and other buildings were all on the extreme north end of the landing ground.

A simple plan was crafted.

Captain Billy Jack Jaxx, accompanied by Club and two SOG operators, would attack the Savoia-Marchetti SM.79 bombers. Captain "Geronimo" Joe McKoy and MSgt. Beckwith would take two men to attack the underground concrete aerial bomb bunkers. Last but not least, Col. Randal, Lovat Scouts Lionel Fenwick and Munro Ferguson, accompanied by Wing Commander Ronnie Gordon, who was beginning to have serious reservations about his impulsive decision to ride along with Col. Randal, would attack the fuel supply tanks.

All the explosive devices had thirty-minute fuses. The raid was to be by stealth. Slip in and slip out with no one the wiser until everything started blowing up.

The plan was to infiltrate the landing ground at 2400 hours, be back at the patrol laager by 0230 hours, drive until dawn, then go under camouflage netting to hide from the inevitable air search.

The night was dark, but with so many stars twinkling it did not seem completely black. Capt. Jaxx led out first with Club on point, followed by Capt. McKoy, then Col. Randal. Infiltrating through the barbed wire marking the south end of the perimeter was not difficult. The rusty strands were sagging, with the bottom one laying on the ground.

Once inside the perimeter, the raiding party stayed together as it moved west across the end of the landing strip. On the far side, Club made a hard right-hand turn and led Capt. Jaxx and Capt. McKoy's parties due north, while Col. Randal continued on straight.

The Savoia-Marchetti SM.79s were parked on the west side of the strip. Club led the two raiding parties wide of the bombers. The Raiders were far enough away they could barely see the airplanes. They patrolled until three quarters of the way down the length of the landing ground.

Club halted. Capt. McKoy silently moved forward. Without a word, the mercenary pointed in the direction of the underground bunkers, then continued on with Capt. Jaxx's team, disappearing into the dark.

Capt. McKoy took his three men and moved toward the bunkers. His party was the first to arrive at their objective. There were four underground bomb storage bunkers. Each man on his team took one.

The bunkers were built according to spec. Three concrete steps down. A long rectangular structure twenty feet wide running for fifty feet in length, with aerial bombs stacked eight high, six across, packed in for the entire length with a narrow aisle down the center. The Raiders started at the back and placed their explosives staggered on opposite sides of the stack of bombs, pulling their fuses as they worked back toward the steps.

Professionals, everyone was calm but excited. When they were done, Capt. McKoy collected his team. Then he began to exfiltrate independently back to the patrol laager.

Following Club, Capt. Jaxx's team reached the end of the line of Savoia-Marchetti SM.79 bombers. Normal practice was for the Italians to station a guard on each airplane. In the past, when Raiding Forces arrived unannounced and unexpected, the guards had all been asleep.

Not tonight. There were no guards at all.

All was not sunshine and happiness, however. The wings of the Savoias were twelve feet high. And the doors were locked.

What to do?

Capt. Jaxx pulled the detonating ring on the fuse lighter of one of the prepared charges. It made a small *CRAAACK.* There was a burning smell. Then he threw the explosive like a football up on top of the wing where it joined the fuselage.

His coach at the University of Texas would have been proud.

The Raiders sprinted from plane to plane, repeating the process until they came to the end of the squadron. When the last charge was in place, Capt. Jaxx began exfiltrating his team back to the patrol laager, with Club leading the way.

On the far western edge of the air base, Col. Randal and his team had reached the aviation fuel storage tanks and were wandering around placing their explosives. Everyone was enjoying themselves, even W/Cdr. Gordon, who was beginning to think there was not much to this raiding business.

KAAAAABLAAAAAM!

One of the charges Capt. Jaxx had tossed on top of a Savoia-Marchetti SM.79 bomber exploded prematurely. The aircraft went up in a fireball. Then the bombs on board the plane, which was tasked with a dawn mission against Malta, detonated.

The ground shook.

A siren wailed. Machine guns firing on fixed lines opened. Tracers crisscrossed the airfield. Searchlights came on and began weaving back and forth in the mistaken belief the landing ground was under air attack.

No one was having fun any longer.

Col. Randal shouted, "Rally!"

The Raiders came to the sound of his voice. A quick count was taken. Everyone was there.

"Follow me," Col. Randal ordered. Taking point, he led the team in a wide loop around the blazing machine guns. By the time they reached the barbed wire, the unmanned MGs, which were firing on fixed lines, had expended all of their ammunition.

"*ARRESTATE*!"

With unerring accuracy, Col. Randal had managed to lead the group into stumbling across the exact spot where all the Italian night security personnel had gathered to camp out for the night instead of standing guard. Not part of the plan.

Col. Randal had been patrolling with his 9mm MAB-38A submachine gun at a modified port arms. In one move, he slung it onto his back by the sling, unlimbered his shoulder-fired Brixia 45mm mortar and discharged a round from the hip. *BLUUUUUP*.

In the same instant, Club and Lovat Scouts Fenwick and Ferguson threw hand grenades—letter-perfect reaction/teamwork.

The soft thud of the Brixia discharging was immediately followed by a satisfying *CRUUUUUPH!* Screams filled the night. Whether he hit anyone or the Italians were merely panicked, no one knew.

Col. Randal had no plans to hang around to find out.

The three hand grenades commenced cooking off extremely loudly. The bomb storage bunkers started detonating, making four separate explosions that, while muffled, shook the ground like earthquakes. Then the fuel storage tanks began blowing up, which was a beautiful sight lighting up the night.

If the Italian defenders were not already rattled they were now.

Col. Randal led off at a trot. His party arrived back at the laager with a winded W/Cdr. Gordon bringing up the rear. The pilot was now of the opinion that maybe there *was* a higher difficulty factor to this raiding business than he first thought.

The gun jeeps rolled out five minutes later, wanting to put as much distance as possible between the patrol and the base before first light. In their rear view mirror, they could see that the Italians had finally manned their air defenses. What looked like millions of tracers were streaking into the sky. The base defenders were convinced the landing ground was under aerial attack.

Now, the Italians were fighting for all they were worth.

CLUB SAID, "I HAVE BEEN ASKED TO WORK WITH SAS ON SEVERAL OCCASIONS WHEN THEY HAD special missions. Have a strange way of doing things, Colonel."

The patrol was en defilade in a wadi under pink and green camouflage netting of a pattern designed by The Great Teddy. The jeeps were practically invisible to aircraft. However, the sensation of hiding under a net the colors of Easter eggs always felt more than a little silly.

"Like what?" Colonel John Randal asked.

Club said, "SAS drop their raiding parties off forty-five to fifty miles away from their objective. The men have to conduct a forced march to the Objective Rally Point, then lay up in the burning sun during the day so they can attack the next night. Then their troops have to do another forced march to a pick-up point at another location somewhere else equally far away."

Col. Randal said, "Why would they do that?"

"I don't know," Club said. "Their jeeps could make a stealthy approach at night and laager just over the horizon out of sight of the target the way we do. Make it a lot easier on the troops. Every now and then, SAS lose an entire team who vanish in the desert after a raid—never make it to the final rally point.

"One other thing, Colonel. SAS does not respect radio security procedures. One day they will pay for that oversight in a big way. Mr. Zargo has informed Major Stirling that his people will no longer accompany SAS patrols."

Col. Randal said, “I don’t think Major Stirling had anyone like Captain McKoy to show him how to operate the way we did.”

Captain “Geronimo” Joe McKoy said, “I always subscribe to trainin’ hard, fightin’ easy *and* smart.”

“That’s a definite Rodge,” Captain Billy Jack Jaxx said.

“The Long Range Desert Group takes the exact opposite approach as SAS, operating almost the same way Raiding Forces does,” Club said. “The difference is, LRDG patrols are all about stealth and arithmetic.

“LRDG conducts two week ‘Road Watch’ missions on the Via Balbia. One of their gun truck patrols will drop off individual trucks five miles apart to set up patrol bases in deep concealment approximately three miles off the hardball. Then at night, working in pairs of two men, Road Watch reconnaissance teams make their way surreptitiously down to the coastal highway where they set up LP/OPs and maintain their position for twenty-four hours.

“The LRDG operators record everything that travels past their location. They are not allowed to offer opinions on what they observe—only record what they see. Then, on the second night, the recon teams are relieved without ever seeing their relief party, who take up another LP/OP position of their own choosing. The first team makes its way independently back to the gun truck, and the two men file their report and rest until time to go back on duty at the road. The intelligence information collected is reviewed, checked against the other recon team’s reports, then relayed to MEHQ.

“Highest order of professionalism—the focus is on accuracy.”

“Wouldn’t work for me,” Capt. Jaxx said. “LRDG never gets to fire up the bad guys, and I’m not good at math.”

“Recon ain’t for everybody,” Capt. McKoy said. “It’s a specialized business. Now, Waldo—he’s the best reconnaissance man ever was. Only, he won’t ever let you know it.

“See if you can get him to tell you about the time Lord Kitchener sent a private train to take Waldo and P. J. Pretorius to track down the German General von Lettow-Vorbeck over in East Africa during the last war, Jack—good story.”

"So, what do you have planned for us next, Mr. Club?" Col. Randal asked.

"I thought you might like to see one of the dummy Luftwaffe airstrips," Club said. Then we can motor past after last light and raid the active base ten miles west of it."

Capt. Jaxx said, "Dummy airstrips?"

"Around-the-clock bombing is now a staple of the RAF and USAAF's new policy," Club said. "The Luftwaffe and Regia Aeronautica have been experiencing serious losses. The Axis have resorted to having planes land during the hours of daylight but fly them out to another location come nightfall. Then they roll out dummy airplanes like the ones Ensign Hamilton concocted for our side.

"The idea is to lure the RAF into bombing the landing grounds where the dummies are lined up."

"Interesting," Wing Commander Ronnie Gordon said. "I had no idea anything like that was taking place."

"Recent development," Club said.

"The second landing ground you want us to raid," W/Cdr. Gordon said, "would that be one of the bases where the planes are diverted to remain overnight?"

"Correct."

"Would it be reasonable to expect there will be twice as many enemy aircraft located there?"

"Affirmative, Wing Commander . . . at least that many."

"Why not do this the easy way?"

"What might that be?" Col. Randal asked.

"We put eyes on target," W/Cdr. Gordon said, "then I call in our four A-20 gunships and let them do the work."

Col. Randal said, "I like that plan."

WING COMMANDER RONNIE GORDON AND CLUB WERE LYING UNDER A SMALL CAMOUFLAGE NET the mercenary carried in his pack draped over them like a blanket. The sun was going down behind them. The two were invisible to the Italians on the Regia Aeronautica airfield a mile away. No one on the enemy base was going to be looking into the burning red globe even though the sun was setting.

W/Cdr. Gordon was studying the airfield through Colonel John Randal's prized Zeiss binoculars he had loaned him for the reconnaissance. Parked on the landing ground was a squadron of twelve Savoia-Marchetti SM.79 three-engine bombers. The SM.79 was the most prolific medium bomber in the Regia Aeronautica inventory.

Ground crews were working to service the aircraft and load bombs for the next days' operation. While the evening refueling was necessary for the planes to be ready to take off to fly a combat mission at dawn, it also made the bombers extremely vulnerable to air or ground attack. Once topped off with aviation fuel and bomb loaded, the SM.79s were big—as in gigantic—incendiary bombs.

"You believe another squadron will be landing?"

"At a minimum," Club said. "Sometimes two."

W/Cdr. Gordon said, "Perfect target for our A-20s."

Behind them, the sun went down in blazing colors. The temperature dropped. It became dark almost immediately.

The two stood up and started the two-mile trudge back to the laager. While they were walking, SM.79s were coming in for a landing at the airfield behind them—exactly as Club had predicted. W/Cdr. Gordon was impatient to message his flight at Oasis X. He had never witnessed an air attack from ground level—unless you counted the BOMBSHELL raid when he and Captain Pamala Plum-Martin landed, taxied up to and strafed a bordello frequented by enemy pilots with the organic weapons on their two A-20s.

Or counted the times he had been bombed.

0130 hours. The gun jeeps were pulled up on line approximately a mile from the landing ground. Captain "Geronimo" Joe McKoy, sitting in the passenger seat of his jeep, was about six inches from Col. Randal at the wheel of his. Captain Billy Jack Jaxx at the wheel of his jeep was pulled up just as close on the other side of Col. Randal, next to W/Cdr. Gordon. All four had Waldo Treywick's unlit cigars in their teeth as they waited for the A-20s to arrive.

"Like going to the drive-in theater on Saturday night," Capt. Jaxx said.

"You are guaranteed to enjoy the show," W/Cdr. Gordon said. "We took our A-20s to the USAAF maintenance people to have them perform field modifications like the fliers in the Pacific have been experimenting with to strafe Japanese barges. Asked them to remove the two 20mms and replace them with six .303s in the nose. The Yanks said, 'Why would you want to do that?'

"They painted the plexiglass nose cone black to eliminate reflections, mounted six Browning .50 caliber machine guns in place of the existing armament and four more on each side of the cockpit in blisters. Then they moved the top gun turret forward, fixed it in place so the gunner was eliminated and the pilot fired the two 50s."

Capt. Jaxx said, "Sixteen forward-firing .50 caliber machine guns—all going at once."

Capt. McKoy said, "Sixty-four forward firing .50s in the flight . . . that's some serious firepower. Each one a' them MGs shoots a bullet the size of a ping-pong ball."

"Tonight," W/Cdr. Gordon said, "the A-20's guns will be loaded with tracer and incendiary rounds. No need for armor piercing since they are only attacking thin-skinned targets."

Col. Randal glanced at his Rolex, "Now's the time, Sergeant Major."

Master Sergeant Mack Beckwith was supervising the team that manned the 81mm mortar set up out in front of the command jeep. He gave the order, "Hang it."

The loader placed the round in the tube.

MSgt. Beckwith gave the command, "Fire!"

The round was away in an instant. In the distance, there was a crack as a parachute flare popped open, illuminating the airfield. Somewhere up in the night sky the four A-20 gunships could see the target. They swung into a line astern formation and dived on the parked SM.79s.

"This shall be quick," W/Cdr. Gordon said, "The A20's pilots have strict orders to make a single pass and return to base."

The attack aircraft came in a shallow dive.

When the lead A-20 opened, three things happened all at once. The massed .50 caliber machine guns made a bizarre, otherworldly yawning sound that did not resemble machine gun fire at all. A solid beam of silver light created by the tracers seemed to switch on. Things started blowing up.

The first three A-20s concentrated on the thirty SM.79s. The last one shot up the fuel storage tanks, then continued on to hose the hangars, barracks, and air control buildings at the far end of the air strip.

The air raid was over in seconds.

A hush fell over the Raiders. Regia Aeronautica SM.79 bombers were exploding, fuel tanks were burning, buildings splintered into matchsticks were smoldering from the incendiaries, fueling trucks and other vehicles were blazing.

Not one single round had been fired at the four intruders in return. The RAF aircrew were already on their way back to Oasis X for a drink before climbing into bed. The flight of A-20s had inflicted more death and destruction in five seconds than Raiding Forces troops could have done in two hours of sneaking around in the dark placing explosives by hand.

Col. Randal asked, "Is that repeatable?"

"As long as you have eyes on target," W/Cdr. Gordon said. "There is no reason we cannot do this anytime you desire."

"Jack," Col. Randal said, not taking his eyes off the flaming fuel tanks and the burning SM.79s—some of which still had their bomb loads continuing to cook off. "You copy that?"

"Roger, sir,"

"Know what to do."

"Yes, sir," Capt. Jaxx said. "I'll debrief the A-20 pilots at Oasis X to get a clear after action report. Then we'll organize an air forward observer school to teach our patrol leaders how to make this happen—teamwork, teamwork, teamwork."

Capt. McKoy said, "Big fifties sure do the dam-dam."

Col. Randal said, "I had no idea a single pass of Havocs could inflict that kind of damage."

W/Cdr. Gordon said, "Pilots love the A-20. It has no vices. Easy to fly. You can toss it around like a fighter. Made the mistake of taking Beverly Blackwell for her check flight in one."

Capt. Jaxx said, "Joy ride, huh, sir?"

W/Cdr. Gordon said, "I would not choose to describe it in quite those words, Jack."

Col. Randal said, "I don't want Pam or Beverly flying ground attack missions."

"Then it shall be up to you to stop them, Colonel," W/Cdr. Gordon said. "Those two do not pay any attention to what I have to say on the subject. They informed me in no uncertain terms that women in SOE and OSS are authorized to perform the exact same duties as men.

"For all I know, both girls were at the stick of one of those Havocs tonight."

Col. Randal said, "That's what I was afraid of."

9
MAJOR MOTION PICTURE

COLONEL JOHN RANDAL WAS IN THE SUITE HE SHARED WITH MAJOR THE LADY JANE SEABORN ON the third floor of Raiding Forces Headquarters. He was napping on the couch while Lady Jane was in the bedroom getting ready for a drive to Cairo for lunch. She was less than thrilled with him for raiding the airfields he had promised were only going to be reconnoitered.

Beverly Blackwell arrived. She was wearing the standard off-duty uniform of cut-off blue jeans and peewee cowgirl boots favored by female personnel at RFHQ. Col. Randal had already given Beverly and Captain Pamala Plum-Martin a hard time about flying the A-20 Havoc missions.

Failed.

Capt. Plum-Martin informed him the RAF was suffering from an extreme shortage of pilots not likely to improve anytime in the near future. With Lend Lease in full swing, the Royal Air Force had more planes than qualified aviators.

Even Beverly stood up to him, pointing out that it was more dangerous to land on a Raiding Regiment patrol's improvised desert airstrip or a poorly lighted Regia Aeronautica emergency landing ground late at night than to make a single gun run on an airfield where the defenders were not manning antiaircraft positions. She invited him to fly with them on their next mission to see for himself.

Col. Randal accepted.

Beverly tossed a copy of the *Hollywood Reporter* on his lap. "You're going to be famous, John."

"What?"

"The only thing better than being a movie star is to have a movie made *about* you," Beverly laughed. "Especially when you're a big war hero."

The headline read, "*JUMP ON BELA* SOON TO BE A MAJOR MOTION PICTURE STARRING TYRONE POWER AND ERROL FLYNN!"

"Jane," Col. Randal shouted, "get out here!"

Lady Jane rushed in from the bedroom, pinning one of her diamond ear studs. "What, John?"

"You did this," Col. Randal said, holding up the paper.

"Me?"

"Probably had one of your business people set this up," Col. Randal said. "Or bought the studio to film it."

"I did not," Lady Jane said. "But only because I never thought of it."

Beverly laughed. "I sent a copy of the book to a friend who's a Hollywood movie producer. He optioned it from your publisher."

Col. Randal said, "I don't have a publisher."

"Actually," Lady Jane said, "you do. I authorized my business agent in New York to arrange to have *Jump on Bela* published in the States."

"You're kidding," Col. Randal said.

"Why are you so upset, John?" Beverly asked.

"Other than the fact Terry and I jumped on the island, not one word in that entire book is true," Col. Randal said. "The admiral's girlfriend had their bags packed when we landed. She set up the whole deal."

"You mean there was no platoon of evil Muslim fanatics with sharp swords?" Beverly laughed. "You didn't order your troops to 'kill 'em all and let Allah sort 'em out', really?"

"No, Beverly," Col. Randal. "There weren't any enemy forces on the island. I never said that since I didn't have anyone to say it to except Terry."

Lady Jane said, "Still, it was a brave thing you two did—parachuting on to a remote island all by yourself on a high-value mission for British

Intelligence. No one knew for sure in advance how it was going to turn out."

"Make a blockbuster true-action movie," Beverly said. "Tyrone Power is perfect to play you. Errol Flynn's a dead ringer for Sir Terry. You'll go along with the project, John—please?"

"Only," Col. Randal said, "if your director boyfriend can get Veronica Lake to play Brandy."

Beverly said, "She's hot."

"I intend to tell Brandy your terms," Lady Jane said. "Who would you cast to play me?"

"You're not in the book, Jane," Col. Randal said. "But if you were—Gene Tierney, only she's not as good-looking as you are. In fact, since none of it's true, no deal unless they write you into the script."

Beverly said, "Wow, Gene Tierney's the most beautiful actress in Hollywood!"

Drop-dead gorgeous Lady Jane rewarded him with one of her patented heart attack smiles without saying a word.

But then, she did not need to.

All was right in the world at RFHQ.

COLONEL JOHN RANDAL AND MAJOR THE LADY JANE SEABORN ARRIVED AT THE GEZIRA CLUB. Flanigan dropped them off. Lovat Scout Munro Ferguson was following the ex-policeman in a jeep in order to take Col. Randal back to RFHQ. Lady Jane had business after lunch.

The pair walked in and were immediately whisked to the back of the dining room to a spot behind a palm. Captain Billy Jack Jaxx was at the bar with Red, who had just returned from the States where she had been teaching airline flight attendants the finer points of air travel espionage on behalf of the Office of Strategic Services. The glamorous Clipper Girl was introducing Jack Cool to a Pan American Airlines stewardess she had met on her trip.

Brandy Seaborn and Captain Penelope "Legs" Honeycutt-Parker were at a table having lunch with Brigadier Raymond J. Maunsell, who liked to be called "R. J." Col. Randal wondered what that could be about. Clearly, it was more than simply a pleasant meal with interesting company. The Chief of Security Intelligence Middle East had his finger in a lot of pies.

Wing Commander Tony Dudgeon was there with his new bride. Her job had evolved into being Lieutenant General Sir Harold Alexander's personal secretary, not merely his social secretary—Lady Jane was still on the hook to help out with the General's social schedule. Col. Randal had missed the wedding while he was out on patrol. Lady Jane, Captain Pamala Plum-Martin and Mandy had attended. They had all known then-Squadron Leader Dudgeon at RAF Habbaniya.

Lady Jane began entertaining Col. Randal with a story as soon as the two of them were seated. "Are you aware that Colonel Menzies, 'C', has a brother named Ian?"

"No."

"He is married to an Austrian woman named Lisel Gartner," Lady Jane said. "She has a sister, Friedi, who is a cabaret 'artiste'."

Col. Randal said, "You mean a stripper?"

Lady Jane said, "Friedi is Admiral Canaris's mistress."

"Are you saying," Col. Randal asked, "that the chief of the British Intelligence Service has a sister-in-law who's sleeping with the chief of the German Intelligence Service?"

"Yes, I am," Lady Jane laughed.

"When we were in Nairobi, didn't you tell me that 'C's sister was divorced from the Earl of Errol," Col. Randal said. "The Italians' man in Kenya?"

"You *were* paying attention." Lady Jane laughed again.

Col. Randal said, "Colonel Menzies has a complicated family life. How does he even get a security clearance?"

"Byzantine—no idea about the clearance."

"Great story, Jane."

"Classified."

"I can see how it would be."

"While we are gossiping," Lady Jane said, "Colonel Menzies was not the Prime Minister's first choice for the job. Neither was Air Marshal Tedder or General Montgomery."

"Really," Col. Randal said.

"Not that it matters," Lady Jane said. "Our side has not been doing so well with first choices."

Col. Randal said, "We'll see what happens with the second string."

Lady Jane asked, "Has anyone briefed you on Mr. Treywick's meeting with the crime lords?"

"Negative, I haven't seen Waldo since we got back from the field."

Lady Jane said, "The conference was held in Moe's private office at the Kit-Kat Club. According to Mandy—who got her information from Major Sansom—Mr. Treywick said, 'I understand you men have a problem with small-deal diamond and gold dealers cutting into your profits.'

"When all five crime bosses agreed that was indeed true, Mr. Treywick said, 'Well, boys, the problem is the solution'."

Col. Randal said, "You're kidding."

Major Vladimir Peniakoff *aka* Popski appeared at their table. The tubby, middle-aged Russian had not been seen by anyone in Raiding Forces for at least three months. After returning from an operation with Desert Patrol, he had gone native and disappeared into the desert with a handful of men from the Libyan Arab Commando on some mysterious mission of his own.

Maj. Peniakoff said, "GHQ disbanded the Libyan Arab Commando while I was away in the desert making things go bang in the dark."

"That's too bad," Col. Randal said.

"Not entirely," Maj Peniakoff said. "Now I am to be allowed to raise my own command, No. 1 Demolition Squadron, PPA."

"What's PPA stand for?"

"Popski's Private Army."

Col. Randal said, "Has a nice, unassuming ring to it."

"PPA is authorized thirty-five officers and men," Maj. Peniakoff said. "Only have half that many at present—find the rest somewhere.

"I am in need of a parent organization. The Long Range Desert Group dissolved into hysterics when I made inquiries as to their interest."

"What sort of parent organization?" Col. Randal asked.

"We lack transportation," Maj. Peniakoff said, "and an administrative tail."

Col. Randal said, "You need jeeps, a source for maintenance, and someone to feed, supply and pay your troops."

Maj. Peniakoff said, "Most definitely."

Col. Randal said, "See Mr. Rawlings at RFHQ. He'll provide you with six jeeps. I'll notify Colonel Stone that PPA will be operating out of Oasis X. He'll have his staff work out the administrative details with Captain Fawcett-Tatum."

"Thank you, Colonel."

Col. Randal said, "In return, I want actionable intelligence—you know what we're looking for, Major. Mr. Zargo's men are overtasked since we expanded Raiding Regiment. Eighth Army's offensive is in the works, so our intel situation will only get worse. Take up their slack, Popski."

"You will never regret your decision, sir," Maj. Peniakoff said.

"If I do," Col. Randal said, "Popski's Private Army won't be getting any more beans, bullets or cold hard cash."

After Maj. Peniakoff departed, Col. Randal said, "I've got a story for you I've been saving."

He told her about Beverly Blackwell's bust being on display at the University of Texas, her personally sculpted nude torso locked in the director of the Art Department's private office, and Billy Jack sneaking in late at night with the professor's student aide to check it out.

Lady Jane thought the story so funny she developed the hiccups.

Capt. Jaxx arrived at their table, having promised Red and the Pan American stewardess he would be right back.

"Beverly told me about your movie deal, sir. Tyrone Power doesn't look anything like you, Colonel. We need Roy Rogers."

Col. Randal said, "I like that, Jack."

Lady Jane started hiccupping again.

MAJOR THE LADY JANE SEABORN HAD AN APPOINTMENT WITH CUTHBERT BOWLBY *AKA* "CURLY," chief of MI-6, the British Secret Intelligence Service, Cairo. She departed the Gezira in her Rolls Royce and was driven to his office by Flanigan, the ex-policeman who was now her bodyguard/chauffeur.

Cuthbert was waiting when Lady Jane arrived. The SIS officer went straight to the point. He was a man who, like the organization he represented, chose not to take women seriously regarding intelligence work. Basically, the SIS chief-of-station tended to view Lady Jane as a wealthy socialite who traded on her family contacts.

In that, he was not entirely wrong.

"Lady Seaborn, it has come to my attention that Colonel Randal has been asked to look into the matter of illicit diamond buying, what is described as IDB. Is that correct?"

"It is."

"An operation undertaken at the behest of the U.S. Office of Strategic Services?"

"Yes."

"I shall require you to keep me informed of all information Colonel Randal or his operatives develop on the subject, specifically as it relates to the DeBeers Diamond Company."

Lady Jane was a highly-trained MI-6 "employee," for lack of a better word, having attended a mind-numbing series of intelligence schools. She was not an operative. All the training was merely a way to keep her occupied by an organization that had absolutely no intention of ever using her as an agent. MI-6 had been keeping her out of harm's way because of her family's history of a longtime relationship with the British Secret Intelligence Service, her great wealth and social standing.

Lady Jane knew SIS considered her a "lightweight."

Even so, Lady Jane—having learned something from all the spy school training—noted Curly did not make mention of industrial diamonds, which she knew were of strategic importance to the war industry. He only said IDB, which was, she also knew, a term coined by the DeBeers Diamond Company to cover any stone bought or sold without paying a commission to the corporation.

"Naturally," Cuthbert said, "this conversation is confidential. You shall not allow Colonel Randal to know you are providing me reports. I shall expect them, at a minimum, on a weekly basis."

"What is it you desire," Lady Jane asked, "exactly?"

Cuthbert said, "Specifically, we are interested in learning what the Americans understand about the extent of DeBeers' control of the international diamond market."

Lady Jane said, "I shall be in touch."

Then she stood up and walked out.

Curly Bowlby was startled. People were not in the habit of abruptly ending meetings with him. *He* ended meetings with him.

Flanigan drove Lady Jane back to Raiding Forces Headquarters. Arriving upstairs in the third-floor suite, she found Colonel John Randal talking to Lieutenant Mandy Paige and Beverly Blackwell. The three seemed to be having a really nice time.

She heard Mandy say, "Roy Rogers?"

Beverly laughed, "Why not the Lone Ranger? Then John and Zorro could both wear masks."

Lady Jane said, "Why don't you take Mandy and Beverly and go teach them your trick of shooting skeet with a pistol?"

It was not really a question.

Col. Randal looked up. "OK—Roger that."

After the three departed, Lady Jane went into her bedroom and retrieved a thin pamphlet from the hidden compartment of one of her jewelry boxes. She took out a piece of paper, scanned through the pages of code and jotted down a message. Next, she prepared a handwritten note in the clear addressed to Colonel Dudley Clarke, A-Force, which she gave to Flanigan, who was sitting at the desk outside the suite. His instructions were to deliver it immediately.

Then, she went downstairs to the Operations Room, walked to the corner bay the Phantom radio operators occupied and said, "Send this straightaway."

"Will there be a response, Lady Seaborn?"

"Most likely it shall be a while."

Decoded, which the Phantom operators had no way of doing, not being in possession of the code, the message read:

> EFFECTIVE IMMEDIATELY I RESIGN MY POSITION WITH THE BRITISH SECRET INTELLIGENCE SERVICE STOP RAIDING FORCES SHALL NO LONGER PARTICIPATE IN JOINT OPERATIONS WITH SIS OR ANY AFFILIATED ORGANIZATIONS STOP
> SIGNED LADY JANE SEABORN, MAJOR RM STOP

The note to Col. Clarke read: *Raiding Forces is severing its relationship with A-Force effective upon your receipt of this message. Security has been instructed not to allow you or any member of your staff access to the RFHQ compound nor shall we accept phone calls or take messages from your organization. This ban remains in effect as long as you and/or your command maintains a relationship with SIS, specifically Mr. Cuthbert Bowlby.*

Lady Jane did not bother sending a note to Special Operations Executive (SOE), Cairo. She did not take them seriously. However, she did order Captain Stephanie Fawcett-Tatum to dispatch a detail to go to James "Baldie" Taylor's room, pack his bags and have them transported to Shephard's Hotel in Cairo.

The British Secret Intelligence Service had underestimated the depth of Lady Jane's loyalty to Col. Randal.

COLONEL JOHN RANDAL, LIEUTENANT MANDY PAIGE, BEVERLY BLACKWELL, RITA AND LANA had repaired to the shooting range Captain "Geronimo" Joe McKoy had set up for handgun practice at Raiding Forces Headquarters.

Col. Randal was struggling with a canvas parachute bag full of an assortment of handguns while the girls all lugged boxes of various kinds of ammunition. Beverly was only armed with the Remington Model 51 pocket pistol her father had given her. Now Col. Randal was going to let her try out the full-size service automatics he had collected, primarily by having shot the previous owner.

He laid out the weapons on the wooden table at the range. The guns were limited to either .45, .38 Super or 9mms because ammunition was readily available. There was a .45 U.S. Army 1911A-1, a 9mm Polish Radom (Vis 35) which was a 1911 knockoff, a 9mm Luger P-08, a 9mm Walther P-38 double action, his 9mm Browning High-Power *aka* P-35 and one of his Colt Government Model .38 Supers, the Raiding Forces' pistol of choice.

Handguns are a highly personal weapon. One size does not fit all. Nor does one caliber. Armchair experts opine on the subject at length in various gun magazines using up barrels of ink expounding on velocity, foot pounds, knock down power, etc. However, those who have actually been in a gunfight know what is vitally important is to get a first-round hit first and keep scoring more hits until the opposition quits or is dead.

Then, shoot him or her at least one more time.

It's not rocket science. You cannot pick a pistol for your personal defense by studying ballistics tables or reading gun magazines. The handgun you want is the one you personally handle best.

To Col. Randal's surprise, Beverly was familiar with all the weapons except the 9mm Walther P-38, the 9mm Polish Radom (Vis 35) and the Colt .38 Super—not the gun, the caliber.

"Daddy has an extensive firearms collection."

Col. Randal said, "You don't have to pick a full-sized service automatic, Beverly. Mandy carries a pair of Sauer .32s I gave her. One in her purse, one at her waist. The idea is . . . I want everyone to *know* you're armed."

Mandy said, "John taught me to put my hand on my weapon the instant I sensed danger and never take it off."

"I'll remember that," Beverly said. For once, she was not laughing. What they were doing was serious business and she was taking it as such.

"We don't have any Remington 51s," Col. Randal said. "So if you decide you want to go with pocket pistols, you'll have to see if your father can send one. We'll find something else you can use until it arrives."

"I'd like to carry a full-size belt gun the way Lady Jane does," Beverly said.

"That's what we're here for," Col. Randal said. "Pick one, let's get started and see which you like best. All you have to do is shoot those steel plates on the Texas Star practice target Captain McKoy made for me."

He did not mention that when she hit one, the wheel holding the rest of the plates would start spinning around and around—fast.

Beverly looked the weapons over, "The Luger is a beautiful weapon, built like a Swiss watch, and fits my hand really well . . . only it jams sometimes. Daddy says never to trust a P-08 for personal protection."

Col. Randal said, "Your father knows what he's talking about."

"Let's try this one," Beverly said, picking up the 9mm Vis 35. "I like the art deco triangle-shaped grips."

Using a two-handed hold, she took dead aim at one of the plates and touched off a round. There was a resounding ring when the 9mm bullet struck the metal. The wheel started spinning.

Beverly laughed, having fun now, and continued to fire—shooting fast. She scored hits with all eight rounds. The UT beauty queen could shoot at a skill level that would qualify her for a spot in Captain McKoy's Wild West Show and Shooting Emporium.

"The Vis 35 is a very nice pistol. I like it."

Col. Randal said, "It's a popular choice with quite a few of Jane's Royal Marines."

Next Beverly picked up the Walther P-38. The weapon was a revolutionary design. Col. Randal showed her how it worked, explaining it was double action, meaning it was fired first round from the hammer down position. "Like a double action revolver."

Beverly raised the pistol and had trouble pulling the trigger because her hands were too small. She missed the first shot. After that, the weapon was single action, meaning it had a substantially lighter trigger pull and she ran the plates.

"I'll pass on this one, thanks."

Col. Randal said, "It's not for me either."

Next Beverly tried one of Col. Randal's .38 Supers. Since she had plenty of practice with her father's .45 Colt 1911 Government Model, she scored all hits even though the wheel was whizzing around at a high rate of speed.

Beverly said, "The .38 Super is definitely a lot easier to control on rapid fire than a .45 ACP."

"So," Col. Randal said, "what are you thinking, Beverly?"

"Browning High-Power," Beverly said. "I grew up shooting Daddy's. Its grip fits my hand like a glove, low recoil, high capacity. You have to get it set up for me the same as yours, John. I love the crisp trigger pull and gold bead front sight."

"No problem," Col. Randal said. "Jane and Captain McKoy had my Browning I tuned at Westley Richards in Cairo. They have the specs.

"Carry mine until yours is ready."

Lt. Mandy said, "You are really a good shot, Beverly."

Beverly laughed, "There's not a lot to do for entertainment on a South Texas ranch."

Now with the serious work done, Col. Randal showed the girls the concept of shooting skeet, or more accurately trap, with a handgun. "Captain McKoy taught me this game. Only, he didn't tell me the trick."

"Typical cowboy," Beverly laughed. "What is the trick, John?"

"The trick," Col. Randal said, "is to wait. When the clay pigeon is going straight away, it rises in an arc. The instant the bird reaches the top of the curve, it's standing still. That's when you touch it off.

"Not easy but it can be done."

With Rita and Lana reloading magazines, they spent a pleasant afternoon *trying* to shatter clay pigeons with their pistols. It was excellent practice.

BRIGADIER RAYMOND J. "R. J." MAUNSELL ARRIVED AT RAIDING FORCES HEADQUARTERS. R. J. had two men in mufti carrying what appeared to be a large heavy suitcase. They went to the third floor and were shown to Rikke Runborg's room by Major the Lady Jane Seaborn.

Inside the suitcase was concealed a portable long distance radio transmitter. The two men were Security Intelligence Middle East (SIME) radio operators. Rocky sat talking to R. J. and Lady Jane while the radiomen worked.

When the two were through, one of them went outside and stood guard in the hallway. The other remained in the room. His job was to eavesdrop on the message Rocky transmitted in Morse Code to make sure she was following the script R. J. provided her.

The message was in two parts. First, what was called "chickenfeed." Something the Nazis either knew or were interested in knowing.

Chickenfeed, as it related to the intelligence trade, is something true but irrelevant. The idea is for the agent sending the message to give the "client," meaning the Nazis, something they can confirm or that they will soon be able to confirm in order to set up the second part of the message.

Which is a lie.

Rocky sat down at the key and spread out the message on the table where she could read it while she transmitted. She was a highly trained professional with a distinctive "signature." The receiving station in Tripoli would have no trouble recognizing her "hand."

No one on the other side would question whether or not it was Rocky who had sent the message.

Rocky started tapping the key. The first part of the message read:

THE UNITED STATES ARMY WILL NOT COMMIT MAJOR GROUND FORCES TO REINFORCE EIGHTH ARMY.

That was true.

Enigma intercepts indicated the German High Command, and Field Marshal Erwin Rommel in particular, were concerned the massive convoy forming in Great Britain was en route to Tobruk via the Cape of Good Hope. If so, that would spell doom for Panzerarmee Afrika.

The second part of the message read:

> MONTGOMERY STATES HE WILL NOT LAUNCH HIS COUNTERATTACK FOR NINETY DAYS.

That was a lie.

With the "Good Source" shut down—gone home to the U.S.—and Captain Seebohm, Rommel's radio intercept genius, dead, Rocky was the Germans' last hope for a highly placed source in Cairo. A-Force intended to exploit that deficiency. Unknown to the Nazis, every single one of their spies in Egypt/Libya was either dead or working for SIME as a double agent. R. J. was an extraordinarily proficient chief of counterintelligence, and he played hardball.

In Middle East Command, the highly vaunted Abwehr was a total bust.

Based on Rocky's transmission, Rommel flew home to Germany the next day to treat his dysentery, malaria and high blood pressure. The Desert Fox may have been famous as a military genius, but he had not been able to take much pleasure from it. Most of his ailments were complicated by stress.

After R. J. and his team departed, Lady Jane walked downstairs and outside to where Col. Randal and the girls were shooting at the clay pigeons, not necessarily hitting them. At the first opportunity, she pulled Lt. Mandy aside.

"Someone you trust is going to come to you in the future," Lady Jane said. "He or she will ask questions about the DeBeers Diamond Company. When they do, inform me immediately."

"Wow!" Lt. Mandy said, having picked up some of Beverly's slang.

"'Wow!' is right," Lady Jane said. "Make that a double 'Wow!'"

COLONEL JOHN RANDAL WAS IN THE THIRD-FLOOR SUITE HE SHARED WITH MAJOR THE LADY JANE Seaborn. He was reading an "Enemy Threat Assessment." Lady Jane was in the master bedroom doing whatever she was doing. One thing for sure, she could entertain herself by herself better than any woman he had ever known.

The way Lady Jane was amusing herself today was lying on the king-sized bed, perusing a stack of U.K. published editions of fashion magazines like *Glamour* and *Vogue,* looking at the pictures . . . something she loved to do. However, this was business, not pleasure. All that time spent in those MI-6 spy schools had not been wasted. What could be found on the glossy pages when you knew what to look for was illuminating.

Unfortunately, what she discovered raised more questions than answers.

There were no pictures in what Col. Randal was reading. It was a Y-Service intercept, a detailed explanation of Afrika Korps armored tactics sent from Field Marshal Erwin Rommel to the German High Command. It made fascinating reading. Rommel described his style of warfare as "concentrating strength at a single point, forcing a breakthrough, rolling up and securing the flanks on either side, then penetrating like lightning deep in his rear areas, causing disruption and panic before the enemy has time to react."

Col. Randal liked the aggressive tactical model: concentration of force, speed, violence of action.

However, it occurred to him Rommel never took into consideration what was going to happen next after he had accomplished the penetration, disruption, etc. The Royal Air Force, the United States Army Air Force, the Royal Navy and Raiding Forces would be attacking his 1,500-mile sea/land logistical tail around the clock. And since the Desert Fox's supply convoys were restricted to the fifty-mile-wide strip of "good going" along the coast, all four outfits would know exactly where to find his thin-skinned vehicles.

For the last eighteen months or so, Afrika Korps, now styled Panzerarmee Afrika, had launched one attack after another. No matter how much initial success he had, Rommel's campaigns always ended the same way. Virtually no tanks left, infantry shattered, having outrun his supply train, with no choice left but to retreat back to the original start line in order to resupply and regroup.

So, what would happen if Panzerarmee Afrika captured Cairo? Then the Nazis would have *really* long supply lines. And the Suez Canal had lost a lot of its strategic importance the moment Lend Lease had gone into effect.

However, if Eighth Army gave up Cairo and retreated east of the Canal, it would then become a virtually impassible defensive barrier for Rommel to cross. The result: a stalemate. Panzerarmee Afrika would find itself tied up in Egypt for no strategic gain.

While neither side could expect much help reconstituting troop strength, resupply from the United States gave the British the advantage in replacing equipment losses. They could do it faster than Panzerarmee Afrika, and the U.S. tanks were improving the quality of Eighth Army's armored divisions.

Logistics were clearly not the Desert Fox's long suit, nor were they trending in his favor now. The thought occurred to Col. Randal that Rommel was attacking to nowhere. What was the point . . . ?

Lady Jane came out of the bedroom, "We need to talk."

10
DIAMOND DEAL

COLONEL JOHN RANDAL, VICE ADMIRAL SIR RANDOLPH "RAZOR" RANSOM AND CAPTAIN "Geronimo" Joe McKoy were sitting at a table in the mess hall at Raiding Forces Headquarters having breakfast. The three were discussing diamond smuggling along the West African Gold Coast. According to initial reports, most of the trafficking was done aboard tramp merchant ships that plied their trade in the squalid ports inhabiting the region. Sierra Leone and the Gold Coast Colony, both having major ports of call, were the most promising places for OSS agents to discover the diamonds.

"I'll be headed out that way," Capt. McKoy said. "Travelin' as me—a federal U.S. Marshal. My cover story is a real story. That way, I can kill two birds with one stone. I'll be makin' a survey of U.S. citizens in the British colonies along the coast, to include Nigeria, which is inland, who are subject to the draft. And I'll be putting steps in place to make sure they get themselves registered to do their duty.

"By steps, I mean bringin' in some retired deputy marshals and Port Authority men to do the registering, working out of the U.S. Counsel's office. What they'll really be doin' is settin' up to drop the hammer on the smugglers just as soon as we can dope out how the IDB deal works."

Col. Randal asked, "You have your people lined up?"

"I do," Capt. McKoy said. "My boys are tired a' bein' retired. They're rarin' to go—handpicked men, law enforcement hard cases. First I have to go check it out. Time spent on reconnaissance is rarely wasted, as we both know from long experience, John."

VAdm. Ransom said, "There are a million and one places to hide stones on board a ship. We need to consider having Mud Cat Ray and Wino Muldoon go back into the tugboat business. Put them in position to gather intelligence. They likely already know most of the captains who ply their trade in that cesspool."

"That's a dang good idea, Admiral," Capt. McKoy said. "Might set Wino and Mud Cat up as buyers too. Have Waldo come in as Mr. Big. Take over control of the diamond trade out there. The smugglers ain't gonna care who they sell to if they get their money quicker and the price is right. Particularly if John goes out there and shoots a few uncooperative sellers to set the tone of the market.

"That'd play in real good with Mr. Big's story in Cairo. He's the kingpin a' diamonds—nationwide."

Col. Randal said, "I heard Mr. Treywick told the Big Five that 'the problem is the solution' in regard to resolving their competition issues with small diamond and gold traders."

Capt. McKoy said, "Waldo ain't a fast learner but once he gets his teeth in an idea he don't let go."

"We have a situation," Col. Randal said. "Lady Jane severed Raiding Forces' relationship with MI-6 and A-Force. Admiral, why don't you go talk to her and see what problems that creates for you?"

VAdm. Ransom asked, "What precipitated her action?"

"Has to do with IDB," Col. Randal said, "Best let Jane explain it to you, sir."

VAdm. Ransom had a string of his "Irregular" fleet of picket boats stationed all down the Mediterranean coastline to intercept Axis fuel tanker blockade runners attempting to transport fuel to Panzerarmee Afrika. He had been feeling particularly cheery due to the fact that last night one of his boats had intercepted the Italian ship *Luciano* and sunk her.

The Admiral was not feeling so great now—he had a relationship with MI-6.

After VAdm. Ransom left, Col. Randal said, "Before he flew out, King warned me to be careful. Specifically, he said when it came to IDB, I would not be able to count on some people I would normally trust my life to."

"King said that, huh? Worth knowin'," Capt. McKoy said. "What is it riled up Lady Jane so bad?"

Col. Randal said, "Cuthbert Bowlby ordered her to report what we found out about DeBeers. Jane was specifically instructed not to inform me she was making the reports. Jane resigned from MI-6, banned Dudley Clarke from RFHQ and had Jim's things moved out of his room here to Shephard's Hotel."

Capt. McKoy said, "Big mistake askin' her to go behind your back. But maybe that's a good thing."

Col. Randal said, "What makes you say that?"

"MI-6 went and smoked out their own selves," Capt. McKoy said. "Saved us the trouble. Now we know from the get-go we can't depend on any British intelligence folks when it comes to IDB. Here or out where I'm headed.

"This diamond deal is gettin' downright interestin'. Could be more to the IDB game than meets the eye. Watch yourself, John—money, greed and politics . . . that's a real treacherous witches' brew."

"You're way ahead of me on this, Captain," Col. Randal said. "I don't have the benefit of your law enforcement background. Keep me posted on your estimate of the situation as it develops."

Capt. McKoy said, "Count on it, John. I've got me a hunch we're playin' for BIG chips."

Col. Randal said, "Who can we trust?"

"Well," Capt. McKoy said, "there's you, me, Waldo, sounds like King warned you to be careful, so there's him. Beverly's OSS, so she's not compromised, and we know for a bona fide fact Lady Jane's reliable. I'd say that's about it for right now, unless you want to throw in Billy Jack."

Col. Randal said, "I've intentionally kept Jack Cool out of IDB so far because he's on permanent standby for GOLDEN FLEECE/RED INDIAN missions."

Capt. McKoy said, "You may want to rethink addin' him to our team.

We're pretty thin on players. I hate to say it, but when it comes to diamonds we have to consider all British personnel suspect until proven otherwise."

Col. Randal said, "That's not good."

He had not failed to note there were a number of people included in his initial briefing on Raiding Forces' assignment to interdict diamond smugglers who were not on Captain McKoy's short list. Which did nothing for his morale.

Capt. McKoy said, "You have any problem with me contacting Wild Bill direct, John?"

"Go ahead," Col. Randal said. "What do want to talk to him about?"

Capt. McKoy said, "Well, for one thing, we need us a confidential line of communication. We're gonna have to be *real* careful about signals security. OSS needs to provide us a secret code nobody else has. That way we can still use Phantom to transmit and receive our messages, only they just won't be able to read 'em because we encode or decode 'em ourselves."

Col. Randal said, "Good idea."

Capt. McKoy said, "What're we gonna call this operation, John—my part?"

Col. Randal said, "What do you recommend?"

"How 'bout," Capt. McKoy said, "OPERATION RODEO. As in, this ain't my first rodeo."

Col. Randal said, "I like it."

COLONEL JOHN RANDAL, CAPTAIN "GERONIMO" JOE MCKOY, CAPTAIN BILLY JACK JAXX AND Waldo Treywick were smoking Waldo's cigars as they sat out by the private pool belonging to the third-floor suite. Major the Lady Jane Seaborn and Beverly Blackwell were in the pool floating on rafts. Whatever they were talking about must have been entertaining because the two never stopped laughing.

Rita and Lana were at a table on the other side doing each other's nails.

Waldo was growing a new beard. He had shaved to play the role of Mr. Big.

Lady Jane had taken him to a tailor to have a white, raw silk suit made for the occasion of his meeting with the Big Five. Capt. McKoy had donated a pearl gray, four-inch brimmed Stetson hat of a style called the "San Antone," commonly worn by businessmen and politicians. The hat was a gift from some well-meaning individual. "Geronimo" Joe had never put it on once, not even to check it out in a mirror. Captain Pamala Plum-Martin had provided a pair of U.S. Army Air Force Ray-Ban flight glasses to the Mr. Big wardrobe. Waldo's Smith & Wesson 38/44 Triple Lock Fitz Special revolver in a chest holster worn to intentionally bulge under his tailor-made suit coat had completed the ensemble.

The purpose of today's meeting by the pool was to bring Capt. Jaxx up to speed on the anti-diamond and gold smuggling mission Raiding Forces had been assigned by the Office of Strategic Services.

Col. Randal said, "Right now we've got our assignment broken down into two elements, Middle East faction and West Coast region. Captain McKoy is heading up the effort in West Africa. That's called OPERATION RODEO. Mr. Treywick is the point man in Cairo and Alexandria and going after the smuggling caravans crossing the desert into Turkey—don't have a name for his mission yet.

"How about," Capt. Jaxx said, "OPERATION LONG LEGS—as in Legs Diamond?"

"That's a dang good name, Jack," Capt. McKoy said.

"It really is," Waldo said. "Some a' his stories in the newspapers even made it out to Abyssinia, bein' only about a year old by the time I read 'em when I's bein' held in servitude. My favorite was a quote by the gangster Dutch Schultz, who had put out a contract on Legs, sayin', 'Can't anybody shoot this guy so he don't keep coming back?'"

"OPERATION LONG LEGS, it is," Col. Randal said. "I'm going to tell Parker you named it after her, Jack."

"Fine by me, sir," Capt. Jaxx said. "Captain Honeycutt-Parker has better wheels than Betty Grable and hers are insured for a million dollars."

Waldo said, "Is that apiece or for the pair?"

Capt. Jaxx said, "I don't know."

Waldo said, "When you get to diggin' around out where you're goin', Joe, lookin' the diamond industry over, you'll find out a bunch a' them sparklers come from the Belgian Congo, which we ain't talked about yet."

"I'll add the Congo to my list, Waldo," Capt. McKoy said

"Yeah, well, you need to be a little careful when you get out there," Waldo said. "Some strange stuff goes on in the Congo."

"Like what?"

"The natives claim a dinosaur goes by the name a' Mokele-mbembe hangs out in the wetlands. People been reportin' it for over two hundred years, which is before nobody hardly even knew we had dinosaurs, accordin' to the professor from the Chicago Museum of Natural Science I was guidin' in Abyssinia before gettin' captured," Waldo said. "He was real interested in the story when I told him about it."

Capt. McKoy said, "What's your connection to the Congo, Waldo?"

"Back in the day, P. J. Pretorius liked to trek where no white man had ever gone before. Next thing I knew he had us workin' our way through a monster-sized swamp somewhere in the Congo 'bout as big as Alaska. We came to some real tall trees. The limbs had all been ate off about eighteen feet up where the green sprouts was," Waldo said.

"We didn't see no dinosaurs, but we come across tracks. Looked like a big bull elephant's, only these tracks had claws. Elephants don't have claws.

"You keep your eyes open out there, Joe."

"I'll make a point to," Capt. McKoy said. "What kind a' dinosaur was it?"

Waldo said, "Sounded like the ones you see on those gas station signs with the long necks. Some a' the natives drew us a picture of it. They claimed it could bite a hippo in half, but I always thought those gas station dinosaurs was supposed to be passive leaf eaters."

"Yeah," Capt. McKoy said, "me too."

Capt. Jaxx said, "Something's not right about this diamond story, Colonel."

Col. Randal said, “Like what, Jack?”

“You said we’re undertaking the assignment at the express order of the President of the United States, sir,” Capt. Jaxx said, “because the U.S. has a shortage of strategic industrial diamonds and the DeBeers Diamond Company refuses to provide us the supply we requested.”

“That’s the official line,” Col. Randal said.

“Is the President aware, sir,” Captain Jaxx asked, “there’s a diamond mine in Murfreesboro, Arkansas?”

“I have no idea,” Col. Randal said. “How would you know about it, Jack?”

“When Texas played Arkansas, sir,” Capt. Jaxx said, “we had a goodwill date exchange the night before the game. One of our football players had a date with one of the Razorback cheerleaders and one of their players had a date with one of ours. I went out with the Arkansas cheerleader.

“She was from Murfreesboro. What do people from small towns talk about? We talk about our towns—she told me all about the diamonds.”

Col. Randal said, “Captain McKoy, you know anything about this?”

“Negatory,” Capt. McKoy said. “And like I mentioned before, John, I spent some time in Arkansas huntin’ down a couple a’ malicious bank robbin’ criminals. Never heard a whisper about any diamond mine.”

Col. Randal said, “How big is it, Jack?”

“Well, that’s the thing, sir,” Capt. Jaxx said. “It’s not a real producing operation. Even though my date said the Arkansas governor’s wife traditionally wears diamond jewelry from the Murfreesboro mine. According to the cheerleader, there’s no commercial mining, but those diamonds had to get out of the ground somehow.

“The way it works is, for a fee, anybody can go to the property, dig and keep what they find.”

Capt. McKoy asked, “People ever strike pay dirt?”

Capt. Jaxx said, “One in ten do—gemstones that is. The cheerleader said most of what’s found is like gravel, which is exactly how you described industrial diamonds, Colonel. But here’s where her story doesn’t make sense. You can’t dig any deeper than four feet down and the company people come around to check—why would that be?”

There was dead silence. It was a good question. No one had an answer.

"What I'm gettin' ready to say, boys," Capt. McKoy said, "can't leave this swimmin' hole. Nobody but us has a "Need to Know" exceptin' Lady Jane and Beverly — who is both cleared, and I reckon Rita and Lana is OK."

Col. Randal said. "Let's hear it, Captain."

"*If* the President of the United States had himself a diamond problem big enough to threaten to cut off sendin' Lend Lease bombers to England because DeBeers wouldn't ship a big enough allocation of industrial grade stones to the USA, then all he'd have to do is nationalize that Arkansas mine under the War Powers Act," Captain McKoy said.

"You ain't wrong, Jack—somethin's dang sure fishy about the tall tale everybody's tellin' us."

Col. Randal said, "Captain McKoy, I want you to postpone your trip to West Africa. You need to fly to Arkansas immediately to check out Jack's story on the ground. Then go to Washington, D.C., and meet with Donovan in person.

"Brief him on what you find at the Murfreesboro mine site—get Wild Bill's reaction. I want your first-hand impression about how Donovan takes the news."

"Just about to suggest you let me do that, John," Capt. McKoy said. "Mind if Waldo comes along? We kinda need to go take a look at some more prime property out on the West Coast while the "Jap Flap's" still on.

"Real estate'll make a good cover story for our trip."

"Fine with me if he can tear himself away from playing Mr. Big long enough," Col. Randal said, "When's your next performance, Mr. Treywick?"

"Bout a month," Waldo said. "Ain't no rush. The plan is to give the "Five" time to whittle down the competition. Let 'em get to feelin' good about the way things is going before we spring our trap. That's when we'll give those criminal gentlemen the word they're gonna be selling all their diamonds and gold direct to Mr. Big, exclusive."

Col. Randal asked, "What do you guess their reaction will be?"

Waldo said, "May not be real excited about the idea when they hear it for the first time."

"I can see how they might not be," Col. Randal said. "All right then, have Red make your travel arrangements. We need to have a better understanding of what we're getting into. There's the off-chance we can't trust what *anyone's* telling us—MI-6, OSS or the President —when it comes to diamonds."

Capt. McKoy said, "There is that possibility."

Flanigan brought the phone out to the pool, trailing a long extension cord. "Miss Runborg for Mr. Treywick."

Waldo took the phone, "I'll be there in a few minutes."

After Mr. Treywick departed, Col. Randal said, "What just happened?"

"Well, John," Capt. McKoy said, "it's all on account a' you."

"Me? What did I do?"

"Assigned Waldo to guard Rocky at Oasis X," Capt. McKoy said. "They've become real close."

"You're kidding."

"No," Capt. McKoy said, "I ain't."

COLONEL JOHN RANDAL, MAJOR THE LADY JANE SEABORN, BEVERLY BLACKWELL AND LANA, who was working as Beverly's bodyguard, were having a late lunch at the Gezira. As usual, they were at a table in the back of the restaurant behind a palm. The place was packed, even at this hour. There was a hum of excitement in the air . . . or maybe it was tension. Eighth Army was marshaling for its long-anticipated attack. Or counterattack, as it might more accurately be described. Rommel's last effort had pushed the Allies all the way east—almost to Alexandria—before running out of steam and being forced to fall back to El Alamein. Panzerarmee Afrika was presently ensconced in massively mined defensive positions, short on fuel and tanks, with little hope of reinforcements any time soon.

Now Eighth Army had a new commander, new U.S. tanks and new hopes of winning a decisive victory.

Col. Randal said, "Let's fly to Oasis X in the morning. I need Terry to bring me up to speed on the status of Raiding Regiment."

"Love to," Lady Jane said.

Beverly said, "Can I come?"

Lana flashed a dazzling smile. She did not say anything. But then, she never did—at least to Col. Randal.

Colonel Dudley Clarke and Commander Ian Fleming, out from England, arrived at their table. In addition to having a mission for Raiding Forces, Cdr. Fleming was in Egypt to meet with Lieutenant Douglas Fairbanks to discuss the idea of forming an OSS RED INDIAN-type team composed of U.S. Navy personnel trained to enter enemy ports during an Allied invasion with the express purpose of capturing classified documents and secret enemy technology.

That was classified.

Col. Clarke said, "Lady Jane, I realize we are not currently on the best of terms; however, Commander Fleming flew in because a RED INDIAN target has been identified. For my part, I need a word with Colonel Randal on a subject of major importance."

Cdr. Fleming asked, "May we sit down?"

"You may, Ian," Lady Jane said, "Dudley, I made it clear that as long as you are associated with Cuthbert Bowlby, you are not a welcome guest."

"I understand Curly offended you, Lady Jane. What he did was inexcusable," Col. Clarke said. "However, the matter I need to discuss with Colonel Randal is larger than A-Force, Raiding Forces, or an ill-advised affront to your personal integrity for that matter. Give me a moment to talk to Colonel Randal, then I shall be on my way."

Col. Randal said, "Let's step in the back."

When they were alone in a corner, Col. Clarke said, "Everything I am about to tell you is classified Top Secret. No one else has the 'Need to Know'. No one."

Col. Randal said, "Understood."

"Great Britain and the United States are in the final stage of preparing to open a second front called OPERATION TORCH. Where is not important.

What you need to know is it's the most ambitious, complex, high-risk amphibious operation in modern history. The British admiral commanding the fleet sailing from England has informed the Prime Minister the Navy will consider his mission a success if he can deliver fifty percent of his ships to the invasion beaches.

"Another fleet will be putting to sea from Hampton Roads in the U.S. to rendezvous with the Royal Navy. Nazi U-boats are on a rampage in the Atlantic and along the Eastern Seaboard of the United States. No one even has any idea how to calculate the odds of it arriving."

Col. Randal said, "Not a very encouraging report, Dudley."

Col. Clarke said, "As you may recall, I mentioned previously there would be A-Force missions you would gladly undertake. TORCH is what I was referring to. I, meaning Great Britain and the United States, need Raiding Forces to help provide cover as to the true location of the invasion beaches."

Col. Randal said, "What is it you want from us?"

Col. Clarke said, "The Axis know an invasion is coming. They do not know where. A-Force is tasked with keeping the enemy guessing. To accomplish that object, I need Raiding Forces to conduct a series of meaningless landings, a deception called OPERATION OVERTHROW, on meaningless beaches that appear to be reconnaissance missions in advance of a major landing. The idea is to make sure the Nazis know your people came ashore in hopes of confusing their intelligence services.

"You cannot allow your troops to know what they are doing is a deception, in the event any of them should be captured. Even you are not cleared for the 'when or where' of OPERATION TORCH. Conversely, it is not out of the realm of possibility that some of the beaches Raiding Forces goes ashore on will turn out to be the true objective.

"This tiff between Lady Jane and MI-6 has come at a terribly inopportune moment."

"Well," Col. Randal said, "it's the real deal. She's not mad. Major Seaborn has made up her mind Mr. Cuthbert Bowlby crossed the line and that's that. She has cut him dead."

"Granted, the man made a grave miscalculation," Col. Clarke said. "It may cost him his job. That stipulated, Raiding Forces is a priceless asset, even more so at this point in time. We cannot afford to lose your services because of a personality conflict. Surely the fact that you and I have a long history working together counts for something."

Col. Randal said, "If it were not for you, Colonel, there wouldn't be any Raiding Forces. Pencil us in to do whatever it takes to support TORCH—maximum effort. However, someone has to do something to get Jane off the warpath."

"What will it take?"

"I have no idea."

After Col. Clarke left the restaurant, Cdr. Fleming refrained from making eyes at Beverly long enough to say, "There is an immediate RED INDIAN target NID would like Small Operations Group to take down. When can we discuss it?"

"Now's fine."

"Here?"

"Why not?" Col Randal said. "We've planned a lot of missions in this restaurant. Hiding in plain sight."

"Works for me," Cdr. Fleming said, reaching down to pick up his briefcase.

"Hold on," Col. Randal said. "Lana, would you go ask Billy Jack to join us? You'll find him at the bar. Feel free to produce your pistol if he's not cooperative."

Captain Billy Jack Jaxx was having a drink with Captain Stephanie Fawcett-Tatum.

When Lana returned with Capt. Jaxx in tow, Cdr. Fleming spread out a map on the table and tapped it with his Parker fountain pen. "There is a German Vorpostenboot, a converted prewar fishing trawler, tied up at the pier located in this tiny coastal hamlet. The place is extremely remote. Intelligence is not even one hundred percent sure of the town's name. It is believed to be Tris Ekklisies.

"Naval Intelligence Division has no idea why a Vorpostenboot would call at that location. There is no reason for it to be there. An RAF photo reconnaissance plane will make a pass prior to sundown to confirm the ship is still docked.

"If it is, I need SOG to pop over tonight and find out what RED INDIAN material might be on the VP-Boat."

Col. Randal said, "Jack?"

"German forces in the area, sir?"

"None," Cdr. Fleming said. "The German 22nd Air Landing Division, which garrisons the island, cannot possibly station troops in every village on Crete. This place is particularly inaccessible, as it can only be reached by boat. Piece of cake, Jack."

Col. Randal said, "What's your thought on why the patrol boat is at Tris Ekklisies?"

Cdr. Fleming said, "The only answer that makes sense is mechanical difficulties. Possibly waiting for replacement parts. Maybe the captain is faking engine problems because he has a girlfriend in the village. Who is to say?"

Col. Randal said, "What's the plan, Jack?"

"Why don't we load up a team of my SOG people on one of Randy's MAS boats," Capt. Jaxx said, "sail over, board the VP-Boat tonight and see what we find."

Cdr. Fleming, who had long experience unexpectedly springing high-priority missions with short time fuses on Raiding Forces—and who had just described the mission as a "piece of cake"—was nevertheless taken aback by how casual the planning process for this one sounded.

"Will that work?"

"Should," Col. Randal said. "The Vorpostenboot won't be alarmed by the arrival of an Italian motor torpedo boat. Might even believe it's bringing the spare part."

"Anything else, sir?" Capt. Jaxx asked.

"If you and Stephanie can manage to tear yourself away from the bar," Col. Randal said, "you two have work to do before it's time to shove off."

Lady Jane and Beverly looked at each other, clearly amused. Jack Cool always did have a weakness for older women. Meaning older than he was.

After Capt. Jaxx left, Beverly laughed, "Billy's eyes always are bigger than his appetite."

Col. Randal said, "Commander, you go with Jack and Stephanie. There will be questions."

Not what Cdr. Fleming wanted to hear. Beverly would be staying at the restaurant. Unfortunately, that part of his mission was not going as hoped.

AT 1830 HOURS COLONEL JOHN RANDAL BRIEFED THE MISSION. PRESENT WERE LIEUTENANT Randy "Hornblower" Seaborn, DSO, OBE, DSC, RN, Wing Commander Ronnie Gordon *aka* "Flash Bang," Captain Billy Jack Jaxx, Captain "Pyro" Percy Stirling, Lieutenant Eddy Ryder, Lieutenant Clint Hays, Sergeant Major Mike "March or Die" Mikkalis, Master Sergeant Mack Beckwith, and twelve men from the Small Operations Group.

"Crete is over there, and we're over here."

As usual, this got a laugh. The SOG troops loved it when Col. Randal briefed. Everyone knew he was intentionally keeping tension down—not trying to be a comedian. No detail would be left out of the briefing while nothing extra would be included. Raiders preparing for a dangerous mission do not need to be overloaded with excessive information.

Keeping it "Short and Simple" was one of Raiding Forces' rules. The SOG knew a briefer who cluttered up his pre-mission Operations Order with unnecessary detail was not demonstrating conviction. Anyone as laidback as Col. Randal had to be confident of success—which was a good thing. He *was* leading the raiding party tonight.

"Mission: A twelve-man team plus attachments under my command, armed with suppressed handguns as their primary weapon in order to ensure maximum stealth, will board an enemy VP-Boat located at the hamlet of Tris Ekklisies on the southern coast of Crete. We will conduct a search of the vessel for RED INDIAN material, prepare the ship for demolition, then withdraw.

"At dawn, Wing Commander Gordon will conduct an aerial bombing attack with a flight composed of two RAF A-20 gunships and a pair of USAAF A-20 medium bombers, the purpose of which is to help obliterate any signs Raiding Forces was ever there.

"Execution: The raiding element, composed of twelve SOG personnel and four officers with Captain Stirling, Sergeant Major Mikkalis, and Sergeant Major Beckwith attached, will board a MAS boat commanded by Lieutenant Randy Seaborn, known to us all affectionately as 'Hornblower' because of his great courage, seamanship and leadership skills, and set sail for a tiny village on the coast of Crete.

"Located at this seaside hamlet is a small pier. Docked at the pier is a German VP-Boat. Our mission is to board the craft by stealth, silently eliminate any crew on board, conduct a search for RED INDIAN materials and egress the area without anyone knowing we were ever there.

"Line of Departure time is 1930 hours—trucks to the dock will move out from RFHQ at that time. Lieutenant Seaborn will put to sea at 2000 hours. The MAS boat will arrive off the objective at 0030 hours.

"Concept of the Operation: The MAS boat will approach to within one half mile of the pier and heave to. At that point, Captain Jaxx and three men will cast off in a rubber raft, silently make their way to the starboard side of the Vorpostenboot and, by the use of grappling hooks, surreptitiously board. After waiting fifteen minutes, the MAS boat will approach the pier from the port side, where a four-man team led by Lieutenant Ryder will land on the pier, move to the land end and set up a blocking party to prevent any of the VP-Boat's crew who may be ashore from returning to the trawler.

"A second four-man team under my direct command will follow Lieutenant Ryder's people off the MAS boat, land on the pier, and board from the port side.

"The party under the command of Captain Jaxx will conduct a search below deck. The team under my command will search top side.

"While the search is underway, Captain Stirling will place demolitions, which will be delivered on board the VP-Boat by his party, consisting of Lieutenant Clint Hays and Sergeant Majors Mikkalis and Beckwith, who will make up the demolitions team.

"Under no circumstances will we remain aboard the trawler longer than thirty minutes. It is imperative our MAS boat reach the safety of USAAF/RAF air cover before first light.

"Administration and Logistics . . ."

MAJOR THE LADY JANE SEABORN AND BEVERLY BLACKWELL DROVE COLONEL JOHN RANDAL TO the dock. Lieutenant Mandy Paige followed in another jeep with Commander Ian Fleming—he would not be accompanying the Raiders. Mandy had been in Cairo when she learned through her intelligence sources that Raiding Forces had an operation in the works and immediately returned to RFHQ even though she played no part in the operation.

Col. Randal stepped out of the jeep with his MAB-38A submachine gun in one hand. "I'll see you girls for breakfast."

As he walked away, Beverly said, "Wow, sometimes I have to pinch myself to see if this is really happening. It's like living a movie."

"It always seems that way," Lady Jane said, "I hate this part of the war the worst—keeping a stiff upper lip while waving good-bye, when what I really want to do is cry. Keep calm and carry on."

Raiding Forces personnel were unloading from the two transport trucks. Col. Randal conducted a brief inspection before the men loaded on the MAS boat.

He pulled Sergeant Major Mike "March or Die" Mikkalis aside.

"Brought you a present from Achnacarry—something new Captain Fairbairn designed called a Smatchet," Col. Randal said. "You were never impressed with his original fighting knife."

Sgt. Maj. Mikkalis' eyes lit up when he pulled the big knife with a leaf-shaped blade out of its sheath. In some ways, the weapon resembled a handier version of the short sword Roman Legionnaires carried. Only deadlier.

"This is more to my taste, sir," Sgt. Maj. Mikkalis said.

"I've owed you one, Sergeant Major," Col. Randal said, "for the Browning you gave me at Calais."

"Miss Blackwell appropriated the Browning, sir?" Sgt. Maj. Mikkalis asked.

Col. Randal said, "She'll give it back."

Lieutenant Randy "Hornblower" Seaborn was waiting on board in command, even though it was not his boat. RED INDIAN missions were absolute top priority but that was not the reason he was along tonight. It had been a while since he and Col. Randal had been on a raid together. Hornblower was not about to pass up the opportunity when he had the chance.

The MAS boat slipped the dock on schedule—Lt. Seaborn ran a taut ship. The Raiders would leave shortly after dark and return shortly after sunrise. The timing was important. The biggest threat to a small craft like a torpedo boat was enemy air.

Col. Randal said, "I'm going down to the skipper's cabin and hit the rack."

Lt. Seaborn said, "I shall wake you up before we arrive back here at the dock, sir."

"I don't think I'll sleep that long, Randy."

Col. Randal liked being at sea. He climbed in the tiny cabin's bunk and was immediately sound asleep.

The pitch of the MAS boat's engine changed. Col. Randal's eyes came open. He glanced at the lime green hands on his Rolex, surprised at having slept a lot longer than he planned. Unless his watch was broken, they were off Crete.

He went up on deck to find Captain Billy Jack Jaxx organizing his rubber assault boat team. The rubber boat was lowered over the side, then Jack Cool and his gang went down, climbed aboard and on the command "give way together" began rowing. The plan called for Lt. Seaborn to wait fifteen minutes, then ease the MAS boat in to the dock. At that point, the raid would commence.

Lieutenant Eddy Ryder had his team ready to go. Col. Randal spoke to him briefly, then linked up with his people. His party consisted of Lovat Scouts Lionel Fenwick and Munro Ferguson and GG. The cook was along because he spoke Italian—as he should since he was a captured Italian soldier who had been a full-fledged member of Raiding Forces since Force N days in Abyssinia.

Col. Randal would follow Lt. Ryder's team off the MAS boat. Scout Ferguson was his number two tonight. Everyone was carrying High Standard Military Model .22s with silencers as their primary weapon. However, they all had MAB-38As slung over their shoulders just in case.

No one was expecting trouble, but all were prepared for it.

On the far side of the VP-Boat, Capt. Jaxx had the raft tight against the stern of the ship in position to see when the MAS boat slid past. Like a ghost it appeared and slipped past right on time. The Raiders silently paddled amidships and the two Raiders in the front of the raft tossed their grappling hooks up and over the VP-Boat's rails.

There was no clang of metal-on-metal contact. Chief Warrant Officer Hank Rawlings had cut strips of rubber from old jeep tires and melded it to the grappling hooks with a blow torch. Capt. Jaxx and his men were up and over the side, going hand-over-hand, not making a sound.

On the MAS boat, Lt. Ryder's men leaped for the pier before it made it all the way alongside. Col. Randal and his team were right behind them. The night was pitch-dark. There were no lights showing on the trawler.

The lack of lights did not present a problem. Raiding Forces had trained exhaustively on boarding ships. Col. Randal knew exactly where the boarding ladder would be located. He led his men straight to it. Their rubber-soled raiding boots were absolutely silent on the ancient wooden planks.

The instant the Raiders stepped on the VP-Boat, automatic weapons fire erupted down the length of the patrol boat. Tracers lit up the night. The volume of fire was staggering.

This was not part of the plan.

While the VP-boat was considered a small vessel, Col. Randal knew there could easily be thirty to forty sailors in its crew. He just had not expected them to be on board, armed with hand-held automatic weapons and willing to fight. Vorpostenboots are normally crewed by civilians . . . typically ex-fishermen, along with a handful of German sailors as stiffeners to man the guns.

In fact, it was fairly common practice for a German NCO to be the skipper.

The volume of fire directed at the Raiders was incredible. Fortunately, it was aimed high by frightened men who were unfamiliar with their weapons. They had been safe in their hammocks one minute and found themselves being boarded by an unknown enemy the next. The enemy sailors were firing out of hatches utilizing the "spray and pray" technique. They were not hitting anything, but they were not presenting themselves as targets for the Raiders either.

Most likely, Col. Randal thought, the sailors believed they were being attacked by Cretan guerrillas intent on murdering them all.

This estimate of the situation took up less than one half of one second to formulate. Col. Randal had his silenced pistol holstered and his MAB-38A submachine gun unslung, returning fire in the time he was making it. Scouts Fenwick and Ferguson were in action, as was GG.

Capt. Jaxx's team on the starboard side of the boat opened, though they could not actually see anyone to shoot at either. All the Raiders were firing at muzzle flashes coming from weapons being held over the bad guy's heads. The goal of the Raiders at this point was to suppress the enemy fire.

Captain "Pyro" Percy Stirling and his team of senior Raiding Forces personnel dropped their demolitions packs and raced to the trawler. The demo team commenced fire on the run.

Col. Randal was pinned down behind a winch, with rounds glancing off it fired by what, strangely enough, sounded like British Sten guns. Capt. Stirling rushed up the boarding plank, dived over him and went into the prone on the other side.

Tracers were crisscrossing back and forth, making it seem like suicide to raise your head an inch.

"Bloody hell!"

Some of the enemy fire had been snuffed out by the combined effect of all three boarding parties engaging. The Raiders had seized control mid-ship and were hunkered down. However, Col. Randal knew things could not remain static.

He had to attack.

Before that thought could be translated into action there was a pop and a parachute flare lit off overhead, turning night into day, allowing Lt. Seaborn's crew to obtain a clear view of the enemy ship. The MAS boat opened fire.

Hornblower had packed the boats in the squadron under his command with heavy, fast-firing automatic weapons for strafing Panzerarmee Afrika convoys running down the Via Balbia at night or for chance encounters with German E-boats along the coast. The boat he was commanding tonight had an improvised quad 20mm cannon mount on the bow. A pair of Oerlikon 20mms riding in a mount on the stern had a .50 caliber machine gun flanking each of them. Every available spot on the boat had a .50 caliber machine gun bolted on.

The MAS boat looked like a cartoon—the little ship was outlined in a bubble of light coming from the combined automatic weapons. The sound was like a hundred, or maybe a thousand, heavy-duty chain saws. Col. Randal was not sure which was worse. Getting shot at by Italian sailors or being on board a ship under fire from Hornblower's bloodthirsty pirates.

At virtual contact range, the 20 millimeter rounds punched right through the VP-boat's hull. With all the added machine guns in the mix, the magnitude of tracers ricocheting off steel, screaming into the midnight sky was amazing. So much for a stealthy mission with nobody the wiser.

This was NOT a "piece of cake."

Aiming low at the waterline of the VP-boat, the 20mm cannon chewed through the wooden pier, almost sawing it in half. The concentrated firepower of Hornblower's little patrol boat was a fight stopper. When the MAS boat engaged, the enemy sailors gave up. It took longer to get Lt. Seaborn's sailors to check fire.

Incredibly, once the VP-Boat was secured, it was discovered not a single person on either side had been killed. That did not seem possible when thousands of rounds had been exchanged at point-blank range.

A search did not produce much of intelligence value other than the radio code books. One item of interest: The VP-Boat's crew *was* armed with 9mm British Sten guns confiscated from prisoners when the Germans captured Crete. Both sides were using each other's weapons. The majority of the Raiders were armed with Italian 9mm MAB-38A submachine guns.

Capt. Stirling had the enemy crew locked in the ship's hold. Col. Randal ordered "Pyro" Percy to open the watertight door and leave it unlocked. GG went in and threatened the prisoners they would all be executed if anyone came up on deck for one hour. He made it sound believable.

Col. Randal and Capt. Stirling decided to forego setting demolitions as planned. However, since the Air Force was coming in at dawn, charges were placed on the 88 mm gun and the antiaircraft weapons mounted topside. There were a lot of those and it was fortunate they had not been manned when Raiding Forces came calling.

Then Col. Randal ordered the Raiders to return to the MAS boat and they set sail for home humbler and wiser men. No one was ever going to take one of Commander Ian Fleming's intelligence reports at face value again. And it would be a long time before any of them described an upcoming mission as a "piece of cake."

For their part, Hornblower's MAS boat crew was jubilant. The sailors thought this was the absolute best Commando raid ever. They had shot it out with a larger enemy ship and emerged victorious.

Standing on the bow of the patrol boat with Col. Randal while the sleek craft pounded for home, speaking for the contingent of SOG ground personnel, Capt. Jaxx said, "You'd have thought we'd learned better by now, sir."

"Roger that."

11
STONE COLD MANDY

LIEUTENANT MANDY PAIGE WAS IN THE THIRD-FLOOR SUITE TALKING TO COLONEL JOHN Randal. He was cleaning his weapons after the night's raid. Major the Lady Jane Seaborn was in the master bedroom packing for their flight to Oasis X.

Lt. Mandy said, "Captain McKoy told me the Chinese have a proverb that might apply to our diamond smuggling problem."

"What's that?"

Lt. Mandy said, "If you sit by a river long enough, you will see the dead body of your enemy float past."

Col. Randal said, "That's very helpful, Mandy."

Lt. Mandy said, "It might work. Nothing else sounds feasible."

Col. Randal said, "I've been wanting to talk to you. That was a cold-blooded plan you suggested. Have the big five crime families knock off their competitors—what's happened to you?"

"You, John," Lt. Mandy said.

"Me?"

"First rule: 'there ain't no rules'."

"There are limits," Col. Randal said.

"'Keep it short and simple'."

"Mandy . . ."

"'Kill 'em all and let Allah sort 'em out'."

"I never . . ."

"'Plan operations backward'," Lt. Mandy said. "We needed a manageable number of illicit diamond buyers. I simply came up with a plan based on everything you taught me. Working to perfection too."

"I'm going to start calling you 'Stone Cold Mandy'," Col. Randal said, feeling a little sick when he remembered she was not on Captain McKoy's short list of those who could be trusted with the full details of IDB.

Flanigan stuck his head in the door, "Wing Commander Gordon, sir."

"Send him in."

Wing Commander Ronnie Gordon came in wearing his flying togs, back from leading the morning mission to bomb the VP-boat.

"How'd it go, Commander?" Col. Randal asked.

"Dry run," W/Cdr. Gordon said. "You sank the boat—or at least Lieutenant Seaborn did. I am rather surprised you could not hear his whoops from downstairs when I informed him the VP-boat only had its masts showing above water when we rolled in."

Lt. Mandy asked, "Does Randy get credit for sinking an enemy warship even if it was tied to the dock?"

"Roger that," Col. Randal said. "We don't call him 'Hornblower' for nothing."

Lady Jane came out of the bedroom, having heard the news, "The Admiralty is always thrilled when one of its captains sinks an enemy ship twice the size of his command, even if they are both small craft—demonstrates pluck."

Flanigan opened the door. "Mrs. Paige, sir."

"Show her in," Col. Randal ordered.

"Is this a bad time?" Veronica asked, walking in with a roll of paper under her arm.

"Just leaving, Mrs. Paige," W/Cdr. Gordon said.

"If you have a moment, John," Veronica said, "I would like to show you a marvelous new development for future MI-9 operations."

"Let's do it."

Veronica rolled out a blueprint on the coffee table.

"When the battle for Crete was lost in May of last year, German and Italian forces garrisoned the island. To everyone's surprise, it was soon learned there were hundreds, if not thousands, of British Commonwealth troops who had never surrendered and were still at large on the run, hiding in the mountains. Special Operations Executive took the lead in rescuing evaders from Crete because they wanted to obtain intelligence concerning enemy activity and SOE needed their assistance to make contact with the Cretan Resistance.

"Because of the rugged terrain, the movement of evaders off the island has to be by sea. The first two ships dispatched to do so were the submarines HMS *Thrasher* and HMS *Torbay.* They landed on a secluded beach below the Preveli Monastery. Under the watchful eye of the abbot, the place had been turned into a refuge for evaders.

"Nearly two hundred men were brought out by the two submarines. This marked the beginning of clandestine operations to Crete carried out by the Royal Navy, supported by the Royal Hellenic Navy.

"Unfortunately, after the first mission, the monastery was occupied by elements of the German 22nd Air Landing Division—putting a stop to using it as a sanctuary. Then the submarines were withdrawn by the Royal Navy for more pressing duties elsewhere. Two enterprising Royal Navy Reserve lieutenants, John Campbell and Michael Cumberlege, somehow secured two small craft, a twenty-foot motorized lifeboat, HMS *Escampador,* and a sixty-ton fishing trawler, HMS *Hedgehog.* They began conducting missions along the coastline of Crete, bringing out an additional one hundred fifty-five evaders.

"In June of this year, the ports along the northern Libyan/Egyptian coastline closest to Crete fell to Rommel, complicating rescue efforts. Then the Royal Navy required its two ships for other duties. Once again, Escape was shoved to the curb. Yesterday SOE informed me it was getting out of the business altogether.

"In future, MI-9 is to 'take the lead in the role it was created for'.

"I spoke with Admiral Ransom. He immediately had the *Hedgehog* and *Escampador* transferred to his 'Irregular' fleet, along with the two young

RNVR lieutenants. Then SOE agreed, astonishingly, to arrange for two Fairmile Type B motor launches to be built for MI-9.

"Admiral Ransom will allow us to use Sea Squadron's MAS boats, the MGB 345 and its PT boats and/or the *Hedgehog* and *Escampador* for Escape until our Fairmiles are ready.

"These are the ML's plans."

Col. Randal said, "Mandy, go find Randy and have him come take a look at these blueprints."

"On the way, John."

"I've got a feeling, Veronica," Col. Randal said, lighting a cigarette with his old battered U.S. 26th Cavalry Regiment Zippo, "we're being had by SOE."

"Why would you believe that to be the case?" Veronica asked.

"Where are these MLs being constructed?"

"In Cairo," Veronica said, "by the Anglo-American Nile & Tourist Company."

"Did SOE mention crews?" Col. Randal asked.

"No, actually they did not."

"Admiral Ransom can get sailors from the Royal Navy Patrol Service," Col. Randal said. "No one else wants 'em. The problem is qualified deck officers—we need at least four. There's none to be had."

"Oh dear," Veronica said. "It is always something."

Lady Jane said, "We shall find a solution."

Col. Randal did not say anything, but he was not so sure. He knew from conversations with VAdm. Ransom that there were not four qualified Royal Navy deck officers unassigned in Middle East Command.

While they waited, Veronica briefed Col. Randal on other MI-9 developments. "The Great Teddy has been sending me a steady stream of notes with suggestions. Have to love him. To date, Teddy has recommended we glue small maps on the backs of playing cards, stick saw blades on combs and hide all sorts of useful Escape tools, to include parts to build radios inside cricket bats."

Col. Randal asked, "Then what?"

"We put everything in Red Cross packages and let the agency ship them to the POWs."

Col. Randal said, "Now, that's a plan."

Lt. Mandy and Lieutenant Randy "Hornblower" Seaborn came thundering up the steps and rushed into the suite.

"Take a look," Col. Randal said, pointing to the blueprints. "Two of these MLs are being built for MI-9 missions."

Lt. Seaborn's eyes lit up as he studied the plans, "Fairmile Type B, one-hundred-twelve feet long with a crew of sixteen. Two petrol engines provide a top speed of twenty knots making an overnight trip to Crete well within its capability if you depart and return in partial daylight. Mrs. Paige, these MLs are truly outstanding craft, perfect for what you want them for."

Brandy Seaborn and Captain Penelope "Legs" Honeycutt-Parker arrived at the suite with their bags ready to travel to Oasis X. Brandy, a prewar, high-speed, open sea competition boat driver, was immediately interested in the ML drawings. She sat on the floor cross-legged next to her son, Lt. Seaborn, and studied them with the seasoned eye of a professional sailor.

Col. Randal watched as Brandy traced the lines of the plans with a scarlet-tipped nail. Capt. Honeycutt-Parker hovered over her shoulder.

Lt. Seaborn said, "The design is based on a scaled-down destroyer's hull with total prefabrication in mind, Mother. Kits are made by Fairmile and shipped out to various shipyards to be assembled. The Type B was originally intended to be a sub chaser; however, the decks are pre-drilled so fittings for other weapons besides depth charges can be mounted.

"Two 650-horsepower Hall-Scott Defender petrol engines . . ."

"Twenty knots," Brandy said. "Not enough speed."

A SMALL CROWD WAS ON HAND TO SEE OFF COLONEL JOHN RANDAL, MAJOR THE LADY JANE Seaborn and the people traveling with them to Oasis

X. Captain Pamala Plum-Martin and Beverly Blackwell were the pilots today. Wing Commander Ronnie Gordon would be escorting the Hudson with his pair of A-20 gunships that were flying back to the oasis. Col. Randal was engaged in a series of brief, last-minute discussions prior to takeoff.

Commander Ian Fleming was at the field. He would not be traveling to Oasis X. His mission to Egypt had consisted of two parts—not counting trying to advance his cause with Beverly. The first being the raid on the VP-Boat. It was a failure from the standpoint of gaining intelligence that would help crack the dreaded fourth rotor on Kriegsmarine Enigma encoding/decoding machines.

The second part of his assignment had yet to be attempted. He had one last chance to take a crack at it—now—before the Hudson took off. While Col. Randal was talking to Lieutenant Randy "Hornblower" Seaborn, Cdr. Fleming approached Lady Jane to ask for a word in private.

"Certainly, Ian," Lady Jane said. The two walked a short distance from the crowd with Happy tagging along.

"I shall be brief," Cdr. Fleming said. "The flare-up between you and Cuthbert Bowlby has created an upheaval in the intelligence community. Naval Intelligence Division believes it to be in the best interests of all concerned for the row to be resolved quickly. For reasons of national security, it is imperative there be no cataclysmic rift between MI-6 and Raiding Forces."

The skin on Lady Jane's razor sharp cheekbones tightened, with the unintended consequence of making her appear even more striking. It was also a warning sign.

"I quite doubt," Lady Jane said, "Cuthbert spoke to me on his own initiative."

Cdr. Fleming said, "I have no knowledge of what the man did nor whether higher authority authorized him to proceed in the manner he chose. My brief, as a neutral third agent, is to inquire how we can resolve the issue to your satisfaction. A harmonious working relationship between you, the Secret Intelligence Service and Raiding Forces is essential to support an imminent joint U.K. and U.S. military action.

"Time is of the essence—how do we make things right?"

"I was instructed to spy on a specific Raiding Forces operation," Lady Jane said, "report details weekly to Cuthbert in private and specifically not to inform John."

"Unfortunate miscalculation on his part," Cdr. Fleming said, feeling slightly ill. He knew quite a bit about women, and he knew Lady Jane was not having a temper tantrum. She was deeply offended. He also knew he was not getting the entire story.

"You tell whichever of your masters you are required to relate our conversation to," Lady Jane said, "MI-6 can go to hell!"

Cdr. Fleming was a fixer. Fixing problems was his job. He was not going to fix this one. The trip to Egypt had turned out to be a total bust. No Enigma signals intelligence obtained, Lady Jane intransigent, and Beverly had not even seemed to notice his advances.

As Lady Jane and Cdr. Fleming were concluding their unhappy chat, Col. Randal was wrapping up his conversation with Lt. Seaborn. "You remember what we did with the French fisherman you captured and had converted to run guns to Enemy Occupied France?"

Lt. Seaborn asked, "You mean replacing the motor with automobile engines, sir? It can outrun the *Arrow.*"

Col. Randal said. "Make your mother happy about those MLs, Randy."

"Aye, aye, sir," Lt. Seaborn said. "Are you thinking what I am thinking, sir . . . about deck officers?"

"Negative, Randy," Col. Randal said. "I'm doing everything in my power *not* to be thinking what you're thinking."

"Good luck with that, sir."

Ensign Theodore Hamilton, OBE, *aka* "The Great Teddy", was standing by to talk to Col. Randal.

"What are you doing here, Ensign?"

"*Frogspawn,* sir," Ens. Hamilton said in a stage whisper. "Colonel Clarke sent me."

"Why would he do that?"

"I'm the new CLO, sir, between A-Force and Raiding Forces, sir."

"What is a CLO?"

"Clandestine Liaison Officer, sir. Only you and I have the 'Need to Know'—and Col. Clarke."

"I thought you and Douglas Fairbanks were involved in some secret project," Col. Randal said. "Sonic deception?"

"We were, sir," Ens. Hamilton said. "However, now we have been temporarily reassigned to plan RAYON."

"I see," Col. Randal said, not having a clue what "RAYON" was. "Do you have a message for me in your new capacity as CLO?"

"Yes, sir," Ens. Hamilton said. "Colonel Clarke desires Raiding Forces to begin conducting a series of beach reconnaissance missions on the island of Crete. I have a list of the target's grid coordinates."

"When?"

"Commencing immediately, sir."

"Go see Admiral Ransom," Col. Randal ordered. "I've already alerted the Razor something along these lines might come up."

Ens. Hamilton was not on Captain McKoy's list of people to be trusted about IDB—he had a connection to several of the intelligence services. It was hard for Col. Randal to believe MI-6 was recruiting teenagers to spy on Raiding Forces or that The Great Teddy ever would. Nevertheless . . .

"Yes, sir."

"Ensign," Col. Randal said, "I don't keep secrets from Lady Jane. You don't have the same relationship with her that I do. But if you value your life, stud, you will never, ever let her know you acted as a mediator between Raiding Forces and A-Force at this point in time.

"Lady Jane can kill an attack dog with her bare hands."

"Understood, sir," Ens. Hamilton said, "loud and clear."

"Good."

Col. Randal glanced in the direction of Master Sergeant Mack Beckwith. The tough paratrooper was at his side in an instant. "Do you know if any of the 575th men who didn't make it through the 'Blood in the Sand' training happen to be auto mechanics?"

"I'll check, sir," MSgt. Beckwith said.

"You do that," Col. Randal ordered. "I need four men—volunteers for hazardous duty involving small boats working for a U.S. government agency so secret its initials are classified."

MSgt. Beckwith said. "If anyone's an auto mechanic, sir, my guess is they'd volunteer for a suicide squad to get out of being stevedores on the docks."

Col. Randal said, "Have to be skilled."

"I'll get Mr. Rawlings to sign off on 'em, sir."

"Do it."

Red walked off the Hudson. She was flying out to Oasis X to visit her boyfriend, Lieutenant Colonel Sir Terry "Zorro" Stone. Today she was a passenger. However, the stunning Clipper Girl could not break old habits. She had been checking to make sure everything in the cabin was ready for boarding.

Red said, "I saw Captain McKoy and Mr. Treywick off to the States this morning. Acted like teenagers. Whatever is a 'Jap Flap', John?"

Col. Randal said, "People living on the west coast of California are afraid the Japanese are going to invade."

"Is that even possible?"

"I don't think so," Col. Randal said. The Clipper Girl was MI-6. She was not on Captain McKoy's short list of people who could be trusted about IDB.

Brandy and Captain Penelope "Legs" Honeycutt-Parker were in deep conversation. Seeing Col. Randal was free, they walked over.

"Parker and I . . ."

Col. Randal said, "Not going to happen, Brandy."

"Yes it is, handsome."

The two globetrotting thrill seekers had a long-standing connection with British intelligence, though which agency was not clear, MI-5 or MI-6. Neither woman was on Capt. McKoy's list.

Lieutenant Mandy Paige drove up with James "Baldie" Taylor and Rita, who hopped out of the jeep and ran over to where Captain Billy Jack Jaxx was showing Lana his pistol.

The MI-6 Chief of Special Operations, Middle East Command, had flown in from the U.S., where he had been meeting with Colonel William "Wild Bill" Donovan, the Chief of the Office of Strategic Services. Jim had been appointed as the MI-6 Special Operations advisor/liaison officer to OSS. He had come straight to the Raiding Forces airfield when he learned Col. Randal was flying out to Oasis X.

Jim did not yet know he had been evicted from RFHQ. He was definitely not on Capt. McKoy's list.

"Colonel, the U.S. Armed Forces, particularly the Navy, has gone completely off its rocker," Jim said. "The Navy formed 'Amphibious Force' at Hampton Roads—a unit so hush-hush, it uses a Post Office Box in New York as a mailing address.

"Admiral Hewitt, the commander, conducted what was supposed to be a Top Secret training exercise for OPERATION TORCH. The landing craft came ashore to find a vendor on the beach waiting to sell ice cream cones to the troops. Then a letter from Walt Disney arrived, offering to design a logo for his new command. So much for security.

"U-boats lurking along the Atlantic coast have sunk so many ships, the U.S. Navy only feels safe conducting landing exercises *inside* Chesapeake Bay . . ."

Lady Jane came over, "James, I would like a word with you."

As the two walked away, Col. Randal said, "Mandy, did you forget to tell Jim he was *persona non grata* at Raiding Forces?"

"No, John, I did not forget," Mandy said. "I simply never mentioned it."

Col. Randal lifted her and Rita's bags out of the back of the jeep. "The General will need transportation back to Cairo. Think Jane will mind him using one of our vehicles?"

Mandy said, "You know her moods far better than I do."

Col. Randal said. "She's a happy girl. But this time it's different."

Jim came back. He was so mad his face was purple. "I am going to kill Cuthbert Bowlby with my bare hands if it is the last thing I do."

Col. Randal said, "Take the jeep."

As they were boarding the Hudson, Col. Randal asked Capt. Jaxx, "What were you showing Rita and Lana?"

"Mr. Treywick asked me if he could have a copy of the nude shot of Rocky on my pistol, sir," Capt. Jaxx said. "Since it was the only one I had, I took it out and gave it to him. Moe at the Kit-Kat Club gave me a couple of promotional photos of Rita and Lana that're pretty hot. One of the girls is in the plexiglass grip on each side of my Colt automatic.

"I'm going to rotate 'em."

Jack Cool.

Once on board the Hudson, Col. Randal sat next to Lady Jane in the front row. He had noted she seemed to need more attention since the dust-up with MI-6. So, he put his arm around her shoulders. "OK, babe, now tell me in simple terms I can understand why you're so upset with Cuthbert Bowlby?"

"Did you call me 'babe'?" Lady Jane asked, as she snuggled against him.

"Short for baby," Col. Randal said. "A form of endearment—it's a California thing."

"As long as you are not referring to me as Babe the Blue Ox," Lady Jane said.

"Now how would you know about Paul Bunyan's pet?"

"I saw a cartoon at the cinema," Lady Jane laughed, "before *Casablanca.*"

Col. Randal said, "You didn't answer my question about MI-6."

"Cuthbert wanted me to be his personal Mata Hari at RFHQ, but what he ordered me to report on had no military value," Lady Jane said.

"Really?"

"All MI-6 wants is to be kept current on information Raiding Forces develops about the DeBeers Diamond Company," Lady Jane said. "In the trade, that's called industrial espionage—attended a course on it. What Curly asked for is of no possible value to the war effort.

"However, from a business perspective, the information could be priceless. Particularly to a secretive international company that has a death grip on the world diamond market."

Col. Randal said, "And that's what made you so upset?"

"No, babe," Lady Jane said. "Cuthbert was ordering me to spy on you."

"Got it," Col. Randal said, wondering if she was calling him an ox.

They didn't say much for the next hour or so, but just enjoyed being together. Lady Jane said, "It is really nice to be able to relax for a change. I am soooo looking forward to our time at the oasis with no one to bother us."

Then she stood up and made her way to the cockpit to visit Capt. Plum-Martin and Beverly Blackwell. Happy was sitting between them, looking out the window. The dog liked to fly.

Col. Randal glanced over at Lt. Mandy, who was sitting with Capt. Jaxx on the other side of the aisle. Lt. Mandy immediately came and took Lady Jane's seat.

"You wanted me?"

"We're not having this conversation, Mandy."

"Seems like we are getting ready to."

Col. Randal said, "Do you have some way to send confidential messages to R. J.?"

"If you are asking if I possess a code to communicate privately with the Brigadier," Lt. Mandy said, "the answer is yes."

Col. Randal said, "I need to know what plan RAYON is. It may be styled OPERATION RAYON."

"Is this time-sensitive?"

"No," Col. Randal said. "I only want the answer."

Lt. Mandy asked, "Who has the 'Need to Know'?"

Col. Randal said, "Until I understand what RAYON stands for, just us."

"I can make an inquiry as soon as we land, John."

After Lt. Mandy returned to her seat, Beverly came out of the cockpit to sit next to Col. Randal, who was happy to see her. The South Texas cowgirl did not have an agenda except to be a part of the team, and she was on the list of people to be trusted about IDB. No way to make a mistake having a conversation with her.

Besides, Beverly was fun to talk to.

Col. Randal was not enjoying the situation in which he found himself because as much as he trusted the people around him, it was not possible to pick and choose who to confide in about IDB. A single slip or a simple response to a harmless-sounding question could result in the death of one or more of the undercover operatives he was putting in the field to ferret out the diamond smugglers.

What made it even more insidious was that the person who learned something from him in a careless moment might pass on that information unwittingly, in response to an innocuous-sounding question, having no reason to be suspicious that someone they trusted was curious about something as harmless as diamonds.

While not a trained intelligence operator, Col. Randal knew that was how human intelligence gathering worked. A house of mirrors. The spy-vs.-spy intrigue was beginning to take a toll on his morale.

Col. Randal said, "How did you grow so much hair?"

Beverly laughed, "Daddy said he put fertilizer on it when I was a baby."

Brandy walked up. She said, "I need to speak to John. Give me a moment, Beverly."

"Yes, ma'am."

Brandy said. "I . . ."

"Forget it, Brandy," Col. Randal said. "But I've been wanting to talk to you. Can you explain to me why Jane is so hostile about this business with Cuthbert Bowlby? She won't let it go."

"Three reasons," Brandy said. "First, Cuthbert asked her to do something that tilted her well-defined moral compass and she did not like that at all. Second, ever since her husband accused her of being a Nazi spy, Jane is deathly afraid you will not trust her. Third, she believes Cuthbert forced her to sever ties to MI-6, slashing and burning a relationship her family has enjoyed with the Secret Intelligence Service for generations. She is holding that against Curly.

"Jane has drawn a line in the sand; she is standing her ground and not backing down."

Col. Randal said, "I see."

"Probably not," Brandy said. "Are you aware that after her meeting with MI-6, Jane instructed her solicitor to make inquiries about becoming a naturalized U.S. citizen? Any idea of the shock waves that would send through British society if word got out?"

"Negative—you serious?"

"I have the impression," Brandy said, "you simply have no true sense of how passionately Jane values your relationship."

Col. Randal said, "How am I supposed to know if she doesn't tell me?"

"That is what you have me for, handsome," Brandy said. "Now, about Veronica's Motor Launches . . ."

BEVERLY BLACKWELL PEEKED OUT OF THE COCKPIT, THEN CAME BACK AND SAT NEXT TO Colonel John Randal again. "Wow, I never saw Brandy so intense."

Col. Randal said, "She's on a mission."

"What kind of mission, John?"

"Brandy and Parker want to command one of Veronica Paige's Motor Launches to extract evaders from Crete. What's your professional opinion, Beverly, in your official capacity as the OSS Escape officer?"

"I think you're teasing me, John," Beverly laughed. "Since you asked, I say let Brandy go for it."

"You think so, huh?"

Changing the subject, Beverly said, "Jane's more like her old self today. Has something been bothering her, John? I've been worried."

Col. Randal said, "Lady Jane was ordered to make a weekly report to Cuthbert Bowlby, the Cairo MI-6 Chief-of-Station, about what Raiding Forces finds out about illicit diamond buying . . . and not tell me she was doing it."

"Oooooooh—that is so wrong!"

Col. Randal said, "Before he left for the States, Captain McKoy informed me there are only five other people besides himself I can trust about IDB—you're one."

"Are you teasing me again?"

"Jane, Jack, Waldo, Rita, Lana, and you, Beverly," Col. Randal said. "That's the Captain's list, and two of the people on it won't talk to me."

Beverly said, "I promise not to let you down, John."

Col. Randal said, "I don't believe you will."

Major the Lady Jane Seaborn emerged from the cockpit. "Pam received a priority message. We have been ordered to return to Raiding Forces Headquarters."

Col. Randal said, "Why?"

Lady Jane said, "No explanation."

Beverly said, "Never know what's going to happen next around here."

Lady Jane said, "Beverly, would you ask Red to advise everyone on board about our change of plans?"

When he heard the news, Captain Billy Jack Jaxx looked across the aisle and gave Col. Randal a thumbs up. Whatever was going on, it would most likely involve his Small Operations Group. The SOG commander was always ready for a mission.

Jack Cool.

Captain Pamala Plum-Martin radioed Wing Commander Ronnie Gordon the change of plans. He acknowledged. The two A-20s would continue on to Oasis X. They were needed to be there to support Raiding Regiment's gun jeep patrols.

The Vargas Girl look-alike Royal Marine pilot put the Hudson into a sharp bank and the plane headed back north. A staff car was waiting on the Raiding Forces airstrip when it landed. Col. Randal was driven to Grey Pillars, where he was immediately ushered into a small, cramped conference room, space being at a premium in Middle East Command Headquarters.

Vice Admiral Sir Randolph "Razor" Ransom, James "Baldie" Taylor, Colonel Dudley Clarke and Commander Ian Fleming were waiting inside.

Col. Clarke chaired the meeting. He said, "*Frogspawn.*"

Col. Randal said, "That's great, since I'm not even supposed to be associating with two of you present."

VAdm. Ransom said, "Most likely you could make that all four of us, Colonel."

Col. Randal said, "That's what I was afraid of, sir."

Col. Clarke said, "We are diligently working on resolving the issue between MI-6 and Lady Jane. Unfortunately, every effort has failed miserably.

I have come up with what is hopefully a satisfactory temporary solution."

Col. Randal said, "What might that be?"

Col. Clarke said, "I propose to compartmentalize different operations. Since Illicit Diamond Buying is the root of the problem, we shall simply all agree not have any conversation about it. It will be off limits. Not a factor in anything this group proposes today or in the future."

Col. Randal said, "I don't think that's going to work, but let's pretend it will."

"One can only hope," Col. Clarke said.

Jim said, "You would not be here now, Colonel, if it was not of national strategic importance to both the U.K. and U.S."

Col. Clarke said, "You were recently alerted Raiding Forces would be carrying out a series of OPERATION OVERTHROW beach reconnaissance deception missions on Crete. Now the operation has been expanded to include Pas de Calais, Sardinia, Sicily and the toe of Italy. We may decide to add Greece at some later date.

"Combined Operations' most experienced small-scale raiding commander was recently killed while on loan to SOE. It is not certain Admiral Mountbatten has anyone with the skills necessary to perform the missions we require in the Pas de Calais region.

"Out here in Middle East Command, Layforce—the Commando Brigade the Prime Minister personally ordered out to Egypt—has been disbanded and its officers and men scattered to the winds. There is the odd Commando unit still in existence, but they are all frightfully amateurish. Afraid that leaves only you, Colonel Randal. Can you do it—carry out OVERTHROW missions against Pas de Calais, Sardinia, Sicily and Italy, in addition to Crete?"

Col. Randal said, "We'll do the job, provided the Admiral can get us where we need to go."

"Calais should not prove to be a problem," VAdm. Ransom said. "The *Arrow* shall work splendidly as sealift. She has been performing cross-channel missions for MI-6. OVERTHROW missions along Crete's coastline are fairly straightforward. Sea Squadron shall find PT boats and MAS boats adequate to land SOG or Duck Patrol Commandos ashore. I should like to have Captain

Hoolihan back from the Commando School in Scotland to command."

"I'll make it happen, Admiral," Col. Randal said.

VAdm. Ransom said, "Sardinia, Sicily and the toe of Italy—now that's a bird of another feather. It might be possible to insert by seaplane, but I do not recommend it. The Luftwaffe controls the skies during daytime with some night fighter capability.

"The only good option is to go in by submarine."

Jim asked, "Will the Royal Navy provide them?"

"Not likely," VAdm. Ransom said. "Even if they do, the skipper might not be willing to risk his craft on a job we are not free to adequately advise the true nature of. Royal Navy submarine commanders have a lot of latitude. Expected to be bold but not reckless, they can cancel a mission on their own authority if they believe it puts their submarine at risk. Subs are in short supply and the skippers are admonished not to lose them."

Col. Clarke said, "A-Force, meaning Supreme Headquarters Allied Expeditionary Force, requires those Sardinian, Sicilian and Italian OVERTHROW missions. I cannot overstate their importance to OPERATION TORCH."

Jim said, "Four U.S. Navy submarines are laid on for Task Force 34—TORCH. I can see if Colonel Donovan is able to have two of them temporarily detailed to Admiral Ransom. OSS should jump at the opportunity to be involved. To use an Americanism—'for the bragging rights'—right down their alley."

Col. Randal said, "Work out the transportation, provide intel on the targets, gentlemen, and Raiding Forces will do the rest. This mission is 'right down *our* alley'."

BRIGADIER RAYMOND J. "R. J." MAUNSELL INVITED MAJOR THE LADY JANE SEABORN TO TEA while Colonel John Randal was at Grey Pillars. He had a close working relationship with MI-6's Cuthbert Bowlby and had gone out of his way to cultivate relations with Raiding Forces. The purpose of the exercise was to see if he could smooth over the problems between the two.

R. J. failed.

12
THEODORE

COLONEL JOHN RANDAL WAS IN HIS THIRD-FLOOR SUITE TALKING TO MAJOR THE LADY JANE Seaborn. There was a knock on the door. Flanigan stuck his head inside. "Sir, Phantom delivered a message for you."

"Bring it in."

The flimsy was typed in code. Mindful of what Brandy had said to him about Lady Jane's fear he might not trust her, Col. Randal handed over the dispatch. The best way he could think of to keep Jane from worrying was to include her in everything concerning IDB.

Lady Jane said, "A coded message from Captain McKoy. Can you decipher this?"

"Why don't you do it," Col. Randal said, picking up the copy of *Jump on Bela* from the coffee table and handing it to her. "Page 32, second paragraph."

Lady Jane opened the book, took out a pen and began to write out the message on a notepad. It said:

> EVERYTHING ABOUT DIAMONDS IS A LIE STOP NO SHORTAGE OF INDUSTRIAL GRADE STONES STOP TAKE NO ACTION UNTIL WALDO AND I RETURN STOP BURN AFTER READING STOP MCKOY STOP

Col. Randal said, "Why not just tear the flimsy into a million pieces?"

"Let's burn it," Lady Jane laughed, "like real secret agents."

She was clearly getting her sense of humor back.

"Jim burned one in front of Terry and me when we first went out to the Gold Coast," Col. Randal said, taking out his old U.S. 26th Cavalry Regiment Zippo and holding the message over an ash tray. "Definitely got our attention."

Lady Jane said, "John, do you have any idea what is actually happening?"

Col. Randal said, "I was going to ask you that. From the very start, Captain McKoy hasn't been buying into the story about diamond smuggling. We need to trust his instincts."

Lady Jane said, "Agreed."

Col. Randal said, "Wondering who to trust is getting old fast."

"It's just you and me, babe," Lady Jane laughed, "with a little help from Jack, Beverly and the girls at the moment."

"Pretty short list," Col. Randal said.

Lady Jane said, "We can do it."

"MI-6," Col. Randal said. "How will they come at us?"

"From all directions," Lady Jane said. "SIS will never give up. No matter how profusely Cuthbert Bowlby apologizes or what he promises, the man is never going to stop trying to discover what we learn about the DeBeers Diamond Company."

Col. Randal asked, "Do you know all the members of Raiding Forces who are MI-6?"

"No."

"That's not good—don't you spies have a secret handshake or something?"

"Like I said, it's just you and me," Lady Jane said, not laughing this time. "Think about bringing in 575th Ranger personnel to expand the antismuggling operation when the time comes."

"Good idea," Col. Randal said. "We also have Travis McCloud, Roy Kidd and Preston Butterfield if we need 'em."

"At some point in the near future," Lady Jane said, "I have to let MI-6 make peace with me. SIS shall be dissembling, as will I. However, it is to our advantage, John, for MI-6 to believe everything is forgiven. A big misunderstanding, all is well."

Col. Randal said, "You did learn something in those intelligence schools."

"Enough," Lady Jane said, "to be dangerous."

Col. Randal said, "Dudley Clarke is going to initiate the offer. His idea is to compartmentalize operations. Any discussion of diamonds will be off the table unless we bring it up."

"How do you know, John?"

"That's what we had to divert our flight for," Col. Randal said. "A-Force has been tasked with organizing a deception program to cover a major Allied invasion—when and where to be announced. He needs Raiding Forces to carry out beach reconnaissance missions in support of his plan.

"I have to do it, Jane."

"Perfect," Lady Jane said. "I shall allow Dudley to make the first move. Then be gracious."

"Sounds like a plan," Col. Randal said, relieved he was not going to need to go behind her back in order to work on OPERATION TORCH.

"Fun," Lady Jane said. "I enjoy the two of us working on the diamond project together—outsmarting the British Secret Intelligence Service."

"Could be dangerous," Col. Randal said. "We're not sure what we're getting into. Never go anywhere without Flanigan—ever."

Lady Jane said, "How do we know *he's* not MI-6?"

"I'll get you two Ranger bodyguards."

COLONEL JOHN RANDAL WALKED DOWNSTAIRS TO THE OPERATIONS ROOM. THERE WAS NOT A lot going on at the moment. Captain Stephanie Fawcett-Tatum was sitting at her desk reading a *Screen Stars* movie magazine.

Col. Randal said, "Is 'The Great Teddy' in the building?"

"I believe so, John," Capt. Fawcett-Tatum said. "Let me dial his room."

Col. Randal could hear the phone ringing. "Ensign Hamilton."

Capt. Fawcett-Tatum held out the receiver.

Col. Randal took the phone, "Be down in the Op Room in the next sixty seconds."

"SIR!"

Capt. Fawcett-Tatum said, "Short and simple."

Col. Randal said, "You never heard that conversation."

Capt. Fawcett-Tatum went back to browsing through her magazine. "That was not a conversation, John."

"Track down Capt. Jaxx," Col. Randal ordered. "I need to see him ASAP. Have him meet me in my suite."

Capt. Fawcett-Tatum said, "Jack can be found lounging at the private pool on the second floor with Red and some of her BOAC girlfriends. I shall send one of the Marines up to deliver your message."

The private pool on the second floor was a restricted area. "Female Personnel Only." Men were only allowed to use it by invitation. Very few were given. The girls liked their privacy.

Jack Cool.

Ensign Theodore Hamilton, *aka* The Great Teddy, came dashing into the Operations Room.

"You wished to see me, sir?"

The two stepped over to a deserted corner of the room.

Col. Randal said, "Time to do a little CLO work, Ensign. Go find Colonel Clarke. Inform him I said that if he wants to try patching things up with Lady Jane, he'd better get here quick. We'll be flying out for Oasis X later this afternoon.

"Tell the Colonel to call first—he owes me one for this."

"Yes, sir."

Col. Randal said, "Take any jeep you want."

As The Great Teddy went tearing out of RFHQ, Capt. Fawcett-Tatum said, "What in the world did you say to him?"

"That's classified, Stephanie," Col. Randal said. "You need to notify everyone who was on board the Hudson earlier this morning that we'll be taking off again at 1630 hours."

"Yes, sir."

"Are you up for coming with us?"

"Very much so."

"Pack your bags."

Col. Randal and Captain Billy Jack Jaxx, wearing his swimming trunks and a Texas Longhorns jersey with the sleeves hacked off, arrived on the landing of the third-floor suite at the same time.

Col. Randal said, "We're going to be flying out to Oasis X at 1630. I want to brief you on an upcoming mission before we take off so you can be thinking about it. Then you can get back to the girls at the pool."

"Yes, sir."

Col. Randal ordered, "Flanigan, don't let anyone in without announcing first."

"Sir!"

The two officers went inside to the small map room/briefing area off the living room of the suite. There was a new map of the entire Mediterranean pinned to the wall. It was a huge chart covering an enormous area.

Col. Randal said, "What I am about to tell you is classified Top Secret. No one but the two of us and Lady Jane have the 'Need to Know' at this point."

Capt. Jaxx perked up. "Understood, sir."

Col. Randal said, "I mean it, Jack. You can't even talk in your sleep."

Capt. Jaxx said, "Colonel, if I talked in my sleep, I'd be a dead man by now."

"What could I have been thinking?" Col. Randal asked. "Here's the deal. A major Allied invasion called OPERATION TORCH is in the works. I have no idea where. My guess is in this part of the world. Two fleets, one sailing from England and one from the United States, will link up to open the long-anticipated Second Front.

"The British admiral claims his fleet will have accomplished its mission if half his ships arrive. No one even knows how to figure the U.S. Navy's chances of making it."

Capt. Jaxx said, "Those are some odds, sir."

"It is what it is, Jack," Col. Randal said. "I want you to hear everything I know so you can appreciate the gravity of the situation."

"Yes, sir."

Col. Randal said, "Raiding Forces has been tasked with providing cover for TORCH. Our mission, OPERATION OVERTHROW, is to carry out a series of reconnaissance missions on beaches the invasion fleet will probably *not* be landing on. The purpose of the exercise is to make sure the bad guys know we conducted the beach survey to confuse their intelligence services as to where the landings will actually take place."

Capt. Jaxx said, "Going to require finesse, sir."

"Yes, it is," Col. Randal said. "OVERTHROW is more complicated than it sounds. While the operation is Top Secret, I have to tell you, Butch Hoolihan, and Roy Kidd at a minimum. The three of you will need to work out the details about how to leave telltale signs behind after you exfiltrate the beach so as to appear accidental when they're found. It won't work if you all leave ammo pouches behind every time."

Capt. Jaxx said, "Got it, sir."

Col. Randal said, "The problem is, since you three studs know we're carrying out a deception, you can't be captured."

Capt. Jaxx said, "But Butch, Roy and I still have to lead the missions, right, sir?"

Col. Randal said, "I can't think of any other way."

Capt. Jaxx said, "We're going to want our troops to believe they're performing actual beach surveys in the event any of them are captured, right, sir?"

Col. Randal said, "Affirmative."

"Tricky," Capt. Jaxx said, "but can do, Colonel."

Col. Randal pointed to the map. "We'll be operating against Sardinia, Sicily, Italy, Crete and possibly Greece. Because SOG still needs to be on stand-by for GOLDEN FLEECE/RED INDIAN targets, I'm going to assign you OVERTHROW responsibility for Crete. That way, you'll only be away from RFHQ overnight.

"What are your questions?"

Capt. Jaxx said, "How are Butch and Roy going to reach all those distant targets, sir?"

Col. Randal said, "Jim's working on the loan of two U.S. Navy submarines."

Capt. Jaxx said, "What's the plan to make sure Butch, Roy and I don't get captured, sir?"

Col. Randal said, "I'm going to send someone along to guarantee you don't."

Capt. Jaxx said, "You mean as in, shoot us, sir, in the event capture is unavoidable?"

Col. Randal said, "Roger that."

"That's not much of a Plan B, Colonel."

"Only one I've got, Jack."

An hour later, after Capt. Jaxx had returned to the pool, the phone rang. The call was for Major the Lady Jane Seaborn. After hanging up, she said, "That was Dudley. He is on the way to RFHQ."

"Showtime," Col. Randal said. "I'm out of here."

Lady Jane gave him one of her patented heart attack smiles. Col. Randal felt better immediately. Seeing Jane getting her sense of humor back was good.

Col. Randal went downstairs to the Operations Room again. Capt. Fawcett-Tatum was away from her duty desk, packing for the trip to Oasis X. Sub-Lieutenant Bentley St. Ledger had taken her place. She was reading the movie star magazine.

"Bentley," Col. Randal said, "did I tell you I met your mother?"

S/Lt. St. Ledger said, "Mother mentioned it in her last letter."

"Really?"

"You made quite the impression," S/Lt. St. Ledger said. "Be careful. Mother is a man-eater. Recently divorced her fourth husband . . . or maybe it was the fifth. Hard to keep track and depends on how you count. She married one twice."

Col. Randal said, "Send a message to Oasis X. I need to meet with Major McCloud when we arrive. Also, I want to talk to Captain Kidd. If either of the two are not currently at the oasis, have Colonel Stone lay on air transport to bring 'em back ASAP."

"Yes, sir," S/Lt. St. Ledger said. "Anything else, John?"

"Do you happen to know where Beverly is?"

"She was in here a few minutes ago," S/Lt. St. Ledger said. "Went back to her quarters, I believe."

Col. Randal said, "Call Beverly, see if she'd like to meet me for target practice."

He did not want to be in the building when Col. Clarke arrived.

S/Lt. St Ledger hung up the phone. "Beverly said to inform you she is on her way down now."

Col. Randal asked, "Is Sergeant Major Beckwith in the area?"

"Believe he is still in the building."

Col. Randal said, "I need to speak to him."

"I shall put one of the Marines on the case," S/Lt. St. Ledger said. "They are like the Royal Canadian Mounted Police. Always get their man."

Col. Randal said, "I just want to talk to him, Bentley. He doesn't have to be in handcuffs."

"I was only teasing. The Sergeant Major is in the billiard room," S/Lt. St. Ledger said. "He complained to me about the billiard tables not having 'pockets', whatever those are."

Beverly came down the stairs with a canvas pistol belt containing her—or rather his—Browning P-35 slung over her shoulder. Shortly after she walked into the Operations Room, Master Sergeant Mack Beckwith arrived.

While Beverly tried to explain to S/Lt. St. Ledger about pool table pockets, Col. Randal held a brief conversation with MSgt. Beckwith. "I need two Rangers to serve as Lady Jane's bodyguards. Who do you recommend, Sergeant Major?"

MSgt. Beckwith said, "Bannon and Clooney, sir. Both men were street cops on the NYPD and MPs in the New York National Guard before their unit got mobilized for active duty. You can count on those two to protect Lady Seaborn, sir. A couple of tough-as-nails Micks, and they don't take nothin' off nobody."

"Thanks," Col. Randal said. "Getting a handle on billiards yet?"

"Negative, sir. That's a finesse game," MSgt. Beckwith said. "I'm an 8-ball man. Try to shatter the Q-ball on the break, then pick off the cripples."

"Stand ready, Sergeant Major," Col. Randal said, changing the subject.

"I'm going to be leaning on you. Raiding Forces has a lot of projects in the works. Expect to play a big part in our future operations."

MSgt. Beckwith said, "Been wondering what was going to happen next, sir, now that our patrol got broken up."

Col. Randal said, "For one, you're going to start sitting in on certain classified meetings with Captain McKoy, Captain Jaxx, Mr. Treywick and myself—I need people around me I can depend on."

"Yes, sir."

"Effective immediately, as in right this minute, you're in charge of supervising Lady Jane's personal security detail. If you feel more than two men are required for the job, that's not a problem," Col. Randal said. "Tell Lieutenant St. Ledger where to locate Bannon and Clooney. If they're on patrol, she'll have 'em flown in on a priority basis."

MSgt. Beckwith realized he had just been tapped to be a member of Col. Randal's inner circle. He had not expected that. "Major Beauchamp ain't gonna be happy, Colonel."

"Why might that be?

"Clooney's the Major's driver and Bannon's his machine gunner, sir."

Col. Randal said, "I'd say Lady Jane's personal security outranks Major Beauchamp's need for a driver and a gunner, Sergeant Major."

"No question in my military mind about that, sir."

When Col. Randal and Beverly walked outside, Lieutenant Mandy Paige and Rita were driving up in a jeep.

"Have a moment, John?"

"Sure."

Lt. Mandy glanced at Beverly.

Col. Randal said, "You can add Beverly to our two-person 'Need to Know' list."

"OPERATION RAYON is an A-Force deception," Lt. Mandy said. "Teddy has a crew building decoy tanks and landing craft here on the river and in Alexandria. All I have been able to find out so far."

"Good enough," Col. Randal said, "Everything I need."

Lt. Mandy said, "What is going on, John?"

"Classified."

"You know I shall find out," Lt. Mandy said. "Why not make it easy and tell me now."

Col. Randal said, "I want to see how long it takes you."

Lieutenant Randy "Hornblower" Seaborn drove up in another of the Raiding Forces' jeeps.

"You were absolutely right, sir," Lt. Seaborn said. "SOE was playing us . . . or rather Mrs. Paige, but not the way you thought."

Col. Randal asked, "What did you find out?"

Lt. Seaborn said, "Grandfather and I spent the morning at the shipyard. Takes six months most places to assemble one of the prefabricated Motor Launch kits. Probably longer in Cairo with the slackers out here doing the labor. Replacing the engine will take a major redesign to the hull. We would need to rebuild the engine spaces and modify the drive train to the screws, so the idea of substituting automobile engines to increase the ML's speed is out, sir."

"I hate SOE Cairo," Lt. Mandy said. "They think they are so smart."

Col. Randal said, "I don't want Veronica waiting six months. What's the plan, Randy?"

"Grandfather is having entirely too much fun commanding a PT boat to release the one he commandeered from Sea Squadron," Lt. Seaborn said. "Besides, he has both MAS boats, my MGB and our other PT out every night patrolling for enemy fuel tankers trying to run the blockade.

"There is no plan, sir."

Col. Randal said, "Beverly, you're the OSS Escape officer. What do you suggest?"

Beverly said, "Why don't we ask Colonel Donovan to ship us another PT boat?"

"OK, do it, Beverly," Col. Randal said. "See what happens."

Lt. Seaborn said, "Mother would like her own PT boat."

Col. Randal and Beverly walked to their skeet shooting range, which consisted of a single thrower they took turns operating. They were throwing the clay pigeons straight away, having fun trying to hit the clays—emphasis on *trying.* What they were attempting to do was almost impossible with a pistol, but extremely good training for real live targets that did not always cooperate by holding still to let you shoot them.

Ens. Hamilton arrived unexpectedly. He reported to Col. Randal. It was not easy. The Great Teddy had trouble remembering to breathe when Beverly was around.

"Colonel Clarke is meeting with Lady Seaborn, sir."

"That's nice," Col. Randal said. "I hope they have a pleasant visit."

"So does Colonel Clarke, sir," Ens. Hamilton said. "He asked me to brief you on a new A-Force deception requirement we received today."

Beverly said, "Pull!"

Col. Randal launched the clay pigeon. Bang! It turned into fine, black mist.

Ens. Hamilton seemed hesitant to say any more.

"Beverly is cleared to hear anything I am," Col. Randal said, which was not exactly true. "Go ahead with your briefing, Ensign—pull!"

The little skeet flew straight away, traveling at a tremendous speed. Bang! It kept right on going—a miss.

Ens. Hamilton said, "When Eighth Army launches its attack, General Montgomery has asked Colonel Clarke if he can create the illusion of an armored division maneuvering against the enemy's rear where none exists, sir."

Beverly said, "Pull!"

Bang! Another puff of black dust.

"Well," Col. Randal said, "can you do that, Ensign? Pull!"

Bang! Missed again.

"Yes, sir," Ens. Hamilton said, "provided I have your help, Colonel."

Beverly said, "Pull!"

Bang! She missed.

"What do you need from me?" Col Randal asked. "Pull!"

Ens. Hamilton said, "One hundred jeeps and drivers, sir."

Col. Randal lowered his Colt .38 Super, not even bothering to fire at the clay pigeon sailing off. "What?"

"Rig up chains on a plank and pull it behind a jeep to create a dust cloud," Ens. Hamilton said. "We can use pieces of metal bars or perforated steel plate, sir. They work even better. The idea is to create a giant dust cloud that looks like an armored division on the move."

Col. Randal said, "Jeeps are not a problem. We have plenty of those. Drivers, that's another story."

Ens. Hamilton said, "Sir, Colonel Clarke ordered me to inform you that creating a phantom armored division was of vital importance to General Montgomery."

"Raiding Regiment has been ordered to make a maximum effort interdicting Axis supply convoys from Oasis X to Tripoli once Eighth Army's attack goes in," Col. Randal said. "Sea Squadron is already overcommitted. I don't have the drivers. Maybe we can use Major Merritt's Sudanese, but that doesn't get us to a hundred."

Beverly said, "I can drive a jeep."

Col. Randal said, "Negative."

Ens. Hamilton said, "If A-Force makes drivers available, Raiding Forces will supply the jeeps and you will command the operation, sir?"

"I will be in overall command," Col. Randal said, "Colonel Stone will have direct responsibility for execution. I'll expect you to travel with the maneuver element, Stud, to supervise."

Ens. Hamilton said, "I shall so inform Colonel Clarke, sir."

The Great Teddy secretly liked the fact that Col. Randal paid him the respect of addressing him as Ensign. He liked it even better when Col. Randal called him "Stud."

Beverly said, "I'll give you a do-over on that last bird, John."

Col. Randal said, "Are you a hustler, Beverly? Shot skeet with a handgun before?"

"I may beat you shooting targets," Beverly laughed, "but you're better than me at shooting people."

Ens. Hamilton said, "Ask Mandy to tell you about the time when we were besieged at RAF Habbaniya and Colonel Randal shot up the entire supply of Boys antitank rounds in one morning sniping Iraqis."

Beverly said, "She has, Theodore."

Ens. Hamilton despised the name Theodore, but it sounded good when Beverly said it.

Col. Randal said, "Pull!"

OASIS X WAS SEMI-DESERTED. MOST OF THE RAIDING REGIMENT PATROLS WERE IN THE FIELD. The only difference now that the 575 Rangers and RAF 2 Armored Car Squadron had arrived were two more gun jeep patrols back in from operations, resting and refitting. Those patrols' vehicles, like all the extra jeeps that had mistakenly been shipped to Egypt for the 575 Parachute Infantry Regiment, were camouflaged under colorful Arab tents.

Colonel John Randal and Lieutenant Colonel Sir Terry "Zorro" Stone immediately went into conference. They were out on the deck of the snow-white apartment chiseled out of the stone face of the cliff, above the river that cascaded down and ran through the lush oasis, then plunged back deep underground. Oasis X was a magical place—like something out of a storybook.

Lt. Col. Stone briefed Col. Randal on developments since he had been away. While it had been less than a month, that length of time seemed like a year in a high-speed raiding outfit. With Panzerarmee Afrika sitting on the Alamein line licking its wounds and Raiding Forces ordered to redouble efforts to attack Petroleum, Oil and Lubrication (POL) installations and resupply convoys, a lot had been going on.

Lt. Col. Stone said, "We have taken our share of casualties, old stick. 575th Rangers suffered the highest rate—as was only to be expected being thrown into the fire, so to speak. Down to four patrols. That said, Major McCloud has performed extraordinarily well. Stays in the field with one of his patrols virtually all the time. His Rangers have turned into our second highest-scoring element.

"RAF Patrol has lived up to expectations. As we thought, it was a good day for Raiding Regiment when Lady Jane recruited Squadron Leader Johnny Page and his lads. They have taken to gun jeeps like ducks to water. Glad to be out of those museum-piece armored cars they had at RAF Habbaniya.

"My cousin, 'Mongo' Farquhar, has proved to be a brilliant raiding tactician. Lounge Lizard Patrol has taken the least casualties. He is a military perfectionist, but casual about it . . . a lot like you. The Duke is most pleased with the reports we send him on the Regiment's operations, and that makes my life easier.

"He wishes more Americans could be assigned. Who would have ever believed that? Yeomanry county regiments, officered by the monied horsey set, being notoriously clannish such as they are.

"Lieutenant Butterfield has Blue Patrol well in hand—perfect fit with his having served in the French Foreign Legion. I have taken the liberty, subject to your approval, to promote him to acting captain, unpaid."

Col. Randal said, "Only in the British Army could you have ranks like that. I'm pretty sure we can get the promotion confirmed through OSS."

Lt. Col. Stone said, "I have a list of decoration recommendations."

Col. Randal said, "Give it to Jane."

There was nothing she liked better than to take care of "her troops." Col. Randal knew that in many units, decorations were often recommended—only to never be heard of again. Lost in the maze of military bureaucracy or due to laziness on the part of staff officers who could not be bothered with the additional paperwork.

When Lady Jane submitted a decoration, God help the fool who failed to follow through on having it approved.

Lt. Col. Stone said, "This concludes my report. I shall supply you with patrol after-action reports, casualty lists, etcetera, so you will have reading material for your leisure time."

Major Travis McCloud and Captain Roy Kidd were inside the apartment talking to Major the Lady Jane Seaborn, and Beverly was waiting to see Col. Randal.

Col. Randal said, "Ask Travis and Roy to step out. Then hang around,

Terry. You need to know what I'm going to tell them.

"After that, we need to talk."

Lt. Col. Stone arched an eyebrow. He and Col. Randal were close friends. The Errol Flynn-looking officer could not remember when he had ever said anything like that. "Sounds serious, old stick."

"It is."

When the three officers returned, Col. Randal said, "I know you men have been overcommitted. I understand there have been casualties. Fairly heavy in Ranger Patrol, but I haven't seen the numbers yet.

"Don't be expecting a break anytime soon. In fact, the pace of operations is getting ready to pick up. The situation is this: Eighth Army under General Montgomery is poised to launch the attack that is designed to push Panzerarmee Afrika all the way back to and out of Tripoli. Approximately in the same time period it kicks off, the U.K. and U.S. will be opening the Second Front somewhere not known to me, OPERATION TORCH. Raiding Forces has been tasked with supporting the Allied invasion by reconnoitering likely invasion beaches.

"Sea Squadron is going to be stretched too thin to handle all the missions it will be asked to perform. In addition, for political reasons, the opposition needs to believe this is primarily an American invasion. The combination of those two things means we're going to be forced to use Rangers to reinforce Major Corrigan.

"Travis, that's going to hit you pretty hard."

"Understood, sir."

"Roy," Col. Randal said, "you'll be flying back with me when we leave. Who do you recommend to take over your Scout I Patrol?"

"Duke Slater, sir."

Col. Randal said, "Make it happen, Travis."

"Yes, sir," Maj. McCloud said, not overjoyed at the prospect of losing his best patrol leader, in addition to an undisclosed number of Rangers.

Col. Randal said, "Major McCloud, be prepared to provide a thirty-man platoon of your Rangers to act as a parachute reaction force for TORCH—Captain Jaxx to command."

"Maj. McCloud said, "That will put a serious strain on the 575th Ranger Regiment, sir."

"Get with Terry," Col. Randal said. "He will temporarily attach another patrol the 575th

to keep you in business."

"Yes, sir."

Col. Randal said, "Bannon and Clooney will be going back to RFHQ with us to serve as Lady Jane's bodyguards. They won't be back."

Maj. McCloud said, "I'll detach them immediately. Major Beauchamp is not going to be happy, sir."

Col. Randal said, "No one ever said serving in Raiding Forces was going to be easy. We are overcommitted to Top Secret missions. We've all got to pull together—teamwork, teamwork, teamwork."

Maj. McCloud and Capt. Kidd left. Neither officer was pleased with the developments. One had been informed his command was about to be reduced. The other was giving up his patrol for an undisclosed assignment.

Lt. Col. Stone said, "What did you wish to talk to me about?"

Col. Randal said, "In addition to all our other responsibilities, Raiding Forces has been tasked with interrupting the illegal flow of smuggled industrial diamonds. Germany has no source of industrial diamonds. Hitler only had an eight-month supply over a year ago but the Nazis have never run out. Why—nobody knows."

Lt. Col. Stone said, "What makes industrial diamonds so special?"

Col. Randal said, "Only diamonds are hard enough to stamp out precision parts for airplane engines, torpedoes, tanks, artillery, the fine wire for military electronics, the jeweled bearings for stabilizers, gyroscopes and navigation systems for submarines and airplanes . . . the list goes on and on."

Lt. Col. Stone said, "Been doing your homework, old stick—impressive."

Col. Randal said, "Without a continuing supply of industrial diamonds, the Nazi war machine will grind to a halt. Raiding Forces' mission is to interrupt what is known as illicit diamond buying—IDB—which results in industrial diamonds being smuggled into Germany."

Lt. Col. Stone asked, "So, why do you think the Nazi supply has not run out by now?"

Col. Randal said, "DeBeers has to be selling industrial diamonds to both sides."

Lt. Col. Stone said, "Not likely, old stick. The chairman of the board of directors and chief operating officer of the DeBeers Diamond Company, Sir Ernest Oppenheimer's son Harry, is the intelligence officer of 4 South African Armored Car Regiment serving in Eighth Army."

Col. Randal said, "The DeBeers Diamond Company has refused to sell the U.S. the allocation of diamonds it ordered. Used every excuse in the book. The one I like best is that they're not able to open the vault storing DeBeers' reserve supply of diamonds in London because the doors are jammed."

"Surely you jest," Lt. Col. Stone said. "Who would believe such a story?"

Col. Randal said, "Gets worse."

Lt. Col. Stone said, "Than what you have already told me? I went to school with Harry Oppenheimer."

Col. Randal said, "Cuthbert Bowlby ordered Lady Jane to report to him information Raiding Forces learns about the DeBeers Diamond Company and not tell me she was doing it. Jane immediately resigned from MI-6, severed all ties with anyone associated with SIS and had Jim's things packed up and moved out of RFHQ to Shephard's Hotel. The end result is a rift between the U.S. and the U.K. over diamonds that goes all the way from the White House to Number 10 Downing Street."

Lt. Col. Stone said, "Bloody fool must have gone temporarily insane to say that to Jane!"

"Yeah, well," Col. Randal said, "now for the *bad* part, old stick. There's a short list of people I can discuss IDB with.

"You're not on it."

Colonel John Randal and Major the Lady Jane Seaborn were sitting out on the deck of their apartment. It was dark. Torches lining the steps down the cliff were blazing. Torches also ran along both banks of the river.

The view was spectacular—in a small way.

Lady Jane said, "How did Terry take being informed you could not discuss IDB with him?"

Col. Randal said, "I explained it was a compartmentalized operation. A police action headed up by Captain McKoy and Waldo. And that IDB would not have any impact on any other Raiding Forces missions."

Lady Jane asked, "Was he OK with that solution?"

Col. Randal said, "He was until I threw in the kicker."

Lady Jane said, "What does 'kicker' mean?"

Col. Randal said, "Slang for something tacked onto the end of a story you don't want to hear."

Lady Jane asked, "What was the kicker?"

Col. Randal said, "I told Terry not to come ask me when MI-6 instructed him to check into what had been learned about DeBeers."

Lady Jane said. "What makes you so sure Sir Terry is MI-6?"

"Terry is an Etonian," Col. Randal said. "Before I jumped into Abyssinia, Jim told me Eton equals MI-6."

Lady Jane said, "I never knew Eton's connection to the Secret Intelligence Service was so pervasive."

"Yes, you did," Col. Randal said. "But, since Terry's the only officer in Raiding Forces who attended, it's not much of a problem. I don't care if Zorro or anyone else is a spy, as long as it's for our side. We'll restrict IDB to Need to Know—problem solved. No one should be offended."

"You're right," Lady Jane laughed. "I knew about Eton. Everybody does."

Captain Stephanie Fawcett-Tatum knocked on the outside of the door leading to the deck.

"Phantom received a message from Colonel Donovan. It is in the clear. I thought you would like to see it straightaway."

The message read:

> SHIPMENT OF PT'S EN ROUTE EGYPT STOP ONE HAS
> YOUR NAME ON IT PROVIDED LADY J. AGREES TO
> LOCATE SUITABLE HQ BLDG FOR OSS SECRET

INTELLIGENCE CAIRO STOP DETAILS OF SI'S REQUIREMENTS TO FOLLOW UNDER SEPARATE COVER STOP SIGNED DONOVAN STOP

"Space is at a premium in Cairo, may prove difficult," Lady Jane said. "Dudley's first office at Grey Pillars was a remodeled restroom in the basement."

13
FROGMAN

COLONEL JOHN RANDAL CLIMBED OUT OF THE B-17 THAT LANDED AT A JOINT U.S. ARMY AIR Force/Royal Air Force base outside of London. He had flown in from Cairo. The travel accommodations had been spartan—an oxygen bottle and a sleeping bag on the deck. Lieutenant Colonel Lionel Honeycutt-Parker, the commanding officer of Raiding Forces, Europe, was waiting. The two stepped into a command car and drove directly to Seaborn House.

Col. Randal was in England on such short notice because he had realized that he needed to brief the Raiding Forces, Europe, operators in person if OPERATION OVERTHROW, the deception plan designed to mislead the Nazis into believing OPERATION TORCH was going to take place somewhere in France, was to succeed.

It was necessary for the Raiders to believe they were reconnoitering actual landing sites. If this were an actual invasion, the word would come directly from him. For a mission of such strategic magnitude as OPERATION TORCH, it would not be convincing any other way.

Col. Randal filled in Lt. Col. Honeycutt-Parker on certain aspects of OVERTHROW as they drove. "TORCH is the Second Front. No one knows where it's going to land. . . at least I don't. Raiding Forces, Europe, has been tasked with surveying beaches in the Boulogne and Calais area.

"What that means, Lionel, is wherever TORCH lands, it *won't* be in

France in the vicinity of Boulogne or Calais."

Lt. Col. Honeycutt-Parker said, "Our mission is a deception, then?"

"Exactly."

The two officers had worked together in Abyssinia and trusted each other explicitly. Raiding Forces, Europe's part in OVERTHROW required careful execution. A mistake could give away the game with catastrophic results for TORCH.

The purpose of military deception—according to Colonel Dudley Clarke—was to get the enemy to "do something." What was wanted in OVERTHROW's case was for Hitler to reinforce France, denying precious military assets to the actual Second Front landing site, wherever that turned out to be. Enemy planes, tanks and troops guarding beaches *not* assaulted by TORCH was the purpose of the exercise.

Col. Randal said, "The south coast of England is going to see a lot of activity in the next few weeks. Hards are going to be constructed on beaches; coastal shipping will be assembled to simulate sea transport; an exercise by the British 3rd Division is scheduled; antiaircraft defenses will be built up; aerial photo-reconnaissance flights will be increased; and there will be an army of dummy tanks and landing craft constructed.

"Your mission, Colonel, is to carry out a series of clandestine beach surveys on likely landing sites, taking pains to make sure the enemy knows Raiding Forces has been there inspecting them."

Lt. Col. Honeycutt-Parker said, "All the while not letting the other side in on the secret that what we are doing is nothing more than smoke and mirrors?"

"Affirmative," Col. Randal said, "That means your Raiders can never know what they're doing is a deception. Nevertheless, Lionel, you're going to have to take someone who's going on each mission into your confidence.

"They'll need to leave behind telltale evidence to let the Nazis know Raiding Forces has been ashore. And you'll have to implement extreme preventive measures to guarantee that whoever it is you take into your confidence does not get captured."

"I understand, sir," Lt. Col. Honeycutt-Parker said, "You were not jesting.

Our part in OVERTHROW is not only multifaceted, it's more than a little sinister. I do not like the sound of certain aspects of your orders."

Col. Randal said, "You don't have to like it, you just have to do it. I've handed you a tough assignment. Now I'm going to make it harder. Send one of the two C/1/575 Ranger platoons back to Egypt."

"Sir…"

"You can retain Captain Longstreet to run the series of OVERTHROW missions."

"Yes, sir."

The two rode along in silence.

Lt. Col. Honeycutt-Parker asked, "How long will you be staying?"

"Flying out tomorrow."

HIS MAJESTY'S YACHT *ARROW,* FORMERLY BRANDY SEABORN'S PERSONAL PLEASURE BOAT, WAS hoved to a mile off a beach east of Calais, France. Colonel John Randal, Lieutenant Tom Green and four Rangers from 2nd Platoon/C Company/575th Parachute Infantry Regiment climbed down into a rubber assault raft paddled by a pair of Lifeboat Servicemen. Silently they made their way toward the shore. Stealth was all important. The Calais region was the most heavily defended region of Enemy Occupied France for the simple reason that it was the closest point to England, being located on the narrowest part of the English Channel.

Col. Randal and Lt. Green were sitting side by side in the front of the raft. They would be the first to go ashore. Tension was high.

Col. Randal leaned over and whispered to Lt. Green, "I'm about to give you a direct order you're never to reveal to anyone—even under extreme duress. Is that clear, Lieutenant?"

"Yes, sir."

"When we hit the beach, make sure to stay in arm's reach at all times,"

Col. Randal ordered. "In the event my capture is imminent—shoot me."

"Colonel, is this some kind of leadership test?" Lt. Green whispered back. He was clearly shaken by the order.

"Negative," Col. Randal said. "Let me hear a 'wilco', Lieutenant."

"Wilco," Lt. Green said. "Try to make sure things don't get to that point, sir."

The night was dark. No moon was out. There were differences of opinion about whether raids should only be carried out when there was moonlight.

Col. Randal was ambivalent on the subject. A full moon gave his men the light to see by. It also gave the enemy the light to see his men.

His policy was, Raiding Forces operated when a mission came up—provided a hurricane was not in progress.

Tonight Col. Randal was clicked on, tenser than usual, possibly a little spooked and not because he had just ordered a hard-charging U.S. Army Paratroop officer to shoot him. Calais brought back bad memories. He had lost a lot of Swamp Fox Force men here—more percentage-wise than in all his operations since. And there had been the bridge teeming with civilians that had to be blown or the 10th Panzer Division would have been able to take the town and then slam into the right flank of the British Army being evacuated at Dunkirk.

Col. Randal hated the place.

Tonight's mission was designed to be a quick in and out. One of the Rangers was going to take a soil sample, under the guise of engineers evaluating it later to determine if the beach would support tanks—that was not going to happen. The rest of the Rangers were to advance fifty yards inland, taking care to make sure there were no landmines emplaced and to see if there were any beach defenses in the way of concertina wire entanglements, bunkers, etc. Then the patrol was to make its way back to the Lifeboat Servicemen waiting with the assault raft at the water's edge.

Col. Randal did not know exactly where they had landed. Navigation was difficult, if not impossible, in pitch-dark. Not that it mattered. All that was necessary tonight was to leave behind some item of equipment to alert the enemy that Commandos had come calling—only the Rangers did not know that.

Col. Randal and Lt. Green were out of the assault raft the instant it crunched ashore. Behind them, the other Rangers fanned out. The night was cool—they were not.

Col. Randal and Lt. Green low-crawled inland. As they advanced, they brushed the sand in front of them with their hands to check for mines. In minutes they reached a single tangled strand of concertina wire strung out like a giant child's slinky toy.

One strand of concertina wire is more for appearance than actual defense against a determined attacker. Col. Randal made a show of inspecting it. No matter how many times he had done it before, there was always the sense of exhilaration when sneaking into the enemy's back yard. It overrode the bad feelings he had for the place.

Col. Randal and Lt. Green were laying side by side studying the wire when, with no warning whatsoever, two pairs of German jackboots appeared on the other side of the entanglement. The Nazis were less than five feet away. A beach patrol, consisting of two bored soldiers who would have rather been back in their bunks than walking the wire on a deserted beach at this time of night, had stopped directly across from them.

Col. Randal looked at Lt. Green and mouthed, "Freeze."

But it was no good. The Germans spotted them. No longer bored, the two enemy soldiers immediately swung into action, unslinging their rifles and shouting, "*Hande hoch.*"

BRRRRRUUUUUP. Col. Randal shot the Nazi closest to him with his 9mm MAB-38A submachine gun, firing a little longer burst than intended, blowing the enemy soldier completely off his feet.

"Hands up" typically being the preparatory command prior to ordering someone to surrender, Lt. Green was trying to decide whether he was supposed to shoot Col. Randal or the other Nazi. The second German ran off screaming, "Kommandos!"

So much for stealth.

"Lead out, Lieutenant," Col. Randal said. "Let's get the hell out of Dodge."

Lt. Green did not need any additional encouragement. He was away in a flash. Col. Randal reached in the billows pocket of his parachute smock, pulled out one of his old green berets with a Raiding Forces flash stitched on the front over a pair of his colonel's eagles and tossed it into the wire. German intelligence was not going to have much trouble determining who had been there—his name was stenciled inside on the headband.

It felt good. Col. Randal was saying, "I'm back."

CAPTAIN PAMALA PLUM-MARTIN, LIEUTENANT MANDY PAIGE AND BEVERLY BLACKWELL WERE waiting at the airfield when Colonel John Randal landed in an Avro Wellington. When he exited the bomber, the tidal wave of Egyptian heat nearly knocked him over. Nevertheless, he was glad to be back in Cairo.

Capt. Plum-Martin and Beverly had flown in to take him back to Oasis X. Lt. Mandy was along because they were all girlfriends and she did not want to be left out of anything.

"Have a nice trip, John?" Capt. Plum-Martin asked.

Col. Randal said, "Long flight laying on a metal deck, breathing out of oxygen bottles both ways."

Beverly said, "We'll take you to the Gezira for lunch. That should perk up your spirits."

Col. Randal said, "I would like that."

Lt. Mandy said, "Captain McKoy and Mr. Treywick are back. They're at Oasis X."

Capt. Plum-Martin said, "King is flying in later this afternoon. Air Marshal Tedder sent his private plane to pick him up from Gibraltar."

Beverly said, "Lady Jane is going to meet us at the Gezira. She's been out looking at real estate for OSS. I think Jane likes riding around Cairo in a jeep with Happy and her two Ranger bodyguards."

Which prompted Col. Randal to ask, "Mandy, do you happen to have a list of the addresses of the Big Five?"

Lt. Mandy said, "I am sure Sammy does."

"Call him from the Gezira," Col. Randal said. "After lunch, I'd like to drive by and take a look before we fly out. Let's check out the lifestyles of the rich and famous Middle Eastern crime lords."

Capt. Plum-Martin, who had served with Col. Randal a lot longer than the other two girls, studied him carefully but did not say anything. The Vargas Girl look-alike Royal Marine knew he never did anything without a reason. She wondered what it might be.

Beverly laughed, "Sounds like fun, John. The crook tour."

When the four walked into the restaurant, there was a message waiting. The maître d' said, "Lady Seaborn asked me to inform you she has been delayed, sir. She will meet you at the airfield prior to take-off."

Col. Randal asked to speak to the manager. He was immediately escorted to his office. "Lieutenant Paige needs to make a private phone call, Wilson."

"Use my telephone, by all means," the manager said. "I shall vacate the premises and let Mandy have it to herself. Tell her to take all the time she needs."

While Lt. Mandy made her call, Col. Randal, Capt. Plum-Martin and Beverly were shown to a table in the back of the room by the manager. As usual, it was partially obscured by one of the potted palms.

Col. Randal said, "Where's Rita and Lana? Beverly, you and Mandy have specific orders not to go anywhere without them."

"We're guarding each other today, John," Beverly said. "Mandy has the girls circulating through the native quarters at the Oasis X. She believes they've picked up indications that one of the locals may be in the pay of the Italian Intelligence Service—SIM."

Col. Randal said, "Won't end well if they are."

Beverly asked, "Why don't you make Pam have a bodyguard like Mandy and me?"

"Pam has the best guarded body in Cairo," Col. Randal said. "She never goes anywhere without at least two fighter pilots with her at all times."

Capt. Plum-Martin said, "Sometimes I make do with one."

Lt. Mandy made her way to the table. "Here are the addresses. Sammy says not to loiter out in front of the houses. The Big Five have armies of security personnel. They shoot first and ask questions later."

Colonel Dudley Clarke appeared at the table, "Welcome back, Colonel."

Col. Randal said, "How did you know I was here?"

Col. Clarke said, "I *am* paid to know things. Might I have a word?"

The two stepped back in the corner.

Col. Randal said, "Did you and Jane kiss and make up?"

"We did," Col. Clarke said. "I suspect her uncle, Colonel John Bevins, who is in truth her godfather, instructed her to make peace."

Col. Randal asked, "Why would he do that?"

"Colonel Bevins has recently been appointed head of the London Controlling Section—better known to those in the know as the LCS," Col. Clarke said. "Jane's godfather is my exact counterpart in London. If Lady Jane refused to work with me because I have a relationship with MI-6, she would not be able to work for him. . . and he has asked her to return to the U.K. to serve as his personal assistant.

"What a tangled web."

Col. Randal said, "Affirmative."

"Never fear," Col. Clarke said. "Lady Jane turned her 'uncle' down flat. In all likelihood a first since her parents were killed. She will not be leaving Raiding Forces for LCS."

Col. Randal said, "What do you want to talk to me about, Dudley?"

"Y-service in England intercepted German reports about the first OVERTHROW beach reconnaissance," Col. Clarke said. "Stroke of genius leaving your beret behind with your name inside. The Abwehr is buzzing with speculation about why you were there and not here. We know, strange as it sounds, that Hitler obsesses over every detail of even the smallest Commando raid against Enemy Occupied Europe—demands every report of one be brought to him immediately.

"Jumped off to a jolly good start—mystify, mislead, misdirect."

Col. Randal said, "A little more excitement than I intended."

Col. Clarke said, "Keep up the good work."

After touring the city and working their way through Lt. Mandy's list of addresses, which were all high-walled, hotel-sized mansions, Col. Randal's party arrived at the Raiding Forces airstrip. The plan was to board the Hudson for the flight to Oasis X. Major the Lady Jane Seaborn was there ahead of them. She had a tall stack of heavy cardboard boxes being loaded on board by her new bodyguards Ranger Clooney and Ranger Bannon.

Col. Randal asked, "What's in the boxes, Jane?"

Lady Jane gave him one of her patented heart attack smiles. "Research."

Col. Randal pulled back the edge of one of the boxes, "Looks like glossy women's magazines to me."

Lady Jane laughed. And that was the end of that.

Sub-Lieutenant Bentley St. Ledger drove up in a jeep. She reported to Col. Randal.

"A message from King arrived. He lands at 1700 hours. Wants to meet with you. Says he is bringing a box of toys.

"Were you expecting a dentist, John?"

"Negative."

S/Lt. St. Ledger said, "A U.S. Navy lieutenant junior grade, who claims to be an orthodontist, reported in from the States. He says he brought three 'frogs' with him."

"I have no idea what that's about," Col. Randal said. "Thanks, Bentley."

Col. Randal walked over to where Lt. Mandy was petting Happy. "Let's talk."

"Love to."

The two walked off a short distance away from the group gathered at the plane.

Col. Randal said, "Lieutenant, in your professional opinion, has enough time elapsed to set up the next meeting with the Big Five?"

Lt. Mandy said, "John, you never called me lieutenant before."

Col. Randal said, "I just did. Seems to me you're running the IDB show in Cairo. R. J. and Major Sansom implement every suggestion you make."

"We could have the sit-down any time now," Lt. Mandy said. "Intelligence indicates the crime lords have been relentless in their pursuit of reestablishing the Big Five diamond brokering monopoly. Blood has run red in the streets.

"We need Mr. Treywick here to do his Mr. Big act.

"Tell Major Sansom to set it up."

"Is there a reason for your rush, John?"

"Eighth Army is ready to kick off its attack," Col. Randal said. "And it's no secret an American invasion is in the works, somewhere. Let's go ahead and get the part you want me to play with the Big Five out of the way—who knows what Raiding Forces will be tasked with once all the fireworks start."

"Good idea," Lt. Mandy said, "I am on it."

Col. Randal climbed on board the Hudson and made his way to the cockpit where Capt. Plum-Martin and Beverly were going through their preflight check.

"Change of plans, ladies. Fly to X. Pick up Captain McKoy and Mr. Treywick. Do a quick turnaround and bring 'em back.

"Take my name, Lady Jane, Mandy and Jack's off your manifest."

Beverly said, "Billy Jack's already scratched."

Col. Randal said, "Why? I only made the decision in the last five minutes—he doesn't know yet."

"Told me he was going out with Brandy tonight," Beverly laughed. "That boy is something else."

"You're kidding."

"Billy Jack has exquisite taste in women," Capt. Plum-Martin said.

Col. Randal said, "Heard he asked you out."

"True," Capt. Plum-Martin said. "Tell Red to board her passengers, John."

"Will do," Col. Randal said. "Both of you are invited to dinner at Mena House tonight."

Beverly said, "I'm game."

Capt. Plum-Martin said, "Pencil me in as a maybe—I may have a date."

As the Hudson was taxiing for takeoff, Col. Randal, Lady Jane, Lt. Mandy and Happy were already en route to Raiding Forces Headquarters in a jeep. The two Ranger bodyguards followed in a second jeep. S/Lt. St. Ledger brought up the rear in hers.

Lady Jane said, "You are quiet, John."

Col. Randal said, "I'm in shock."

Lady Jane said, "Whatever is the matter?"

"Beverly told me Jack Cool has a date with Brandy tonight."

Lady Jane turned and looked Lt. Mandy. The two burst out laughing.

Lt. Mandy said, "No, John. What Jack said—he was *going out* with Brandy."

"What's the difference?"

Lady Jane said, "The OSS/MI-9 PT boat arrived yesterday. When Colonel Donovan said it was en route, he was not exaggerating. The Razor, Randy, Parker, Veronica and a scratch team of sailors from the Sea Squadron boats are running Jack and a few of his SOG operators over to Crete tonight to conduct one of Dudley's reconnaissance deceptions on a totally isolated beach."

Lt. Mandy laughed, "A sea trial to check out the PT boat—Jack decided to kill two birds with one stone."

Col. Randal said, "Nearly got one more—me."

Still laughing, Lady Jane said, "Billy Jack may be a 'life taker and a heart breaker'. A date with Brandy—not that cool."

Col. Randal said, "Yeah, that's what I thought."

Lady Jane said, "You were jealous."

KING AND JAMES "BALDIE" TAYLOR WERE WAITING AT RAIDING FORCES HEADQUARTERS. THE MI-6 Special Operations Chief, Middle East Command, was working his way back into Major the Lady Jane Seaborn's good graces. She had allowed him to move back into his room at RFHQ.

Colonel John Randal, King and Jim immediately went into conference in the third-floor suite he shared with Lady Jane.

King went first. "I had Air Marshal Tedder's pilot divert to an alternate airfield because of the off-chance the Air Marshal might be on hand to meet the plane. For reasons of my own, I prefer he not be able to recognize me by sight."

The Merc opened a metal footlocker. Inside were stacks of neatly packed individually boxed wristwatches. All made by manufacturers specified on the list provided by Air Marshal Tedder.

Col. Randal said, "How did you manage to make this happen?"

"So easy, Chief, it was laughable," King said. "Change of plans. Instead of a clandestine flight to Enemy Occupied France, RAF flew me to Gibraltar. I crossed the border into Spain using my passport, then caught a Spanish Air flight to Switzerland. Once in Zurich, I purchased the watches. No problem, Swiss watch companies have a backlog of inventory. Losing the ability to trade with the U.K. due to the war has been hard on the premium timepiece business. England used to buy a lot of luxury watches."

Col. Randal asked, "How did you pay for 'em?"

"Captain McKoy and Waldo financed the buy with money borrowed against the gold coins they have not been able to convert to cash. I had letters of credit waiting when I arrived."

Jim asked, "What route did you use coming back?"

"Same way in reverse," King said. "My only concern on the return was crossing the Spanish border into Gibraltar. No problem. The guards merely glanced at my Swiss passport and waved me on. Did not even inspect my luggage."

Jim said, "I can make sure they never do. MI-6 has half the Spanish Civil Guard on the payroll. Money talks in Spain."

Col. Randal said, "What's the plan, King?"

"I would like you to deliver the watches to the Air Marshal," King said. "Present him the bill, which includes a thirty-percent markup. You score points with the RAF. Captain McKoy, Waldo and I make a profit."

Col. Randal said, "Can do."

Jim said, "You need to charge a bigger commission. The RAF is desperate for the wristwatches. They will gladly pay more. Thirty percent is standard peacetime middleman profit."

"We get rich on the deal as it is," King said. "These are expensive wristwatches. The RAF needs them by the thousands."

"Good job, King," Col. Randal said, "Glad you're back. Raiding Forces is about to be very busy."

"You can count on me, Chief," King said. "I made arrangements for a business agent to handle the transport of the watches to Gibraltar. The occasional trip to Zurich to make sure everything is running smoothly is all the travel necessary for me in the future."

Col. Randal said, "Raise your commission—fifty percent sounds about right. I understand the mark-up on luxury goods is often over twice that in peace time."

King said, "If you say so, Chief."

Col. Randal said, "I'll try to see Tedder today. Get you your money."

Jim said, "You made a lot of friends in high places, King."

As the mercenary was leaving, Col. Randal picked up the phone. "Bentley, will you send the dentist up?"

Jim said, "Dentist?"

"Don't ask," Col. Randal said. "I have no idea what this is about."

As they waited, Jim said, "I would like to try to make something perfectly clear, Colonel, if I can. The fact MI-6 asked Lady Jane to report information without your knowledge does not mean the Secret Intelligence Service would ever—under any circumstances—take any action that would result in injury to Raiding Forces personnel.

"All it means is SIS wants to know what you know about a certain subject—gathering intelligence is what they do. MI-6 sees nothing immoral or unethical about it. The inelegant way Cuthbert Bowlby went about it is what created the problem."

Col. Randal said, "All's well that ends well."

Jim said, "I am relieved you feel that way. Our relationship is far too valuable to let the likes of Cuthbert wreck it. That stipulated, and we are not having this conversation, MI-6 showed its hand."

Col. Randal said, "In what way, Jim?"

"Certain people in high places in the government have an unusual interest in the DeBeers Diamond Company. What begs the question is why? The curiosity may or may not have anything to do with the war," Jim said. "In all my years in intelligence, I have never seen anything to quite match this situation."

"I appreciate you telling me, Jim," Col. Randal said. "I've decided anything having to do with DeBeers will be limited to the small group of people actually involved in the operation."

Jim said, "Not being on the Need to Know list is not going to hurt my feelings. I am no toady gathering industrial espionage in the service of big business or members of government who have been paid off. I pride myself on being a Direct Actions/Special Operations officer.

"You and I need to concentrate on killing Nazis, Colonel."

What Jim failed to mention was that William Stephenson, MI-6's senior officer in the United States, who liked to call himself "Intrepid" even though no one else on his staff ever used that name, had grilled him about Raiding Forces, DeBeers and Col. Randal's intentions *vis-à-vis* IDB. Someone with enough influence to get to Stephenson had an intense interest in the subject. Whoever it was might be higher in government than imagined.

Jim intended to find out the who, what and why if he could.

Col. Randal said, "How was your trip to Washington?"

"OSS is on a slippery slope," Jim said. "The military services all have their long knives out for Donovan. Seems everyone in the prewar establishment hates the idea of an Office of Strategic Services—particularly the FBI Director, J. Edgar Hoover.

"For his part, Colonel Donovan is thrilled by Raiding Forces' performance. Making plans to fly out to visit you in the very near future."

"Really?"

Not what he wanted to hear. All Col. Randal needed right now was a visiting fireman.

"Wild Bill claims he wants to accompany one of our gun jeep patrols."

"Well, that's not going to happen."

Col. Randal noted Jim had used the word "our." Maybe things were getting back to normal. Good.

Changing the subject, Jim asked. "Do you believe there is any possibility

Captain McKoy is sending private minutes to the President?"

Before Col. Randal could respond, Flanigan announced, "Lieutenant Taylor to see you, sir."

Thirty-three-year-old Lieutenant Junior Grade Jackson Taylor, USNR, marched into the room and threw Col. Randal what could only be described as the worst salute in the history of the United States Navy, an organization known for sloppy saluting.

Col. Randal said, "This is the general."

LtJG Taylor looked confused, then started to salute again.

Jim said, "Not necessary, Lieutenant."

Col. Randal said, "What can I do for you, Lieutenant Taylor?"

"Sir," LtJG Taylor said, "my team was initially assigned to England, but Colonel Donovan switched our orders to Egypt. I'm reporting for duty."

"I see," Col. Randal said. Which meant he did not have a clue what LtJG Taylor was talking about. "Is this a temporary assignment or a permanent change of station?"

"My understanding is permanent change of station, sir."

"In that case, Raiding Forces will have the best teeth in Middle East Command," Col. Randal said. "I wasn't expecting a dentist."

"I'm not a dentist, sir," LtJG Taylor said. "I mean. . . I am a dentist, just not a military dentist."

"What are you, then?"

"A Frogman, sir."

Col. Randal said, "I wasn't expecting a Frogman either. Were you, General?"

Jim said, "Negative."

Col. Randal said, "Why don't you take it from the top, Taylor."

"I'm an orthodontist, sir," LtJG Taylor said. "My office is in Hollywood, California. Before the war came along, I spent my time fixing movie starlets' and aspiring actresses' bad teeth and sailing my thirty-two-foot Catalina. I was happily minding my own business making a fortune—you have any idea how many girls want to be in the movies, sir?"

"I do," Col. Randal said, not mentioning he was from the same place.

"Then the Japs bombed Pearl Harbor, sir," LtJG Taylor said. "Since I liked to spend every spare minute sailing, I joined the United States Navy. Because I was capable of navigating, they sent me through a crash course on how to be an officer, then assigned me to a destroyer escort.

"For reasons never clear, the navy reassigned me to be trained on the use of the Lambertsen Amphibious Respirator Unit, LARU, sir. Then the navy, in its wisdom, decided not to adopt the LARU.

"What to do?

"I was in Washington, D.C., trying to figure out my next move when I picked up scuttlebutt that there was a secret organization created to perform exotic secret missions employing highly creative and unusual methods. Supposed to be so hush-hush even its name was classified, to include the initials, sir.

"So I asked a taxi driver to take me, not knowing the name or address of the place. He said, "Oh, you mean the OSS." Drove me straight there. No one seemed to mind my just popping in.

"The following day, sir, I was demonstrating the Lambertsen Amphibious Respirator Unit to Colonel Donovan and a few of his principal staff in the swimming pool at the Shoreham Hotel. Next thing I know, orders came through assigning me to the Office of Strategic Services in command of the OSS Maritime Unit, MU.

"Now I'm in Egypt reporting to you, Colonel," LtJG Taylor said. "I understand the subs USS *Barramundi* and the USS *Bluestreak* are being attached to Raiding Forces for immediate operations in support of OPERATION OVERTHROW, whatever that is. My team, consisting of a Boatswains Mate 1st class and two Coxswains, specialize in operating out of submarines."

Jim asked, "What type of missions?"

LtJG Taylor said, "Beach surveys. Obstacle demolitions ahead of amphibious assaults. Things like that, sir."

Col. Randal said, "So, what is a Frogman, exactly?"

LtJG Taylor said. "Maybe I should give you a demonstration in the pool outside. You'll get the picture, sir."

Col. Randal said. "I can hardly wait."

After LtJG Taylor departed to don his Frogman gear, Jim said, "Colonel, do you ever get the impression we live in an Alice in Wonderland type world?"

"Pretty much sums up the total of my entire military experience," Col. Randal said. "A Frogman orthodontist from Hollywood. What more could you ask for in one day?"

COLONEL JOHN RANDAL, MAJOR THE LADY JANE SEABORN AND JAMES "BALDIE" TAYLOR DROVE to the dock where Brandy Seaborn, Captain Penelope "Legs" Honeycutt-Parker, Vice Admiral Sir Randolph "Razor" Ransom, Lieutenant Randy "Hornblower" Seaborn, Captain Billy Jack Jaxx and three of his SOG operators were preparing for the mission to Crete in the newly arrived PT boat.

The plan was to shove off an hour before dark.

The PT boat was a beauty. Sleek and deadly. Its primary weapons were four Mk XVIII torpedo tubes. There was a twin .50 caliber Browning mounted on the stern. Mounts for four more .30 caliber Lewis guns were located two to a side port and starboard, with a single 20 Oerlikon on the bow. Originally one of four 77-foot Elco PTs built for the Royal Dutch Navy to use off Java after the Japanese invaded the island, the boats had been diverted to Egypt.

Colonel William Donovan had been able to have one assigned to MI-9, which was a joint OSS mission. The U.S. Navy was glad to comply, not caring what the British did with the PT boats. And the Royal Navy had no objection either, as it had little use for torpedo boats in the Mediterranean at this stage of the war. Once again, Raiding Forces was being issued hand-me-down equipment no one else wanted—and was glad to get it.

VAdm. Ransom said, "First opportunity, we shall remove the torpedo tubes. The plan is to load up on light, fast-firing antiaircraft cannon and machine guns. My guess is enemy air will be the biggest threat. We intend to limit risk by operating strictly at night as much as possible but have plenty of firepower on board should air attack ever occur."

"Sounds like a plan, Admiral." Col. Randal said.

"As you know, Colonel," VAdm. Ransom said, "I can get crew from the Royal Navy Patrol Service replacement depot in Alexandria. What is not available are deck officers."

"I'm sure," Col. Randal said, "that makes Brandy and Parker happy."

"I do not like it," VAdm. Ransom said. "However, with the Blitz on, making a high-speed run to Crete and back under cover of darkness is a lot safer than the average citizen having dinner out in a restaurant in London. Or going to church on Sunday, for that matter."

Sub-Lieutenant Bentley St. Ledger drove up in a jeep. Lieutenant Junior Grade Jackson Taylor had his team and their gear piled on board.

Col. Randal said, "Admiral, let me introduce you to a Frogman."

While VAdm. Ransom and LtJG Taylor were talking, Col. Randal pulled Capt. Jaxx aside.

"Change of plans, Jack," Col. Randal said. "I want you to let the OSS Maritime Unit do their stuff. You're an observer tonight. Give me a report when you get back in the morning."

"Yes, sir."

"You brief Lieutenant Taylor about leaving something behind," Col. Randal said. "What was your plan?"

"A canvas compass case with U.S. stenciled on the front, sir."

"That works."

"May run out of ideas, Colonel," Capt. Jaxx said. "We need to coordinate what we leave behind with Sea Squadron and Raiding Forces, Europe. Don't want to use the same item twice—Nazis may be dumb, but they ain't stupid, sir."

"Good point, Captain. I've been worried about duplication. Get with Lady Jane to handle coordination," Col. Randal said. "Keep on thinking like that, Jack."

Lieutenant Mandy Paige arrived in a jeep driven by Lovat Scout Munro

Ferguson, who was pulling duty as her bodyguard today. Col. Randal walked over to speak to her.

Lt. Mandy said, “The meeting with the Big Five is scheduled for 2200 hours tonight in Moe’s office at the Kit-Kat Club. Captain McKoy and Mr. Treywick are en route to Lady Jane’s suite at Mena House. Everyone will assemble there for final coordination at 1930 hours.”

“Great,” Col. Randal said. “Jane and I will head that way as soon as I wrap up here.

“Mandy, at some point tonight we have to talk.”

“Sounds serious, John.”

“It is.”

Two hours later, as the sun was being swallowed up by the desert, Col. Randal, Captain “Geronimo” Joe McKoy and Waldo Treywick were smoking Waldo’s cigars as they sat out by the private pool at Lady Jane’s suite, which was, in fact, a detached bungalow.

The plan was for room service to cater dinner. Then Lt. Mandy would give her briefing. Brigadier Raymond J. Maunsell, who liked to be called “R. J.”, and Major Sammy Sansom would be arriving shortly.

Capt. McKoy said, “We stopped by to visit Colonel Donovan on our way out west. I told him about you swearing me and Waldo into the OSS. He thought that was the funniest thing he’d ever heard.”

Waldo said, “Wild Bill wanted to know if you issued us our secret decoder rings. Turns out there ain’t no OSS oath of enlistment.”

Capt. McKoy said, “Donovan’s got hisself a genuine puzzle palace goin’, John. Hiring mostly educated idiots, like Beverly said. Ain’t nothing but bird watchers, archeologists and professors a’ one kind a’ science or another on the payroll. Lots a’ foreigners too. Wild Bill’s real happy with Raiding Forces. But Special Operations is small change at the Office of Strategic Services—Secret Intelligence is all the rage.”

Col. Randal said, “Why might that be?”

Capt. McKoy said, “Donovan’s playin’ the long game. I’m guessin’ he’s wantin’ to set up a national intelligence service and run it after the war. Secret Intelligence is what counts at OSS and that’s too bad. Cause, MI-6 ain’t never goin' to let him in on a game they got a total monopoly on."

"You're probably right," Col. Randal said. "Tell me about the diamond mine in Arkansas."

Capt. McKoy said, "Well, Billy Jack had all his facts straight. The cheerleader he went out with from Murfreesboro knew what she was talkin' about. There's a thirty-seven-acre diamond mine all right. Accordin' to custom goin' back to the 1840s, the governor's wife wears stones mined out of it, and, according to witnesses I talked to, they are high-grade sparklers.

"The mine is owned by the Arkansas Diamond Company, which is a shell company set up by a buddy of Sir Ernest Oppenheimer, the Chairman of the DeBeers Diamond Company—which is not commonly known locally.

"There's no commercial quarryin' for diamonds at all. The official stated reason bein' that, due to the high wages paid to union labor in the United States, it ain't profitable. That's a lie. What happened was, the engineer who designed the mining equipment intentionally built it so it was too expensive to operate.

"So what they do is let people, meaning locals and tourists—of which there ain't very many in Murfreesboro—come in and do a little surface mining for a daily fee. It's set up sorta like a local park. One in ten people pull out a gemstone diamond, only nobody can dig deeper than four feet—like Jack told us.

"You don't have to be Dick Tracy to know somethin' ain't right with that picture."

"Good report, Captain," Col. Randal said. "How did you manage to find out all those details?"

"I'd met the Sheriff," Capt. McKoy. "He'd provided a little assistance on the bank robbin' couple that Frank Hamer and I eradicated back in the day. Knows everybody and everythin' goin' on in his county. Claims the Arkansas Diamond Company is a crooked deal but it don't pay to ask too many questions."

Waldo said, "Me and Joe went to the mine and done a little diggin'. We didn't find any good rocks but there was a ton a' that industrial diamond gravel. Enough to last a million years. The USA don't need to buy any from

DeBeers; that part's a big whopper."

Col. Randal asked, "Find any real estate you liked in California?"

Capt. McKoy said, "Still givin' it away on the West Coast. Don't make sense. The Japs can't invade California. Try tellin' the locals that."

Waldo said, "The Sons a' Nippon occupied a couple a' islands off Alaska and that's got folks real spooked. Didn't have a whole lotta time this trip but we optioned some stuff around Carmel and the Big Sur. Beautiful country."

Col. Randal said, "I understand you and Rocky are having dinner in one of the Mena House Hotel restaurants, Mr. Treywick. You'd better get a move on. Don't get suited up in your Mr. Big outfit until afterwards. We wouldn't want anyone to see you and be able to identify you later."

Waldo said, "Least of all me."

Col. Randal said, "Captain, would you ask Mandy to step outside, then hang around the door to make sure no one interrupts our conversation."

"I can do that, John."

Lt. Mandy walked out to the pool. "Why is Beverly allowed to attend the Big Five sit-down tonight and not me?"

Col. Randal said, "Beverly has a Texas accent and you don't. You know we want diamond buying to appear to be an American-run OSS operation with the cooperation of MI-6 and R. J.'s SIME. What we don't want is for the Big Five to ascertain your involvement and kill you, Mandy."

Lt. Mandy said, "Is that why you have been so insistent about bodyguards lately?"

"It is."

"The Big Five are known to be vengeful," Lt. Mandy said. "Despicable—possibly the most debased criminals anywhere in the world. You are right, I will cooperate—it pays to take precautions."

Changing the subject, "Col. Randal said. "Mandy, would you say we're friends?"

"Friends!" Lt. Mandy said, "We are a *lot* more than friends."

Col. Randal said, "If I ask you a question, will you tell me the truth, even if you don't want to or feel you shouldn't answer?"

"You know I will," Lt. Mandy said. "As long as it is not about my sex life."

Col. Randal said, "Are you now or do you have plans in the future to work for MI-6?"

"Why do you ask?"

"You didn't answer my question, Mandy."

"I do not now, nor do I have plans to join the Secret Intelligence Service," Lt. Mandy said. "MI-6 prefers not to have female agents working for it. Most women in SIS are merely what are described as 'employees' or 'assets'.

"Besides, I am a Raiding Forces, Royal Marine officer on loan to SIME. I work for you, John, 100%."

Col. Randal said, "Mandy, I'm getting ready to do something everyone, to include certain members of MI-6, have advised me against. So I have to trust you. Can I?"

Lt. Mandy did something completely out of character that caught Col. Randal completely off guard. She teared up. He could not recall ever seeing her cry, even after he shot her horse, Blackie.

"I cannot believe you actually asked me that," Lt. Mandy sobbed. "You do not trust me… after *all* we have been through together."

Col. Randal said, "You have to answer my question."

"You know you can trust me, John," Lt. Mandy said, still sobbing.

"OK," Col. Randal said. "Here's the deal, Mandy. For some reason, your country and mine appear to have conflicting national interests when it comes to diamonds—don't ask me why. Acting on the advice of intelligence officers from the U.S. and U.K., I intend to limit the Need to Know list about plans to interdict diamond smuggling to a handful of non-British personnel and Jane.

"Now, that's a problem when it comes to you, Mandy," Col. Randal said. "I want you in on the operation with me. But I had to ask if you had a conflict of interest."

Lady Jane walked out to the pool to find Lt. Mandy with her arms around Col. Randal's neck. "Are we good?"

Col. Randal said, "We are now."

Lady Jane put her arms around both of them.

Today had been one for the books. And, as had been pointed out, it was not over yet. Col. Randal wished, not for the first time, that he had never heard of industrial diamonds, DeBeers or IDB.

KING DROVE COLONEL JOHN RANDAL AND BEVERLY BLACKWELL TO THE KIT-KAT CLUB IN Major the Lady Jane Seaborn's Rolls-Royce. Officers from all the Allied countries and branches of service, plus wealthy locals, were streaming in the front door. If past experience was any indicator, one or two enemy agents could be expected to be in the crowd. Raucous music blared out every time the doorman opened the heavy front door.

King came around and held the limousine's door while Col. Randal and Beverly stepped out. Col. Randal was wearing his forest green Commando beret, a set of tailored U.S. Army pinks and greens with his highly-polished brown Coracan paratroop boots bloused. Since tonight was pure theater, he was wearing four rows of valor ribbons—having been decorated by the U.S., U.K., France and Abyssinia—parachute wings, and a silver and black Raiding Forces flash on his left shoulder.

Beverly was stunning in a skintight white sheath she had borrowed from Lady Jane—they were the same size. Her role, besides being the Office of Strategic Services representative at the sit-down, was to give the impression she was Col. Randal's mistress. The Big Five appreciated good taste in women.

However, only a very confident person would bring his girlfriend to a high-level meeting of crime lords. Or a fool. Col. Randal was intentionally disrespecting the heads of the five crime major families.

Tonight was men's business. Women were not welcome. Not in a serious sit-down.

The Kit-Kat was pulsating. When they walked in, a Hungarian expatriate was performing an erotic dance that did not seem anatomically possible. More of the crowd turned to stare at Beverly than watched the performer.

Moe, the manager, was waiting. He escorted Col. Randal and Beverly through the maze of tables down a narrow corridor to his office.

By design, they were the last two to arrive.

Waldo Treywick *aka* Mr. Big said, "I'm sure everyone knows Colonel Randal, at least by reputation. Miss Blackwell is a representative of the United States Office of Strategic Services."

Col. Randal and Beverly sat in the two empty chairs that had been purposely saved for them at the big round table, next to Mr. Big. Cigar smoke in the room was so thick it looked like blue fog. None of the Big Five had been expecting the commander of Raiding Forces—a unit known to all present as killers of Germans, Italians, Vichy French, Iraqis, Arabs and anyone else who crossed them—to attend the meeting.

The heads of the crime families did not like surprises. And they did not like being disrespected. However, not one of them—or in fact all five combined—could put an army on the street to rival Raiding Forces, which gave the Big Five something to think about.

No one around the table was smiling. Except Beverly. She draped one very toned arm over Col. Randal's shoulder, with her scarlet nails splayed on his chest. None of the Big Five believed she was there solely as the representative of the Office of Strategic Services.

Mr. Big did not explain the purpose of Col. Randal being at the meeting.

What had been a jovial mood among a group of contented criminals who had been allowed, even encouraged, by British intelligence to eliminate their rivals in the lucrative diamond brokering business had taken a dark turn. Col. Randal was a wild card. The Big Five did not like uncertainty.

Mr. Big said, "Now that everyone is present, time for business, gentlemen—diamonds. You've got 'em. I want 'em."

None of the crime bosses understood exactly what that meant. However, no one present had any objection to establishing a new buyer. Now, with the low-level competition wiped out, they had a lot more diamonds to sell. Possibly, prices might increase.

Another big buyer sounded attractive.

Mr. Treywick dropped the bomb. "Effective immediately, starting tonight, you will only sell your diamonds to me. My appraiser will evaluate each stone and I'll pay a reasonable price per karat. For industrial diamonds, I buy by the pound. For both, and I set the price."

The five crime bosses went pale. Brigadier Raymond J. "R. J." Maunsell stared off into space. Major Sammy Sansom stroked his toothbrush mustache. Mr. Big touched up his cigar with the flame from a solid gold Dunhill lighter.

Beverly removed her arm from Col. Randal's right shoulder.

The Egyptian called "The Cobra"—because he liked to poison his enemies and watch them die, even sometimes filming it—asked, "What if we choose not to sell our diamonds exclusively through you, Mr. Big?"

Col. Randal produced one of his Colt .38 Supers and shot him through the heart. *BLAAAAAM!*

The room was soundproofed, which meant no one outside could hear the gunshot. However, the soundproofing, which consisted of thick, red leather padding on the walls and low ceiling, only served to make the handgun sound even louder going off inside Moe's office. The Cobra was blown out of his chair. He lay on the floor dead.

Everyone sat there in shock, ears ringing.

Col. Randal had violated the most cardinal rule of Big Five sit-downs—no violence during a conference. Beyond any question now he was a rogue player.

Everything changed in an instant.

A new enforcer was in town, and there was nothing the crime bosses could do about it. Lined up against them was the combined weight of the United States and Great Britain's intelligence services, Special Forces and Cairo's Security Police. No one knew what rules they played by—if any.

Mr. Big said, "Questions?"

In the limo on the way back to Mena House Hotel, Beverly said, "John, you are the worst negotiator."

"With criminals like the Big Five, you can go a long way with a pistol and a smile," Col. Randal said. "But you can do pretty well with just the pistol."

"Daddy's going to love this story."

14
MR. BIG, ET AL

COLONEL JOHN RANDAL, MAJOR THE LADY JANE SEABORN, CAPTAIN "GERONIMO" JOE MCKOY, Captain Billy Jack Jaxx, Lieutenant Mandy Paige and Beverly Blackwell were in Lady Jane's Rolls-Royce, driving to an address located in the exclusive heart of Cairo that Col. Randal provided King. The car was followed by Master Sergeant Mack Beckwith and the two Ranger bodyguards, Privates Clooney and Bannon.

"The Big Four," Capt. McKoy said, "doesn't have the same snap as the Big Five."

"Where are you taking us, John?" Lady Jane asked.

Col. Randal said, "It's a surprise."

Beverly said, "I know where we're going."

Lt. Mandy said, "Me too."

Col. Randal said, "Give me a report, Jack."

"Brandy shoved off right on schedule, sir," Capt. Jaxx said. "The new PT boat can fly. Felt like we were shot out of a cannon. Admiral Ransom said that after the torpedo tubes and some of the other gear is removed it will pick up a few more knots.

"Legs Parker's probably the best navigator in Raiding Forces, Colonel. We hit the beach right on the money—only we never actually saw it. We hove to a mile off shore. Lieutenant Taylor and one of his coxswains were standing by in their rubber Frogman suits and immediately went into the water.

"Two hours later, they were back. We pulled them on board and hightailed it for home. Nothing much to report, sir. The swimmers were underwater the whole time except for when they crawled up on the beach."

"You think there's anything to the Frogman concept?" Col. Randal asked.

"I don't want to be one," Capt. Jaxx said, "but yes, sir, once we figure out the best way to use 'em, the Frogs are definitely going to be an asset. Lieutenant Taylor said last night's mission was easier than what they routinely practiced in training."

"If the Frogman thing doesn't work out," Beverly said, "Jackson can still do our teeth."

Lady Jane asked, "How did Brandy like the PT boat?"

"Love at first sight," Capt. Jaxx said. "She ordered me to hurry up and find more beaches to recon. And when we got back, she told Mrs. Paige to crank up her MI-9 rescue missions."

Col. Randal said, "Still no word on crew for the boat?"

Capt. Jaxx said, "Brandy, the Admiral, and Randy are en route to Alexandria to visit the Royal Navy Patrol Service Depot as we speak, sir. They intend to be back tomorrow with a full complement. Brandy wants to start sea trials immediately."

Lt. Mandy said, "I want to go on one of her missions."

"Negative," Col. Randal said. "Now would be the time, Beverly."

"John, you are no fun," Lt. Mandy said.

"Close your eyes, Lady Jane," Beverly said, taking a black silk scarf out of her handbag. "I'm going to blindfold you."

Lady Jane laughed, "Do I get a last cigarette?"

King turned into a long, private drive at the end of a cul-de-sac.

Beverly said, "Now, John?"

"Do it."

When the blindfold came off, Lady Jane saw a sprawling, three-story, walled mansion inside a high-walled, gated compound of an architecture style that could be best described as Taj Mahal. It was surrounded by a platoon of field security police. Major Sammy Sansom was standing by the front gate.

He was waiting for them.

Lady Jane said, "Why are we here?"

Col. Randal said, "Will this do for OSS Headquarters? I understand there's over thirty thousand square feet."

"Oh, yes," Lady Jane said. "Perfect. How did you discover it, John? There is not a stick of space available for lease anywhere in the city."

"Just came on the market," Col. Randal said.

Beverly said, "The previous occupant doesn't need it anymore."

Lady Jane asked, "Who does this property belong to?

"Waldo is the owner of record," Col. Randal said. "Captain McKoy's his silent partner."

Capt. McKoy said, "The deed says 'Mr. Big, et al'."

As they were getting out of the limousine, Lady Jane said, "Is this the residence of the criminal overlord...."

Maj. Sansom said, "I called from the club last night and ordered my men to secure the estate before our meeting broke up at the Kit-Kat. By the time they arrived, the house was already being abandoned. A team swept the place this morning after first light to make sure it was empty. Other than one poor soul found imprisoned in a cell in the basement, no one was here."

Beverly asked, "Where did everyone go?"

"Being a family member of a major crime family has its highs and lows," Capt. McKoy said. "When the head man gets hisself killed, that's a low."

Maj. Sansom said, "As a professional courtesy for services rendered—reporting enemy agents operating in Cairo, etc.—before the bulk of my police detail could arrive, I had a car deliver the news to the guards stationed at the front gate that their boss was dead. The security people simply abandoned their posts and fled into the night as fast as they could.

"My men said the family members inside had vacated the house within ten minutes after they arrived. Everyone escaped on foot. We did not allow any vehicles to depart the compound and we did not allow any luggage or handbags to leave the premises. They got out with only the clothes on their backs.

"Everyone was strip-searched."

Beverly said, "I don't understand."

Maj. Sansom said, "The four surviving crime bosses were dividing up the spoils of their deceased associate's empire before you and Colonel Randal pulled away from the curb at the Kit Kat last night. The instant a crime lord shows any sign of weakness or dies, the others turn on him. . . and that includes his family. A desperate life living on the run and always looking over their shoulder awaits any member of the Cobra's clan who manages to survive the blood purge to come. The Cobra's family can never return to Cairo or reside in any major city in the Middle East without risking a horrible death.

"I shall forego the details."

Beverly said, "Wow!"

Lt. Mandy said, "Middle Eastern crime bosses are animals, Beverly."

Lady Jane said, "How does this work, Major?"

"Mr. Treywick and Captain McKoy own the real estate," Maj. Sansom said. "The Brigadier said you inherit everything inside the walls of the compound that is not classified as real property—free to dispose of it as you wish, Lady Seaborn. My understanding is the Office of Strategic Services will be occupying the building at some later date.

"Until such time as OSS arrives, my field security police shall provide constant around-the-clock protection."

Beverly asked, "What's real property?"

Maj. Sansom said, "Anything attached to the structure. For example, Lady Seaborn owns the curtains, but Mr. Treywick and Captain McKoy own the curtain rods bolted to the wall."

Capt. McKoy said, "We got us a real good deal—ten dollars and other valuable consideration."

Lt. Mandy said, "Reminds me of the Iraqi general's suite in the basement of the RAF Habbaniya Bachelor Officers Quarters. . . only about twenty-five times larger. Wonder what is hidden inside?"

Lady Jane said, "Let's go find out."

JAMES "BALDIE" TAYLOR ARRIVED FROM EIGHTH ARMY HEADQUARTERS. HE AND COLONEL John Randal were sitting in an empty living room on the ground floor in what was being called "the Palace" by Major the Lady Jane Seaborn and her entourage. The interior of the late Cobra's mansion was decorated in Hollywood-meets-King Tut, art deco design. Jim was briefing Col. Randal on the upcoming Eighth Army offensive OPERATION LIGHTFOOT. While he talked, a preliminary search was in progress for hidden and not-so-hidden treasure.

There was a lot being found.

The Cobra had enjoyed a lavish lifestyle. Money had clearly been no object. Spectacular was the best description of his residence.

Most likely, the gangster did not employ the services of any of the Cairo banks. In his line of work, it paid to be liquid. The question was, where had he kept his money?

Jim said, "General Montgomery is an unknown quantity. He is not part of the landed gentry or upper-class elite military establishment. The man spent most of his military career serving in lackluster regiments, having to live off his army pay. He was not first choice for command of Eighth Army.

"However, he distinguished himself in France in the last war, did as well as anyone during the debacle with the British Expeditionary Force coming out through Dunkirk commanding a division. The general is known as an exceptional planner, obsessive organizer and demanding trainer of men. It remains to be seen how well he will perform commanding an army.

"Most officers I have spoken with find the man insufferable. Montgomery has a tin ear and apparently does not realize when he is offending someone."

Col. Randal said, "Command's not a popularity contest."

Jim said, "I am merely providing background, Colonel. Some of which I know you have heard before. The well-loved, highly respected, upper class commanders we have enjoyed in the Middle East thus far have all suffered indignities at the hands of the vaunted Desert Fox."

Col. Randal said, "That is a fact."

Jim said, "Monty, as he likes to be called, is a weird duck. He tried wearing an Australian sundowner's hat with regimental badges pinned all over it.

Looked like a silly tourist. When he went to visit the Royal Tank Regiment, as he was climbing into a Lend Lease Grant tank to inspect it, one of the tankers loaned him his black tankers beret because he was concerned the General's hat would be knocked off in the tight quarters inside. Now, General Montgomery has adopted that man's black beret with the RTR regimental badge as his personal trademark.

"Never takes it off—troops seem to take to him immediately."

Col. Randal said, "What does Eighth Army expect of Raiding Forces?"

"I spoke with General Montgomery," Jim said. "When the balloon goes up, he does not want anything different—only more of it."

Col. Randal said, "Raiding Regiment has been patrolling with no break since before Rommel pulled up short at Alamein. We have plenty of jeeps. But we peaked on manpower a month ago. You can't keep running the kind of long-range missions we do without losses, and there are no replacements.

"Sea Squadron has been mining the Via Balbia nightly. Randy's boats are constantly out on blockade duty, trying to prevent fuel from reaching Panzerarmee Afrika by sea. Dudley Clarke has requested Raiding Forces to execute a long list of deception targets to cover the TORCH landings. Air Marshal Tedder wants me to ramp BOMBSHELL back up to take out enemy pilots. And OSS wants to put a stop to illicit diamond buying.

"So, General, how do you propose for me to step up the pace?"

Jim said, "'Geronimo' Joe told me a story about a smuggler he arrested for running guns. The judge sentenced him to twenty years in the Arizona State Penitentiary. The gun runner said, 'Your Honor, I'm eighty-three years old. I don't think I can make it.'

"The judge said, 'Do the best you can'."

Col. Randal said, "That's very helpful, General."

Captain Roy Kidd arrived. He had been flown in from Oasis X on Col. Randal's orders. As he came in, Jim strolled up a double-wide spiral staircase to inspect the wonders of the rest of the mansion.

"What is this place, sir?"

"It will be OSS Headquarters once Colonel Donovan sends someone to take possession," Col. Randal said. "Used to be a gangster's house."

"Pretty incredible."

Col. Randal said. "Roy, you're headed back to the *King Duck* to take command of Duck Patrol again."

Capt. Kidd said, "Yes, sir."

He did not sound happy about it. Capt. Kidd liked plinking trucks from long range with a scoped Boys .55 caliber antitank rifle.

"I need Sergeant Major Mikkalis for another assignment," Col. Randal said. "Once OPERATION LIGHTFOOT kicks off, I don't think sniping trucks is going to have the same high priority."

"Understood, sir."

Col. Randal said. "There's another reason, Roy. I need to keep you close by. Raiding Forces has a classified mission that can only be entrusted to U.S. personnel. I'm putting together a small team. You'll be part of it at the appropriate time."

Capt. Kidd said, "Like the sound of that, sir."

Col. Randal said, "Once the fireworks from LIGHTFOOT and another operation called TORCH settle down, we're going to be going after diamond smugglers all over Africa."

"Diamonds?"

"I'll explain later," Col. Randal said. "Right now, you'd better double time on up to the third floor. Captains McKoy and Jaxx are in the gun room, making an inventory of the weapons in the previous owner's massive collection. Pick out what you want. Make sure to get a battery of best grade English sporting rifles for after the war."

"Yes, sir!"

Master Sergeant Mack Beckwith marched in, "Brigadier Maunsell is outside, sir."

"I'll go talk to him," Col. Randal said. "You better shove off with Captain Kidd. He's headed to the gun room. Find anything you like, it's yours.

"Thanks, Colonel."

Col. Randal said, "When you're finished, I want you to go to the docks. Spread the word to the 575th Parachute Infantry Regiment—people who failed the Blood in the Sand selection course, we'll be holding another one. You think any of the men will be interested?"

MSgt. Beckwith said, "I'll be surprised if they're not, sir. Working as stevedores in this Egyptian heat is pure murder."

"Good."

Col. Randal walked out the front door. A locksmith was changing the lock. Brigadier Raymond J. "R. J." Maunsell was standing on the lawn, talking to a Royal Engineer lieutenant in charge of a small party of troops. The engineers were armed with equipment he had never seen before—hand-held mine detectors.

"Borrowed from Eighth Army," R. J. explained. "Five hundred units were flown out from the U.K. for LIGHTFOOT. Remains to be seen how well they shall work finding landmines, but they should be quite helpful locating anything buried inside the compound.

"General Montgomery did not want to loan out even the pair," R. J. said. "However, after I explained to General Alexander why I needed them, he ordered the general to release them immediately."

"What are you sweeping for," Col. Randal asked, "exactly?"

"Anything the Cobra may have buried on the grounds," R. J. said. "This is Lieutenant McDonald, he will flag anything he gets a hit on for you. Excavate the target at your convenience.

"Explain to Colonel Randal how the detectors work, Lieutenant."

"What we have is the Polish Mine Detector, sir," Lt. McDonald said. "Also known as the Mine Detector Mk 1. Before the war, the Department of Artillery of Poland's Ministry of Defense put out a request for proposal to develop a device that could locate dud rounds on artillery training ranges. The design by AVA *Wytwornia Radiotechniczna* was accepted. Unfortunately, before the devices could be manufactured, the Germans invaded. When the Polish Army's General Headquarters displaced to the U.K., the project was restarted—but this time as a land mine detector.

"The Mk1 has two coils. One is connected to an oscillator, which generates an oscillating current to an acoustic frequency. The other coil is connected to an amplifier and a headphone. When the coils come into proximity of a metallic object, the headphones report the signal with a high-frequency screech."

"I see," Col. Randal said. Which meant he did not have a clue what the Royal Engineer was talking about.

R. J. said, "Like crates containing gold."

Col. Randal said, "Got it."

Leaving the engineers to their work, he went back inside. Lady Jane was in the living room, hanging up the phone.

"I called the Cairo Museum to ask if they could recommend an art appraiser. OSS gets to lease the building, but they are not about to have the furniture and artwork.

"I called Parker to come help sort things out."

"What's the plan?"

"We shall sell the fine art," Lady Jane said. "Not my taste. How about you, John?"

"My idea of fine art is old movie posters."

"Captain McKoy said he and Waldo might like to have the furniture and the large mirrors for the houses on the ranches they bought." Lady Jane laughed. "Cairo in the Wild West.

"He wants me to be their interior decorator."

Col. Randal said, "Jane, you need to search behind each painting, every mirror, any wall covering. There should be hidden safes and possibly even hidden rooms. That's what we discovered at Habbaniya."

Lady Jane said, "Jim says the Big Five would hire contractors. Then, when the workers finished, kill them so they could never reveal to anyone what they built. He has people on the way here to start inspecting the walls and crawlspaces."

Col. Randal said, "You've got a big project."

Lady Jane laughed, "We are having great fun."

Captain Pamala Plum-Martin and Captain Stephanie Fawcett-Tatum arrived.

COLONEL JOHN RANDAL WAS IN ONE OF THE LIVING ROOMS ON THE GROUND FLOOR OF THE late Cobra's mansion. He was reading a document Phantom received that morning from Colonel William Donovan stamped: OFFICE OF STRATEGIC SERVICES. Captain Penelope "Legs" Honeycutt-Parker had brought it with her when she drove in from RFHQ.

Capt. Honeycutt-Parker said, "I understand you bought this house, John."

Col. Randal said, "That would be Captain McKoy and Waldo."

"You negotiated the purchase?"

Col. Randal said, "How'd the mission go last night?"

"A breeze," Capt. Honeycutt-Parker said. "The PT boat is a dream, a pleasant surprise considering the U.S. Navy only sends us prototypes that fail their sea trials. Brandy and her father are fighting over armament."

"About what?"

"Brandy wants rapid firing 40mm cannon fore and aft. The Razor vetoed that idea in favor of something the U.S. Navy shipped with the PT boats but did not have time to install—a pair of NH 96505, Elco 20mm Quadruple Gun Mounts."

"Eight 20mms per mount," Col. Randal said. "That's a lot of concentrated firepower."

"Admiral Ransom is of the opinion they should discourage low-level air attack. High-level bombers will be wasting their time trying to hit us in a nimble PT," Capt. Honeycutt-Parker said.

"Do you believe we shall find hidden treasure here like we did in the BOQ at RAF Habbaniya?"

"I do," Col. Randal said. "You and Mandy know the drill."

While Capt. Honeycutt-Parker went in search of Lady Jane, Col. Randal resumed his reading. The title of the OSS document was WORLD PRODUCTION AND TRADE IN INDUSTRIAL DIAMONDS 1942.

It was stamped SECRET.

Following typical military and intelligence protocol, the SUMMARY came first so the reader would know what to look for while reading the document. . . or maybe decide to skip the rest.

Industrial diamonds have become increasingly essential to mass production. The greatest demand for diamonds is in the manufacture of war material. Since the principal source is limited largely to areas in Africa, far removed from the U.S., industrial diamonds are of particular strategic importance to the prosecution of the war. Annual U.S. requirements are between 4 ½ and 5 million carats, or about one-half of the total world output.

The U.S., because of its highly mechanized industry, would be particularly affected by any interruption in the supply of industrial diamonds. The production and sale of industrial diamonds are largely controlled by the West, but the location of most of the African diamond-producing areas makes them strategically vulnerable.

Diamonds, because of their hardness, which is greater than that of any other natural or artificial substance, are the most important gemstones used in modern industry, and they have become essential in the development of precision machinery. Without diamond abrasive wheels and other diamond tools, the mass production of machine tools and precision instruments would be impossible.

The small size and light weight of diamonds are out of all proportion to their strategic importance but also make it very difficult to control their shipment. For example, the total world output of all types of diamonds in 1940 weighed only slightly more than 3 short tons. A quarter of a million carats of industrial stones thus weigh about 125 pounds. The weight limit in the diplomatic pouch is usually about 100 pounds, and therefore the quantity of industrial diamonds that could be shipped by diplomatic pouch assumes considerable importance. . .

Captain "Geronimo" Joe McKoy wandered into the living room, "You better come on up and check out the guns, John."

"Here," Col. Randal said, handing him the OSS document. "Take a look at this."

Capt. McKoy squinted at the report. When he finished reading he said, "Sounds like shuttin' down diamond smuggling is gonna be like tryin' to herd cats.

"I'm beginnin' to have some thoughts."

Col. Randal said, "I wish I'd never heard of IDB or industrial diamond smuggling."

"Now, John," Capt. McKoy said, "don't go lettin' them problems with Cuthbert Bowlby throw you."

Col. Randal said, "Nearly fractured Raiding Forces—still might."

"Naw," Capt. McKoy said. "All ol' Cuthbert did was what MI-6 always does and that's they don't have much use for women. I've got it on good authority Colonel Menzies, 'C'—he's a closet womanizer. But the word is, C don't have very good taste in his choice a' ladies, which has resulted in a lack a' respect for women, the man thinkin' they're all the same.

"What it was, as a result of the MI-6 culture, Cuthbert figured Lady Jane would do whatever he said, no problema. Nobody in the Secret Intelligence Service saw her reaction comin', which gives you somethin' to cogitate on when it comes to analyzin' SIS's predictive ability."

Col. Randal said, "Good point."

Capt. McKoy said, "Now, back in the day when you and Zorro was a-chasin' women, you two boys was runnin' 'em pretty hard. But then Lady Jane come along and—*boom*—you realized why eat hamburger when you can have steak?

"Get my drift?"

"Not exactly."

"Look at it this way. A lot a' the things we do, they ain't exactly concrete," Capt. McKoy said. "But we do 'em anyway, all them deceptions. This diamond business, it's the *real* deal in black and white, with an exclamation point tacked on at the end—strategic.

"Ain't gonna be any 'fracture' in Raiding Forces. You know when to fish or cut bait."

Col. Randal said, "Which one are we doing?"

"Fishing," Capt. McKoy said. "Let somebody else cut the bait."

Major the Lady Jane Seaborn appeared at the door of the living room. "John, I would like a word with you."

Col. Randal stood up and the two walked out in the hall.

"What's going on?"

"You need to come up to the gun room," Lady Jane said.

Col. Randal said, "Captain McKoy came down to get me."

Lady Jane said, "Inspect all the guns in the collection, but whatever you do—on no account—select a pocket pistol for yourself."

"I see," Col. Randal said. Which meant he had no idea what she was talking about.

Lady Jane said. "Beverly is upstairs having a panic attack."

Col. Randal said, "Why would she do that?"

Lady Jane said, "Beverly wanted to give you a Christmas present. She made a great effort to find you the appropriate gift—not easy. You are a hard man to buy a gift for.

"I explained to Beverly we do not give Christmas or birthday presents in Raiding Forces, but we do gift each other from time to time."

Col. Randal said, "So, what does that have to do with pocket pistols?"

Lady Jane said, "Make a point not to take one."

Col. Randal said, "I can do that."

Capt. McKoy, Lady Jane and Col. Randal walked up the sweeping spiral staircase to the gun room. Lieutenant Mandy Paige and Beverly were talking to Captain Stephanie Fawcett-Tatum outside in the hallway. Captain Billy Jack Jaxx, Captain Roy Kidd and Master Sergeant Mack Beckwith were inside inspecting the weapons, having taken over the task of cataloging them.

Col. Randal said, "Beverly, you and Stephanie help me pick out a couple of handguns."

Capt. Jaxx said, "More privately owned firearms in this room than I've ever seen in one place, sir. A lot of 'em are antiques. There's a ton of Super

Grade shotguns from the finest gunmakers in the world. A lot of purpose-built big game rifles—mostly large bore doubles."

Col. Randal said, "I'm interested in pocket pistols."

Lady Jane gave him a glare that would have melted the frontal armor of a Panzer Mk III.

Capt. Kidd said, "You'll find those in the glass-topped table over there, sir. Extensive selection to choose from."

Col. Randal, Capt. Fawcett-Tatum and Beverly walked over to the display. Over fifty small handguns from a dozen different countries of manufacture were encased in the glass box. Most of the little pistols were heavily engraved; some had gold inlays of animals, birds or nude women; and they all sported handgrips made of ivory, pearl or some other exotic material.

Col. Randal said, "Stephanie, you need a small pistol to carry in your purse. Pick out a pretty one."

"Thank you, John."

"Beverly," Col. Randal said. "If you see something your father doesn't have in his collection, let's send it to him."

Beverly said, "Daddy will love that."

Col. Randal glanced at Lady Jane and was rewarded with one of her Super Grade heart attack smiles, which was dangerous—standard issue were lethal enough.

While the two women were studying the collection of pocket pistols, Col. Randal walked back to where Lt. Mandy was standing with Lady Jane. He slipped her the OSS report. "Go find a quiet spot and read this. I want your impression when you're finished."

Lady Jane looked at him.

"Intel on IDB," Col. Randal said, "I'll go over it with you later tonight when we can take our time."

Capt. McKoy strolled over, "The late Mr. Cobra was a pure-dee gun nut. He had hisself just about one a' everythin' but it's mostly top a' the line European make. The man was a little short on American hardware, but he had some real interestin' stuff from our frontier days."

Lady Jane said, "What do you recommend we do with the collection, Captain?"

"Well, I'm thinkin' we'll crate up everythin' that might be of interest to anyone in Raiding Forces or that we can use for tradin' with rear echelon units that has gear we need. Maybe the navy too—Admiral Ransom likely'll have some thoughts," Captain McKoy said.

"Then, we'll put out feelers to find out which of the unit commanders who might be useful to Raiding Forces likes guns or hunts. We'll present each of 'em with a firearm from us to them with no strings attached, but of course there will be."

Col. Randal said, "I like it."

Capt. McKoy said, "The antique weapons, we probably need to get us an appraiser in here to take a look like you're plannin' on doin' with the paintin's. Major Sansom's family is in the insurance business all over the Middle East. Mandy can probably get him to find us somebody knows guns. I ain't exactly up to snuff on the value a' fifteenth-century wheel locks and the like. Once we know the numbers, we'll throw ourselves an auction."

"Perfect," Lady Jane said. "John, you should shoot a major crime lord more often."

Col. Randal said, "We need the four that're left."

Capt. McKoy said, "I spotted somethin' you might be interested in for yourself, John. I know you ain't a collector, but you oughta take a look."

The two walked over to one of the glass showcases. In it was a display of handguns from the American West, .45 Colts, Smith & Wesson No. 3s, .44 Russians, Remington 44–40s, Merwin & Hulbert Pocket Army .44s. . .

"I remember you told me one time," Capt. McKoy said, "you grew up shootin' a Colt 38–40. Well, there ain't one a' those and we couldn't find any ammo for it if there was, but layin' right there's a brand-new, unfired, ivory-stocked four and three-quarter-inch .45 Long Colt Peacemaker with a interchangeable .45 ACP cylinder. Lots a' .45 ACP around.

"Thought you might like to have you a single action to do a little target practice with, John."

"I would," Col. Randal said. "You can teach me how to twirl it like you do in your Wild West shows."

"Get Beverly to," Capt. McKoy said. "She's probably better at it than I am. Word is she's been givin' you a run for your money shootin' skeet."

"That is a fact."

Walking out of the gun room, Col. Randal went in search of Lt. Mandy and found her down the hall in one of the mansion's countless living areas. She was all alone, reading the intel report. He sat down next to her on the couch and waited until she finished.

Col. Randal said, "What do you think?"

Lt. Mandy said, "We are never going to be able to stop diamond smuggling."

Col. Randal said, "That's my take too."

Lt. Mandy said, "Allowing me to read this intelligence assessment makes me feel like you trust me again. When I cried last night, it was because you hurt my feelings."

"I know," Col. Randal said. "You didn't even cry when I shot Blackie."

Lt. Mandy said, "I was unconscious at the time."

Beverly came into the room, "Are you two making out in here?"

Col. Randal said, "Read this, Miss OSS."

Beverly took the file.

Col. Randal said, "Just the summary."

Beverly sat down on the couch. When she finished, the blond Texas girl looked up. "Interesting."

Col. Randal said, "What's your thought?"

"No one's telling us the whole story."

"And why might that be?"

Beverly said, "Because preventing diamond smuggling doesn't have anything to do with diamonds?"

Col. Randal said, "Could be."

15
GERMAN TANK PROBLEM

COLONEL JOHN RANDAL WAS SITTING AT A TABLE IN THE MESS HALL AT RFHQ TALKING TO Sergeant Major Mike "March or Die" Mikkalis and Master Sergeant Mack Beckwith. The room was pretty much empty, the evening meal having been over for about an hour.

Col. Randal asked, "How many of the 575th men on the docks are interested in re-testing Blood in the Sand?"

MSgt. Beckwith said, "Out of the one hundred twenty-three men who did not pass, only nine of 'em are not interested in trying again, sir."

"No kidding?"

"Tough duty being a stevedore," MSgt. Beckwith said. "Manhandling crates on and off ships, stacking 'em on the dock or working down in the holds in this heat, sir. Those paratroopers are in the best shape of their lives right now. Probably drink too much nights—get in bar fights.

"Willing to do nearly anything to get off those docks, sir."

Col. Randal said, "Eighth Army is going to launch OPERATION LIGHTFOOT any day. When that happens, Raiding Regiment will have to keep all its patrols in the field all the time. Going to take even more casualties. We need a source of replacements.

"Do you two men think you can conduct a shortened version of Blood in the Sand, in say. . . a week?"

Sgt. Maj. Mikkalis asked, "The idea is to get as many men qualified as possible, sir?"

"Affirmative," Col. Randal said. "We won't organize patrols. The men who meet your standards will be stationed at Oasis X as a manpower pool. Sir Terry can use 'em where needed.

"In that case, Colonel," Sgt. Maj. Mikkalis said, "four days are enough."

Considering his nickname—"March or Die" came from service in the French Foreign Legion—Col. Randal thought those four days could be rough. "Do it. ASAP."

"Yes, sir!"

Col. Randal asked, "Anything you need?"

Sgt. Maj. Mikkalis said, "Could we have Mad Dog come down and help to run the re-test, sir?"

Col. Randal thought, "Uh-oh!"

"I'll have Captain Reupart flown in tonight," Col. Randal said. "Try not to kill anybody."

The looks the two tough-as-nails sergeants gave him were not reassuring.

Col. Randal walked upstairs to the third-floor suite. King was on duty at the security desk on the landing outside the door. The Merc said, "Lady Seaborn gave me strict orders that no one was to be allowed inside, Chief."

"Really?"

"She said that included me," King said. "No mention of you."

"Who's in there?"

"Mandy and Beverly."

Col. Randal said, "Why don't you ring the room and ask."

King picked up the phone, dialed and spoke into the hand piece. "Lady Seaborn says you have permission to enter, but no one else."

Col. Randal said, "What do you think they're doing in there?"

"No idea, Chief."

Col. Randal opened the door to the suite and walked inside. Lady Jane, Lt. Mandy and Beverly were all sitting on the floor with glossy magazines spread out everywhere. There were other boxes of magazines stacked up.

Lady Jane had a yellow legal pad with notes scribbled on it.

"What's going on?"

"Research," Lady Jane said. "We were planning to do it at Oasis X but since we never seem to get there..."

"Here's one," Beverly said excitedly. She handed the magazine she was flipping through to Lady Jane. There was a photograph of the Queen of England at a reception.

"What is the date on the magazine?"

"August 1938."

Lady Jane jotted the information down on her legal pad.

"What kind of research?" Col. Randal asked.

Lady Jane said, "The Queen wears diamond jewelry almost exclusively. As I recall, that was not always the case. What we are trying to establish is *when* Her Royal Highness began her love affair with diamonds."

Col. Randal said, "And what will that tell you?"

"Maybe nothing," Lady Jane said. "According to all those MI-6 classes I took, intelligence is like putting a puzzle together. The only difference is, one never knows if all the pieces fit or if you will have a picture that means anything when you get through."

Col. Randal said, "You must have some idea where you're going with this."

Lt. Mandy said, "We want to know if DeBeers is bribing the Royal Family."

"So, what do you think?"

"What we *know* is," Lady Jane said, "shortly after the coronation in 1937, the Queen virtually stopped wearing emeralds, rubies, sapphires or any other precious stones. Most likely we shall not be able to discover the reason why.

"You can never tell anyone we are doing this, John—ever!"

Col. Randal sat down on the floor, "Give me some magazines."

RECENTLY-PROMOTED BRIGADIER GENERAL WILLIAM "WILD BILL" DONOVAN, WHO BORE A striking resemblance to the actor James Cagney, flew in to Cairo the next morning. He was there to check out the new Cairo Office of Strategic Services, Secret Intelligence Headquarters, and to make a tour of Raiding Forces, Middle East. Wild Bill was a man of action. He liked to see things for himself.

There was very little advance notice of his arrival. The last thing BG Donovan wanted was a canned dog and pony show. His idea was to observe Raiding Forces' normal day-to-day operations and make his own assessment.

Major the Lady Jane Seaborn and Beverly met BG Donovan at the Pan American sea plane terminal. Colonel John Randal had flown out the night before for Oasis X, unaware the general was en route to Egypt. Drop-in inspections have their drawbacks as well as their advantages.

The first thing BG Donovan did, right in the terminal, was to award Beverly a Silver Star for her mission to destroy the tanker bringing fuel to Panzerarmee Afrika. The little ceremony caused a stir among the crowd of high-ranking VIP passengers deplaning or waiting to board. Wild Bill could be a bit of a showman.

Beverly was shocked.

BG Donovan said, "Air Marshal Tedder has authorized me to inform you, Beverly, he will be presenting you the Royal Air Force Distinguished Flying Cross at a later date as soon as we can figure out how to award you some branch of military pilot's wings first. My good friend, your father, is going to be most impressed when he hears the news."

Lady Jane said, "We only received notice you were arriving this morning, General. Unfortunately, John departed for our secret forward-operating base, Oasis X, last night."

BG Donovan said, "Can you contact him?"

"We can."

"Inform the Colonel I shall be taking a tour of the new OSS facility, then I want to fly to Oasis X and accompany one of the Raiding Regiment's patrols."

Lady Jane said, "I notified John the moment we learned you would be landing today. He suggested you might like to observe the 'Death in the Sand' test for aspiring candidates for Raiding Forces, then inspect our Sea Squadron. Major Corrigan, the commander, is en route to escort you to Alexandria where the squadron bases."

BG Donovan said, "Outstanding! I would dearly love the opportunity to see your selection process. Sea Squadron is at the top of my list of things to see and do, as well."

Lady Jane did not mention that Col. Randal had instructed her to order Major Taylor Corrigan not to allow BG Donovan to go ashore with Duck Patrol. If Wild Bill insisted, then Captain Roy Kidd was to find some nice, quiet, isolated stretch of the Via Balbia and let him participate in a much abbreviated mission to mine the road in relative safety.

King drove them to "the Palace." BG Donovan loved the nickname. "OSS will have to make arrangements for office furniture," Lady Jane said. "Beverly and I shall be glad to assist in acquiring what you need as soon as you have someone provide us a list."

When they arrived inside the walled compound, BG Donovan was thunderstruck by the Palace. "Outstanding! Exactly the statement OSS wants to make. Who owns this place and how much is it going to cost?"

Lady Jane said, "Captain McKoy and Mr. Treywick, whom I believe you met when they were passing through Washington recently, are the owners of record. The rent will be based on the current market rate, General."

"What a pair," BG Donovan said. "An old Arizona Ranger and a legendary African scout from the last war. How in the world did they come to acquire this magnificent piece of real estate?"

Beverly said, "Originally it was the private residence of one of the five Middle Eastern crime lords. There are only four now."

"What happened to number five?"

"John shot him."

"Why?"

"We were in a meeting explaining how OSS intended to corner the diamond market and the crook asked too many questions."

"How many was too many?"

"One," Beverly said.

BG Donovan said, "I want to hear the story from start to finish. Sounds like you have been getting around, young lady."

Lady Jane said, "You have no idea, General."

SOMEWHERE OFF THE COAST OF EASTERN EGYPT

THE MAS BOAT COMMANDED BY LIEUTENANT RANDY "HORNBLOWER" SEABORN POUNDED toward a rendezvous with the Landing Craft Tank *King Duck.* Brigadier General William "Wild Bill" Donovan was standing next to him on the bridge of the captured Italian motor torpedo boat. He was having the time of his life.

"Originally there were three of these Italian torpedo boats in a covered dock up a river off the Red Sea, sir," Lt. Seaborn said. "Colonel Randal discovered them. When we went back to retrieve them several months later, the roof had fallen in and one was damaged beyond repair. Our squadron consists of the two surviving MAS boats and the two PT boats you provided us.

"The last seventy-seven-foot Elco you arranged for Raiding Forces has been requisitioned by MI-9, sir."

BG Donovan said, "Mrs. Paige briefed me on Escape. I understand your mother is the skipper of the PT? A bit unorthodox."

"Yes, sir," Lt. Seaborn said. "There was no one else available, General."

BG Donovan said, "I understand Brandy is a highly experienced speed boat racer. Special Operations Executive uses women in all capacities—parachutes them into Enemy Occupied France as undercover agents, radio operators and the like. I intend to follow the same policy in OSS. Total war. Can't see any reason MI-9 should *not* have a PT boat captained by a qualified woman.

"Pretty hard to say no to your Mom, huh, Lieutenant?"

"Virtually impossible, sir."

"I can see how it would be."

"Colonel Randal is less than thrilled by the prospect, sir." Lt. Seaborn said. "Lady Jane formed the Royal Marine Detachment to pack parachutes and handle our administrative duties, then things spiraled out of control."

"What types of missions do you run, Lieutenant?"

"Mostly we conduct small raids and mine the Via Balbia farther up the coast to the west than the *King Duck* can reach and retreat to the safety of the RAF's air umbrella before daylight, sir," Lt. Seaborn said. "Lately it has been primarily interdiction patrols to prevent tankers carrying POL from reaching Panzerarmee Afrika by sea."

The lookout called, "Ship four points off the starboard bow."

The MAS boat warbled alongside the *King Duck.* A landing net was hanging over the side.

Acting Provisional Sub-Lieutenant Skipper Warthog Finley, DSO, OBE, DSC, RNPS, leaned over the rail with a nasty-looking stub of a cigar clenched in his teeth.

BG Donovan called, "Permission to come aboard?"

Skipper Finley said, "Permission granted."

BG Donovan said, "Thanks for the lift, Lieutenant. OSS will be in touch. You can use a few more PT boats in your squadron."

Lt. Seaborn said, "Good luck, sir."

As soon as BG Donovan climbed over the rail, the *King Duck* got underway, sailing west. Skipper Finley took the Director of the Office of Strategic Services, an officer who had absolutely no legitimate reason being only a few miles off the coast of Enemy Occupied Libya, on a tour of his ship. The ungainly LCT was packed with men, equipment, gun jeeps and DUKWs.

BG Donovan said, "I understand you sank two Kriegsmarine submarines, Captain Finley."

"Affirmative."

"Very impressive."

Captain Roy Kidd showed BG Donovan his command DUKW. It was

even more cram-packed with weapons, gear and equipment than the LCT.

BG Donovan said, “How does the combination of DUKWs and gun jeeps work?”

Capt. Kidd said, “Five DUKWs will go ashore, four carrying gun jeeps and one with a crane mounted, sir. The crane DUKW will unload the jeeps. Then the five DUKWs will set up a perimeter while the gun jeeps drive to the Via Balbia, which parallels the coastline.

“Tonight, sir, we’ll mine the road, employing horse apple landmines.”

BG Donovan said, “What, pray tell, is a horse apple landmine?”

Lt. Kidd showed him one of the little mines.

BG Donovan said, “What genius thought this idea up?”

Capt. Kidd said, “When we were surrounded at RAF Habbaniya, sir, Teddy Hamilton, The Great Teddy, who’s now a teenage officer serving in Raiding Forces, came up with the idea to paint squirrels orange and parachute ’em onto the Iraqi positions at night.

“Ted also invented the mines. He really is sort of a genius, sir.”

BG Donovan said, “Orange squirrel paratroopers and horse apple landmines. Any other strange and unusual exotic weapons?”

“Well, there’s the camel chip mines, sir.”

“Outstanding,” BG Donovan said, as he weighed one of the camel paddy mines in one hand and a horse apple mine in the other. “OSS will definitely want the specs to manufacture these two toys. How do I get in contact with this fellow, The Great Teddy?”

“I believe he’s on detached assignment at A-Force, working on a Top Secret project with Lieutenant Douglas Fairbanks, sir.”

“The actor?”

“Yes, sir.”

“Lt. Fairbanks is one of us—OSS,” BG Donovan said. “I understand you were at the Siege of Habbaniya, Captain Kidd—serving in an Indian Army Regiment. Were the odds as lopsided as I’ve heard?”

“Probably worse, sir.”

“Which DUKW do you want me in?”

“The crane…”

"Not a chance, Captain."

"I was afraid you were going to say that, sir," Capt. Kidd said. "You're on me, General."

COLONEL JOHN RANDAL, LIEUTENANT COLONEL SIR TERRY "ZORRO" STONE AND CAPTAIN "Geronimo" Joe McKoy were in the Operations Room at Oasis X. They were discussing the current state of Raiding Regiment. The unit was overcommitted and paying a price for it.

The Long Range Desert Group rested patrols between missions, at times having all of them on stand-down. The Special Air Service went weeks, or even months, between operations. Raiding Regiment was in the field patrolling every day. The old proven routine of two weeks out, one week in had gone by the wayside.

Now it was all hands on deck, all the time. A-patrol would return to base, re-arm, re-equip, pull maintenance, then move out within forty-eight hours. The pace was taking a toll on men and vehicles. Due to the fortunate miscalculation of a harried supply officer who had shipped Raiding Forces jeeps based on the strength of a full regiment of parachute infantry, replacement vehicles were not a problem.

Troop strength was. Raiding Regiment was being degraded one Raider at a time from the unrelenting pace. Lt. Col. Stone had reached the tipping point where his patrols were having to be cannibalized.

Sub-Lieutenant Tabitha Walpole, WRNS brought Col. Randal a message. It read:

> DONOVAN FLYING TO X STOP ACCOMPANIED ROY ON MISSION TO MINE VIA BALBIA STOP EXPRESSED DESIRE TO GO ON JEEP PATROL STOP SIGNED JANE STOP

"Well," Col. Randal said, "that tears it."

Lt. Col. Stone said, "Problems?"

Col. Randal handed him the flimsy.

When the CO of Raiding Regiment finished, he handed it to Geronimo Joe.

"No big deal," Capt. McKoy said. "We'll put together a scratch patrol. I'll take Mr. Wild Bill out in the desert, get him lost, stay out a week. Circle around Oasis X twenty miles out or so. The man'll never know the difference. Not a chance a' gettin' killed or captured—go back to Washington with a good war story to tell."

"I like it," Col. Randal said. "Four jeeps enough?"

"That'll do fine, John."

"I think we can manage to spare enough people to man four gun jeeps," Lt. Col. Stone said. "Temporarily."

Col. Randal said, "Let's do it."

The Hudson arrived the next morning, piloted by Captain Pamala Plum-Martin. Brigadier General William "Wild Bill" Donovan, Captain Billy Jack Jaxx, Beverly, Red and GG were on board.

Major the Lady Jane Seaborn had put GG on the plane in anticipation of his going on patrol to cook for Wild Bill.

Capt. Plum-Martin and Beverly transferred to one of the Ro.63s and immediately took off for RAF Habbaniya.

Capt. Jaxx explained to Col. Randal while Lt. Col. Stone gave BG Donovan a tour of Oasis X.

"Pam's taking Beverly to the RAF Flying School to take her pilot's qualification exams, sir."

"Why would she do that? She's already a rated pilot."

"It's complicated, sir," Capt. Jaxx said. "Air Marshal Tedder plans to award Beverly the RAF Distinguished Flying Cross. However, according to regulations, she needs to be a military pilot to qualify.

"The RAF only awards Air Transport Auxiliary wings to females. That's what Pam wears, even though she occasionally flies combat missions, sir. The United States Army Air Force does not have any female pilots. The bill authorizing them stalled in Congress.

"However, sir, a small band of American women—all qualified pilots—traveled to England as a group to serve in the ATA. So, Air Marshal Tedder decided to waive the flying requirement, have Beverly take the written exams and award her British ATA wings since there was no U.S. equivalent."

Col. Randal said, "That is a little complicated, Jack."

Capt. Jaxx said, "It gets worse, sir. Word came down that the Congressional bill finally passed, so now the U.S. will have Women Auxiliary Service Pilots—WASPs. On learning the new development, Air Marshal Tedder and the new commander of the 9th USAAF in Cairo, General Brereton, agreed to a reciprocal deal. Female pilots from the States who qualify for ATA wings will be retroactively awarded WASP wings."

"Jack…"

"The problem is, sir," Capt. Jack said, "nobody has ever seen a pair of WASP wings."

"That's the least of our worries," Col. Randal said. "The commander of the flying school at Habbaniya is a coward who loves to flunk pilot candidates and hates women."

"Not a problem, sir," Capt. Jaxx said. "Pam told me Air Marshal Tedder personally called the 'Butcher' and threatened to have him transferred to flying duties in a frontline bomber squadron if Beverly fails to qualify.

"I have the impression the Air Marshal likes Beverly, Colonel."

Col. Randal said, "Who doesn't?"

COLONEL JOHN RANDAL WAS SITTING OUT ON THE DECK OF THE APARTMENT HE SHARED WITH Major the Lady Jane Seaborn at Oasis X. Unfortunately, Jane was in Cairo. Lieutenant Colonel Sir Terry "Zorro" Stone had disappeared with Red. Captain Billy Jack Jaxx was off somewhere flirting with Sub-Lieutenant Tabitha Walpole. Waldo and Rikke Runborg were in Rocky's suite having a nightcap, and Captain "Geronimo" Joe McKoy was conducting a patrol meeting with his hastily put-together team in preparation for taking BG Donovan to the field.

It was a magical night. Millions of stars stacked up in the sky. Torches lined the banks of the river. Rita Hayworth and Lana Turner grew bored with leaning over the rail surrounding the balcony, staring down into the picturesque village, and came to sit with him at the small table.

Col. Randal said, "Did you two ladies get your bad guy?"

The only response was a pair of beautiful smiles. That meant yes.

"So, what happened?"

Lana got up from the table, went inside and came back with a pen and a piece of paper. She laid it on the table and wrote a single letter: "Z."

Col. Randal was surprised. Writing was a new form of communication. The girls steadfastly refused to talk to him. It had something to do with the fact they were both Zār Cult priestesses—a vow they had taken when he was under their care after having been clawed by a lion.

Col. Randal said, "Zorro?"

Both girls shook their heads, "No."

"Mr. Zargo?"

Big smiles.

That could only mean the local suspected of spying had met a sticky end. Having Rita and Lana around made for pleasant company. It was almost like being back in Abyssinia—only nothing was going to creep up and eat him. At least he did not think so. One of his Colt .38 Supers was laying on the table just in case.

BG Donovan came out on to the balcony. "I've been wanting a chance to speak to you alone."

"General, have you met Rita Hayworth and Lana Turner?"

"No," BG Donovan said. "Everyone at OSS has heard about your two slave girls. Colonel Bonner Fellers says they are local celebrities in Cairo—dancers."

"Bonner Fellers…"

"The former Military Attaché to Middle East Command. He works for me now," BG Donovan said. "Head of PsyOps."

Col. Randal knew Psychological Operations was at the bottom of the career totem pole. The U.S. Army did not place the same emphasis on PsyOps the British did. Poor Bonner Fellers was paying a heavy price for using a code the Germans could read to file his reports. A code he had made a written protest against—suspecting the Germans could read it—but was ordered by the State Department to continue using despite his concerns.

"They're not my slaves, sir."

"Bonner claims the girls say they are."

"I'm going to want them to be able to relocate to the U.S.," Col. Randal said, "when the war's over."

"What is their citizenship currently?"

"Unknown."

"Lady Seaborn has beaten you to it, Colonel," BG Donovan said. "She provided me a list. Rita, Lana and GG. She and Mandy Paige are interested in establishing dual citizenship. Not only am I the director of the national intelligence agency, I'm also a partner in a high-powered New York law firm.

"We shall simply enroll everyone on Lady Seaborn's list in OSS. When the war ends, as a reward for services rendered, they will be issued green cards. I shall personally be their sponsor. You see, I know a thing or two about taking care of my troops—like you, Colonel."

Col. Randal said, "One more thing I don't have to worry about, sir. Thank you, sir."

BG Donovan said, "*Frogspawn.*"

Col. Randal said, "Where in the hell did you pick that up, General?"

"Lady Seaborn."

"I'm all ears, sir."

"How much do you know about the statistical theory of estimation, Colonel?"

"Not a thing, sir."

"We'll save the details for another time," BG Donovan said. "Suffice to say, if our OSS analytical people can lay their hands on the serial numbers stamped on the parts of German tanks—preferably the gear box, they will be able to calculate how many tanks the Germans are building per month. Information of priceless strategic importance to our war planners."

"I see," Col. Randal said, which meant he did not have a clue what Wild Bill was talking about.

"On paper, ascertaining enemy tank manufacturing capabilities would appear to be a Secret Intelligence function," BG Donovan said. "However, our SI people do not frequent the battlefield where German tanks are likely to be found."

Col. Randal said, "Neither do we if we can help it, sir."

BG Donovan said, "I need you to come up with a plan to obtain those serial numbers."

Col. Randal said, "A plan, sir, or do you expect Raiding Forces to acquire them for OSS?"

BG Donovan said, "Both."

"Love to," Col. Randal lied.

BG Donovan said, "I knew we could count on you."

Col. Randal had just about had enough of people springing new assignments on him. He had noticed there was no mention of any kind of support to help obtain the serial numbers. How was Raiding Forces supposed to get a serial number off of a German tank?

BG Donovan said, "I'm rolling out at dawn with Joe McKoy on a week-long patrol. You did not happen to order the old Arizona Ranger to drive me around looking at sand dunes a million miles from any possibility of enemy contact, did you?"

"Sir," Col. Randal said, "that's exactly what I did."

AFTER BRIGADIER GENERAL WILLIAM "WILD BILL" DONOVAN HAD DEPARTED FOR BED, exhausted from his travels and the road mining mission with Sea Squadron, Colonel John Randal walked downstairs to the Tactical

Operations Center. Things were quiet. The room was cool and comfortable. It had a dark golden glow around the edges from the oil lamps. The Phantom operator on duty in the radio bay was reading a paperback book.

"Encode these two messages, Ingersoll, and get 'em out right away."

"Sir!"

The first one was to Captain Roy "Mad Dog" Reupart.

ADVISE SOONEST NUMBER WHO DID NOT PASS THE BLOOD IN THE SAND RE-TEST STOP DO SO BEFORE YOU ANNOUNCE THE RESULTS TO THE MEN STOP RANDAL STOP

The second message was to Chief Warrant Officer Hank Rawlston.

SECRET STOP REPORT TO ENEMY TANK IDENTIFICATION RANGE AT MIDDLE EAST COMMAND INCOUNTRY ORIENTATION
SCHOOL ASAP STOP DEVELOP A CHECKLIST OF ALL PARTS
WHERE SERIAL NUMBERS ARE STAMPED ON ALL MODELS OF
GERMAN TANKS STOP SIGNED RANDAL STOP

Col. Randal had a plan.

16
ABYSSINIAN RULES

SOMEWHERE IN THE DESERT

COLONEL JOHN RANDAL WAS DRIVING THE LEAD JEEP OF A FOUR GUN JEEP PATROL WITH NO name. Brigadier General William "Wild Bill" Donovan was riding shotgun. GG was manning the twin Vickers K machine guns on their pedestal mount in the back. Black Club, one of Mr. Zargo's mercenaries—who was an entirely different operator than Zargo's intelligence operative Club—was also in the back, armed with an M1941 .30 Johnson Light machine gun. The Via Balbia was approximately ten miles straight ahead. The sun was a glowing ball, dropping fast. When it went down it would get dark—like flipping off a light switch.

The plan was to ambush the Via Balbia.

Unfortunately, that was not working out. A German Me 110 had spotted the patrol and banked around, swooping in low to make an attack run. The pilot began firing his machine guns and dropped a pair of small bombs that missed because of the evasive maneuvers the jeeps were making—hard 90-degree turns. The bombs detonated harmlessly, but the sound was titanic. *KAAAAABOOOM! KAAAAABOOOM!*

The explosions ripped the breath out of the Raiders' lungs. The patrol immediately initiated SOP countermeasures for air attack. Every machine gun in the patrol that could be brought to bear, which meant the eight pedestal-mounted .303 caliber Vickers K machine guns, immediately engaged. Every man, except drivers, who could not acquire the target with their machine gun was firing his .30 caliber Colt Monitor, a chopped, highly modified BAR, or an M1941 .30 caliber Johnson LMG at the Me 110.

The intensive return fire from the four jeeps had a telling effect. The German pilot, trailing smoke, broke off his attack. That did not mean he had not radioed for reinforcements. There was nowhere to hide, so Col. Randal pressed on, hoping the sun would get down.

The orange sphere seemed to have stopped setting.

A Ju-87 bomber appeared within minutes. The enemy bomber immediately went into the attack. The enemy aircraft went after the gun jeeps one by one, firing wing- and tail-mounted machine guns as it screamed over. The Nazi pilot also dropped bombs, and these were much larger.

The thunderclap detonations made the desert shake like an earthquake.

The patrol continued to drive at speed, waiting until the enemy airplane committed to its attack run before initiating evasive maneuvers, making hard right- or left-hand turns and accelerating. The small, fast-moving jeeps made difficult targets in the fading light. Somehow none were hit.

When a bomb went off, it created a massive dust cloud. The jeep driver nearest the explosion immediately raced into the cloud seeking to hide. It did not take the German pilot long to wise up to that tactic.

As soon as a bomb detonated, the Ju-87's gunners began machine gunning the sand cloud. The problem the enemy pilot had was being constantly forced to jink left and right to dodge the streams of concentrated automatic weapons fire squirting his way. His aircrew never hit a thing.

Finally, the Ju-87 ran out of bombs and ammunition. The plane turned for home.

Col. Randal pulled up and circled the wagons to get a bomb damage report.

"Well, General, enjoying desert ops?"

BG Donovan said, "I may have gotten a piece of the Me 110. This Colt Monitor is a beast. I intend to ask Colt to manufacture a special lot for OSS."

Col. Randal said, "We had ours modified in theatre."

Captain "Geronimo" Joe McKoy and Captain Billy Jack Jaxx walked up. Capt. McKoy said, "No vehicles damaged. No personnel injured. That don't mean we'd like to do it again, though."

Col. Randal said, "Roger that."

Capt. McKoy said, "Notice anything about our Ju-87 attack?"

BG Donovan said, "You mean other than not wanting to be hit by one of the bombs?"

Capt. McKoy said, "Couple of 'em failed to explode."

Col. Randal said, "I saw that."

Capt. McKoy said, "Ain't normal."

BG Donovan said, "The Nazis are reported to be using slave labor in their munitions plants. Intel out of Germany indicates the forced workers sabotage as much war materiel as they can get away with. Possibly we just experienced sabotaged bombs first-hand."

"Good for those forced workers, sir," Capt. Jaxx said.

A Phantom operator walked up to the jeep and handed Col. Randal a flimsy.

TWENTY-THREE MEN FAILED TO SUCCESSFULLY COMPLETE THE RE-TEST STOP SIGNED REUPART STOP

Col. Randal said, "Send Captain Reupart the following, 'How many of the twenty-three no-go's would you not serve with under any condition?'"

"On the way, sir."

"Hang on," Col. Randal said. "Send the following to Captain Plum-Martin, 'Extract four PAX at 0230 hours at coordinates. . .' Black Club will provide those to you momentarily."

"Will do, Colonel."

Black Club strolled up to the command jeep. He had dismounted to make a recon of the area to the immediate front on their line of march.

"Colonel, you might want to come take a look. The Via Balbia can be observed over the rise ahead."

Col. Randal and BG Donovan followed the mercenary to a low, sloping ridge. It overlooked the only paved highway in the Libyan/Egyptian desert. The sky was purple and scarlet preparatory to turning black, but there was still light to see. A convoy of German Mark III tanks on tank transporters was rolling past, east to west.

BG Donovan whispered, "Incredible!"

Col. Randal said, "Too bad we didn't have an ambush set up. Panzerarmee Afrika only has about fifty of those tank carriers, General. I've been reliably informed that if we could knock out all of 'em, the war in the desert would be over."

BG Donovan said, "That's what I understand."

Black Club said, "Before the light went, I could see a white roadhouse a half mile west of here. There were approximately thirty vehicles parked beside it, with soldiers walking around."

Enemy traffic was widely dispersed, rolling past in twos and threes. The precaution dashed hopes of setting up an ambush. One of the vehicles was an antiaircraft gun with four Nazi soldiers in their coal scuttle helmets, sitting upright like robots. The recent RAF air interdiction campaign was making the Axis drivers take extra precautions.

BG Donovan said, "Was that truck carrying giant tree trunks?"

Black Club said, "Never know what you are going to see next out in the blue, General."

"The blue?"

"What we call the desert."

The three stayed in place and watched the enemy traffic until it became pitch-dark.

Col. Randal said, "Most of the trucks are stopping at the roadhouse. That's all we need to know."

They returned to the patrol with no name.

Col. Randal went to the Phantom jeep. "Message Wing Commander Gordon—'Five Mark III tanks on transporters traveling east at approximately twenty miles per hour', and give him the time and our present coordinates."

"Yes sir, Colonel. Your response from Captain Reupart arrived."

Col Randal said, "What was the number?"

"Eight, sir."

At 1930 hours, Col. Randal issued a comprehensive patrol "frag order." Everyone paid rapt attention. The troops were all veterans. They had done this before. Most of the men were from the 575th Parachute Infantry Regiment Rangers. The navigator was ex-LRDG, the Phantom team had been with Col. Randal all the way through Abyssinia, as had GG. Waldo Treywick was driving—meaning in command of—one of the jeeps as was Capt. McKoy. Capt. Jaxx was along as BG Donovan's escort officer—at least in theory. He was not doing much escorting. Jack Cool was driving a jeep.

Following the frag order, the Raiders ate a cold dinner. Maintenance was pulled. Weapons were cleaned. Magazines were topped off after all the firing at the two Luftwaffe aircraft. Grenades were checked. Personal weapons were dusted off with shaving brushes.

Then the troops rechecked everything they had just done. Action was imminent. Everyone was impatient to get going. But they had to wait until the appointed Line-of-Departure Time.

With time to kill, Capt. McKoy was holding court.

"Now boys, there's a couple a' things you need to always keep in mind, bein' special operators and all, such as you are. For example, if at first you don't succeed, maybe jumpin' outta airplanes ain't for you.

"And if the time ever comes you get to thinkin' you reached the point where you got a lot a' influence, just try ordering another man's dog around—only that particular one don't apply to Lady Jane. She done stole Happy, Colonel Randal's hound, fair and square."

The men all laughed.

"Now, there's two more things a man has to know in order to be a full-fledged success in Raidin' Forces—don't tell everythin' you know and...."

After a few long seconds of silence, Waldo said, "Good 'un, Joe."

With dark, the desert cooled rapidly. While it probably was not very cold, it felt cold. BG Donovan slipped on the sand green parachute smock Capt. Jaxx had loaned him.

"Where did Raiding Forces obtain these?"

"British Airborne Forces issue, sir," Capt. Jaxx said.

"I shall be procuring these for OSS," BG Donovan said. "Outstanding piece of gear."

Capt. McKoy said, "Germans designed 'em for their paratroops. British copied the pattern for theirs. Now the U.S. is gettin' ready to issue it to some a' our jumpers. Come full circle."

Waldo said, "Why reinvent the wheel. . . it's round."

Col. Randal was dozing in a canvas folding chair with his cutdown bush hat over his face. He sat up, glanced at the lime green hands on his Rolex, and then gave the command, "Saddle Up."

It was 2200 hours.

BG Donovan said to Waldo, "How did he manage that trick—wake up exactly on time?"

Waldo said, "Been doin' stuff like 'at as long as I've known him."

The patrol pulled out, driving slow, traveling cross-country paralleling the Via Balbia.

In the command jeep, Col. Randal ordered, "Stand ready."

Waldo told his men, "This is it."

"Fire on my command," Capt. McKoy instructed his crew. "Shoot straight, boys."

"Lock and load," Capt. Jaxx said. "Time to boogie."

Jack Cool.

As they rolled along, intending to drive a half mile past the roadhouse before turning back and pulling up on the Via Balbia, Col. Randal said, "I'll open first, General. Then you commence with your Vickers Ks. Aim low and keep firing. Don't bother about short bursts."

"Wilco."

"Still enjoying gun jeep operations, sir?"

"Listening to Geronimo Joe's yarns tonight took me back to my 'Silk Stocking Boys' days on the Mexican border," BG Donovan said. "My first command."

"Did you know Captain McKoy, sir?"

"No, but he was a living legend," BG Donovan said. "The Punitive Expedition did not account for many of Pancho Villa's rebel bandits, but it was said McKoy's Scouts killed a third of the total body count."

"Changing the ammunition drum on a Vickers K can be tricky," Col. Randal said. "If you have a problem, General, Black Club will climb over the back of the seat and provide assistance."

BG Donovan said, "Let's hope I will not need it."

The patrol closed up as Col. Randal turned north toward the Via Balbia. There were three trucks driving past, heading east. They were heavily loaded with supplies under tarps that were covering their beds. He waited a few minutes, then drove onto the hardtop following behind them.

The speed was a tooth-grinding twenty miles per hour.

Col. Randal swiveled his pair of .303 Vickers K machine guns hard to the left until they hit the stop, then backed them up until they were at an angle. GG had his guns pointing in the same direction. BG Donovan had his pair all the way against their stop, which had them almost at the same angle as Col. Randal's.

Cat's eyes lights appeared in front of the command jeep. Then seven empty trucks passed the patrol with no name, going in the opposite direction, returning from delivering their load.

"This defies belief!" BG Donovan said, "You drive behind enemy lines, roll up on the Axis main line of communication in traffic and nobody seems to notice."

Col. Randal said, "They're getting ready to. Still having fun, General?"

"Not as much as I was," BG Donovan said. "I probably should not get captured."

"No problem, sir," Col. Randal said. "That's why Black Club is sitting behind you."

Up ahead, the Italian *casa strata* swam into view. Like all the others on the Via Balbia, it was built to the standard design: a basic two-story building with a gravel parking lot on the west side of the main building. Two tall fuel tanks at the back of the parking lot contained the gasoline for trucks needing to top off.

The parking lot was packed. More vehicles had arrived since Black Club last had visual contact with the target. Some were in the process of parking as the patrol with no name rolled up.

Cigarettes could be seen glowing.

Col. Randal reached down, picked up his 45mm Brixia shoulder-fired mortar and laid it on the hood of the jeep in front of him. "GG, you aim for the fuel storage tanks. The rest of us will concentrate on the parked trucks. When we come level with the roadhouse, I'm going to try to take down the door with my 45mm.

"Everyone remember to shift your fires to the door and ground floor windows of the building as we roll by."

The four gun jeeps all had cat's eye lights like all German and Italian vehicles, so no one was paying any attention to them as they drove up. Besides, the *casa strata* was 400 miles behind Panzerarmee Afrika's lines at Al Alamein. How safe could you be?

"Commence fire!" Col. Randal commanded, as he pulled the trigger on the twin .303 Vickers K machine gun mounted on a swivel in front of the jeep's steering wheel. The drum was loaded with tracer, incendiary and armor-piercing rounds, with the mix being five rounds of AP and incendiary every other round to one round of tracer. There was no need for standard ball ammunition since most of Raiding Regiment's shooting was at vehicles, enemy aircraft or structures.

Adjusting his fire to the tracers, Col. Randal was aiming low so his rounds were striking the ground. That was exactly what he wanted. Full metal jacket machine gun rounds ricochet. A skilled gunner can bank them into his target almost like a pool shark.

Col. Randal wanted to get at the vehicles' gas tanks.

Vickers K machine guns were designed for use on RAF aircraft. The weapons had a cyclic rate so high the guns made a screaming sound. Multiplied by six and the terrifying noise alone was almost a fight stopper.

The enemy truck drivers in the parking lot were either swept off their feet by the hailstorm of bullets or instantly went to ground hoping to hide. Col. Randal's rounds performed exactly as expected, seeming to jump off the gravel into the undersides of the parked trucks. Fires broke out immediately.

BG Donovan was firing into the closely parked vehicles, turning them into cheese shredders. The canvas tops began to smolder, and several burst into flames. One of the trucks he was engaging was loaded with ammunition.

It exploded in a massive fireball, sending shrapnel screaming in every direction. That was a hazard of raiding a *casa strata*. The Via Balbia ran right next to the parking lot and the building—range was point blank.

The blast nearly blew Col. Randal's lead jeep off the road. Everyone on board was already night blind and nearly deaf from the machine guns. Now they were dazed.

Then the two fuel storage tanks GG was engaging went up like twin volcanos.

Behind the command vehicle, the second jeep, with Waldo at the wheel, engaged. Because of the spacing between the jeeps, the old African scout avoided most of the blast. The concentrated fire from the number two jeep added to the chaos—in machine gunner's terms, the parking lot had become a beaten zone.

Col. Randal was driving slowly. . . barely crawling. Picking up his 45mm Brixia, holding it in the crook of his left arm, he fired a round into the open doors of the building. A muffled *KAAAAABOOOOM* came from inside, followed by the sound of men screaming.

It was a chip shot. Point blank. He had not expected the big double doors to the roadhouse to be open.

BG Donovan and GG shifted their fires as instructed. Black Club was shooting at whatever struck his fancy with his .30 M1941 Johnson LMG. Driving with one hand, Col. Randal dropped the Brixia on the floorboard and went back to his Vickers Ks, but the jeep was already past the building and the stops on the traversing mechanism prevented him from ranging on it.

The temptation was to speed up now. However, he needed to give the last two jeeps time to fully engage. The risk to the follow-on gun jeeps was that other trucks loaded with ammunition would begin exploding in the parking lot. Nearly all the vehicles were on fire.

Third in line, Capt. McKoy's gunners went into action with a roar. Since night had turned into day, visibility was excellent. Nothing in the parking lot escaped the fire from his gun jeep or Capt. Jaxx's—who was following behind tail end Charlie.

At such close range, it seemed as if the whole world was blowing up. This was hell in a very small place. The patrol had accomplished a textbook perfect raid. Surprise, speed, violence of action and gone.

In times past, Col. Randal would have continued on down the Via Balbia looking for targets of opportunity. Not tonight, with BG Donovan along. He had a rendezvous at an abandoned Regia Aeronautica emergency landing strip thirty miles away.

It took a great deal of self-control to turn off the hardball and drive into the desert. What Col. Randal really wanted to do was go find those tank carriers and light them up.

A quarter mile off the Via Balbia, he pulled to a stop and waited.

Capt. Jaxx soon appeared at his jeep, having made his way on foot up the column. "No one killed. No one seriously wounded. A few minor burns, scrapes and abrasions—two men peppered by shrapnel. All vehicles in good shape. . . or at least still running. We nearly blew ourselves up back there, sir. We're all shell-shocked.

"I'm having a little trouble walking straight."

Col. Randal said, "Good report, Jack. Let's get the hell out of Dodge."

THE PATROL WAS SITTING ON THE ITALIAN EMERGENCY LANDING GROUND FIFTY-FIVE MILES FROM the Mediterranean coast. While it was only a few miles into the Great Sand Sea, there was virtually no chance of encountering German or Italian forces. Contrary to constant news reports that the enemy were skilled desert warriors, the Axis did not venture into the Great Sand Sea. With the exception of a few small, desert-capable Italian units, they restricted their operations to the 1,500-mile-long, approximately fifty-mile-wide "good going," hard ground along the Mediterranean coast.

Brigadier General William "Wild Bill" Donovan, Colonel John Randal, Captain Billy Jack Jaxx, Captain "Geronimo" Joe McKoy and Waldo

Treywick were standing by to be extracted by air and flown back to Raiding Forces Headquarters outside of Cairo.

While they were waiting, BG Donovan said, "Malta is the key to the war in Middle East Command. German Airborne Forces were staging for a drop, to be followed up by a seaborne invasion of the island, like they did so successfully on Crete. Then Rommel demanded re-inforcements for Panzerarmee Afrika. The High Command did not want to give them to him, but Hitler intervened and overruled his generals. The paratroops were the only troops available. They were frittered away here in the desert, useless without organic transport. Now the Nazis don't have any airborne capability left in this part of the world.

"Without the Airborne Forces, the invasion of Malta had to be canceled. If the Germans had captured the island, it would have blocked our sea lanes and the war in Middle East Command would have been kaput."

Capt. McKoy said, "Sounds like we dodged a bullet, General."

BG Donovan said, "We have intelligence indicating that after the high casualties suffered on Crete, Hitler no longer believes Airborne Forces have strategic value."

Col. Randal said, "I believe a drop on Alexandria during Rommel's last push might have been decisive, sir."

Capt. McKoy said, "Yeah, it would have. Nazis ain't as smart as everybody believes they are. They sure ain't military geniuses."

Black Club and a team were spread out down the length of the dirt airstrip. On signal from Col. Randal, they lit off red railroad flares and placed them along the perimeter. Right on time the Hudson came in, landed and wheeled around ready for a quick take-off. The party to be airlifted out climbed aboard.

Overhead, one of the captured Italian Ro.63s circled. It was a rule all Raiding Forces Aircraft fly in pairs over the Great Sand Sea. In the event one went down, the other could mark the location.

Col. Randal climbed into the Hudson's cockpit and sat in the copilot's empty seat next to the Vargas Girl look-alike Royal Marine pilot, Captain Pamala Plum-Martin. As soon as the door to the passenger cabin closed, she took off. When the plane was airborne, the Ro.63 joined up on the left wing to fly in a two-ship formation.

"How's your life been, Pam?"

"Busy," Capt. Plum-Martin said, "Ronnie radioed he was able to intercept the Mark IIIs you reported. Five panzers being transported on tank carriers. Not anymore."

"Very good," Col. Randal said, "I wasn't sure he would be able to locate the convoy with the sketchy information provided."

"The tank transports were still rolling east when he arrived on station," Capt. Plum-Martin said. "Ronnie's two A-20s made short work of them."

In the passenger cabin, BG Donovan said, "I have a professional interest in the Force N Abyssinian Mission, Joe. One of the primary responsibilities of OSS is to organize, arm and lead guerrilla armies. What can you tell me about it?"

"Well," Capt. McKoy said, "you need to let Waldo lead off. He was there from the day John and Headhunter Hoolihan jumped in. I came into the picture later, after Force N was already just about gettin' itself organized."

Waldo said, "I was livin' a peaceful existence as the slave of an evil, baby-rapin' ras, minding my own business one day when a airplane flew overhead and these parachutes came floatin'...."

In the cockpit, Col. Randal said, "We're not having this conversation."

Capt. Plum-Martin turned and gave him a dazzling smile. "I love it when you talk sexy."

"I mean it, Pam," Col. Randal said. "This is serious."

"Yes, sir."

"Raiding Forces has been ordered to investigate the problem of industrial diamond smuggling," Col. Randal said. "Are you up to speed on that?"

"Only to the point of Lady Jane having the mother of all rows with Cuthbert Bowlby over the DeBeers Diamond Company," Capt. Plum-Martin said. "My flying duties have kept me occupied. I have very little contact with MI-6 these days."

"Here's the deal," Col. Randal said. "I no longer trust the SIS not to attempt to learn what we uncover about DeBeers in the course of our trying to put a stop to diamond smuggling—not that I care. If Bowlby would have asked me, I would have provided the information. It's not clear what SIS's true motive is, but there seems to be a rift between the U.S. and U.K. over the Diamond Company.

"What I don't want is to put you in a situation where you have to decide between the British Secret Service and Raiding Forces."

"I should not like to have to make that choice, John," Capt. Plum-Martin said. "You should be aware my ties to MI-6 are practically nonexistent."

"Well," Col. Randal said, "here's the solution I've come up with. When it comes to The Diamond Company, whatever we uncover will be restricted to Need to Know.

"You won't be in the loop."

Capt. Plum-Martin said, "Fine by me, John."

"I don't want your feelings hurt," Col. Randal said. "I have a lot of respect for you, Pam. We have too much history."

"Yes, we do," Capt. Plum-Martin said. "Consider my feelings officially not hurt."

"My guess is there's going to be a lot of flying in places we've never been, chasing down smugglers," Col. Randal said. "I want you to be our pilot. We just won't talk about DeBeers."

"Works for me, Love."

In the passenger compartment, BG Donovan said, "No gold or rifles to recruit guerrilla troops. So you and Randal went from village to village shooting man-eating lions to win the hearts and minds of the locals, hoping to entice them to enlist?"

"Force N wasn't interested in no hearts and minds," Waldo said. "We just needed us some troops. Now, the Colonel didn't show hardly no aptitude…"

Col. Randal said, "Had a chance to get over to the future OSS headquarters, Pam?"

"Not yet," Capt. Plum-Martin said. "I hear it's fabulous. Lady Jane said she was saving things I could put in my hope chest."

"Hope chest?"

"Girls do that, John. For when they get married."

"I'm having a hard time picturing you married," Col. Randal said. "Planning to get Jane to introduce you to one of her rich friends?"

"Not a chance," Capt. Plum-Martin laughed. "In case you failed to notice, divorce among the English upper class is virtually assured. Admiral Mountbatten, the King's cousin, Dickie—you met him at Combined Operations. He and his wife both have *friends.* Sometimes the couples double date."

Col. Randal said, "No kidding."

Capt. Plum-Martin said, "Maybe you can introduce me to some American millionaire bachelors."

"I don't know any," Col. Randal said. "Beverly's father's rich, single, likes women and he's a colonel in the USAAF. Get her to fix you up with him."

"Sounds like my type," Capt. Plum-Martin said. "If I marry Colonel Blackwell, when Lady Jane throws you over to go back to her husband, you could marry Beverly and that would make me your mother-in-law."

Col. Randal said, "Maybe we could double date."

In the passenger cabin, BG Donovan said, "Let me get this straight, when Force N captured an enemy village or Model Farm, the troops raped the women before taking them captive to sell as slaves and killed the men—Randal let your people do that?"

"Wasn't any stopping 'em," Capt. McKoy said. "Murder's the national sport."

Waldo said, "To the victor goes the spoils and in that godforsaken country, General, it didn't pay to be the spoils."

Capt. McKoy said, "We called it Abyssinian Rules."

COLONEL JOHN RANDAL HAD BREAKFAST WITH BRIGADIER GENERAL WILLIAM "WILD BILL" Donovan, Captain Roy "Mad Dog" Reupart, MC, Chief Warrant Officer Hank Rawlston, Sergeant Major Mike "March or Die"

Mikkalis and Master Sergeant Mack Beckwith in the mess hall at Raiding Forces Headquarters.

Col. Randal said, "This conversation is classified Top Secret."

The men at the table became very quiet.

"While we were on patrol, General, Chief Rawlston has been busy working on a project for you."

BG Donovan said, "Oh?"

Col. Randal said, "Middle East Command has a two-week in-country indoctrination program for all new incoming officers. Part of the course is enemy tank identification. For that block of instruction, the students are taken to a range where captured enemy tanks are on display. Chief Rawlston has been there learning where the serial numbers on stamped parts are to be found, sir."

BG Donovan looked at Col. Randal in surprise, "Outstanding!"

"Maybe, sir, you would like to explain to us what you expect along those lines," Col. Randal said, "exactly."

"Expect?"

"You want the part recovered, sir, or will recording the serial number work?"

BG Donovan said, "If we can recover removable parts with serial numbers, they can provide information of significant intelligence value. However, I understand the Germans have a highly aggressive tank recovery program, so you may have to fight for a damaged tank. In that case, obtaining the serial numbers will suffice nicely."

Col. Randal said, "Captain Reupart, do not make any announcement about pass/fail—let's keep that to ourselves. Send the men who passed the Blood in the Sand retest to Oasis X. Of those who still failed to meet your standards, pull out the eight men you would not serve with in any capacity and return them to the docks. Divide the rest into four-man teams—two jeeps per team.

"Station a team with each division in Eighth Army. Their mission is to go to the scene of the most recent tank action and record the serial numbers off knocked-out enemy tanks before German recovery vehicles have time to show up and tow 'em off."

"Yes, sir."

Col. Randal said, "Sergeant Major Beckwith, I want you to select worthy Rangers we can promote to corporal to be team leaders.

"Questions?"

MSgt. Beckwith said, "Is this a temporary assignment, sir?"

"Negative," BG Donovan said, "OSS can expect to be collecting the serial numbers for the rest of this war."

"Yes, sir."

Capt. Reupart asked, "What do we call this operation, sir?"

BG Donovan said, "My HQ does not have a codename designated. Any recommendations?"

Col. Randal said, "Let's keep it simple, sir. Call it OPERATION PURPLE. Name your teams Purple 1, Purple 2, etc. Understand, PURPLE is Need to Know. Only the team members and the people sitting at this table have the need at this time.

"Call a formation of the Purple Team members in one hour. The General and I will brief their mission."

Capt. Reupart asked, "Do I command OPERATION PURPLE, sir?"

"Negative," Col. Randal said. "Get it organized, then report back to Oasis X as soon as the Purple Teams deploy to their divisions. You're too valuable as a patrol leader and trainer to use in a position that's purely administrative. The Purple Teams will be spread out all over Eighth Army and they'll never operate as a unit."

Walking up the stairs to the third-floor suite, BG Donovan said, "You are taking the men who failed to qualify for Raiding Forces for the *second* time and using them to collect tank part serial numbers for OSS."

"Yes, sir. They're good men, just not good special operators."

"That's brilliant."

"We have a rule, General—Right Man, Right Job," Col. Randal said. "So how do you feel about inducting the Purple Teams into the OSS?"

BG Donovan said, "Provide a list of names. The teams will need credentials when they are eventually attached to U.S. Army divisions. We don't want local commanders not understanding, interfering with, or failing to support Purple

Team operations. I will get with Colonel Clarke later today and have his forger, 'Twitters the Taster', prepare orders they can use during LIGHTFOOT."

Flanigan was sitting at the duty desk on the third-floor landing. "Ensign Hamilton is standing by inside, as instructed, sir."

"Ensign," Col. Randal said when he walked in. "You have fifteen minutes to give General Donovan a rundown on everything you've been doing since the day we met."

"Sir!"

Col. Randal continued on into the bedroom.

Drop-dead gorgeous Major the Lady Jane Seaborn was lying on the bed, playing with a pile of jewelry.

"Trophies from the Palace?"

"These are some of the best pieces I picked out for my Royal Marines," Lady Jane said. "We found trunks and trunks of jewelry. I had it trucked to RFHQ for the girls to rummage through. There were guns by the hundreds, an impressive sword collection, arguably the largest assemblage of the most vile child pornography on the planet…"

"No hoard of gold bars?"

"There was hardly any gold," Lady Jane said. "A surprise, actually."

"What about buried on the grounds?"

"We located underground bunkers," Lady Jane said. "They contained an arsenal of military-grade small arms. Roy Kidd has been having the time of his life with all the weapons."

"No gold?"

Lady Jane said, "While there was a substantial stash of bundled U.S. currency and British pound notes, the total did not total up to what one would have thought. I expected to find bales of paper money and a mountain of gold coins and bars.

"What a letdown."

Col. Randal said, "You think the family spirited it away before Major Sansom's men arrived?"

"No," Lady Jane said. "Sammy put out an all-points bulletin from the Kit-Kat. Police converged on the Palace from every direction within minutes. No one could take anything from the premises. No suitcases were confiscated, the men had to hand over their wallets and the women were not permitted to take purses.

"Major Sansom allowed those in residence to leave with only the clothes on their backs."

Col. Randal said, "Pretty cold."

Lady Jane said, "Not getting sympathy from me. Those people personified the word evil. The police acted on the belief the people fleeing might have maps to caches or financial instructions secreted away.

"That did not prove to be the case."

Col. Randal asked, "What do you think happened to the loot?"

"We searched the house, then we went back and searched it again. Even used the mine detector to see if there was anything concealed in the walls or buried under the floors or in the basement. Nothing." Lady Jane said.

"Then, as we were giving it up as a lost cause, I noticed the suitcases the police had confiscated and placed behind a door in the foyer. No one had gone through them.

"Look what was inside."

Lady Jane opened the drawstring on a blue velvet pouch laying on the bed. She poured out a sparkling stream of diamonds.

"Every suitcase contained the equivalent of a crook's bailout bag like Raiding Regiment has on board each gun jeep in case the crew has to abandon their vehicle to escape and evade. These are all the sparklers."

"Paper money's too bulky for a quick getaway," Col. Randal said. "Gold's too heavy. Diamonds make sense."

"Few people have ever seen as many high grade diamonds in one pile," Lady Jane said. "Who says crime does not pay?"

"It paid you," Col. Randal said.

"I know where these will end up," Lady Jane laughed. "What do you suggest we do with these sparklers for the time being?"

Col. Randal said, "I think you just financed Mr. Big's monopoly."

Seated in the living room of Colonel John Randal and Major the Lady Jane Seaborn's suite were Brigadier General William "Wild Bill" Donovan, Captain "Geronimo" Joe McKoy, Captain Billy Jack Jaxx, Captain Roy Kidd, Waldo Treywick, Lieutenant Mandy Paige, Ensign Theodore Hamilton *aka* The Great Teddy and Beverly Blackwell.

When Col. Randal and Lady Jane walked in, BG Donovan was saying, "It has been a pleasure talking to you, Ensign Hamilton. Fascinating stuff. I want you to fly to Washington at your earliest convenience to brief my staff at OSS about your deception activities.

"I shall expect you at 2200 hours sharp."

"Sir," Ens. Hamilton said, "I am currently wrapping up the planning of a naval sonic deception with Lieutenant Douglas Fairbanks. Then I have a commitment to A-Force to support OPERATION LIGHTFOOT. It may be a while until I am free to travel."

"Who do you report to?"

"Col. Randal, sir."

BG Donovan said, "I shall ask him to arrange for you to travel to the States as soon as you can be released, Ensign."

Col. Randal walked The Great Teddy out the door. When they were on the landing he asked, "What do you and the General have going at 2200 hours?"

Ens. Hamilton said, "He wants me to take him to the Kit-Kat Club, sir."

Back inside, Col. Randal said, "General, allow me to introduce our IDB team. I believe you've met everyone except Lieutenant Mandy Paige. With the exception of Lady Jane, Mandy is the only British subject currently a full-fledged member of the IDB interdiction team. I trust her with my life—that's all we're going to say about that."

"Nice to meet you, Lieutenant Paige," BG Donovan said. "Your reputation has preceded you. Colonel Randal tells me you're as brave as a lion."

"John said that?"

"We call her Lieutenant Mandy, sir," Col. Randal said. "She specializes in counterintelligence."

"Looks like a fine group," BG Donovan said. "I am interested to hear your plans. Do you have a code name for the operation yet?"

"We do, General," Capt. McKoy said. "Waldo told us a tale about the time he and P. J. Pretorius was huntin' for a dinosaur supposed to be livin' in the Belgian Congo."

BG Donovan said, "A dinosaur?"

Waldo said, "Mokele-mbembe—native drawin's show it to be like one a' those longneck monsters on the gas station signs. They're supposed to be passive leaf eaters, but the tribesmen claim this one can bite a hippopatamus in half. Me and P. J. never saw no dinosaur, but we did find us some tracks the size of a hippo with claws.

"Hippopotamuses—they don't have no claws."

"Interesting."

Col. Randal said, "We're planning to call our diamond interdiction program OPERATION LEAF EATER. No one will ever figure that one out, sir."

BG Donovan laughed. "Great name."

Col. Randal said, "Captain McKoy, why don't you brief the General on the strategy you and Waldo devised."

"Well, we've got us a two-part plan for openers," Capt. McKoy said. "The idea is to take control of the diamond market here in Cairo, which is the heart of the entire diamond trade on the continent a' Africa. To do that, General, we had a sit down with the Big Five crime lords. We introduced Waldo, who was posing as Mr. Big from the United States, and made it clear he had the backing of Security Intelligence Middle East, MI-6 and OSS. . . unofficially, that is. He done bribed 'em—at least that's what they was led to believe.

"At that meeting, Mr. Big authorized The Big Five to rub out all their competitors who was buyin' and sellin' diamonds, cuttin' in to their profits, so we'd only have to deal with the five a' them. Mandy suggested the idea for simplicity and it dang sure worked. Blood was a-runnin' in the streets.

"Then, after they'd murdered all the competition, we called us another meetin'. It was explained that as of right that minute, they all had to sell one hundred percent of their stones to Mr. Big exclusive. That's when the Big

Five became the Big Four, John havin' shot one of 'em right there at the table, as you already heard about.

"The idea is, we buy up all the diamonds. Then we sell 'em to smugglers. The smugglers load their goods on camel caravans headed for Turkey, where they'll be sold to Nazi agents who intend to smuggle 'em over into Greece, which the bad guys occupy, and on into Germany.

"But that ain't exactly how it'll play out, General. We'll have the caravan intercepted by one a' Raiding Forces' gun jeep patrols somewhere in the middle of the Great Sand Sea. Take back all the rocks we sold to the smugglers. So not only will we corner the diamond market, but we'll make us a big profit resellin' the stones to the same smugglers at a higher price later. Nobody can tell one uncut diamond from another."

BG Donovan asked, "Do you believe you can recover all the stones?"

Capt. McKoy said, "Probably not, General. But we can drive up the price per karat so high the Nazis can't afford 'em anymore."

"Oh," BG Donovan said, "that is OUTSTANDING!"

"Meanwhile, phase two is goin' on simultaneously. I've been infiltratin' ex-lawmen into West Africa," Capt. McKoy said. "They're out there now a-dopin' out the lay a' the land, figurin' out the good guys from the bad guys. I'm gettin' ready to head out there myself and start puttin' a crimp in the diamond trade, most a' which is stones or industrial grade rocks bought here in Cairo, then transported on tramp merchant ships to different places where Nazis agents can pick 'em up."

BG Donovan said, "Let's get back to cornering the diamond trade from the four surviving crime families. You will need OSS to supply the buy money?"

"Negative, sir," Col. Randal said, "Raiding Forces will finance LEAF EATER."

"Now *that* is impressive," BG Donovan said. "One of the reasons I went to the trouble to come to Egypt was because I felt it was important for me to personally talk to you face-to-face to tell you how vital putting a stop to the illicit diamond trade is to the war effort.

"You men have gotten off to a fast start. Thought things through and have developed a truly remarkable plan. However, somehow I sense your heart is not really in LEAF EATER. If that is indeed true, I want you to understand in no uncertain terms, shutting down the Nazi diamond smuggling channels may be the single most important OSS operation of the war.

"Even more critical to victory than GOLDEN FLEECE/RED INDIAN."

BRIGADIER GENERAL WILLIAM "WILD BILL" DONOVAN FLEW BACK TO THE UNITED STATES THE next day. Before he departed, the Director of OSS had a private conversation with Colonel John Randal. "Slight change of mission. When you track down the diamond smugglers, kill every single one.

"Abyssinian Rules are in full force and effect."

17
WORLD'S BIGGEST FIRE BOMB

COLONEL JOHN RANDAL, MAJOR THE LADY JANE AND BEVERLY BLACKWELL WERE SITTING IN the terminal of the Cairo International Airport. Col. Randal had orders to fly to the United States and report to the commanding officer, Western Task Force. He had no idea who, what or why.

OPERATION LIGHTFOOT had kicked off two days previous. Eighth Army launched its attack against Panzerarmee Afrika sooner than A-Force had advertised to the Nazis, through lanes cut in the extensive German minefields that were not much wider than a sidewalk. The Axis had been caught off-guard. Field Marshal Erwin Rommel was not even in the country, thanks to Rikke Runborg.

The last thing Col. Randal wanted was to leave Raiding Forces with the battle raging. Not that there was much he could do. The commanders of Raiding Regiment and Sea Squadron knew their jobs. They did not need him looking over their shoulders.

There was a buzz among the VIP passengers waiting in the lounge—all twenty-six of them, the total number the plush Douglas C-54 Skymaster was rated to carry. Everyone was speculating about the battle.

Red came off the airplane and walked into the lounge. She had volunteered to work the flight. While a stewardess from a British airline serving on a United States Air Force aircraft was unusual, the USAAF had contracted with qualified flight attendants from civilian airlines to serve on their VIP flights. Her Clipper Girl background guaranteed a spot on the crew, plus she had impressive Office of Strategic Services credentials that made it virtually impossible to turn down her offer to fly.

Col. Randal suspected Lady Jane had asked Red to make the trip.

The two women disappeared, leaving him alone at the table with Beverly. The blond Texas beauty reached in her purse and produced a small box wrapped in plain brown paper with a ribbon on it. She slid it across to Col. Randal.

"I wanted to give you something for Christmas," Beverly said. "Lady Jane said we don't do Christmas or birthday presents in Raiding Forces. She told me it's OK to give gifts other times."

Col. Randal picked up the box. It was heavy, which was a good sign. Generally, he did not care for presents because he did not like surprises. However, he really liked Beverly and was not about to hurt her feelings.

The bow was knotted tight. Col. Randal produced a switchblade jump knife and sliced the ribbon. Inside the package was a box with the logo of the Remington Arms Company on it. When he flipped off the top, he found a Model 51 pocket pistol.

Beverly said, "It's just like mine except mine's a .32 and this is a .380. Daddy said you'd probably want the bigger caliber."

"Well, he was right about that," Col. Randal said. "Personally, I believe this is the best small handgun ever made."

"So, you like it?"

"Oh, yeah."

"Remington doesn't manufacture Model 51s anymore—too expensive," Beverly said. "Daddy called the president of the corporation. He found one for sale, wrote a check for the pistol and had his gunsmiths completely rebuild it for you. Like you told me, John, don't leave home without it."

"Don't worry," Col. Randal said. "I won't."

He meant it.

Colonel John Randal was sound asleep on the C-54. At least he had been. Red reached down to shake his shoulder. His eyes came open before she touched him, startling her. "Return your seat to the upright position, John. We are preparing to land. You have been asleep ever since we took off from Gibraltar."

Col. Randal said, "Great flight."

"How would you know?" Red asked. "Lady Jane told me you were exhausted."

"I'm not now."

Red had seated him in the back next to the stewardess lounge to keep an eye on him during the flight, so Col. Randal was the last passenger to deplane. When the two of them came down the metal steps, Major General George S. Patton Jr. *aka* "Blood and Guts" was waiting. He was magnificent in his ivory-handled pistols and a gleaming helmet liner with two silver stars denoting the rank of a major general on the front.

Unknown to Col. Randal, Maj. Gen. Patton was the most powerful army officer in the continental United States after General George C. Marshall, Chairman of the Joint Chiefs of Staff. It was said "what General Patton wants, General Patton gets." While the instruction to meet an "agent or agents known to you" had not been issued prior to the flight, it was now clear who he was supposed to report to.

Most of the other VIP passengers had waited around on the tarmac to see who the general was meeting.

Col. Randal saluted. Maj. Gen. Patton returned the salute crisply and clapped him on the shoulder. "I'm taking you to my headquarters, Colonel. One of my aides will transport your luggage to your hotel."

"Won't be necessary, sir," Col. Randal said. "I'd like you to meet Red, General. Lady Jane arranged for our hotel's car to pick us up. Red can take my bags."

"What hotel?"

"The St. Regis."

Maj. Gen. Patton said, "Don't get comfortable, Colonel. You'll be checking out in the morning."

"Yes, sir."

Fluttering on the fenders of the Buick Super Eight command car transporting them was a pair of red flags with two white stars, denoting a major general. Once they were inside, Maj. Gen. Patton said, "I'm the commander of the Western Task Force of OPERATION TORCH. Largest armada in the history of the United States to ever set sail with the intention of invading a foreign power, the greatest amphibious gamble since Xerxes crossed the Hellespont in the fifth century B.C. I am about to fulfill my destiny of commanding a large army in battle.

"And you're about to fulfill yours as the nation's premier leader of special operations."

"I see, sir," Col. Randal said—which meant he did not have a clue what old Blood and Guts was talking about.

"You are aware of TORCH?"

"Only peripherally, sir. My Sea Squadron is conducting a series of reconnaissances of beaches you probably *won't* be landing on to confuse the bad guys."

"Think that's going to work?"

"I have no idea, sir."

"Worth a try," Maj. Gen. Patton said. "Stonewall Jackson set great store by misleading the opposition."

"So I've heard, sir."

"I have a mission for you, Colonel," Maj. Gen. Patton said. "Truscott will brief you on it when we get to my HQ. He's commanding my Sub-Task Force Goalpost. I recruited him because of the time he spent observing Mountbatten at Combined Operations Headquarters. We need an insane commander for a screwball operation, so I told Lucian, 'let's get that crazy son-of-a-bitch, Randal'."

"Nice to be appreciated, General," Col. Randal lied. The last thing he needed was to get involved in another operation a long way from where Raiding Forces was committed to supporting LIGHTFOOT.

"Don't be too hasty . . . wait until you hear the plan," Maj. Gen. Patton said. "You're going to think we've been drinking and doing drugs while pulling our tactics out of a Marvel comic book. And maybe we have—the funny-book part."

Col. Randal said, "Lovely."

Maj. Gen. Patton's Western Task Force headquarters, in the Munitions Building in Washington, D.C., was a beehive of activity. Recently promoted Brigadier General Lucian Truscott, dressed in a blood-red leather A-2 bomber jacket, silk scarf, riding breeches and boots, was waiting when they arrived. Col. Randal had met him once before at COHQ prior to the Dieppe fiasco. Then Col. Truscott had merely been an observer. Now he was a principal commander in the first U.S. invasion of the war.

The three officers immediately went into conference in Maj. Gen. Patton's office. BG Truscott briefed. "Sometime in the immediate future, Task Force 34 will set sail from Hampton Roads in New York, transporting the Western Task Force under the command of General Patton. I will be in command of Sub-Task Force Goalpost—made up primarily of the 60th Regimental Combat Team 'Go Devils' of the 9th Infantry Division and attachments. My primary objective after landing ashore is to capture an all-weather airfield. Seventy-seven P-40 USAAF fighter planes aboard the only escort carrier available to Goalpost, the USS *Chenango,* a converted oil tanker that can launch but not recover aircraft, and Wellington bombers from England will be flown in to use the airfield.

"My orders are to 'capture, hold and supply' said airfield, which will remain unnamed at this point in time for reasons of security."

BG Truscott picked up a pointer as he flipped over the cloth covering a schematic sitting on a three-legged tripod. The map, if you could call it that, looked like something a third-grader might draw. There was what Col. Randal thought might be the ocean: a long—very long—winding channel that made a big loop inland marked "river" and a rectangle that was labeled "airfield." There appeared to be a high ridge on one side and a marsh on the other. A narrow, oval-styled "lagoon" fringed by what looked like cliffs bordered a third side of the airfield.

"General Eisenhower, General Patton, Twelfth Air Force, and most of the Allied High Command have all come to the conclusion the quick capture of this hard-topped airfield on the first day is paramount to the overall success of TORCH and follow-on operations.

"Colonel Randal, you will take command of a seventy-five-man detachment composed of troops drawn from the 10th Ranger Battalion, land ashore, force entry onto the airfield and secure it by sundown on D-Day. Sealed orders containing detailed instructions, maps, aerial photos, etcetera, will be provided to the captain of the destroyer USS *Dallas,* which you and your Rangers will be sailing on. You are only authorized to open the orders once you are at sea.

"Questions?"

"What's the bad news, sir?"

Maj. Gen. Patton said, "The airfield is twelve miles upriver, the enemy holds both banks with a huge fort guarding it and a heavy chain boom stretching across the channel blocking passage. Oh yeah, forty-five enemy tanks can be expected to reach the airfield in under an hour."

LATER THAT EVENING, COLONEL JOHN RANDAL AND RED WERE HAVING DINNER AT THE restaurant in the lobby of the exclusive St. Regis Hotel. Red said, "I had a drink in the bar with one of the VIPs from our flight while waiting for you to arrive. Seems there's been friction at Supreme Allied Headquarters Europe. High anxiety. Passionate disagreements. Personality clashes.

"Things had become so heated, General Eisenhower wanted to find a way to communicate his feelings about various generals, admirals and politicians to his boss here in the States, General Marshall. According to the VIP, Ike did not want to send a message in the clear calling someone a 'son-of-a-bitch'. He thought SOB was too obvious, so he came up with YBSOB meaning 'yellow bellied son-of-a-bitch'."

Col. Randal said, "You making this up?"

Red said, "The brigadier general I was talking to in the bar was returning from a fact-finding mission to England and the Middle East. He claimed Eisenhower was happily dispatching YBSOB messages to Marshall when a cable arrived from the President inquiring what YBSOB stood for. Seems FDR had been reading Ike's messages and was unable to find that particular acronym on the list provided him by the War Department."

"Uh-oh."

"The President thought it was hilarious."

"I can see how he might."

Major General George S. Patton Jr. appeared at their table. "Colonel, could I have a word in private?"

The two made their way to the lobby of the hotel and found a secluded spot in a corner where they could talk without being overheard. Maj. Gen. Patton said, "If you repeat a syllable of this conversation I'll have you transferred to the North Pole, then shot. Is that clear?"

"Crystal, sir."

"Are the French going to fight?"

Col. Randal realized instantly there were only two places TORCH could be landing and he was sure Maj. Gen. Patton knew he knew. One of those was France, which was not going to happen. The other was Vichy French North Africa. He said, "Yes sir, they will."

Maj. Gen. Patton said, "My State Department advisors say no."

"Sir, I've fought Vichy French on two occasions so far. French officers have a twisted sense of honor. They'll resist the initial landings. If they feel they're acquitting themselves well—for the glory of France, they'll continue fighting."

Maj. Gen. Patton said, "Do you believe Rommel will drop what he's doing in Egypt and rush west to lead the counterattack against the beachhead?"

"I doubt it, General."

"What makes you say that?"

"He's in Germany on medical leave, sir."

"How do you know, Randal?"

"We tricked him, sir—that's classified."

Maj. Gen. Patton said, "Port Lyautey Airfield—see you there."

The next day, old "Blood and Guts" sailed on the USS *Augusta* (CL/CA 31), a Northampton class cruiser.

COLONEL JOHN RANDAL AND RED ARRIVED IN NORFOLK, VIRGINIA, BY TRAIN. THEY TOOK A CAB to the Nansemond Hotel. Col. Randal dropped the Clipper Girl off with their luggage and continued on to meet with Colonel Cyrus J. Wilder, the executive officer of the Port of Hampton Roads.

Col. Wilder was arguably the most overworked, stressed-out officer in the United States Army at the moment. His mission was to get Task Force 34 off to sea. He was the go-to guy in a military three-ring circus involving the Army, the Navy, Merchant Marine and longshoremen. All manifests, boarding orders, marrying up of the various elements of the 90th Combat Team with their ships, loadings, last-minute requests, fuel, ammunition, supplies, victuals and the ordering of troops and ships went through his office.

A nightmare assignment.

Since Task Force 34 had sailed, Col. Wilder should have been able to heave a big sigh of relief, prop his feet up on his desk and be accommodative to Col. Randal when he arrived. Not the case. The phones in his office were ringing off the hooks, and all the callers were desperate.

Col. Randal said, "It always like this?"

Col. Wilder said, "One of my staff had a heart attack day before yesterday. I understand you're on the *Dallas.* The 10th Rangers have already boarded. However, we have a situation. While I'm not cleared to know where TF34 is headed, I do know your mission is to capture an airfield somewhere on Planet Earth, up a river that is no more than seventeen feet deep."

Col. Randal said, "Roger that—didn't know about the seventeen feet part."

Col. Wilder said, "There is no reason for you to capture an airfield if our planes don't have any fuel once you take it. My bean counters were checking bills of lading and discovered a big doughnut hole. There's no aviation fuel being transported by TF34 on a ship capable of navigating seventeen-feet-deep waters."

Col. Randal said, "What's the plan?"

Col. Wilder said, "TF34's already requisitioned every ship capable of sailing across the Atlantic. However, we finally located one with a shallow enough draft that just arrived, a real—this is no joke—banana boat . . . the *Contessa.* And I found aviation fuel. Two thousand cans, each one weighing four hundred pounds. They are already drummed, standing by at Craney Island on loading barges ready to be transferred to the *Contessa.* In addition, nine hundred tons of munitions are waiting to be loaded as well."

Col. Randal said, "The world's biggest fire bomb."

Col. Wilder said, "There's that, but the aviation fuel is vital, and TF34 sailed without the munitions, which are high priority. To make things tricky, there's major repairs that have to be made to the *Contessa.* General Patton gave me orders the ship has to sail independently with the workmen still onboard to complete repairs if they are not finished once the fuel and munitions are loaded.

"You're supposed to board the *Dallas* for a high-speed run to catch up with TF34 as soon as you arrive, which means now."

Col. Randal said, "Sounds like you've got things under control."

Col. Wilder said, "Not even close. The *Contessa* is short almost half its crew, some twenty-nine men. The sailors had been granted leave after her last voyage because the ship was scheduled to go into dry dock. They're scattered to the wind. I called Standard Fruit Company headquarters in New York, the *Contessa's* owners, and talked to their personnel officer. The rep advised that we would be better off looking for sailors in Hampton Roads than trying to track down the men on leave, and he volunteered to fly down here to help."

Col. Randal said, "Why not replace 'em with Navy personnel?"

Col. Wilder said, "You're not going to believe this, but TF34 has sucked up every available sailor. The U.S. Navy can't provide one single hand."

Col. Randal said, "You're right. I don't believe you."

Col. Wilder said, "TF34 has been a total SNAFU and it's about to turn into a FUBAR. The Army doesn't know what it's doing. The Navy doesn't want to do it. Interservice rivalry has been the worst I've ever experienced. One captain refused to lower his loading nets so the troops on board his transport could practice carrying out disembarking drills because he claimed his sailors had not been trained how to operate the nets. The naval aviators on the USS *Ranger,* the only purpose-built aircraft carrier in TF34, are so inexperienced they're not going to be allowed to practice take-offs and landings on the trip over. General Doolittle, the Twelfth Air Force commander, reported seventy-two percent of his airmen are only partially trained."

Col. Randal said, "I'm supposed to believe the U.S. Navy can't provide twenty-nine sailors for TORCH?"

Col. Wilder said, "It's not like anyone has any actual experience conducting a large scale amphibious operation. The last time a U.S. fleet sailed to invade someplace was the Spanish American War. In case anyone ever asks, we're winging WWII.

"For the record—no, the U.S. Navy cannot provide twenty-nine sailors."

Col. Randal said, "My orders are to make the capture of the airfield happen. I can't sail until we have this worked out."

Col. Wilder's secretary stuck her head in the door, "General Kirkpatrick is on the line, Captain Johnson is holding, as is the president of the Longshoreman's Union."

"That's my boss," Col. Wilder said to Col. Randal. "The navy captain is TF34's senior port officer—both calling to check on my progress finding crew for *Contessa.* I can guess what the union wants. It's against safety regulations to load fuel and munitions at the same time. We'll have to declare a wartime emergency and obtain special dispensation."

Col. Randal stepped out into the outer office to let Col. Wilder take the calls. He glanced at his Rolex. It was 0845 hours, Sunday.

While he waited, the Standard Fruit Company representative from New York arrived and was soon joined by two of the local reps from Newport News and Norfolk. Lieutenant Albert Leslie, USN, who would be sailing as the co-skipper of the *Contessa,* walked in to see if he could help. Since he did not bring twenty-nine sailors with him and did not know where to find any to fill out the crew, about all he could do was stand by and look on anxiously.

Col. Wilder took the group into a conference room. They began to check rosters, call other shipping agents and even tried to reach *Contessa's* missing sailors. By the middle of the afternoon they had only been able to reach one seaman who would be arriving the next morning. Capt. Johnson called back with the word there was a possibility the navy could supply the sailors. That hope was dashed an hour later when a Lt. Cdr. Nelson called to inform Col. Wilder it was not going to be possible.

With no new sailors being found and the sun going down, Col. Randal returned to the hotel. It was practically empty since all the officers involved with TF34 either had sailed or completed their assignment and returned to their normal duties.

Col. Randal had dinner with Red.

She said, "I went shopping this afternoon. There are no silk stockings in any of the stores. A clerk told me military procurement officers came in unannounced and bought up all they had on the shelves and in their warehouse. The girl claimed none of the stores in their chain nor any of their competitors have any stockings left anywhere on the Eastern Seaboard.

"Do you know why, John?"

"Not a clue," Col. Randal said, "On another subject—the next question I ask you is classified."

Red said, "Understood."

"Have you ever heard of Port Lyautey?"

"I have; it is in Morocco."

"How far would you say from Gibraltar?"

"Two hundred, two hundred fifty miles by air."

"Tomorrow Red, you travel to New York. Go shopping for a couple of days, then I need you to fly straight back to Cairo and hand-carry sealed instructions for Billy Jack."

Red said, "What about you, John?"

"I'm going on a cruise."

Col. Randal arrived at Col. Wilder's office at 0700 hours, Monday. There was good news. The War Shipping Administration had located another hand, an intern from the Merchant Marine Academy. Then later, even better news came in. Seven seamen from a tanker that docked at Hampton Roads overnight had volunteered.

The civilian skipper of the *Contessa,* who would be sharing command with the Navy's Lt. Leslie during TORCH, phoned to say he had one more recruit. His brother-in-law, a salesman, had always wanted to go to sea. Now was his chance.

Lt. Leslie arrived, as did the Standard Fruit Company representatives. They immediately went into conference with Col. Wilder and Col. Randal. The desperate phone calls kept coming; General Gross phoned and wanted to know if the *Contessa* had sailed. Colonel Franklin called to ask the same thing.

At that point, having hit a wall in their efforts, there was a surreal quality to the meeting. Gloom hung heavy. Here they were in one of the greatest shipping capitals of the world and they could not find eighteen sailors, U.S. Navy or Merchant Marine, for the first U.S. invasion of WWII.

Every possibility had been exhausted.

Col. Randal said, "Why not phone the Norfolk County Jail and see how many sailors got arrested over the weekend."

It was not really a question.

Col. Wilder rushed to call the Norfolk County Sheriff. The Sheriff called the County Judge for approval to release incarcerated sailors with minor offenses. By 1430 hours, the senior Standard Fruit Company representative was at the jail located on East Main Street in Newport News, to conduct job interviews. There were fifty mostly hungover sailors who had decided to volunteer for hazardous duty.

Eighteen were chosen, released from jail, driven to a navy launch and in a freezing sleet storm motored out to the *Contessa,* who had steam up and was making ready to sail.

Col. Randal went on board the *Dallas.* The destroyer immediately put to sea, running at full speed, twenty-five knots, to catch up to the TF34 convoy.

For the *Contessa's* part, the Standard Fruit Company banana boat was going to have to make the 4,500-mile journey, counting all the zigzagging to dodge Nazi U-boats, all alone with her motley crew of ex-jailbirds—some of whom were having second thoughts about the wisdom of their decision when they learned of the ship's cargo.

FOR TWO DAYS A STORM RAGED. THE *DALLAS* BUCKED LIKE A WILD MUSTANG. COLONEL JOHN Randal spent most of the time in Lieutenant Commander Robert Brodie's cabin studying the sealed orders for the capture of the Port Lyautey airfield. The destroyer's skipper had allowed him the use of the tiny room for the duration of the passage. The Navy officer intended to spend the entire trip on the bridge, staying within easy voice distance and only catching cat naps on a pallet nearby when he had the chance. Being the captain of a warship underway was a trying job even when not actually engaged in battle.

The plan was pretty straightforward. The Sebou River was the demarcation between Red and Green's Beaches off Port Lyautey. Concrete jetties had been constructed on both sides of the mouth of the river. There was a boom across the entrance to the river consisting of a pair of cables supported by small boats. The cables held up antisubmarine nets—no one had mentioned the nets. Some distance up the river a heavy chain was stretched across the channel to block it.

A scratch seventeen-man team of U.S. Navy demolition men, hardhat divers flown in from Pearl Harbor and hastily trained on explosives, would blow the cable supporting the antisubmarine nets and then move upriver in a Higgins boat to knock out the chain boom prior to the *Dallas* entering the river at dawn on D-Day.

The Port Lyautey airfield was on the south side of the river. It was protected, sort of, by an ancient fort called the Kasbah, a mile up the Sebou.

The 2/60/9ID was to land ashore, march on the Kasbah and effect its capture before the *Dallas* made its way upriver. The fort's 75mm cannon, manned by tough French Foreign Legion artillerymen, posed a serious threat to the destroyer and her passengers. The Rangers would be crouching on her bow in anticipation of launching rubber assault rafts to paddle ashore when the ship reached the airfield.

On the north bank of the Sebou, 3/60/9ID would land on Red Beach, fight its way inland past the airfield on the opposite bank, capture the bridge spanning the river, cross over and support the 10th Rangers attack. In the event the bridge was defended and could not be taken, the 9th Division troops would be carrying rubber assault rafts with them to make a river crossing.

The 10th Rangers were to be delivered to their objective by the *Dallas,* disembark into rubber assault rafts, paddle ashore and attack Port Lyautey airfield—the prize of the TORCH expedition. The field was reported to be defended by French Moroccan troops described as "Goumiers." Trenches honeycombed the perimeter of the objective manned by what were described as "French troops," whatever that meant, and batteries, exact number unknown, of 75mm cannon and smaller caliber antiaircraft guns crewed by French Foreign Legion artillerymen. There was no intelligence providing information on the state of morale, fighting quality or what numbers the enemy troops would be in.

While the mission statement was straightforward, it was also suicidal.

On the third day, the skies cleared. Task Force 34 warships in nine columns stretched across the horizon as far as the eye could see. There was a sense of majesty, power and being a part of something big. Col. Randal and Lt. Cdr. Brodie had a chance to share a cup of coffee in the wardroom at the Captain's Table behind a curtain that could be pulled shut to provide privacy. What they had to talk about was not for public consumption.

Lt. Cdr. Brodie said, "So, what's your estimate of our mission?"

Col. Randal said, "Can you get us up the river?"

Lt. Cdr. Brodie said, "We have a French Port Authority pilot on board who has spent years navigating the inshore waters of Port Lyautey. Claims to know the Sebou like the back of his hand. He's not sure we can make it.

Shifting sand bars, possible obstructions he doesn't know anything about that might have been placed in the river by the Vichy French to impede passage since he escaped Morocco and the fact the *Dallas* can only draw seventeen feet make the run upriver chancy. That's not taking into account being shot at from both banks."

Col. Randal said, "Yeah."

Lt. Cdr. Brodie said, "If I get us there, can you take the airfield?"

Col. Randal said, "Intelligence is a little sketchy, but I can take the airfield. Anybody mention the forty-five tanks, which I'm guessing to be Renaults, that can arrive in less than an hour?"

Lt. Cdr. Brodie said, "No, they did not."

Col. Randal said, "If the tanks counterattack, we won't be able to hold the airport even if both battalions of the 60th Infantry Regiment arrive on schedule as planned. I recommend you drop the Rangers off, do a quick turn-around and get the hell out of Dodge back to open water as fast as you can."

Lt. Cdr. Brodie said, "Can't do that. The *Contessa* will be following us up the river. Besides, my orders are to support your attack with our four 4-inch guns and our single 3-inch gun. I'll provide you with a fire control team to take ashore with your command party. The battleship *Texas* is supporting Goalpost. She'll be on call to the 10th Rangers—14-inch guns. Plenty of naval fire support."

Col. Randal said, "You have any idea what's going to happen to that Standard Fruit banana boat when all those tanks start shooting at it, Commander?"

Lt. Cdr. Brodie said, "I've been sitting here thinking about that."

COLONEL JOHN RANDAL HAD SPENT TIME DURING THE STORM FAMILIARIZING HIMSELF WITH THE Remington Model 51 .380 pocket pistol Beverly had given him. He was very pleased with the little handgun. However, weapons were a subject he was going to have to address. He was armed with one of his Colt .38 Supers, his Browning 9mm P-35, the R51 and virtually no spare ammunition for any of them.

His personal lack of firepower was on his mind as he made his way to the fantail of the ship to introduce himself to the officers and NCOs of D Company, 10th Ranger Battalion—the men who would be leading the attack on Port Lyautey Airfield. This was going to be an important first meeting. Col. Randal had to take charge while not appearing to be a martinet, which he was when it came to preparing for a mission. At the same time, he needed to convey the clear impression he was a professional who knew his business without seeming to brag.

Not entirely easy.

The group assembled had spent a rough trip so far. Most of them had never been to sea. Some of the Rangers had been seasick while the *Dallas* was still tied up at the dock. For them, things had gone downhill during the storm. Those men who had sailed before most likely never experienced anything as choppy as the *Dallas* the last two days.

First Sergeant Ned Jaworski called, "ATTENTION!"

"As you were," Col. Randal ordered casually. "My name is Colonel Randal. Are you prepared to accept a Warning Order?" If the Rangers' small unit leaders had been expecting a casual meet-and-greet, they were badly disappointed. But he had their attention.

"Situation: We're somewhere in the Atlantic Ocean. On 8 November 42, we'll arrive off an enemy shore somewhere else. Exact time and place to be disclosed at a later date.

"Mission: D Company, 10th Ranger Battalion, is to conduct an amphibious attack on an enemy airfield.

"Execution: At zero-six-hundred hours, dawn on 9 November 42, the *Dallas* will enter the mouth of an undisclosed river, travel twelve miles upstream, D Company will land ashore behind enemy lines, force entry to and secure a hard-topped airfield in anticipation of relief by elements of the 60th Regimental Combat Team, 9th Infantry Division attacking overland.

"Concept of the Operation: D Company Rangers . . ."

Col. Randal wrapped up with. "Major Pfluger—issue your Warning Order to your troops as soon as we fall out. Officers Call in the wardroom in one hour. Fall out."

As the briefing was breaking up, Col. Randal said, "First Sergeant, I don't have a primary weapon. Can you find something for me?"

1SG Jaworski said, "I've got a spare M1 Carbine, sir."

"What's that?"

"A dinky little shooter manufactured by Winchester that they assign to officers, certain NCOs and members of crew served weapons, sir," 1SG Jaworski said. "I'm an '03 Springfield man. You can have my carbine, Colonel."

"Thanks, Top."

One hour later, Col. Randal arrived in the wardroom to find the Company D officers assembled. He had each man stand up and introduce himself. He had already memorized their names from the company roster; now he could put faces with the names. The Ranger officers were Major Walter Pfluger, Battalion XO who was in command of the Ranger detachment; Captain Tom Hathcock, D Company Commander; Lieutenant Griff Dooley, 1st Platoon Leader; and Lieutenant Jeff Lansdale, 2nd Platoon Leader.

There were only two thirty-man platoons in a 10th Ranger Battalion Company. Compared to a standard line infantry company, they were short men, NCOs, and officers.

Col. Randal said, "I'm not going to lie to you gentlemen. This is one of the toughest assignments I've ever been handed. There are a lot of moving parts. Many things that can go wrong.

"Not one of you has ever heard a shot fired in anger unless it was by a jealous husband. Don't let that bother you. The 10th Rangers are one of the most highly trained units in the army. In battle, hard training pays off—you fight how you train.

"Here's what we're going to do. Major Pfluger, you will serve as my Operations Officer. We will develop a Concept of the Operation. I'll issue an Operations Order to the officers and NCOs. Then, based on that briefing, the element leaders will develop their own order specific to their mission and issue it to their teams.

"Starting immediately, we're going to commence intensive mission prep for the remainder of the voyage. Captain Brodie has given the Rangers the run of the deck. I want to see weapons training, PT, hand-to-hand combat, assault raft loading drills, etc. We'll build a mock-up of the objective to study. Do not waste a minute of daylight. Then, work into the night—disassemble and assemble weapons in the dark. Is that clear?"

"CLEAR, SIR!"

"Do it."

Col. Randal provided Maj. Pfluger with his folder on the Port Lyautey Airfield. He gave him specific instructions on how he wanted 10th Rangers to attack the airfield, and he revealed that arrangements had been made for Captain Billy Jack Jaxx, flying out of Gibraltar aboard a pair of C-47s, to make a platoon-sized drop on the airport. That would bring the combined number of U.S. Forces attacking to slightly over one hundred, not counting the two battalions of the 60th Regimental Combat Team who might or might not arrive. Even with Capt. Jaxx's paratroopers, the ratio of attackers to defenders was still not good.

Maj. Pfluger was left to get on with his planning.

1SG Jaworski brought Col. Randal one of the brand-new .30 M1 Carbines. The little weapon was not a true carbine in that it was not a smaller version of the .30 M1 Rifle, and while they were both listed as .30 caliber, the rounds were completely different. The Carbine had been developed to replace the M1911 .45 automatic pistol because it was difficult to train soldiers to shoot pistols well. Especially with all the draftees coming into the army who had no previous experience with weapons.

1SG Jaworski said, "Either you like this toy or you don't, sir. It ain't for me."

Col. Randal said, "Seems pretty handy, Sergeant, for up close, fast work at night."

1SG Jaworski said, "I prefer bolt action thirty-ought-six, sir—slow but sure. Hit what you aim at. Kill what you hit."

Col. Randal immersed himself in the Rangers training program. Everywhere men were climbing ropes, practicing hand-to-hand combat, jogging around the perimeter of the *Dallas's* deck, walking through rubber assault raft drills.

One group was sitting on the deck cleaning their weapons. The troops had the parts spread out on OD wool blankets working on them with toothbrushes and shaving brushes tipped in oil. Col. Randal joined them, "OK, who's going to show me how to disassemble this M1 Carbine?"

The next day Col. Randal was getting ready to climb, gripping a rope that was tied off to the rail running around the upper deck. There were two other ropes dangling down with Rangers standing by, ready to go up. Rope climbing had turned into a series of races. The troops at the rope station were cheering on the three on the ropes. No one said training could not be fun.

Ranger Private Wally Malinowski said, "Smoke 'em, sir."

Col. Randal did not "smoke 'em."

After the noon meal, Maj. Pfluger gave Col. Randal his Operations Order. While it was a worthy first effort, he was not satisfied. He ordered, "Bring in all your element leaders, company, platoon, squad, fire team. Issue them this Op Order the way you gave it to me. Then have each of the leaders work out his individual scheme-of-maneuver. Incorporate all their actions-on-the-objective into the Mission Operations Order, rebrief the leaders, make adjustments or additions as necessary, then issue it to me again.

"Have Captain Hathcock serve as your assistant S-3. I want this mission planned in microscopic detail from start to finish. Provide me with a contingency plan for every conceivable scenario. The devil's in the details."

Maj. Pfluger said, "Yes, sir."

Col. Randal said, "Concurrently with you giving me the revised Operations Order, have the element leaders be issuing their Warning Order to their troops. Then once I've signed off on the plan, have the element leaders give their individual Op Orders they developed for you to their men. We'll allow everyone two or three days to rehearse, and then I'll issue the Mission Operations Order to everyone in D-Company plus all attachments so the men can see the big picture."

Maj. Pfluger said, "Will do, sir."

Col. Randal said, "Have a detail start constructing a mock-up of the Port Lyautey Airfield."

"The *Dallas's* carpenter is working on that now, sir."

"Understand, Major," Col. Randal said, "that when we attack, I'm not expecting things to go as planned."

Col. Randal spent the next two days going from one station to another, training with the troops. On the breaks, he would sit on the deck of the *Dallas* with the men gathered round and talk to the Rangers. Pretty much he said the same things over and over. The idea was not so much for him to get to know the men but for them to get to know him.

"We attack at dawn," Col. Randal said, passing around a package of Camel cigarettes. "We always attack at dawn. I've never heard an Op Order that says, 'We'll attack in midafternoon'."

The troops laughed.

Col. Randal said, "When we go in, men, have the mindset that the only thing standing between the success or failure of OPERATION TORCH is the 10th Ranger Battalion.

"You Rangers are handpicked studs. Self-reliant, able to think for yourselves and you never quit. The idea going back to Roger's Rangers in the French and Indian War is to be more clever than the enemy. Plan in detail, study your objective, and always find the easy way in. Then, neutralize the opposition with the least amount of effort, exhibiting controlled violence—professionally."

After Maj. Pfluger and Capt. Hathcock produced a plan that was acceptable to Col. Randal, he issued it the same day. The explosion of activity that had characterized the Rangers' voyage so far intensified. Mission prep began in earnest.

Col. Randal spent the next seven days at the large mock-up of the objective showing the twelve-mile approach up the Sebou River and the Port Lyautey Airfield. The ship's carpenter had constructed it. He watched and listened to the Ranger officers and NCOs briefing their troops on their individual actions on the objective. The recurring theme emphasized over and over was something he had said: "Exhibit controlled violence—professionally."

The Rangers liked that concept.

Col. Randal had stamped his brand of thinking on D Company, 10th

Ranger Battalion. He was confident the men were as well-prepared for their baptism by fire as any troops could ever be. He only wished they were combat veterans. Port Lyautey Airfield was a tough target.

Whoever was responsible for the idea to ride to the attack on a destroyer up the winding twelve-mile river behind enemy lines should have been required to accompany the officers and men who had to carry it out.

18
TAKING IT HOME

0300 HOURS 8 NOV 42. TASK FORCE 34 WAS ON STATION UNDER COVER OF DARKNESS OFF Morocco, ready to launch OPERATION TORCH after a 3,000-mile voyage that had been turned into a 4,500-mile trip due to all the zigzagging in an attempt to throw off Nazi U-boats. The Navy's navigation had been perfect. The landings were to begin in one hour.

The last stage had an eerie element to it, as Sub-Taskforce Goalpost steamed silently past Rabat. The city was not enforcing blackout restrictions, and its lights were clearly visible out to sea. The convoy was running blacked out, giving the ships a ghostly presence as they cruised along the coastline past it to their landing beaches.

Off the mouth of the Sebou River, Colonel John Randal was standing on the bridge of the *Dallas* with Lieutenant Commander Robert Brodie. The skipper said, "I can't see a thing."

Col. Randal said, "At times like this, one of my officers likes to say, 'It's always darkest before pitch-black'."

Lt. Cdr. Brodie said, "I'd rather not dwell on that."

The plan called for Sub-Taskforce Goalpost to land before dawn. At 0030 hours, landing craft infantry (LCI) began to be lowered into the water and steered toward their designated troop transport ships, with the intention of loading the men going ashore at 0130 hours. Problems began immediately. There were difficulties with winches, cables, divots and loading nets.

Once launched, the landing craft set out independently for the troopship from which they were assigned to pick up their passengers. The swarms of LCIs resulted in a sea-going traffic jam. The sounds of all the small craft swarming around could be heard on the bridge of the *Dallas.* The noise on the water somewhere out there in the dark was not reassuring.

Because of the blackout restrictions, some of the LCIs became disoriented and steered to the wrong troop transport. Radio silence was in force until 0500 hours, so there was no way to use wireless to bring order to the mounting confusion. Megaphones were broken out on the LCIs. Lost landing craft skippers could be heard inquiring as to the identity of the troopship they had pulled up to.

Brigadier General Lucian Truscott, the Goalpost commander, realized the invasion was in trouble. The General clamored down into an LCI, believing he could best provide command leadership from the water since there was no way to communicate by radio or signal lamp. It seemed like a good idea. However, the troopships would not respond to his megaphone requests for them to identify themselves—was the unexpected voice in the dark coming from an enemy agent?

Things got worse. Other ships not involved in the initial assault became confused about their positioning. They drifted into the loading area, contributing to the pandemonium.

Making the mother of all understatements, Lt. Cdr. Brodie said, "Inexperience in a sea-going operation of this magnitude is a real handicap."

Col. Randal said, "Roger that in spades."

He did what he always did when waiting for his part in an operation to kick off—started running over the plan in his mind as they stood by for the Navy demolitions party to report. The sailors had gone in aboard their Higgins boats to blow the cables supporting the submarine nets across the entrance of the Sebou River to allow the *Dallas* to start her run upriver to Port Lyautey Airfield.

Col. Randal was not entirely comfortable with the demolition team—if for no other reason than the sailors were not completely comfortable with being demolition men. The people on the team had been assigned the mission because they were hard-hat divers—not because they were demolitions men. The sailors had taken a course on explosives, but it had only lasted three days before they had to board the *Dallas.*

For what had to be the one thousandth time, Col. Randal repeated to himself, *"there's a sandbar at the mouth of the river slightly over seventeen feet deep. There's a boom across the Sebou up river. Vichy French troops are stationed on both banks, with a fortress located approximately a mile upriver on the south side."*

The width of the runways at the airfield was in excess of 5,000 yards. Too big for the small Ranger company to secure for any length of time. Help had to arrive or the enemy could retake it even without the arrival of the 45 Renault R35 tanks laagered less than an hours' distance away. The good news: the Rangers had six small, handheld antitank rocket launchers called bazookas. The bad news: none of the troops had ever fired one.

There were three prongs of attack comprising TORCH: at Mehdia, Casablanca and Safi. Sub-Taskforce Goalpost, commanded by BG Truscott, would land at Mehdia in three columns. The northernmost column would be attacking above the jetty marking the entrance to the Sebou River. The 3/60th was to race inland twelve miles, capture a bridge, and cross the river in order to assist the Rangers in taking and holding the airfield. In the event the bridge could not be taken, rubber assault rafts transported in half tracks were to travel with the battalion to be used to ford the river.

Col. Randal thought it was a tall order for the 3/60th to make an amphibious assault at Blue Beach, fight their way ashore, overcome the beach defenses, cut their way through enemy lines, travel twelve miles inland, capture a strategic point type target—the bridge—support the attack on the airfield and then participate in its defense until relieved.

The central Goalpost assault would land at Mehdia Beach. It was expected to encounter the fiercest resistance.

The southern column, formed around the 2/60th, had an assignment even more difficult than its sister battalion on the opposite bank. It was to go ashore at Lac Sidi Boughaba on Green Beach, near the highway between Rabat and Port Lyautey. The battalion was responsible for what was arguably the most difficult target of the entire TORCH invasion: capturing or reducing the Kasbah fortress located a mile upriver from Mehdia, which it was to supposed to bounce on the run en route to the primary target—the airfield.

While the main battle of the first wave was being fought at Mehdia, 2/60th and 3/60th, having landed on opposite sides of the Sebou River, were to skirt the fighting and race inland for the airfield. Except the 2/60th had to pause to reduce the Kasbah on the way.

Not to downplay the 3/60th assignment. In addition to all the other tasks it was expected to perform, it had to send one company to seize the bridge and another company to cross the river in rubber assault boats to assist in the capture of the airfield. The remainder of the battalion would be held in reserve, ready to exploit whichever of the two companies achieved success first.

While all that was taking place, 1/60th was to land south of Mehdia on Blue Beach, move around the southern edge of the lagoon, then set up a road block to attempt to prevent those 45 Renault R35 tanks at Rabat from reaching the TORCH beachhead or the airfield. This might be a stretch since the battalion did not have sufficient antitank weapons—except for the bazookas, which none of their troops had ever fired either.

Lt. Cdr. Brodie was to sail up the Sebou River to the Port Lyautey Airfield and land D Company, 10th Rangers, ashore.

None of that seemed very doable to Col. Randal. Particularly the *Dallas's* mad dash up the river to the Port Lyautey Airfield. The plan would have been overly complicated for a stateside peacetime training exercise, much less the first U.S. invasion of a foreign country in WWII.

The skipper of the destroyer interrupted his thoughts. "We won't be seeing any air support until *after* you capture the airfield. We only have the one aircraft carrier in TF34, USS *Ranger*. The *Hornet, Lexington, Wasp* and *Yorktown* were all sunk by the Japs, so it was the only one available. The little escort carriers supporting Goalpost can launch fighters, and they will just as soon as you capture the airfield, but the planes can't land back on board once they take off because the jeep carriers, as we call them, don't have any arresting gear. No pressure, huh?"

Col. Randal said, "All the air support we need after the fight's over."

"I guess you don't want to hear the news that half the bluejackets on the two escort carriers assigned to support Goalpost are making their first sea voyage."

Col. Randal said, "Lovely."

A signalman appeared and handed Lt. Cdr. Brodie a message.

"The demolitions team came under heavy fire on approaching the boom and were not able to reach the submarine nets," Lt. Cdr. Brodie said. "They'll try again tomorrow morning, same time."

Nothing could be worse at this stage than a last-minute postponement.

Col. Randal was disgusted and frustrated but chose not to show it. 10th Rangers were keyed up, ready to go into action. Now they had to wait. "I need to red light my paratroopers on Gibraltar."

Lt. Cdr. Brodie said, "My communications division have their frequency. I'll make it happen, no problem."

Captain Billy Jack Jaxx's two C-47s would be airborne before they received the stand-down order. If they failed to receive it and jumped, there would be a catastrophe. He would be responsible.

Sensing Col. Randal's concern, Lt. Cdr. Brodie said, "I'll let you know as soon as your people acknowledge the order to abort."

Col. Randal asked, "Mind if I borrow your loud hailer?"

"Be my guest."

"NOW HEAR THIS," Col. Randal said into the handset. "RANGERS STAND DOWN. I SAY AGAIN STAND DOWN. WE ARE ON A TWENTY-FOUR-HOUR HOLD. THAT IS ALL."

Col. Randal went down on deck to talk to Major Walter Pfluger and Captain Tom Hathcock. When he got there, the two officers were not happy, not knowing what to be unhappy about other than the postponement. Not that the reason mattered. Waiting played havoc with morale.

Col. Randal ordered, "Immediately commence mission prep all over again. I want you to keep the Rangers busy. We don't want 'em sitting around all day doing nothing but waiting, wondering."

"Yes, sir."

"Don't worry," Col. Randal said. "We'll go tomorrow if I have to take a team in broad daylight and blow the obstruction myself. Tell the men I said that."

"YES, SIR!"

"In fact, start organizing a Ranger demolitions party and let everyone know you're doing it—call for volunteers."

Col. Randal returned to the bridge. Almost immediately an alarm sounded. Lt. Cdr. Brodie pointed out the lights of five unknown ships heading directly toward the Sub-Taskforce Goalpost convoy. Signal lamps from the intruders began flashing a warning: "Be forewarned an alert on shore has been ordered for 0500 hours."

Lt. Cdr. Brodie said, "There goes the element of surprise."

Confusion still reigned among the LCIs. Each battalion of the 60th Regimental Combat Team "Go Devils" was assigned a control ship around which to rally and prepare for a synchronized school solution, clockwork combat landing under cover of darkness. At least that was the plan. In fact, it was nearly sunrise before the landing craft began to straggle their way toward their designated beaches. The sun was up by the time 3/60th made it ashore at Blue Beach.

As the first waves hit the beach, enemy shore batteries opened fire.

Lt. Cdr. Brodie said, "State Department got it wrong. The French plan to fight—as you predicted, Colonel."

Col. Randal said, "There was never any chance they weren't going to."

U.S. Navy warships immediately commenced counterbattery fire. Red and green tracers began arching toward the shore. The morning sun was soon pale gray, partially obscured by the smoke. Because she was loaded with Rangers on her deck, the *Dallas* did not join in the firing.

Situation Report: 3/60th has encountered an extremely steep escarpment just off the beach and are mired down in fine, white sand, making it problematic hauling heavy weapons and the rubber assault rafts inland in a timely fashion.

To add insult to injury, the battalion had just been strafed by four French fighters flying off of the Port Lyautey Airfield—the one the 10th Rangers should have captured at dawn. The incoming artillery fire and the appearance of the French Air Force caused the transport and cargo ships to pull back farther out to sea. The fleet's move created a ripple-down effect. Now the ships were out of shore-based radio range, so communications broke down and messages had to be carried by hand back and forth between the beach and the fleet aboard LCIs. It took longer to transport follow-on troops to the beach. And it took longer for empty landing craft to return to the convoy to begin ferrying the desperately needed heavy equipment, like bulldozers and artillery, ashore.

Disembarkation slowed to a crawl. Even so, supplies began to pile up haphazardly on the beaches. With the odd artillery round screaming in and blowing up, the sailors manning the landing craft wanted to get off the beach as fast as possible and they were not adhering to the rigid unloading plan. Artillery, heavy equipment and stores were sitting idle, buried in the fine white sand where they had been dumped, not making their way inland where it was needed. A high number of landing craft ran aground and became stuck as well.

An epic logistical crisis was in the making.

> Situation Report: 1/60th has fought its way ashore in good order, moved inland, cut the Rabat road and set up a roadblock to stop enemy tanks from advancing on the beachhead.

The 1/60th did not have to wait long. Armed with two Browning M-2 .50 caliber machine guns and one of the new bazookas, the antitank team at the roadblock held their fire until the Renault R35 tanks were within fifty yards. The bazooka's rocket missed the tank but turned a eucalyptus ten yards behind it into matchsticks.

The French column halted, apparently believing 1/60th had moved up heavy antitank artillery. The cautious troop commander sent out reconnaissance patrols to attempt to locate the nonexistent battery. So far, so good.

> Situation Report: 2/60 experiencing difficulty organizing but has finally gotten off Green Beach. The battalion has advanced up the Sebou to the Kasbah fortress where they are pinned down by French Foreign Legion 75mm artillery and U.S. Navy gunfire.

Taking fire from both sides, the battalion withdrew, crossed the northern tip of the lagoon and occupied the high ground. From there, having misunderstood their orders to reduce the Kasbah, 2/60th marched on Port Lyautey Airfield eleven miles distant. As they moved out, French infantry and tanks counterattacked, driving the battalion back to where it started between Mehdia and the Kasbah. At that point, the battalion was again pinned down by the Foreign Legion artillery and incoming fire from the U.S. Navy. The Go Devils 2nd Battalion was not having a good day.

> Situation Report: The 3/60 is situated on the high ground opposite the Port Lyautey Airfield. None of the heavy equipment, artillery or the assault rafts have made it off the beach. A naval fire control party has been established in caves overlooking the airport across the river. Large numbers of French troops have been observed running when rounds impacted the airfield.

A message arrived on the *Dallas.* "3/60th spotted a French steamer heading down the river. The ship was intentionally scuttled at a bend on the north side of the Sebou River in an attempt to block it."

Lt. Cdr. Brodie handed the message to Col. Randal, "Navigating the river without a ship blocking it was going to be difficult enough."

Col. Randal said, "It's always darkest before pitch-black."

Rene Malevergne, the French inshore pilot, glanced at the flimsy, "*Merde!*"

Then a message arrived stating that the Kasbah had been captured and the cable supporting the submarine nets across the mouth of the Sebou River was down. Another message quickly followed, ordering the *Dallas* to storm the airfield.

Tension on the bridge shot sky-high.

Pilot Malevergne said, "Crossing the sandbar was possible three hours earlier. Now, at low tide, sadly it cannot be done. If commanded, I am willing to attempt to take the ship upriver. Understand, Captain, it is impossible."

Lt. Cdr. Brodie said, "Colonel, you OK with this?"

Col. Randal said, "You get my Rangers past the Kasbah and we'll do the rest."

Lt. Cdr. Brodie said, "How about we cruise by the mouth of the Sebou and see if the enemy battery there has been neutralized and if the submarine nets are down before we commit to the run upriver?"

The Frenchman shrugged.

Col. Randal said, "Sounds like a plan."

Orders started going out to D Company, 10th Rangers, over the ship's public address system. Troops began double-timing to their debarkation stations. Men were shouting. Equipment was rattling. The PA system kept blaring instructions.

The wait was over.

Lt. Cdr. Brodie and the pilot consulted on the best strategy. The idea they devised was to run past Mehdia to see if the ship drew fire. The *Dallas* surged forward in a sweeping semicircle, eventually running parallel to the sandbar known to be at the mouth of the river. Splashes of gunfire could be seen landing behind the ship but not aimed directly at it. The idea was to break forty-five degrees to port and enter the estuary at all ahead full.

Still no incoming rounds aimed at the *Dallas,* so the ship powered toward the jetties. The communications officer arrived on the bridge with all the confidential documents that had been on board and heaved them over the side in a weighted canvas sack to prevent them from falling into enemy hands. That was an attention getter.

As the *Dallas* reached the point of committing to its run up the river, a message arrived with the information the Kasbah had not been taken. Then the batteries near the jetties opened fire directly at the ship. And from the bridge, they could see the boom had not been cut. Lt. Cdr. Brodie immediately brought the ship hard about, ordered a smokescreen and departed the area at flank speed.

Now the Rangers had to stand down for a second time.

As the sun went down on the Sub-Taskforce Goalpost beachhead, only ten percent of the supplies needed for the 60th Regimental Combat Team Go Devils had made it to shore.

9 NOV 42 D-DAY PLUS 1. THE WEATHER WAS NOT COOPERATIVE. THE SURF WAS AT SIX FEET AND rising. Rain began to fall.

The boom had still not been blown by daybreak. Colonel John Randal signaled his intent to take in a team to cut the cable. Brigadier General Lucian Truscott sent a terse response, ordering him to stand down and leave the job to the Navy. He did not want the Rangers going up the river since not one of the tasks that had to be accomplished in order for them to have any chance of success had been completed.

Col. Randal read the message to the troops gathered on the bow of the *Dallas.* Their reaction was loud boos. Not only from the scratch demolition team who were psyched up ready to go make it happen, but also from the men who wanted to get up the Sebou and close with the enemy guarding the Port Lyautey Airfield.

> Situation Report: 2/60th still unable to capture Kasbah. The fortress has been heavily reinforced overnight by Foreign Legionnaires from Meknes.

The Go Devil 2nd Battalion was badly disorganized and not performing well. Only thirty to fifty men per company could be accounted for—a third of normal strength. Where were the other troops—captured, wandering around lost, stragglers hiding out on the beach?

> Situation Report: 3/60th rubber assault rafts have arrived. I Company to make river crossing.

Only a single hand pump came with the rafts. The battalion struggled to get them operational. So much noise was made trying to inflate the rubber boats it attracted the attention of the Vichy French, who promptly responded with a barrage of artillery, causing numerous casualties.

> Situation Report: 3/60th battalion commander ordered the bridge over the Sebou to be captured and the river crossing to take place by the end of the day.

> Situation Report: 1830 hours. K/3/60 ambushed when it was within twelve hundred yards of the bridge. Battalion commander ordered a withdrawal.

After a frustrating day, K/3/60th was right back where it started.

> Situation Report: 1900 hours. I/3/60 launched rubber assault rafts. Crossed Sebou and are now dug in on south side of the river.

Follow-up messages revealed I Company's crossing of the Sebou was more involved than the Situation Report announcing it had made it sound. A lack of preparation turned the exercise into a nightmarish SNAFU. Since none of the Go Devils had rehearsed rubber assault raft river crossings prior to TORCH, when they tried it for the first time, the little boats were almost unmanageable in the river. It took seven trips to transport the entire company across.

Col. Randal thought to himself, *poor prior planning produces poor results. The word "preparation" could just as easily be substituted for "planning" in this case.*

Once on the airfield side of the river, I/3/60 found itself floundering through a black silt mud bottom in growing darkness. Instead of heading inland toward firm ground, for some reason the company commander decided to parallel the river—a route that took them into the heart of the swamp. The men were covered in mud, being attacked by at least one million mosquitoes, and their weapons were mostly all unserviceable.

Then I Company turned west on an azimuth that had them paralleling the airfield instead of advancing on it. The French detected their presence and immediately brought down indirect fire, causing a number of casualties and thoroughly dispiriting the already muddy, exhausted, mosquito-bitten Go Devils. The decision was made to retrace their steps to the river bank and wait for the sun to come up.

I/3/60th was right back where they were when the company initially crossed the Sebou.

Outside of Mehdia, BG Lucian Truscott was not having a good start to his war. Tomorrow would be day three of OPERATION TORCH. The other two Sub-Taskforce commanders had already successfully accomplished their missions while his Goalpost troops had still not secured a single one of their D-Day objectives. His boss, Major General George S. Patton Jr., was not pleased with his performance and let him know it in no uncertain terms—something at which old Blood and Guts was extremely capable.

BG Truscott sat down on the beach, lit a cigarette in violation of his own orders not to smoke during the hours of darkness, and dispatched four directives. The first went to Colonel Fredrick de Rohan, the commander of the 60th Regimental Combat Team Go Devils. "You are to personally take command of the 2/60th. Attack and capture the Kasbah at dawn." By that, BG Truscott meant for the colonel to fix his bayonet and lead the charge.

The second order was to the Navy demolitions team. "Blow the obstacles obstructing the Sebou River and report back to me no later than 0200 hours *at all cost.*"

The third order went to the battalion commanders of 1/60th and 3/60th. "At first light, move to support the attack on the airfield by D Company, 10th Ranger Battalion."

The fourth order went to Lieutenant Commander Robert Brodie. "Enter the Sebou River at sunrise and deliver D Company, 10th Rangers, to the Port Lyautey Airfield, then stand-by on call to support the attack with your ship's 3-inch guns."

On the *Dallas*, a message arrived addressed to Col. Randal from Maj. Gen. Patton. "Make me proud."

0500 HOURS 10 NOV 42. THE *DALLAS* BEGAN ITS APPROACH TO THE JETTIES FROM THIRTEEN MILES out. Lieutenant Commander Robert Brodie, with Pilot Rene Malevergne standing beside him on the bridge and Colonel John Randal keeping out of the way but in a position to observe everything taking place, called for a speed of fourteen knots. The idea was to reach the mouth of the Sebou precisely at daybreak.

At 0545 hours, as the ship was running in to the jetties, the waves washing over her stern were pushing the destroyer toward the entrance to the river at a higher rate of speed than desired. Lt. Cdr. Brodie ordered speed reduced to ten knots.

It was still dark; however, a thin sliver of light was beginning to be visible on the horizon. The water the ship was passing over started to show yellow, indicating a sandy bottom. The *Dallas* was closing on the mouth of the Sebou.

Pilot Malevergne asked to take the wheel and Lt. Cdr. Brodie surrendered it to him. It was still too dark to see the jetties, which stuck out from the shore several hundred feet.

Unsure of his exact position, Pilot Malevergne called for the engines to be cut. When the turbines quit throbbing, an unnatural stillness came over the *Dallas.* The PA system blared, jarring the silence: "Now hear this, now hear this. All hands on deck, to include Rangers. Keep a sharp lookout for land."

The Frenchman cocked his head, listening for the "growl" made by waves crossing over the sandbar he knew to expect from piloting other ships up the river in days past. Pilot Malevergne steered a few points to port. The rising sun backlit the pile of rocks marking the south side of the jetty. He brought the *Dallas* around to starboard at forty-five degrees. Now it was possible to see waves breaking on the rocks.

To the south, Mehdia came into view in the pale morning light. Equipment, supplies, vehicles and the occasional LCI stuck in the sand littered the beach. Major General George S. Patton Jr. and Brigadier General Lucian Truscott were standing there watching the *Dallas* come in. Col. Randal saw them through the powerful binoculars Lt. Cdr. Brodie had loaned him.

Maj. Gen. Patton raised the field glasses he wore around his neck. For a brief moment he and Col. Randal were locked on, staring at each other. Neither of them made any gesture before Col. Randal swung his glasses back to the rapidly approaching jetties.

The *Dallas* yawed as Pilot Malevergne pointed the ship toward the channel, first veering toward the rocks, then bobbing back in the direction of the shoal side of the jetties. The waves became choppier as the ship approached the sandbar. This was the moment of truth.

The PA blared, "Now hear this. Now hear this. Stand by for impact. All personnel brace yourself."

As the *Dallas* bore down on the sandbar, the swell increased. A cannon shell screamed in and detonated thirty yards in front of the ship, throwing up a giant plume of water taller than the mast. A heart attack moment for everyone on board.

Lt. Cdr. Brodie said, "Won't need my morning cup of coffee to get me rolling after that."

A second shell came over—making the tearing sheet sound artillery rounds give off as they pass by—and detonated behind the *Dallas.* Now the French gunners had the ship bracketed. At three minutes after 0600 hours, the destroyer hit the bar.

The *Dallas* vibrated from stem to stern. The ship hung, shuddering on the sandbar. Then, inch by inch, she fought her way forward and made it over. Pilot Malevergne ordered full speed ahead—twenty-five knots.

The engine room reported the ship was at full power.

Lt. Cdr. Brodie looked over the side, "We're barely making five knots."

Pilot Malevergne said, "My guess is no more than three."

Lt. Cdr. Brodie leaned over the rail and checked toward the stern. Muck churned to the top of the water. "We're scraping bottom."

Dallas fought her way forward agonizingly slowly, but eventually began to pick up speed.

As the ship approached the Kasbah, Col. Randal studied the scene of intense fighting through his field glasses. The rattle of rifle fire and automatic weapons could be heard. Dead bodies of 2/60 soldiers littered the ground in front of the ancient structure. Other troops were at the giant wooden double doors banging on it with the butts of their M1 Rifles. Go Devil machine gunners were firing on the fortress to no observable effect. The Vichy French inside were shooting back.

Col. Randal said, "Can you raise General Truscott?"

Almost instantly the response was, "Can do."

Col. Randal said, "Advise the General the 2/60th is not making progress. See if he can send a naval fire support team to the Kasbah and have the *Texas* reduce the fort with its 14 inch guns."

Lt. Cdr. Brodie said, "Uh-oh!"

Col. Randal looked where he was pointing. The boom blocking the river had only partially been cut. At this point, the Sebou was approximately a quarter mile wide. The cable stretched about halfway from the south bank to the center of the river.

Pilot Malevergne said, "To the north side of the river, where the cable is down, the Vichy French have planted mines."

Col. Randal said, "Nobody said anything about mines."

Lt. Cdr. Brodie looked grim.

"Toward the south bank are shoals," Pilot Malevergne said. "Captain, there is not enough depth there."

A machine gun fired on the *Dallas* from the Kasbah, but the blue tracers indicated they were out of range as the rounds fell short.

"Lt. Cdr. Brodie ordered, "Ram it dead center."

Pilot Malevergne said, "Ring for eighteen knots."

The PA announced, "Now hear this. Now hear this. Stand by for collision. All personnel stand by for collision."

The destroyer hit the chain. It made a loud screeching sound.

Col. Randal glanced over at the pilot. He had his eyes clinched shut.

Dallas sliced through the boom and surged ahead into deeper water. On both banks of the river, Go Devils stood up from their fighting positions and started cheering. The Rangers were waving back, shouting and giving rebel yells—making a real life charge better than any movie. In the distance, the Port Lyautey Airfield swam into sight.

Then another obstacle loomed just ahead of the next bend in the river, which narrowed at its many sharp curves. Instead of one French ship being scuttled in an attempt to block the river, there were two—the *Batavia* and *Saint Emile.*

This was a problem.

Pilot Malevergne found himself faced with a dilemma. The gap between the two ships was barely large enough for the *Dallas* to squeeze through, the French sailors had got it wrong. However, at the bend, the river was shallow, and the current was strong. If he slowed too much, the ship might be swept against the bank or pushed back into the two ships blocking the channel. If he went too fast, the destroyer might not make the turn in the river and run straight into the bank.

The French inshore pilot rolled the dice, "Full speed ahead."

No one on the ship was cheering now.

First the *Dallas* swayed to starboard. Then she rolled to port. The destroyer righted herself, then shot the gap between the two scuttled ships. And somehow, amazingly, she got around the bend in the river, driving hard for the airfield. Now D Company, 10th Ranger Battalion was the leading element in the Goalpost invasion of Port Lyautey.

The *Dallas* was taking it home.

Col. Randal said, "Whatever they're paying you, Mr. Malevergne, it ain't enough."

Sounding a lot more relieved than he would have probably liked, Lt. Cdr. Brodie said, "Affirmative."

Col. Randal said, "I'm rejoining my troops."

The Rangers gathered around when he arrived on the bow. Up ahead they could see their objective. The men were anxious to get ashore.

All the time Col. Randal had spent working with the troops on the voyage was now paying off. He was one of them—not just some senior officer assigned to command the mission at the last minute. The Rangers were glad to see him—hanging on his every word. He was going to lead them on their first combat mission.

Col. Randal said, "You men all know your job. Each Ranger squad has as much firepower as a TO&E infantry platoon—two BARs and four Thompson submachine guns. Light 'em up when we hit our objective. Controlled violence—professionally.

"Sequence of debarking and order of march, Major Pfluger, my command party, Lieutenant Dooley, Lieutenant Lansdale, and Captain Hathcock."

Two C-47s roared over the *Dallas,* missing her mast by inches. The Dakota troop transports had taken off from Gibraltar and had been racetracking overhead, observing the destroyer's progress up the river. The planes wiggled their wings as they thundered past.

Col. Randal could clearly recognize Captain Billy Jack Jaxx arching out the door of the lead aircraft spread eagle, as if he was performing a jumpmaster inspection. He was checking out the *Dallas.*

Col. Randal said, "That's Jack Cool, boys. A life taker and a heartbreaker. He's going to jump no matter what, so let's go get him."

The Rangers cheered.

The *Dallas* shuddered to a stop, run hard aground. The destroyer was firmly stuck in the middle of the river. She was not going any farther.

This was not part of the plan.

Col. Randal ordered, "Away all boats. Let's go—now."

The Rangers began frantically lowering their rubber assault rafts over the starboard side. The *Dallas* was a sitting target, clearly visible to the gunners on the airfield. The French began to shell the ship and one incoming round struck the port side.

The explosion was extraordinarily loud. While it did not cause any casualties, it had the effect of motivating the Rangers to even greater efforts to get the rubber assault rafts away. Maj. Pfluger's team was over the side and swarming down the nets like mad men.

A pair of P-40 Tomahawks screamed over, firing their .50 caliber machine guns. The *Dallas* opened for the first time with a thunderous roar, smoke rings blowing out the barrels of the ship's three-inch guns. The French guns went silent.

As he was going over the rail leading his command party down the landing net, Col. Randal glanced up at the fighters. The P-40s must have launched from one of the escort carriers—which meant they had no place to land until the Rangers captured the airfield.

As soon as the command party scrambled into the raft, it shoved off on the command of, "Give way together."

Everyone was paddling furiously. With every stroke, the Rangers were shouting, "Go, go, go . . ."

The distance to shore was less than a hundred yards. The rubber assault boats were flying across the water. Up ahead, Major Walter Pfluger's team scrambled up the bank and immediately set off on the double for their objective—the airfield's base headquarters complex.

Col. Randal's command party landed. It consisted of his radio operator, First Sergeant Ned Jaworski, a naval fire control team from the *Dallas,* and a two-man security detail. They moved out, traveling fast.

Lieutenant Griff Dooley's team came right on their heels. Lt. Dooley was responsible for securing the airport's troop barracks.

Lieutenant Jeff Lansdale's team was next. He was responsible for attacking any enemy gun position still firing when D Company arrived on the objective.

Last in the column was Captain Tom Hathcock. He commanded the company reserve. The situation on the airfield would dictate what action his team would take, subject to Col. Randal giving him the go-ahead to commit the reserves.

Shortly after landing, Col. Randal's command party encountered the point element of I/3/60th exiting the muddy bottom they had been trapped in. The frustrated, bug-bitten, exhausted Go Devils were looking to get payback for all the misery they had endured. Without slowing, Col. Randal ordered the platoon leader to inform his company commander to secure the near side of the runway.

Several things happened almost simultaneously at the Port Lyautey Airport that turned out better than what the original and overly ambitious battle plan had called for. Only in this case, three days late.

The two C-47 Dakotas roared down the length of the airstrip at six hundred feet altitude. Thirty jumpers of a provisional platoon, drawn mainly from the 575th Parachute Infantry Regiment commanded by Capt. Jaxx, hit the silk. The effect on the defenders was immediate. The French troops in fighting positions guarding the runway ceased firing and fled for their lives, it being a well-known myth that parachutists did not take prisoners. Naturally, they fled in the three directions away from where the parachutes were drifting down.

That was a mistake.

To the south, A/1/60th, a company that had performed extremely well from the moment it landed in the first wave on D-Day, was racing to be the first to capture the airfield. To the north, M/3/60th saw the defenders of the bridge over the Sebou flee when they too saw the first parachute crack open. M Company immediately charged across, determined to be the unit that captured the airfield. But almost immediately they ran headlong into the French troops escaping the base. After a brief, one-sided firefight, the infantry company hunkered down, creating a blocking force with dead enemy troops strewn out in front of their position as a warning: "don't come this way." And from the river side, I/3/60th and D Company, 10th Ranger Battalion, were driving on the airfield as hard as they could go.

Everyone wanted to be in at the kill. And they were. The airfield was completely sealed, and a slaughter incurred.

The provisional platoon from the 575th was the first in action. Armed entirely with Colt Monitor Model BARs, .45 caliber Thompson submachine guns and 9mm MAB-38A submachine guns, they put out a massive volume of fire. The Rangers chopped down the fleeing enemy troops who were caught on firing range-type terrain that offered no cover.

Maj. Pfluger's team hit the built-up area base HQ complex second. Col. Randal's command party was right with it when they went in. The fighting was intense. While the 10th Rangers did not have as many automatic weapons as Jack Cool's men, they had enough. The roar of fire was deafening.

Col. Randal found himself caught up in the firefight—which was not what he intended. He wanted to be free to command the overall action on the objective.

Maj. Pfluger's Rangers rushed in and immediately took control of the ground floor of the two-story building. Heavy firing from the second floor prevented them from getting up the single stairway.

As Col. Randal arrived, a sniper on the four-story control tower located fifty yards away began firing. By reflex the handy little .30 caliber M1 carbine came up to his shoulder, Col. Randal saw the post front sight clearly through the ghost ring rear aperture, placed it center of mass on the rifleman and *BLAAAM* . . . shot him with no conscious thought of doing it. The shooter cartwheeled down in slow motion.

Then Col. Randal rushed inside the building where the fight was raging.

Rangers were firing up through the ceiling. Enemy troops on the second floor were firing down through it. Col. Randal recognized instantly that this was not going to end well for either side. He did not want to take casualties in a fight with misguided Frenchmen possessed of a confused sense of honor.

"Pull everyone out," Col. Randal ordered Maj. Pfluger. "Break out the bazookas."

"Yes, sir!"

"Knock the building down."

"With pleasure, Colonel."

While the Rangers had not had a chance to fire the bazooka antitank rocket launchers, it was not going to require much skill at point-blank range. When everyone was clear of the building, three scratch bazooka teams knelt down and commenced firing, first making sure no one was behind them—they knew that much. The bazookas, being recoilless, had a back blast. Anyone struck by it would be severely injured or killed.

While the rest of the team gave covering fire, the bazooka gunners started working on the second floor, firing as fast as their loader could slam in a new rocket and shout, "UP!" A steady drumbeat of *BLAAAAM, BLAAAAAM, BLAAAAAM* shattered the wooden structure.

Not speaking one word of French and with no inclination to take a survey to find out if any of the Rangers did, Col. Randal shouted, "Cease firing and come out now or we'll burn the building down."

White flags, towels, undershirts and even typewriter paper started fluttering out the second-story windows. Resistance at the airfield HQ complex had ceased.

Maj. Pfluger said, "That worked."

Which 60th Regimental Combat Team Go Devils unit hit the airfield next was not clear. A flurry of firing broke out all around. However, it was brief and one-sided.

Capt. Jaxx, accompanied by King, arrived at the HQ complex. Jack Cool handed Col. Randal one of Waldo's cigars. "Mr. Treywick wanted to come along but he had a Mr. Big performance that conflicted with his schedule."

Lighting the cigar with his old battered U.S. 26th Cavalry Regiment Zippo, Col. Randal said, "Nice job, Jack."

They stood and watched as the Rangers raised the Stars and Stripes on the flagpole on the control tower. 1SG Jaworski shouted, "Hand salute!"

Everyone did. It felt good. Damn good.

Soon officers from all three companies from the different battalions showed up to report their area of the airfield secured. Col. Randal ordered his radio operator to raise the Brigadier General Lucian Truscott's Goalpost Headquarters. "Mission accomplished. Airfield secure."

As the message was being transmitted, a lone P-40 Tomahawk lined up on the end of the airfield and came in for a landing. After a short run, it crashed into a bomb crater. The pilot climbed out of the plane uninjured.

Then his wingman came in and tried to land on the ground alongside the concrete landing strip. Unfortunately, the ground was soggy, his wheels became mired and the undercarriage was ripped off. The pilot from the first plane ran up to Col. Randal shouting, "Signal the *Chenango* not to launch any more aircraft."

The message went out, to no avail. Planes kept arriving. Before long there were twenty-three crashed P-40s littering the Port Lyautey Airfield, and they kept coming. It was insane—like the pilots had a death wish.

As Col. Randal and the 575th PIR's provisional paratroop platoon boarded an LCI that had been sent up the Sebou to take them back to BG Truscott's Command Post, Capt. Jaxx asked, "How do you explain the USAAF being so stupid?"

Col. Randal said, "You got me."

When the little *Contessa,* having never caught up to Task Force 34 and sailing the entire way across the U-boat infested Atlantic Ocean all by herself, made her way up the river to the airport later, with the same French pilot at the helm who had guided the *Dallas,* she became stuck fast on the exact same sandbank as had the destroyer. At least he was consistent.

No navy vessel would come anywhere near the Honduran-flagged fruit boat because of her cargo of aviation fuel and aerial bombs, so her skipper had to hire native barges to transport it the one hundred yards to shore. Since the Moroccan rivermen did not have a union to protest handling the high-risk cargo and since money talked, the locals went to work with a will.

Two days behind schedule, Maj. Gen. Patton had his all-weather air base—the prize of the entire invasion. Port Lyautey Airfield had its aviation fuel and bombs. However, not one of the fighters that landed on the base from the escort carriers flew a single combat mission in support of OPERATION TORCH.

TWO DAYS LATER, THE C-47S FLEW IN FROM GIBRALTAR AND LANDED ON THE NOW OPERATIONAL Port Lyautey Airfield to take the Raiding Forces personnel back to RFHQ. As they were loading, Colonel John Randal noticed Captain Billy Jack Jaxx and a party of his paratroopers manhandling crates aboard the aircraft.

"What's going on, Captain?"

"You're not going to believe this, sir," Capt. Jaxx said. "The United States Army went to the trouble to bring six tons of silk stockings to Morocco to trade to French women and then just left it all sitting on the beach to rot. I'm taking about half of 'em back to RFHQ with us."

Jack Cool.

TO BE CONTINUED IN TIP OF THE SWORD—
BOOK XIII IN THE RAIDING FORCES SERIES

The Raiding Forces series continues . . . all the way to VE Day.
To be on our notification list for the next book, contact phil@philward.com

ABBREVIATIONS
Orders & Awards

Bt Baronet
CB Companion of the Bath
CMG Companion of the Order of St. Michael & St. George
DCM Distinguished Conduct Medal
DFC Distinguished Flying Cross (Royal Air Force)
DSC Distinguished Service Cross (Royal Navy)
DSM Distinguished Service Medal
DSO Distinguished Service Order
GC George Cross
GCB Grand Cross in the Order of the Bath
GM George Medal
KBE Knight Commander of the Most Excellent Order of the British Empire
KCVO Knight Commander of the Royal Victorian Order
LG Lady Companion of the Order of the Garter
MC Military Cross
MM Military Medal
MVO Member of the Royal Victorian Order
OBE Order of the British Empire
SS Silver Star Medal (U.S. Armed Forces)
VC Victoria Cross

STRATEGIC SERVICES

ACRONYMS

AO Area of Operation
AP Armor Piercing
ATA Air Transport Auxiliary
BAR Browning Automatic Rifle
BMNT Beginning Morning Nautical Twilight
BOAC British Overseas Airways Corporation
BOQ Bachelor Officer's Quarters
CLO Clandestine Liaison Officer
COHQ Combined Operations Headquarters
DUKW A 2 ½-ton swimming tank
DZ Drop Zone
ETO European Theatre of Operations
GHQ General Headquarters
HMS His Majesty's Ship
IDB Illicit Diamond Buying
ISLD Inner Services Liaison Department
KIA Killed in Action
LARU Lambertsen Amphibious Respirator Unit
LCA Landing Craft Assault
LCI Landing Craft Infantry
LCS London Controlling Section
LD Line of Departure
LMG Light Machine Gun
LP Listening Posts
LRDG Long Range Desert Group

MAS *Motoscafo armato silurante,* torpedo armed motorboat (Italian)
MEHQ Middle East Command Headquarters
MG Machine Gun
MIA Missing in Action
ML Motor Launch
MU Martine Unit (OSS)
NCO Noncommissioned Officer
NID Naval Intelligence Division
OD Olive Drab
OP Operations (Orders)
OSS Office of Strategic Services, previously Office of Coordinator of Information
POL Petroleum, Oil and Lubrication (facilities)
PPA Popski's Private Army
PT Patrol Torpedo
PWE Political Warfare Executive
RAF Royal Air Force
RFHQ Raiding Forces Headquarters
RON Remain Overnight Position
SAS Special Air Service
SI Secret Intelligence
SIM *Servizio Informazioni Militare*, Military Intelligence Service (Italian)
SIME Security Intelligence Middle East
SOE Special Operations Executive
SOG Small Operations Group
SOP Standard Operating Procedure
TO&E Table of Organization and Equipment
USAAF United States Army Air Force
VP-Boat *Vorpostenboot*, patrol boat (German)
WASP Women's Auxiliary Service Pilot
WRNS Women's Royal Navy Service or Wrens

STRATEGIC SERVICES
LIST OF CHARACTERS

ACM Sir Arthur Tedder
Acting Provisional Sub-Lt. Skipper Warthog Finley, OBE, DSO, DSC, RNPS
Beverly Blackwell, SS
BG Lucian Truscott
BG William "Wild Bill" Donovan
Black Club
Brandy Seaborn, GC
Brig. Raymond J. "R. J." Maunsell
Capt. Billy Jack Jaxx, MC
Capt. Butch "Headhunter" Hoolihan, DSO, MC, MM, RM
Capt. Dan Morgan
Capt. Earl Longstreet
Capt. "Geronimo" Joe McKoy, OBE
Capt. Pamala Plum-Martin, DSO, OBE, DFC, RM
Capt. Pat Porteous
Capt. Penelope "Legs" Honeycutt-Parker, OBE, GM, RM
Capt. Roy Kidd, MC
Capt. Roy "Mad Dog" Reupart, MC
Capt. "Pyro" Percy Stirling, DSO, MC
Capt. Stephanie Fawcett-Tatum, RM
Capt. Tom Hathcock
Cdr. Ian Fleming, RNVR
Club
Col. Cyrus J. Wilder

Col. Dudley Clarke
Col. John Randal, DSO, OBE, DSC, MC
Col. Stewart Menzies, DSO *aka* "C"
CWO Hank W. Rawlston
Ens. Theodore Hamilton, OBE *aka* "The Great Teddy"
Lt. Cdr. Robert Brodie
Lt. Col. Lionel Honeycutt-Parker
Lt. Col. Ralph Livesay
Lt. Col. Sir Terry "Zorro" Stone, KBE, DSO, MC
Lt. Gen. Bernard Montgomery
Lt. Gen. Sir Harold Alexander
Lt. Col. the Lord Simon "Shimi" Lovat, DSO
LtJG Jackson Taylor, USNR
Maj. A. W. "Sammy" Sansom
Maj. David Stirling
Maj. Desmond Barrymore
Maj. Everard Beauchamp
Maj. Taylor Corrigan, DSO, MC
Maj. the Lady Jane Seaborn, LG, OBE, RM
Maj. Travis McCloud
Maj. Vladimir Peniakoff *aka* "Popski"
Maj. Walter Pfluger
Maj. Gen. George S. Patton Jr.
Maj. Gen. James "Baldie" Taylor, OBE
Maj. Gen. Lewis H. Brereton
Mr. Cuthbert Bowlby *aka* "Curly"
Mr. Zargo
MSgt. Mack Beckwith
Pvt. Bannon
Pvt. Clooney
Pvt. Wally Malinowski
Raquel St. Ledger
Red the Flying Clipper Girl

Rene Malevergne
S/Lt. Bentley St. Ledger, WRNS
S/Lt. Tabitha Walpole, WRNS
Sgt. Maj. Maurice Chauncy
Sgt. Maj. Mike "March or Die" Mikkalis, MC, DCM, MM
VAdm. Louis "Dickie" Mountbatten, DSO, RN
VAdm. Sir Randolph "Razor" Ransom, VC, KCB, DSO, OBE, DSC
Veronica Paige, OBE
Waldo Treywick, OBE
W/Cdr. Ronald *aka* "Flash Bang" Gordon
W/Cdr. Tony Dudgeon

1
MURDER IN CAIRO

The two C-47 Dakotas were winging their way across the desert enroute to Oasis X from the Port Lyautey Airfield in Morocco. The aircraft were piloted by Wing Commander Tony Dudgeon and Squadron Leader Paddy Wilcox, two of the most experienced long-distance pilots in the Royal Airforce. Onboard the two aircraft were Colonel John Randal, Captain Billy Jack Jaxx, the mercenary known as King, Master Sergeant Mack Beckwith and twenty-nine paratroopers from the 575th Parachute Infantry Regiment (Separate) (Special) aka "Rangers". They were returning from invading North Africa.

The plan was to drop off Capt. Jaxx and the Rangers at the oasis then Col. Randal, MSG Beckwith and King would continue on to Raiding Forces Headquarters on the coast north of Cairo. Col. Randal had been gone a month. Raiding Forces had a number of high priority classified missions in various stages of progress when he had been unexpectedly called to the States to participate in Operation Torch. It was time to get back.

Col. Randal was asleep in the tail of the C-47 laying on a pile of X-type parachutes. Capt. Jaxx walked down the aisle to wake him. As Jack Cool leaned down, before he could reach out to touch the Colonel's shoulder, his eyes came open.

"Squadron Leader Wilcox needs a word with you sir."

When Col. Randal arrived in the cockpit the tubby Squadron Leader was flying with his trademark black pirates eyepatch turned up. The former

Canadian bush pilot had perfect eyesight in both eyes wearing the eyepatch, he claimed, to strengthen his eye muscles. He rotated it.

Sqn. Ldr. Wilcox said, "We need to divert to Cairo International Airport. Bad news I'm afraid, Colonel. Lady Seaborn has been reported shot...

ABOUT THE AUTHOR

Phil Ward is a decorated combat veteran commissioned at age nineteen. A former instructor at the Army Ranger School, he has had a lifelong interest in small unit tactics and special operations. He lives in Texas on a mountain overlooking Lake Austin.

Other books in the Raiding Forces Series:

Those Who Dare
Dead Eagles
Blood Wings
Roman Candle
Guerrilla Command
Necessary Force
Desert Patrol
Private Army
Africa 1941
The Sharp End
Raiding Rommel

www.ingramcontent.com/pod-product-compliance
Lightning Source LLC
Chambersburg PA
CBHW030548310726
48979CB00010B/2078/J

* 9 7 8 1 7 3 2 7 6 6 9 1 4 *